Dialogues of a Crime

For David –
I can't tell you how
happy I am that
you enjoyed this!
What a friend.
John

Dialogues of a Crime

a novel by

John K. Manos

First Edition ISBN 13: 978-1-937484-13-2
AMIKA PRESS 53 W Jackson Blvd 660 Chicago IL 60604 847 920 8084
info@amikapress.com Available for purchase on amikapress.com
Edited by LJM. Designed & typeset by Sarah Koz. Body in LTC Cloister, designed by Morris Fuller Benton in 1913–15, digitized by Jim Rimmer in early 2000s. Titles in Zigarre, designed by Jim Rimmer in 2006. Thanks to Nathan Matteson.

For
Leah

1

From the top of the empty building the river cannot be seen, but its presence seeps through the air like a sense of winter on the northern wind. Blood swells around the wire binding the muscular man's wrists, and his long blond hair is matted with more blood, just now coagulating in streaks across the duct tape sealing his mouth and muffling his periodic cries. Able to see little more than a red mist through his swollen eye sockets, he flinches away as something round and hard, a thick dowel perhaps, leaves stinging stripes across his back and thighs. Thick hands clutch at his shredded clothing.

Not yet in shock and with his lungs straining to somehow split the tape, he senses a void at the edge of his consciousness, pebbles on the brittle tar spraying and clattering as in agony he is forced to shuffle forward, shoeless but not feeling the frozen roof.

1972

1

A pounding on the thin panels of the dormroom door invaded the young man's sleep. He dreamt briefly of the caissons being driven for the Hancock Center construction when he and his father and older brother visited the site in Chicago in 1968, but the banging woke him in time to hear the door opening. What he saw first against the weak early-spring light from the windows was a tall, disheveled, middle-aged man with short salt-and-pepper hair wearing an inexpensive suit. *Cop?* was his first thought. The man glanced around the messy room, then stared down at the student as another heavier officer moved through the entranceway, holding aside a burlap screen the young man's roommate had hung between the room and the closets. Finally a remotely familiar short bald man with a beard entered quickly, looked down at the young man and said, "That's him." The bald man pivoted and disappeared. The young man thought he recognized the beard, but not the bald head or the tie.

"What?" the young man breathed as the heavier cop twitched away his blanket and with an air of perfunctory finality clutched his upper arm, pulled him upright, turned him toward the windows and clipped handcuffs around his wrists. Salt-and-pepper rummaged through the top drawer of his desk and pulled out his checkbook. The young man sat naked on the bed with his hands cuffed behind his hips.

The heavier cop stared down at him, then seemed to relent and said, "You're under arrest." An inane idea entered the young man's mind—he thought it was an April Fool's joke. The door to his room stood open, and he could hear activity down the hall, more pounding on doors.

Salt-and-pepper opened the checkbook and said, "Michael J. Pollitz. That you?"

"You don't know who I am?" Michael felt a rush of sleepy terror. His narrow face reddened.

"We know," said the heavy cop. Both men moved around the

room, opening drawers in the desks and small dressers. They walked across his clothing. The heavy cop kicked aside some junk food wrappers on the floor and used his foot to rearrange a pile of papers and books. Salt-and-pepper opened one of the closets, looked down at the pile of clothing, luggage, books and trash, and shut the door again. It occurred to Michael that they weren't searching for anything, their indifferent examination a matter of going through the motions. Both seemed bored.

"Can I put on some clothes?" Michael asked. He was well-muscled in a way that echoed high school athletics, but he was small and felt shriveled and unbearably vulnerable, nude and handcuffed. His nineteen-year-old mind flashed a brief homophobic panic, even though he knew he was dealing with police. The freeze-dried fantasy included a grisly murder. The heavy cop exchanged a look with salt-and-pepper, then nodded. Michael stood and turned, and the detective removed the cuffs. Michael self-consciously shifted his body as he grabbed a pair of threadbare blue-and-white-striped bell bottom pants from the floor and pulled them on. He picked up a wrinkled blue work shirt and buttoned it, and he tied his tennis shoes without sitting. He combed his long hair away from his face with his fingers before the detective replaced the handcuffs, and Michael sat again.

"Feel better?" salt-and-pepper asked with an ironic smile. Then he left the room. The heavy cop positioned himself in the entrance, in front of the flimsy curtain, and stared impassively. Michael looked at the windows, brighter now as dawn filled the sky. Almost to himself, he said, "What is this?"

"You're under arrest," the detective repeated.

"Why?"

The detective didn't answer, and Michael wasn't able to endure his stare. He looked through the windows again. His room was at the end of a long hall on the top floor in one of the older dormitories on the small campus, a three-story building with just two floors of rooms, the building shaped like a T with a central staircase that led down to the Student Union. The noises from the hall had died down, but he could hear voices. Still bleary, he couldn't sort out his thoughts. Why was he being arrested? He hadn't done anything. It was something with the bald guy, but he couldn't fill in the blanks.

His friend John Calabria's father came into his mind. He was suddenly overcome with a desire to be sitting in the office at Dominick Calabria's farm northwest of Chicago, untouchable, waiting for the man's sharp smile to fade as he offered a serious solution. What would Dominick Calabria do? Nothing. He would say nothing at all and wait for his lawyer. Lawyers. An army of lawyers.

"Can't you tell me what's going on?" Michael asked, overcome by confusion and anxiety. The heavy detective's expression didn't change even as salt-and-pepper returned.

"Set?" the heavy detective asked.

"Yeah. Let's go." Both cops stepped to the bed and raised the young man by his arms.

As they walked down the hall, Michael said, "I need to piss," nodding toward the common bathroom. The cops followed him to the urinals, and the heavy detective removed the handcuffs. When Michael finished, they didn't replace the restraint. The young man felt a childish flush of relief that was almost pride for the miniscule favor: He was trustworthy, they could see that. And this added an absurd hope that the arrest was a mistake that would soon be clarified.

Outside, a friend from the sophomore class, Pat Kinnealy, whose room was down the hall from Michael's, stood in handcuffs near an unmarked car in the small parking area next to the dorm. It was brightening into a lovely day. Michael glanced up at the sky, then back toward the parking spaces. Behind the unmarked car were one local squad car and three state cruisers. State troopers stood near their cars. Strangers were seated in the backseats of two of the state vehicles. He could see another acquaintance, a man two years older who lived in an apartment in town, with another stranger in the backseat of the local car. Both sat with the awkward tilt of handcuffed prisoners. Two freshmen from the floor below Michael's stood in the parking area, also with their hands manacled behind their backs, and a small comprehension formed: The two roommates sold reefer, LSD, mescaline and amphetamines in small quantities from their room—he had purchased from them. Michael suddenly felt conspicuous without handcuffs, caught somewhere in the hostile twilight between Us and Them.

He and Pat were ushered into the backseat of the unmarked car. The two freshmen were placed in one of the state cruisers. "Why aren't you handcuffed?" Pat asked. Beneath a taut strain of somnolent shock, his pallid face was a mixture of relief and accusation.

"They took them off when I peed," Michael said. "They didn't put them back on." The cops were talking outside the cars.

"Did you recognize the bald guy?" Pat asked.

"Not really."

"I think I sold him some white cross last fall," Pat said mournfully. "Dan brought him over with another guy," nodding toward their friend in the local squad car. "I think he was wearing a stocking cap, but I recognize the beard." Pat seemed on the verge of tears, the skin pale around his eyes.

"I never sold him anything," Michael mused, feeling relieved and silently reassuring himself that a mistake was being made. His roommate had from time to time sold an ounce or two of excess grass; they must have intended to arrest him instead. A straw to grasp. He didn't know about the strangers in the state cars, but even though the two freshmen usually had hallucinogens or speed to sell, they weren't serious dealers, and he, Pat and Dan weren't dealers at all. Not in the sense of buying quantities and selling again for a profit or even for a supply of free drugs. But he had an uneasy feeling. He thought he recognized the bearded bald man as well, and Pat confirmed it. He thought he had met him once, when Dan brought him to his room in search of drugs. Michael had shown him to the freshmen's room several months earlier, before Thanksgiving. Could that be it? It seemed too inconsequential to be real.

2

The young man's college was located in a small city in central Illinois, its population only about 35,000, even though it was a county seat. The college was also small, with just some 1,300 students enrolled in 1972, but even this comparatively insignificant student body had managed to enrage the surrounding voters with miniature demonstrations against the Vietnam War and a one-night occupation of a historic campus building in 1970—the little liberal arts school's reaction to the Kent State shootings in May. The great majority of students were drawn from affluent suburbs of Chicago, often the wealthy North Shore communities, almost exclusively the offspring of comfortable parents in any case. Michael had written in the school newspaper, "However thinly attended our protest rallies may have been, the noise has been loud enough to stir resentment in the town's working population. They find in their confused patriotism the voice with which to express their bleak, suspicious anger that the well-off, educated white people who so bitterly oppose this damn war are not those who are dying in it." This simple, well-written note had provided him with some notoriety, but he never met anyone who truly understood what he was trying to say. Dom Calabria had read the letter and shrugged, smiling fondly, and asked Michael what made him so sure he understood what the townspeople were thinking. "Although I can see that you might have a better idea than some of your classmates," Dom had concluded.

A scholarship student who was attending the expensive little school on personal loans, Michael was anomalous in terms of family money, and he understood the local community's injured pride better than most of his peers. He could be forgiven for believing there was a political aspect to his arrest, but he had the nature of the politics wrong. As he and the other prisoners were led through a side door into the small police station just three blocks from the campus, he harbored naïve fantasies of some vaguely conceived martyrdom—*to what?* he would later wonder. *Recreational drug use?* But at the moment he was unable to recall any good reason to be fingerprinted and photographed, and he blurted out, "What the hell is this?" to an indifferent technician who rolled his fingers across a blotter and shrugged.

Salt-and-pepper disappeared, leaving the heavy detective to run his name and process him. Michael never again encountered either the older officer or the heavyset cop who had arrested him, and he would never suspect the pity with which each had regarded his naked helplessness and the soft, boyish contours of his startled, groggy face as they had cuffed him. He answered the detective's questions politely and sat, still without restraints, as the detective left his desk to run his name through the state files.

"You never even had a traffic ticket," the detective said, shaking his head. "What are you doing here?"

"I wish someone would tell me," Michael replied, feeling even more confident that everything would soon be all right.

The detective finished with another form and said, "That's it, kid. Just wait there," and rose to leave.

"What's next?" Michael asked, unable to mask the fear in his voice.

"This is a state operation," the detective replied. "We're just processing you here. You'll be taken over to the county jail when we're done with everyone." He paused to gaze briefly at the young man, thinking that the timing of the arrest might make assembling bail tough, especially for the five townies who had been arrested along with the five students. He added compassionately, "Don't worry about it, kid. I don't think there's more than five guys over there right now."

It took more than two hours to process all ten men, and the sky was bright when they were led back outside to a line of waiting state police cars for the short ride to the county jail.

The small, Civil War-era stone and brick building was located directly across the street from the south end of the college campus, its deep-set, tall windows barred with thick, rusted iron. Above the front entrance was a small apartment for trustees in which one of the young man's friends who had been arrested for marijuana possession had spent six consecutive weekends.

The men filed through a side entrance and, after a brief check-in, were each issued a rolled foam mat, sheets, a pillow and an enameled pail with a lid. They were told to find an unoccupied cell. The jail was decrepit, with a small barred entrance onto a large common room with tables and a small bookshelf. An opening screened by a heavy lattice of overlapping strips of steel on the long wall facing the door swept up two stories; a small gate led to three tiers of six- by eight-foot cells, six cells per tier. At the end of the bank of cells were two toilets sitting on the floor. Next to the toilets was a single open shower, the spigot hanging from the wall above a drain in the floor. The cells contained only a shelf for the foam mattress; the enameled pail was the nighttime toilet. Michael followed Pat into the cellblock. The detective's estimate had been too high; only three men were incarcerated, but three of the local men who had been caught in the same sweep as the students rushed to the unoccupied floor-level cells. Michael and the other students carried their mattresses up to the second tier. The windowless cells had hinged, barred gates that faced the deep outer windows. Michael couldn't shake a sense of unreality, as if he was having a bad dream. He dropped the rolled pad onto the shelf and set the other items beside it, feeling dislocated in time in the ancient jail. It occurred to him that he should have called his parents from the police station, but he hadn't thought to ask for a phone, and besides, the person who kept entering his mind was Dominick Calabria—he certainly knew good criminal lawyers.

Michael stepped out of the cell and put his hands on the rail of the cantilevered gangway, feeling numb. He glanced toward the other cells as Pat stepped out, his face pale. Behind Kinnealy, Dan and the freshmen emerged, their eyes wide and frightened but also showing traces of the otherworldly confusion he could feel fogging his own thoughts. As they descended toward the common room, they heard their names being called from the entrance. Peering at them from behind the bars was the agitated face of the student-affairs director, a man no more than nine years older than Dan named Reynolds Muldaur, himself a graduate of the school. He wore his red hair stylishly long and parted down the middle. They moved toward him with a mixture of embarrassment and profound relief, but his news wasn't encouraging.

"Listen," he began. "You're in a lot of trouble. The charges are all felonies." Michael raised his hands in protest, but Muldaur cut him off. "Mike, Pat and Dan—you're facing $50,000 bonds. You two," he faced the freshmen, "are looking at $100,000 apiece." He let the sums sink in.

Finally, Dan overcame his dismay and asked, "What do we do?"

"Bail is ten percent," Muldaur answered, "and there won't be any banks open until next Monday." After a lengthy pause he went on, "I don't know if the college has $35,000 on hand, but we may. The county may accept our guarantee on the bail.

I don't know. We've called your parents."

Pat began to break down but regained control.

"I just wanted to be sure you were all okay. There's a student-administration meeting in an hour. I'll come back when that's over," Muldaur finished.

"What meeting?" one of the freshmen asked. His voice was like a man emerging from anesthesia. Muldaur didn't answer, which was an act of kindness—none of them needed to know that a fierce debate was developing, with the student-assembly president arguing vigorously that the school wash its hands of the five "pushers," as he phrased it. That evening, Michael would announce in rage, after half a bottle of wine, "I'm going to knock some teeth out of that student-council weenie," but his friends would prevent him from hunting down the student leader.

"Look," Muldaur said, "try not to worry too much. One way or another, you should all be out of here soon." He looked from face to face and nodded. "I'll be back this afternoon, either way."

They moved away from the bars and into the common room. Dan, Pat and Michael sat on either side of one of the tables. The two freshmen sat on the floor, leaning against the wall. Neither would speak another word the entire time they were in the jail. Pat held his head in his hands, tugging at his lank blond hair. Michael studied one of the townies, who had spread his foam mattress on the floor and was stretched out on it, and made an obvious observation—the man was a heroin addict, and the early stages of withdrawal were underway. One of the jailers also noted the man's agitation and sweatshine and remarked familiarly, not without sympathy, "Looks like a long day, don't it?" The townie shuddered with his eyes closed.

"Jesus, five grand," Pat moaned.

"What a shitty place," Dan said, looking at the thick brick walls and patched mortar.

"It's an old jail," Michael replied. His thoughts again returned to Dominick Calabria. If necessary, he would call John and ask if his father could lend him the cash to make bail. He could hear John's piercing laugh on the line, "What the hell you doin' in jail, Mikey?" He smiled to picture their reaction to this beat-up old county jail, this relic of the 1860s with enameled pots to shit in. Dom wasn't the laughing type, and Michael didn't think he would share John's amusement about his arrest, but he would have the money and a kind word, perhaps even reassurance. Although Dom had never been in prison, Michael couldn't think of a single man among the dozen or so he had regularly seen over the years at their sprawling home who hadn't done some time. Three years here, five or six there. Salvatore Bruno had once done an eight-year jolt, Michael recalled hearing years before, and like all the others he spoke about it with a matter-of-fact bravado, as if it was just another aspect of existence, like eating, breathing and dying. Angelo DeMicco had said once, when Michael and John asked, "It ain't fun. No one likes it." He had paused to idly trace his forefinger along the scar that creased his face from the left side of his mouth up to his cheekbone. "It's just somethin' ya get through, kid, and that's that." Sal had grunted agreement but added with a rumbling laugh, "It's worth avoidin', if ya can."

Despite an adolescent tendency to romanticize things, Michael didn't glamorize the Outfit. He had spent too much time around thugs. That this was a drug charge would probably make Dom angry, Michael realized, but he knew without thinking about it that his friend's father would be a reliable shoulder to lean on, if he needed one. He tried not to think about his parents or older brother.

The guy on the floor was getting bad, twitching with panicky eyes and a running nose, when Reynolds Muldaur returned in mid-afternoon with the welcome news that the college had posted bond. The five students were sent back to the cells to retrieve the mattresses and other goods, and they were released. They emerged into the cool April air, the low sun casting a bronze light through the budding trees, and walked across the street to the campus and across the broad quad to the dean of students' office. Michael wearily combed back his dirty hair with his fingers and said, "Thanks for getting us out, Reynolds."

"Save your thanks for Dean Walker," Muldaur answered.

3

Dean Howard Walker met them in his outer office. A tall, imposing, silver-haired man, he looked more weary than angry, Michael thought, but he glowered impressively without speaking. *This is all I need,* was Michael's despondent reaction. "What can you tell me?" Dean Walker asked, looking from one to another. Almost simultaneously they shrugged. Dan drew a breath, but the dean raised his hand to stop him. "Let's do this in order," the dean said, grumbling authority with his resonant voice. "First, you two," he announced to the freshmen, waving them into his office. Muldaur followed them in, and as Walker grasped the doorknob, Michael heard him say imperiously, "I'm told you two have been selling drugs from your room..." and the door closed.

Pat sat heavily on the couch and held his head in his hands. After his turn in the dean's office, his eyes were red and puffy, and he hurried out; Dan had still looked shell-shocked. Michael didn't appreciate going last.

"Mr. Pollitz," the dean intoned, standing behind his elegant walnut desk. "I can't believe a scholarship student with your academic potential would risk everything in this way." He paused, and Michael suddenly realized the dean was sincere.

"Dean Walker, I still have no idea what the charge against me is," he said, thinking, *What possible difference can my academic potential make?*

"No?" the older man asked. He shook his head incredulously. "You have no recollection of any of the men who arrested you this morning?"

Michael raised his hands, baffled and beginning to feel frightened again. "Pat said he thought he knew one guy, but I wasn't sure."

"You're going to be charged with assisting in the sale of a controlled substance," the dean said slowly. "That's a felony." He paused again.

"This is nuts," the young man argued. "I don't deal drugs."

"I said 'assisting in the sale'," Walker emphasized. "If you knowingly helped an agent obtain drugs, you committed a crime."

Michael was stunned. He felt immeasurably stupid.

"Can you afford an attorney?" the dean continued. "I spoke with your father some time ago, because the college must be immediately remunerated for the bond. I gather that money is an issue."

Michael shook his head in confusion. "I don't think my parents can afford the bond. Forget a lawyer."

"I spoke with our attorney," Walker said, "when we were assembling the money earlier. He's worked with the college for years. I would recommend him. He handles criminal cases."

"What does he cost?"

"I'm sure you can make financing arrangements." When Michael looked away, still shaking his head in bewildered panic, the dean added, "Or you can use a public defender." He studied the young man for a moment and softened. "Were you planning to go home for the term break?"

Michael nodded dumbly. "Yeah. I was planning to go in the morning."

"Well, you aren't supposed to leave the county until you've been arraigned," the dean said, but he held up one hand when trapped anguish flashed across Michael's face. "No, don't change your plans," he said, trying to be reassuring. "As I told the others, I can invoke *in loco parentis* and release you to leave." He smiled beneficently. Michael had no idea if what the dean was saying was true. "Go home and discuss the situation with your parents. But don't delay on your decision. Your arraignment is scheduled for two weeks from yesterday, and it's best to have an attorney present."

4

Two of Michael's friends on his floor gently held his arms. One tugged at his sleeve, trying to lead him toward the bathroom.

"Come on, Mike," the student said, quietly measuring his tone, cajoling, comforting. "Let's get your hands cleaned up."

The other student stared at the hole in the wall and the diamond shapes of the deformed metal lattice beneath the broken plaster. Matching lacerations on Michael's knuckles bubbled blood. "Yeah," he added, "let's get out of the hall, man."

Michael stood with his forehead pressed against the wall and his loose fists hanging at his sides, barely aware of the pain emanating from his hands. He dimly felt the solicitation of his friends and appreciated their kindness. They had emerged from their rooms at the sound of him pounding a hole in the solid plaster.

"Come on," one said again.

"This isn't like you, man," the other added, still pulling gently to direct him away from the damaged wall.

"Maybe it is," Michael slurred, but he allowed them to drag him toward the bathroom.

"God," one of the young men said, "how are you going to make the train tomorrow morning?"

"We'll go on the late train," the other answered. "We were planning to ride together anyway. Wow! This is wild."

"I've never seen you drunk," the first young man said, and then he looked over Michael's head. "Have you ever seen him drunk?" He laughed lightly, intrigued by this unusual turn.

"Nope, not me, either. Mike, man, you're usually the one who keeps it cool." The second friend was amused as well, now that the desperate anger and wall-breaking was done. "What gives?"

"Pam in the Chip gave me a free patty melt tonight," Michael said, referring to a middle-aged woman who worked the counter at the student coffeehouse/snack bar two floors below in the Student Union, a traditional gathering place that had operated under its odd nickname for decades. He blearily tried to recollect if anyone had spoken to him when he was there, a few hours earlier, but the effort was too great. He had a clear image of Pam, though, handing him the sandwich without charging him, offering it with a sad, sympathetic smile. "Wasn't that nice?"

"Pam has always liked you, man."

"Like her too," Mike answered with a grunted belch.

"What's the story, Mike?" one of his friends asked.

"Got arrested today," Michael burbled with a small chuckle.

"Yeah, we know. That was all over the grapevine. But why?"

"Showed some guys a room downstairs," Michael guessed, but his friend interrupted.

"I don't mean that. I meant, why the wall?"

"Oh." Michael paused, straightening. "Jesus. I don't know." He looked at his hands as if noticing the torn skin and swelling ache for the first time.

The other friend started laughing in earnest. "Of all the

people I might have guessed was out here beating a hole in that wall," he said, "you would have been, like, at the end of the list, Mike. Man!"

The pair continued to laugh as they led their stumbling friend into the bathroom, gleeful in their youth and innocence.

5

Michael replaced the phone's handset in the cradle and looked through the front window of his parents' small home. The trees lining their Barrington street were already laced with a touch of green. Such a fine spring day would be early in the year for the Chicago area. He stretched sleepily, deeply inhaling the odor of bacon, and glanced at a print of one of Monet's haystacks next to the stairway leading up to the bedrooms. He liked the image. It made him think his mother had good taste. He followed his nose into the cramped kitchen. His father and older brother were seated at the table as his mother poured coffee. She looked up at him and smiled warmly, but the atmosphere was taut, as it had been when he arrived home the night before.

"Morning," he said softly.

"Who were you calling?" his father asked with aggressive suspicion. His eyes narrowed above his large nose.

"John."

"Why?"

"I was going to go over today."

"You don't think you got enough trouble? You gotta go see those Mafias, those crooks, maybe find some more?"

"Let's just have a nice breakfast," his mother said, her small mouth tight as she tried to be firm.

"John's my best friend," Michael responded, his immediate defiance sounding childish even to his ear.

"I'm not talking about John," his father snapped. He sipped coffee. "I'm talking about his father."

Michael picked up a spoon and reached for a grapefruit half. "Pa," he said quietly, "I'm going to need an attorney."

"Calabria's got to know some good ones," his brother said, smirking slightly but not seriously taunting.

Michael knew his brother could sense the gathering storm and understood he was trying to soften the tone. "That's what I figure," he said.

"You want a mob lawyer now?" his father asked.

"I just want a good lawyer," Michael said. He set the spoon on the table and stared at his father. It occurred to him that he was thankful he had not inherited his father's close-set, watery blue eyes. He glanced at his mother as she nervously placed a platter of eggs and bacon on the table. Following on his irrelevant digression, he studied her brown eyes and smiled, feeling crazily detached from the building argument with his father. His mother smiled back, ready to hope for the best until the worst arrived.

"And who will pay for this good lawyer?" His father glared across the rim of his coffee cup. "Answer me that."

Michael focused and stared across the table, his appetite gone. "I will," he finally said.

His father snorted. "How? Maybe take a bigger student loan? Maybe the bank will agree to that." He sipped coffee again, his face reddening. "You can go to the bank today, tell them you need more money because you've got this little problem with the police, yeah? Or maybe you were thinking the mobster would lend you the money."

"But Pa, he might be able to help me!" Michael pleaded.

"Yeah? Yeah?" his father sputtered. "His kind of help, it don't never go away!" He slapped the table with his palm. Michael's brother stopped buttering toast. His mother started to speak but held back, almost visibly. "We don't need to ask for help from a criminal!" his father shouted. "Maybe you want I should go to that gangster, ask him to borrow me the five thousand dollars I gave your school, yeah?"

"Come on, Pa," Michael began, but his father cut him off, banging down his coffee cup so violently that the saucer cracked.

His father held his hands in front of Michael's face, his long fingers moving with agitation, as if independently they would throttle the boy, irrespective of his father's wishes. "I work with these hands, honest work, every day! That money was almost everything I have! Maybe you shoulda thought about who you are before you started dealing in drugs!" He slammed both hands down on the table.

"I never sold drugs!" Michael shouted back. Suddenly the ache in his bruised hands was sharper, and he realized he was clenching his fists.

"No?" his father almost screamed. "Then I must have imagined writing a five-thousand dollar check to your college!"

"You'll get the money back, Pa! It's a bond!" Michael slid his chair away from the table. "You'll get it back after the trial!"

"You know what I don't understand?" his father yelled. "No guilt. Where's the guilt? You should be ashamed!"

"For what? For using drugs?" The young man stood in anguish and rage.

"Where the hell you think you're going?"

"Out! Anywhere else!"

"Then you'll go there on foot!" When Michael turned toward the back door, his father howled into the kitchen, "God damn it! You go ask for help from that gangster, don't bother to come home! You hear me?" His father pursued him to the door, still shouting, spit flying from his mouth. He threw open the door behind his son, violating the still April air with his angry voice, "You live in this house! You'll listen to me!" He stared at his son's back, sputtering his fury in Polish, a language he never used at home. "You'll listen, God damn it!"

6

John Calabria was standing at the farm's kitchen window, finishing a glass of orange juice, when he saw Michael walking up the long drive from the gate. He set the glass down and crossed to the back door. "Ayyy, Mikey!" John bellowed, laughing expansively as his friend neared, opening his arms with a grin stretching his broad face. They embraced, then John held Michael at arm's length, chuckling as he stared down into his eyes. "What'd you do, walk here?"

Michael nodded miserably. "I had an argument with my pa," he said.

"Jesus, Mikey, that's a long fuckin' walk," John laughed. "Musta been some argument. You ain't even wearing a coat."

Michael shrugged. "It's a nice morning," he muttered.

John grabbed his hands and squeezed painfully. "Hey! What's this?" He laughed when Michael flinched from his grip.

"I guess I punched out a wall," Michael replied, feeling sheepish. "Don't remember real clearly. Had too much to drink."

"You? Drunk and slammin' shit outta a wall? Now I've heard everything."

Michael shrugged again.

"Don't look so worried, man," John advised. "This is just bullshit."

"I hope you're right," Michael said.

"Sure, I'm right," John announced. "What the fuck?" He laughed suddenly, his huge mouth gapping wet across his wide face. "Don't it figure, Mikey? Here I am, gettin' into the game, and you're down in Hicksville gettin' busted!" John found it hugely amusing.

Michael tried to borrow some of John's humor but couldn't shake a pervasive uneasy feeling that seemed to be making it hard to breathe. "I wonder if your dad has a few minutes," he said hesitantly.

"No sweat, Mikey. He said he wanted to see you when you came over. He's back in the office with Sal and Angie."

As they stepped into Dominick's office, Salvatore Bruno instantly flared up, rasping, "C'mere, Michael," and reaching with one large hand to grab the young man's head. Bruno looked as wide as a boxcar. "Whatchoo doin' fuckin' around wit' drugs, God damn it?" Bruno shouted into Michael's face, his annunciation heavy with Taylor Street, the old Italian neighborhood on Chicago's near west side. The big man pinched hard on his neck with one immensely powerful paw. Michael grimaced with pain. Bruno shook him from side to side.

"Asshole!" Angelo DeMicco snarled, stepping away from Dom's desk and leaning his scarred face into Michael's line of sight. He raised one hand, barely able to restrain his desire to slap the student. "What's the matter with you?" he said, the phrase common among the men who came and went from the Calabria farm, always a rapid string of heavily accented disgust: *What's da matta witchoo?* He popped Michael's forehead with the heel of his hand, lightly, making a point. "I always thought you was smarter'n this."

"None of us has anything to do with drugs," Bruno spat into his ear. "You wanna know why? Drugs is bad news! Bad news, you hear me?" Michael ineffectually tried to pry the heavy man's hand from his neck. John Calabria bubbled with laughter as his friend's face flushed and his knees started to cave in under the pressure of Bruno's drilling thumb. John found the outrage hilarious—half the men in the crews were perfectly fond of the chemical set, and everyone appreciated the income.

DeMicco slapped the side of Michael's head with his fingertips. "Asshole!" he repeated. "Stick with booze, for Chissakes. You get drunk, all that happens is you wake up with a hangover. Then it's over. You wanna be an addict? Some runny-nosed dopehead?" He raised his hand again, getting worked up and loading a solid slap.

"Knock it off," Dominick Calabria snapped. DeMicco stepped away, muttering and glaring at Michael. Bruno gave him another shake and finally released his grip. He shifted the mass of his shoulders and ran a palm across his thinning hair. Michael winced and rubbed the back of his bruised neck. He had no clear idea of the pecking order among the men who surrounded his friend's father, but he knew Bruno and DeMicco were several steps above the common thugs, seemingly in the rank immediately below Dom. And Dom was unquestionably in charge.

Dom wasn't as tall as Angelo DeMicco, nor did he have the sheer bulk of Sal Bruno—the young man had never met anyone else who did, not even John came close—but Dom casually carried a lethal air of command that the young man imagined was replicated only in the military. They all seemed dangerous, but where Bruno and DeMicco might be cutlasses, he thought, Dom was a rapier. An aura of violence surrounded all of the men, but it was colored by impulsive emotion in Sal and Angie. In Dom's glittering eyes there was dispassionate precision. The difference extended even to their characteristic gestures. When expressing some particular point they wanted to make, Sal and Angie habitually raised their shoulders in all-purpose shrugs, arms bent and palms facing upward, typically with their fingertips closed lightly to the tips of their thumbs.

Dom was more likely to modify his stillness only slightly, no shrug, palms down and fingers extended, sweeping his hands outward to close his emphasis. The metaphor that occurred to Michael was the difference between steam and frost.

"It's done," Dom said. He stood behind the large mahogany desk near one wall of his spacious office. To the side were French doors leading out to the pool and patio area and facing north to a view of the main horse barn and a fenced pasture that continued downhill to a distant tree line. Michael could walk the property in his sleep. Dom gazed briefly, his thin lips pursed, then lifted the lid of his cigarette box for a smoke. He lit up and inhaled deeply. His eyes flashed to Michael's hands, but he did nothing to acknowledge the injuries. "So, Mike," he finally said. "We got a problem." He released a cloud of smoke across his desk and sat.

Michael nodded unhappily, but he felt greatly relieved by the word 'we.' When Dom gestured toward the leather armchairs in front of his desk, Michael sat. Sal took the other chair. DeMicco and John sat on the matching couch.

Dom nodded along with Michael, dragging on his cigarette. He exhaled twin plumes of smoke through his nostrils and leaned back. "Tell me," he said.

"I get arraigned a week from Thursday," Michael began.

"From the beginning," Dom interrupted, raising one hand with the index finger extended. "What'd you do?"

"I'm not entirely sure," Michael answered uncomfortably. "One of the guys that got arrested with me thought he recognized an agent that identified us when we were arrested, on Good Friday, last week. But I don't know." He continued to meet Dom's intent gaze. Dom stared at length. He was thinking about an eight-year-old boy.

"Tell me the truth, Mike," Dom said casually, as if it were a matter of little consequence. "Were you selling drugs?"

"No."

Dom nodded thoughtfully. "So what are you going to be charged with?"

"The dean told me it was assisting in the sale of a controlled substance."

"This sounds like bullshit," Bruno interjected.

"Yeah," Dom agreed, "it does." He stubbed out his smoke and looked again at the young man. "What was your bond?"

"Fifty thousand dollars."

"Who put up the five large?"

"The school did, to get us out. My pa paid them back." When Dom failed to mask a small surprise, Michael added, "He had it in savings."

"Do you have an attorney?"

"No," Michael answered. "I was hoping to get some advice from you."

"Of course," Dom said.

"But I can't afford much," Michael continued, nervously drawing a breath. "I wonder..."

"Forget the money," Dom said brusquely, "that ain't an issue." He studied the young man's discomfort for a moment and came to an accurate conclusion. "What does your father say about all this?" he asked.

Michael gazed through the French doors before answering. "He feels I should use what I can afford. That means a public defender at school." John snorted. Anger flashed in Dom's eyes as he shifted his glance to the couch. Michael studied his hands.

"Nothin' against your father, Mikey," Bruno said suddenly. "But that's not the smart move. This kind of problem, you wanna make it go away. Even for bullshit, you want the best lawyer you can get."

"Listen to Sal, Mikey," DeMicco barked. "He's tellin' you the truth." The young man glanced at the couch, then turned back to Dom.

"We've all known you since you were in the fourth grade,

Mike," Dom said with a fond smile. "We want to help you. I hope your father understands that."

"He's proud," Michael answered.

"Nothing wrong with that," Dom replied. "I understand. That's why he didn't want you to borrow your tuition money from me. A man should be proud." He nodded and reached for another cigarette. "But this is different, Mike. You don't want to screw around with this shit." He lit the cigarette and held it between his thumb and index finger, European style. "What did you say the charge is again?"

"Assisting in the sale of a controlled substance," Michael said. "It's a felony."

Bruno snorted. "Shit. What'd you do, anyway?"

"If I'm remembering the guy right, I showed an agent to a room in my dorm where he bought some drugs. Speed or LSD, I guess. From a couple of other guys. I wasn't there for the whole thing."

"What a bunch of bullshit," DeMicco laughed. "Hell, a half-decent lawyer'll plead it out to a misdemeanor. A good one'll string it along until it disappears, for Christ's sake. This ain't nothin'."

Dom shook his head noncommittally. "Angie's right," he said, "but the key there is 'good.' You never know what'll happen otherwise. 'Specially down in some hick town in the armpit of nowhere."

"Maybe you could give me a couple of names," Michael said tentatively but feeling a rising confidence as these experienced men responded nonchalantly to his charges.

"I'll be happy to," Dom said. "Best choice is Jim Allegretti. Guy about my age. He's very good."

"You better believe that," Angie threw in.

Dom sent a stream of smoke toward the couch. "But you're going to have to talk to your father, make him see that we're reaching out a hand in friendship."

Michael nodded, and Dom smiled again. He glanced at John.
"Hey, Mikey," John said. "We got a couple new foals out in the barn. Wanna see 'em?"

7

Dom and Angie watched through the kitchen windows as John and Michael raced down the driveway in John's car.

"We still gotta deal with that fucking kike," DeMicco said, holding rein on his meat-grinder voice.

"Did he cough up our money?"

"Gonna deliver tonight."

"Then that's when we'll deal with it," Dom said, his eyes expressionless.

"I'd like to rip the cocksucker's head off," Angie growled.

Dom nodded indifferently. "Don't worry about it. No one's going to miss the point," he said. "Bring a few guys. Epstein may have some of his crew along."

"You got it." Both men glanced away from the window when Dom's wife walked into the kitchen.

"Toni," DeMicco nodded. "How you doin'?"

"I'm fine, Angie. How's Yvonne?"

"Great, as always." He smiled and nodded again. "Where'd Sal go?" DeMicco went outside. Dom and his wife watched him leave. She stared at her husband.

"What's wrong with Mike?"

"Why do you ask?"

"I saw him outside with John." She kept staring, her wide-set hazel eyes neutral but uncompromising. "From upstairs."

Her face flashed mild impatience with Dom's answer. "Something's wrong."

"What, just from the way he walks around?" Dom smiled. Toni said nothing. She crossed her slender arms beneath her breasts. "You know him," Dom said at last.

"Yes, I do."

"He's got a problem at school. A legal problem."

"Is it serious?"

"It shouldn't be. But drugs are involved."

"Mike's not a drug user!"

"Not in any real way, as far as I can see," Dom agreed. "I didn't ask."

"He wouldn't lie about it."

"No, he wouldn't. You're right there. He wouldn't lie about it." He looked through the window again. "That kid never lies about anything. Never did." He chuckled. "Remember when he and John tried to torch the barn?"

"How could I forget?" Toni smiled, fine lines etched at the edges of her full lips. The boys had made flares out of cattails. One of them set fire to a can of gas somehow. The can got kicked over, almost certainly by John, and the flames splashed up the siding.

"I wasn't here."

"No."

"You told them to keep quiet about it."

"I did." Toni smiled.

"Like I wouldn't notice the fresh paint when I got back."

"I know. John hid. Mike stood there in the driveway and confessed."

"He even blamed himself, and I know damn well John was the one who stuck the burning cattail in the gas." Dom laughed, picturing the boy, all terrified contrition, with his head bowed as he stood in remorseful fear next to the car. "Never said he was the one who started the fire. Just took all the responsibility for it." Dom laughed again.

"I'm going to have a grapefruit," Toni said. She walked to the refrigerator. "You want some?"

"Sure." Toni always had to occupy her hands when she was distressed. Dom's eyes softened.

"So what happened?" she said into the refrigerator.

"Mike got involved, in some way, in a drug sale. A guide, maybe. Months ago. He got arrested on Good Friday."

"Can you help him?"

"Of course. If he'll let me." He watched as she lifted a pair of bowls from a cabinet. "You think he will?" he asked.

"It depends," she answered. She cut the grapefruit.

"That's what I'm afraid of," Dom said. He opened a drawer and pulled out two spoons. "That's precisely what I'm afraid of."

"I hope nothing bad happens," Toni said. "He's one of my favorite people."

"Mine too," Dom answered.

8

"No!" his father shouted, instantly enraged. All four members of the family sat in the cramped living room. His mother looked haggard, as if she had been arguing for less volatility all day long without success.

"Pa," Michael breathed, by inference pleading for a calm discussion, "I've got to have a decent attorney, someone with experience with criminal charges."

"So you turn to these," his father waved a hand in the air, "these mobsters! What did I say this morning? What did I say?" he shouted furiously. "What did I say last night? And you! You defy me!"

"I won't go against you, Pa." *Why do I have to be plaintive?*

"We won't ask for help from criminals!" his father shouted.

"Why do you need a hot-shot lawyer?" his brother asked.

"These are serious charges," Michael said, relieved by the distraction.

"I don't understand," his mother said. "You said you weren't selling drugs."

"I wasn't, but it's a felony to tell someone where they can buy them," Michael replied.

"How do you know that?" his father asked, raw curiosity somewhat quieting his reflexive fury.

"The dean at school told me. And these charges, they can mean up to five years in jail and a twenty-five thousand dollar fine!" When his father slapped his hands onto his balding head, pinching at his short-cropped hair and coughing out undefined horror, Michael added, "That's why I need a good lawyer."

"Tell me again exactly what happened," his brother said, trying to avoid another explosion from their father. The young man felt a wash of gratitude and nodded. He again described the scenario that he believed led to his arrest.

"I don't see how they could send you to jail for that," his mother said hopefully. She smiled again and smoothed the dust cover on the couch with a thick palm.

"Me, neither," his brother agreed.

"It seems to me anyone could have done that," his mother added.

"How do you know this, this... fine?" his father asked, struggling to grasp the enormity of the calamity.

"I looked up the penalties at the library this afternoon," Michael answered.

"At the public library, here in Barrington?"

"Yeah, Pa. They've got law books there. They're a little out of date, but I don't think the statute's changed."

"My God!" his father exclaimed. "Twenty-five thousand dollars!" He shook his head in shock, muttering, "That's more than we paid for this house." Then he exploded again. "You think I'm rich? I'm not rich! I have my little plumbing business, puts food on the table! Our savings are already at your college! I wrote the check!"

"Don't be so melodramatic, Pa! This isn't the time to score points!"

"Points?" his father shouted. "Points? You smarty!" Inarticulate in his rage, he responded as though they were all ten years younger. He waved his big hands in the air. "We can't afford no big-time lawyer!"

Michael stared at his father with a dismal sense of defeat. His father looked away. Finally, Michael said, "I better get back down to school and see who I can find for representation."

"Yeah, you better," his father snapped.

9

"Jesus, Mikey. This don't make no sense." John Calabria's broad forehead was wrinkled with disbelief.

"It's the way it is, John," Michael said, holding his head stiff with inconsolable fatalism. "Let's not talk about it."

"Whaddaya mean, let's not talk about it? You're nuts." John hefted his friend's duffel bag and casually tossed it into the trunk of his Trans Am. "This is crazy. Why not just use one a my dad's lawyers and forget about it? Who's gonna know?"

"I can't do that to my pa," Michael answered. He stared across the roof of the car. The afternoon was clouding over, with a sharp chill in the air. He shook his head. "Just drop me at the train station. I'll let you know what's happening."

"What, in Barrington? Forget about it. I'll take you downtown." John yanked open the car door. "Get in, man. We ain't done."

Michael climbed into the car and grunted noncommittally as the car bounced with his friend's weight. John slammed the car into gear and floored it, squealing away from Michael's house. He pulled open the ashtray and removed a joint. "Take it easy, for Christ's sake," Michael said. "I'm already in enough trouble." John boomed out a laugh as he lit the joint and offered it. Michael shook his head.

"Listen up, Mikey," John coughed. "'Member what Sal an' Angie were sayin'? They know what they're talkin' about, man." He again dragged deeply on the joint and paused while he held his breath. "This is a bullshit deal," he exhaled. "It's nothin'. Lemme just get one a Dad's lawyers to make it go away, huh?" He took another huge hit from the joint and again offered it to Michael, who accepted it.

"I can't, John," Michael said with weary resignation as he exhaled. He stared out at the passing trees as John roared south toward the Northwest Tollway to Chicago. "If it's as small a thing as they're saying, a local lawyer ought to be able to handle it."

"Don't be an asshole, Mikey," John snapped. He was distracted briefly by a song on the radio. 'Saturday in the Park' by Chicago. John was nuts for the band. Michael didn't share his enthusiasm. John drummed the steering wheel and sang, doing a good job of reaching the high notes. Michael handed him the remains of the joint. John inhaled deeply again and sniffed smoke from the roach, pinching the stained scrap of cigarette paper in his fingertips. He coughed and shook his head. "Why's your dad so set against this?"

"It's not that he's against anything," Michael lied. "He figures I should face up to my own problems, here."

"No offense, Mikey, but that's stupid." Michael shrugged, his face closed, but John persisted. "My dad wants to help, man. He can't believe your old man's being so pig-headed about this."

"Let's leave my pa out of it," Michael answered with some heat. He doubted that Dom had said anything, one way or another, about his father. "I don't think he's trying to be stubborn. He's pissed that I'm in trouble at all."

"What? This ain't trouble, for Chrissakes." John shook his head. They rode without speaking for a few minutes, listening to the radio.

"Beautiful day," Michael said dreamily, gazing across the fields south of the expressway. John stamped on the gas, and the Trans Am rocketed onto the highway. John's method of merging was to floor it and let the other drivers make way. Michael cringed as a semi blasted its horn. John laughed and flipped the finger at his rearview mirror.

He thumped the heel of his hand on the steering wheel in time to the radio and glanced from side to side. "Let me tell you, Mikey, all of this, it's gonna get built up." He nodded toward the open land on either side of the highway.

"What do you mean?"

"All of this." *All a dis.* "It's gonna be developed. The family's puttin' money into it. Shopping centers, apartments, you name it."

Michael experienced an incongruous flash of insight: He wondered how it came to be that John, raised in Barrington Hills, ended up sounding like he lived on west Grand Avenue or in Cicero or Elmwood Park, someplace where immigrant and first-generation Sicilians were concentrated. Where had the accent come from? For that matter, why did guys like Sal Bruno and Angie DeMicco talk like such stereotypical mobsters? They had always talked that way, but Dom didn't. Michael thought about it. He knew Italians who weren't connected to the Outfit, and they didn't all talk like Sal and Angie. On the other hand, he also knew non-Italians who did, like one of his Polish uncles. In a way, the style of speaking reminded him of the up-talk adopted by some of his classmates, inflecting their words with a disingenuous wide-eyed faux sincerity. Maybe it was simply an affectation that stuck. Maybe it was lazy, like the unjunctured central-Illinois twang he heard from some of the townies at school. Maybe it was a defensive thing, like the guy on his floor whose Missouri 'country' accent was a lot more pronounced now, as a sophomore, than it had been last year. Maybe because Sal and Angie, and John, never interacted with anyone who wasn't punching an exaggerated inarticulate Chicago tough-talk style, and they just all communicated in perpetual imitation of one another. *They probably just* want *to sound like a bad movie,* he concluded.

"You still here?" John asked.

"Huh? Sure," Michael smiled. "I was just thinking."

"'Bout what?"

"I was wondering why you all sound like such clichés when you talk."

"What the hell?"

"You, Sal, Angie, Marbles, everyone but your dad. How come you all sound like you're making a movie about gangsters?" He ignored John's glare. "I mean, you and I grew up together, but we sound like we come from different planets."

"Fuck you, Mikey. I mean, I'm sorry I ain't got your brains, asshole."

"That's not what I mean. For God's sake! I'm not putting you down. I just wonder where the accents come from." Michael realized he was too high for this conversation. He should have kept his mouth shut.

"It's just the way I talk, you prick."

"Come on, John. I don't mean anything by it. I'm just stoned and curious. Forget it." He leaned forward to catch his friend's eye. "Forget it, right? No offense intended." John shrugged. Michael looked through the window. "All this construction you're talking about. You involved in it?"

"Not so much, me. The family for sure. Lotta dough there. Not me, though. Just a little, you know, hearin' about it. I think I'm gonna run one of our restaurants."

"Yeah?"

"Yeah. I think it oughta be fun, you know?"

Michael shrugged. He was intrigued by the concept of John's career plans. He had never really thought about his own future in any particular way. For the first time he consciously realized that he and John were headed along profoundly different trajectories. "I don't think I'd like the hours," he said.

"Ahhh, I'm up mosta the night anyway." John grunted out another laugh, easy again. "Anyhow, that's what my dad wants me to do." He nodded with his lips pressed together. "I'm gonna work there for a while, figure out the business."

"Which one?" Michael wasn't sure he knew all of the Calabria family restaurants and was asking with an automatic politeness.

"The supper club out on Rand," John answered. "You know, kinda out in the country, out by Cuba Road. Got a big concrete bear out front."

Michael knew the place. "How many restaurants does your dad own now?" The marijuana was making his speech slow and deliberate.

"None, if you ask the IRS," John giggled. "Tell you the truth, Mikey, I don't know for absolute certain. It's gotta be a half-dozen or so." He shook his head, immediately abandoning the effort of cataloging the locations in his mind. "So. What're you gonna do?"

Michael watched a jet on its way into O'Hare and was distracted by a sudden intense desire to get on a plane and fly away, just disappear. "I've never been on a plane," he said.

"What the fuck you talkin' about?"

"I'm going to find an attorney I can afford down at school," Michael replied. He was feeling scared again, but the drug softened his apprehension. "That's what I'm going to do."

John jammed in the car's cigarette lighter and withdrew another joint from the ashtray. "Mikey, that's stupid," he declared.

"I hope not," Michael answered softly.

John clenched the joint in his teeth and suddenly punched Michael in the shoulder. The force of the blow rammed him into the passenger-side door.

"Jesus!" Michael yelped. He felt as though he had been kicked by a horse. He twisted in his seat and returned the blow, swinging as hard as he could in the confined space of the Trans Am.

John laughed gleefully. "That your best shot?" He reached for the cigarette lighter. "Come on, Mikey. Do the smart thing here."

"I can't. Let's drop it, okay? It's the way it is." He laughed suddenly as Marc Bolan hit the first chords of 'Get It On.' Michael played air guitar for a second and laughed again. "I'll worry about it when I get to school. Turn up the damn radio."

10

Randall McKay was an attorney known to Dean Walker who also covered public-defender cases as a small sideline to his three-member law firm's primary practice, which consisted mainly of personal wills, small-company incorporation, real estate transactions and rare civil lawsuits. McKay had worked criminal cases for four years as a junior prosecutor in the state's attorney's office immediately after law school, twenty-three years earlier, so he handled the light but steady caseload of local criminals who could not afford representation by firms that specialized in criminal defense. For McKay's partnership, it was reliable income, and for McKay personally, it provided the opportunity to maintain a connection to the inner mechanisms of the county criminal-justice apparatus, which otherwise he would have missed. Those connections were also very useful when it came to zoning variances. In eighteen years of public defense, McKay had yet to represent an innocent defendant, and he had personally litigated fewer than twenty cases. Nearly everything that crossed his desk ended in a plea bargain of some kind, and the instances in which he had been forced to go to trial had invariably been a consequence of a clueless defendant's insistence. On the two or three occasions that a realistic defense had actually been available, McKay had been smart enough to bring in more-experienced criminal lawyers and had executed his role as the defendant's primary attorney competently, in the sense that he helped construct a reasonable payment schedule with the criminal-advocacy firm.

Michael didn't find McKay personally appealing, but the other two public defenders he met had between them three years' experience practicing law, and McKay had received Dean Walker's personal recommendation. McKay's deal with the young man was a hybrid between public defense and private advocacy, which Michael didn't fully understand beyond the fact that representation would cost him only three hundred dollars overall.

McKay was a tall man with a stylish haircut whose weight was concentrated in his rump and thighs. His hips seemed to be as wide as his shoulders. But he was affable and confident and clearly had a line into the local legal world—when Michael first met him, on the second floor of the imposing, limestone county courthouse, McKay was deep in conversation with the state's attorney who would later prosecute the young man.

"You're Michael Pollitz!" McKay boomed across his extended

hand before the young man spoke. McKay winked. "It's easy to tell a student around here," he explained, grinning as he looked up and down the courthouse hall. "Howard Walker told me you'd be coming by!" He glanced at his watch. "Excellent timing. What can I do for you?"

Michael was surprised by the question. "I understand you take public-defense cases," he began, but McKay interrupted.

"Howard gave me some background," he smiled, "and I'm sure we can work something out. Don't worry about that." He led the young man toward the stairs. "Why don't you tell me, in your words, what happened."

"I don't know," Michael answered.

"Well, you're going to be arraigned in a few days," McKay said over his shoulder, leading the way down into the center of the courthouse's first floor, where its two halls crossed and fed out to the four exterior doors, one facing each compass point. "We'd better go over the events and the procedures, just so you know what will be happening. First, though," he said as he sat on a bench against one wall, "we need to take care of our business." He fished in his briefcase for a pen and some forms. "This is just a standard agreement you'll need to sign. It states that I am representing you as a public defender, plus some boilerplate about what your rights are and the nature of your representation. It's a basic contract. If you'd like, I can just give these to you, and you can return the signed copies to me tomorrow." McKay offered the sheets. "It's probably better if you read them over and give everything some thought. Why don't you bring them by my house tomorrow morning?" He slid a business card from his briefcase and jotted his address on the back. "Tell you what. I'll find out what I can about the arraignment, and I'll walk you through the process tomorrow."

The young man nodded dumbly and stood along with the attorney. He followed McKay outside, barely noticing the chill in the overcast day, even though he wasn't wearing a coat. Mc-

Kay grinned in an odd way, with his even teeth closed. "I'll see you in the morning," he said. "If it helps, jot down your ideas or recollections, something that will help us reconstruct the basis for the charges against you. Meantime, I'll get the arrest records and everything else that's relevant right now. Sound okay?"

"This seems so unreal," Michael muttered.

11

He thought about Linda. He thought about how beautiful he thought she was and how she didn't agree. She didn't like the round end of her nose; she thought she was too short. She thought her breasts were too big. He could see her point about that, but he thought they were fine. She ironed her hair. He thought it looked lovely, dark and flowing away from her face. They had been together long enough for him to see her hair unironed, and he thought it looked pretty good as it came. He liked dating Linda. He liked it when they studied together. He liked making love with her. He liked the noises she made. He wished nothing had occurred to mess things up. He wished he could curl up in her bed in her dorm and not come out until the whole mess had disappeared.

"You may as well go find her," his roommate announced. "Beats whining about her all night."

Michael smiled at his roommate. He was convinced that Phil would end up in the ministry some day. Phil was from Ohio, a spare man with long blond hair and a political earnestness that Michael envied. Phil affected a randy insouciance and a small-time commitment to marijuana that Michael guessed were both quite temporary, probably confined only to his undergraduate years. Michael's fond suppositions regarding his roommate all proved to be accurate.

"If I had some idea where to look, I guess I might," Michael mused. "I don't think she's at the dorm. Maybe the library."

"Go see her," Phil urged. "It might be good for a blow job."

"If that's all the good that comes out of this hellish mess," Michael answered, "then I'm in really deep shit." They laughed with sophomoric titillation, but Michael knew that what he wanted more than anything else, including sex, was a few minutes of silent comfort.

12

"Who's this McKay asshole?" Dom barked.

Bruno raised his hands in bafflement. "I'm supposed to know?"

"Mikey says he's the public defender down there," John answered.

Dom glanced at his son, his lips tight with impatience. John lowered his eyes. "I meant," Dom said slowly, "find out who this McKay asshole is. I want to know." He glared at John and Sal. John kept his eyes on the floor. "A goddamn public defender!"

Sal shrugged. "I'll make a couple a calls, if you want."

"That's better," Dom replied with an angry smile. "Much better. See how easy it can be?"

"Hey, don't expect too much," Sal grumbled. "Mikey ain't goin' to school in the center of the fuckin' universe. Might be better to get a word from Allegretti."

Dom Calabria drummed his fingers lightly on the top of his

desk, breathing slowly through his nose. He leaned forward to reach for a cigarette and took his time igniting it. He reclined in his chair and released a stream of smoke toward the ceiling. "Who do you think I'm going to call in about two minutes?" he asked with scathing courtesy, speaking slowly and modulating his voice. "All I want you to do, Sal, is find out what kind of asshole this asshole is. What kind of cases he handles. If anyone we know knows him." His eyes glittered through the pall of smoke in front of his desk. "If you don't mind."

"Take it easy," Sal groaned. "I'll get what I can."

"Why can't Allegretti just take over?" John asked.

"I won't embarrass Mike like that," Dom answered. "You understand? He'll do what he's got to do. I just want to keep on top of it." He gestured at his son with the lit cigarette. "That means you don't give him any shit about what he's doing, and we don't tell him what to do. Understand?"

13

"It's all procedural," McKay said with as much reassurance as he could muster. "Don't let the process worry you."

Michael was terrified. The courtroom was filled with people, and practically none of them had anything to do with anything involving him. Yet all of them did. The recorder, the guards—everyone had a piece of him if they wanted it. The judge walked everyone through a few *pro forma* steps, as McKay had warned, and consulted with McKay and the state's attorney.

"What are these guys doing here?" Michael whispered into

McKay's ear. McKay glanced at two of the men from town who had been arrested along with the students. One was the junky whose withdrawal Michael had noticed in the county jail.

"They're also my clients in this case," McKay answered simply. "You're all being arraigned together." He gestured with his head toward the courtroom doors, and the young man saw his schoolmates and the other townies filing in with their attorneys.

The young man felt lost. The courtroom smelled of cigarettes and fear. People were moving, talking, interacting, and he had no idea what was going on, what his place in this machinery might be. He had an uneasy feeling that he could end up the star of an ugly show.

14

"I don't know how to keep going to class," Michael said. It was a cool night, and he wrapped his arms around his legs. The bleachers next to the soccer/lacrosse field seemed wet beneath his ass. He wanted Linda to wrap herself around him; he wanted to make love there on the bleachers.

"I think you need to put it out of your mind," she said. He reached for her, yearning. "Don't," she said.

He understood. He leaned back with his arm draped across the back of her hips. "It still has this unreal feeling to me," he said. He took a small swig from a bottle of sweet, cheap wine. She reached for the bottle.

He let his eyes rest on the track surrounding the athletic field. The oval around the newer baseball venue was asphalt, but this track was still cinder. The bleachers were only ten tiers in a brick enclosure. Behind them, separating the field from the road circling the campus, was a wall of evergreens, hawthorns and other plantings that were particularly lovely in the fall. It was a very civilized place to watch lacrosse. One hundred fifty yards away was the field house, of newer vintage than the bleachers. He looked across the campus and could see, through the trees, his dorm. A light was on in his room.

"I wish we could just back the calendar up a month," Linda said. She leaned against him.

"From what I understand, I'd have to back it up a lot farther than that to make this all go away," he answered.

"Dan said his attorney is filing for a continuance. So is Pat's," she answered.

"That's because they can afford real attorneys," he laughed with a touch of bitterness.

"How is this with your parents?" she asked, wondering briefly if it was appropriate. Linda had yet to meet Michael's family.

He shrugged. "How is it with *your* parents?"

"Not good," she answered. He appreciated her honesty, but he could tell she was withholding something. He assumed that their present conversation would be unwelcome news to Linda's parents.

"They are aware, aren't they, that I'm not a drug dealer?"

"I'm on your side, Mike," Linda replied.

He leaned back, resting his elbows on the next row of seats, but he left his fingers on her back. He ignored the moisture seeping through his coat sleeves. "It's pretty much over for you and me, isn't it?"

"No!" she protested, vehement, unhappy. She turned to lean across his body and kiss him deeply. He put his hand in her hair, hungry for the kiss.

15

"The news ain't good," Salvatore Bruno announced, flat and unemotional.

"Tell me," Dom said simply, lifting a cigarette from the box on his desk and staring away through the mullioned windows of the doors. His head disappeared in a wreath of cigarette smoke.

"This McKay," Sal said simply, his voice like the rumble of distant earth-moving machinery. *Dis McKay.*

"Well?"

"What he does, he mostly has wills and probates, insurance claims, that sort of shit. Like last century he was in the AG's office for a couple of years, which is how come he does PD cases. Might be okay if Mikey was lookin' to buy some real estate." Sal shook his massive head slowly. "This," he concluded, annunciating the *dis* with finality, "is one useless, cocksuckin', motherfuckin', piece a shit. Two of the other students, they already got continuances."

Dom's posture did not change, but his eyes narrowed slightly. He nodded, wisps of smoke trailing from his nostrils. Then he reached for the telephone and punched a few numbers. He held his cigarette in front of his eyes while he waited. "Get John," was all he said. He glanced again through the French doors, then at Sal. He smiled when his son came on the line.

"John, do you have Mike's number at school?" He exhaled another cloud of smoke. "Good. Do me a favor. Give him a call, tell him I think it would be a very good idea if Allegretti took over his case. As in immediately." He paused and listened for a moment. "Yeah, exactly that. Let me know what he says." He paused again. "Is that what I said?" he snapped. "Did I say that?" He waited for a couple of beats. "Just let me know what he says."

Dom carefully dropped the handset into the cradle. He stubbed out his cigarette and reached for another and glanced across his desk. "What?" he asked.

"Take it easy, Dom," Sal growled. "How bad can it be?"

"Who the fuck knows?"

"Just take it easy. Mikey, he ain't gonna do the smart thing here."

"Mike will do whatever he thinks is the right thing to do."

"That's what's got me worried," Sal groaned.

16

"Man, what a poem," Michael said softly, rereading Auden's 'Musée des Beaux Arts.' Several heads in the small class swung in his direction.

"That's one way of putting it," his professor said. She smiled. "Would you mind elaborating?"

Michael squirmed. He hadn't intended to be heard and was embarrassed that he had voiced his thought. He straightened in his seat. "It just does such a good job of exploring how insignificant we are," he began. "And I like how he lets us know that he knows his own thought isn't a new one, that artists have conveyed it time after time. It's sly."

"I like that," she said. " 'Sly.' A great word for Auden," and the discussion swirled away through the ten other students in the twentieth-century poetry class as a splendid May day glazed the tall windows of the small room they occupied in the oldest building on the campus. Michael basked in the conversation, almost completely lost in the contemplation of art as the school year neared its end and he was blissfully unaware that, as the only one of the five arrested students who was still there at the end of the term, he remained an object of almost continuous speculation.

17

"This is it?" Michael's father asked, staring up at the imposing stone courthouse. Its clock tower loomed above them.

Michael nodded apprehensively and wished his mother would stop wringing a handkerchief. He squinted in the glare of June sunlight reflecting off the pale limestone blocks of the building. "We're supposed to meet McKay on the second floor," he said. He forced himself to touch his mother's arm, using the distraction to get his feet to move on the hot asphalt of the parking lot. His father stretched his neck uncomfortably, unaccustomed to the pinch of a necktie. Spots of sweat dotted his shirt beneath his pectoral muscles. "Let's go," the young man said. He glanced across the street at his college campus. It looked different in the summer sun, pastoral but somehow sterile without students walking between the buildings. His mother took his arm, holding her head bravely upright.

"What do we do?" his father asked.

Michael pulled open one of the tall double doors at the top of a flight of stone steps. "We meet McKay on the second floor," he said.

"I meant…"

"I know what you meant," Michael said. "But I don't know any better than you do, Pa."

McKay was seated on one of the benches lining the walls outside of the courtrooms on the second floor. He effusively introduced himself to the young man's parents and ushered them into an empty courtroom. He gestured toward a table. McKay held a chair for Michael's mother, who thanked him self-consciously. McKay answered with his closed-toothed smile. He sat and opened his briefcase, talking as he removed a legal pad, a pen and a few documents. "We have a number of options today," he explained, glancing from face to face as he arranged items on the table, "but in essence, you're here to enter a plea." He stood suddenly and removed his suit jacket. "As I'm sure you know, there are only two pleas, 'not guilty' or 'guilty.' The difference, and where the options come in, is what happens next, depending upon how you plead."

Michael glanced at his father, who said nothing. His father seemed overawed by the courthouse's bustling attorneys and solemn air of power. He had greeted McKay with excessive deference, Michael thought. Finally, Michael said, "Why don't you explain the differences."

"Well, nothing's guaranteed. I can just give you my best guesses. With me so far?" He again produced his smile. "The simplest thing, albeit with a few drawbacks, is entering a 'guilty' plea. Then today's hearing is the only hearing." He raised a hand as Michael began to protest. "I have already discussed this and the other possibilities with the state's attorney, so I could give you an informed view, but let me go through your options before you accept or reject any." He waited for the young man to indicate assent. "Good. As I say, a guilty plea ends your case today. The state's attorney has agreed to a plea bargain that will clear your record, after a probationary sentence, although this requires approval from the judge, of course, but he'll probably go along with the prosecution's recommendation. On the other hand, if you plead not guilty, then the case goes to trial. Our choice at that point, depending on what course the state's attorney and judge wish to pursue, will be to decide whether to request a jury or a bench trial." He paused again to glance around the table. "Before we go into any details," he concluded, "I should say that my gut feeling is a 'guilty' plea is your best choice."

"How so?" Michael asked, carefully trying to maintain an objective air. "You just said it has a few drawbacks."

"The drawbacks are the obvious ones," McKay answered breezily. When the young man's parents glanced at one another in confusion, he paused. "As the law is written, Mike is guilty," he explained. "The attitude of the court is to take drug-trafficking charges very seriously, and there are always advantages to expanding the time frame in a case like this. I mean, we could find some gray areas. The law isn't always black and white. Certainly not in a courtroom."

"And if I plead guilty, I'm putting myself at the mercy of the court."

McKay smiled at the melodramatic phrasing. "If you want to see it that way," he replied.

"Then what are the advantages of pleading guilty today?"

"Well, there are several. Foremost, it will mean the prosecution does not have to continue to prepare a case and thus has an incentive toward leniency, whereas if he must take it to trial, that incentive disappears. Simply put, the prosecution would like to get the case off the docket as quickly as it can." Michael's hands and mouth moved, but no sounds came out. McKay raised a finger to slow him and continued, "You see, the state's attorney feels a conviction is assured, if we go to trial. He has the testimony of the Illinois Bureau of Investigation agent, and by statute, that will be sufficient. The charge is assisting in the sale. The agent will testify that you accompanied him to the room where he purchased drugs, and that you knew beforehand that said purchase was his intent. That makes you guilty of a felony, according to the law. Based on this reality, as the prosecuting attorney sees it, if we decide to try the case, he has told me that he views a plea of not guilty a bit more aggressively."

"What does that mean?" Michael asked.

"In practical terms, it probably means he will push for penalties, if you are convicted, whereas if you enter a guilty plea today, no fine will be requested." McKay looked down at some notes on his legal pad while the young man and his parents stared at one another.

"I can't pay a fine!" his father breathed, panicky and out of his depth. Everyone else seemed to have inside information, seemed to know what was going on in ways that were being withheld from him. "How much?" he asked weakly.

"The statutory maximum is twenty-five thousand dollars," McKay answered, looking up from his legal pad.

"My God!" the young man's father moaned.

"My feeling is, if we take it to trial and lose, we will be facing a fine of some kind," McKay said, his voice neutral. "And most likely a prison term of two to five years."

"How is this possible?" Michael asked. "I didn't do anything!"

McKay raised his eyebrows, as if it was unnecessary to disagree, as far as the law was concerned. Michael's father snorted and shook his head with disgust. He tried to concentrate. "What should we do?" he stammered, a forgotten accent creeping into his voice.

"As I suggested earlier," McKay said patiently, "my recommendation is a plea of guilty, a negotiated plea. The benefit is, your record will be expunged, once you've completed a probationary period. And there will be no fine levied. But it's not my decision to make." He stared expectantly at Michael.

"What happens if I want a trial?" Michael asked. "I mean, what if I plead not guilty?"

His father snorted again.

"Well, a trial date will be set today." McKay shrugged. "I can continue to represent you as a public defender, but I would recommend that we involve others in my office or at other firms. This would require that we move outside the public arena." He shrugged again as the young man's father shifted uncomfortably in his seat.

"How much longer would it go on?" Michael whispered, feeling defeated already, wishing his father wasn't in the room.

"I would guess that it would continue through the summer," McKay answered. "It depends on how vigorously you wish us to present your defense, or rather," he caught himself, "how much you are willing to extend this situation. Perhaps the trial would be next fall. Such a delay might offer some advantages," McKay continued, "but I have to warn you, it also involves some expense." As it happened, this obvious tactic would be followed by all of the other students' defense teams; one of the freshmen who actually had been selling drugs wouldn't settle with the state's attorney until nearly two years later, when the local office was sufficiently worn down to agree to a misdemeanor charge that had nothing to do with controlled substances and required only a fine of a couple of thousand dollars as retribution.

"Am I allowed to change my plea later on?"

"You mean if you plead not guilty today?" When Michael nodded, McKay shrugged. "Yes, of course. It's not at all unusual to negotiate a plea at a later date. However, the state's attorney will have prepared a case, as I said, and will probably demand somewhat harsher terms than he is offering now."

"What, precisely, happens if I plead guilty?" Michael asked, trying to keep a tone of trapped despair out of his voice.

"First and foremost, it gets all of this behind you that much sooner," McKay nodded, trying to be reassuring, "but everything else is up to the judge. I can discuss it with the state's attorney," he added. "My guess is they won't be too hard on you."

Michael looked at his father, who didn't return his gaze. "It ends today if I plead guilty?" he asked.

McKay nodded and smiled reassuringly.

"Let's get it over with," Michael breathed, lost and hopeless. He felt as though he had just stepped off the edge of a scaffold with a rope around his neck.

"Good," said McKay. "I think it's the right decision. Let me talk with the prosecutor." He rose, sifting through his notes and forms and stuffing documents into his briefcase. "This is going to take a few minutes." He looked at his watch. "Maybe you'd like to get some lunch?"

"We'll wait here," Michael's father declared.

"Fine," McKay smiled. "I'll be back when we're ready for the hearing."

18

"Am I correct in understanding this issue is settled?" the judge asked, his eyebrows lifted as he glanced from the state's attorney to McKay. Michael stared up from the defendant's table in confusion, feeling a rising sense of alarm as both attorneys nodded. It seemed to be happening too quickly. He and his parents had waited for more than an hour while McKay spoke with the prosecuting attorney, and now it felt as though they would be in the courtroom only a few minutes. The judge studied a file folder for a moment, gazed over his glasses at the young man, then looked back at McKay. "And your client is ready to enter a plea?" he asked.

"That's the entirety of the agreement," McKay said softly, reaching up to the bench with another file folder. "With these addenda." The state's attorney muttered something, and the judge nodded. Michael couldn't hear everything that was being said at the bench. It made him uneasy.

The judge nodded down at the prosecutor and McKay in turn, and as they returned to their tables, he spoke softly to the court reporter and leaned back, steepling his fingers as he studied the young man. The judge waited as Michael stood, then asked if he was ready to enter a plea. Michael nodded.

"You'll have to address the court," the judge said in a warm tone. "Say 'yes' or 'no,' we can't record a nod." He smiled indulgently.

"Yes, your honor," Michael said.

"What do you plead?"

The young man glanced at McKay, who responded with an unruffled nod, his lower lip jutting out, his odd smile meant to reassure. Michael had a momentary thought that McKay was going to wink at him. He faced the judge. "Guilty," Michael said. It felt like bile was creeping into his throat as the judge nodded again and ran through the procedural recording of the plea.

The judge paused and stared down at the documents in front

of him. Michael stood with his hands at his sides, feeling utterly helpless. The judge glanced at McKay. "As agreed, we will proceed to sentencing today." He cleared his throat while he waited for McKay and the state's attorney to indicate their assent, then returned his attention to Michael. "You are to be remanded to the custody of the state police and taken to a correctional institution, where you will serve a sentence of not less than thirty days and not more than ninety days," the judge intoned. Michael's eyes widened and his mouth opened into a small slot, but he managed to maintain a composed expression, even though he felt like his stomach had just fallen onto the floor. His mother gasped behind him. "After which time," the judge went on, "you will be placed on probation for a period of two years, commencing when you begin your sentence. I have heard the arguments for leniency in this case and feel they have merit, based on your age and lack of a criminal record." He looked down at the young man, pausing for effect. "If you complete your probationary period without further incident, all records of these proceedings will be expunged." He paused again. "You committed a serious crime," the judge continued, but Michael shook his head with his mouth working soundlessly, confused and with white noise filling his mind, shocked protest growing in his thoughts, *I didn't do anything. I walked a guy to a room!* barely hearing the judge's voice as he was overcome by the terror of prison, "but it is the opinion of this court that you are not a flight risk. Consequently, you will be given a week to present yourself at Astoria Adult Correctional Facility, where you will serve your sentence." Another weighty pause. "Let me give you a piece of advice, son," the judge said. "You are being given an opportunity. Complete your sentence and your probation, and stay out of trouble, and this will all be behind you."

As the judge closed the proceedings, the young man's attorney said, "Thank you, your honor," and Michael was too stunned to scream. It seemed that his mother cried the entire ride back to Barrington. Michael remained in a state of numb shock. *A blessing,* he vaguely recognized, *better than the fear.* But there wasn't enough air in the car.

19

"You *pleaded* guilty?" his brother screeched, aghast. "How can that be? You're going to jail? I can't believe this!" He squeezed his head, his sideburns emerging comically from beneath the heels of his hands, as he stared from the young man to his mother and father. "How could this happen?"

"It was Mr. McKay's advice," his father finally replied. He sat heavily in his easy chair, weary and beaten.

"McKay."

"Michael's attorney," his mother answered, drained and dry-eyed now, trying to make sense of what seemed to be a senseless outcome.

"He said Mike should plead guilty?"

"He thought it would be even worse if it went through a trial." Some heat crept into his father's voice. "The judge! He said it. A serious crime, he said!"

"Worse?" the young man's brother stormed, waving his hands in the air. "How could it be worse? What more could they do than send you to jail?" He stood with his mouth hanging open in disbelief, looking from his father to his brother, finally turning to his mother. She shrugged with miserable confusion.

"Pa's referring to possible fines," Michael said at length, his voice almost a whisper. "Maybe a longer prison sentence. I don't know."

"A serious crime, the judge said!" his father shouted. "This is what happens!"

"I can't believe this!" His brother's face was red. "What the hell kind of attorney was this?"

"You get what you pay for," Michael muttered. He dropped his sport coat onto a chair as he moved across the room, tugging at his loose tie to pull it from his collar. His mind felt swollen, like a hollow, empty roar was filling his ears with a lonely solitude too immense to comprehend. He walked slowly upstairs to the bathroom and stood staring into the mirror. He barely recognized the ashen face he saw. There were tears moistening the stranger's cheeks.

20

"Astoria!" John shouted. "What the fuck's Astoria?" The question seemed directed at the ceiling of Dominick's office.

"I know the place," Angelo DeMicco said. "It's a medium joint, down somewheres near Peoria, around there someplace."

"Ahhh, Mikey," John moaned. He reached out a big hand to drum softly on the young man's shoulder. "How can this be?"

Salvatore Bruno frowned with regret as he rose from the leather couch. "Yeah, I know the dump too. 'S fucked up, kid," he said. "A real bitch, goin' away on this bullshit."

Michael shook his head in utter misery, unable to speak.

"This shouldn't be happening!" John blurted. "Mikey didn't do nothin'!"

Sal and Angie exchanged pitying glances. Right and wrong

meant nothing to them. The issue was only what you got stuck with. "It ain't gonna be as bad as you think," DeMicco said.

Bruno stepped around DeMicco to gather the young man into a massive hug. He then held him at arm's length, Michael's shoulders disappearing in the grip of the big man's hands. "Listen, Mikey. I'll tell you what to do. Doin' time, it's just a part of life," Sal rasped. "It's just something you get through." *Somethin' ya get troo.*

"It ain't part of Mike's life," Dom snarled, a cold cigarette trapped in his taut lips.

Bruno glanced at the desk and shrugged. "It is for the next month or so," he grunted.

Dom looked away, his face a stone mask. He drummed his fingers on the desk and controlled himself with visible effort, finally reaching for the cigarette lighter with a slight nod.

"Here's what you do," Sal continued. "It ain't a heavy place, a medium work farm. You ain't doin' a long stretch. Just do the time and get the fuck outta there. Understand? Don't try to make no friends, don't do nothin' except get it over with."

Michael nodded almost studiously, still in a state of confused desolation. Bruno released his grip.

"When do you have to surrender yourself?" Dom lit the cigarette and exhaled a thin stream of smoke, still looking away.

"No later than six days from now," Michael answered. "I guess I'll just go tomorrow," he added, trying to keep a quaver out of his voice.

"How come all of this shit happened so fast?" John asked, his tone strained and pitched higher than normal.

"I wanted it over with," Michael replied. He felt immensely stupid, like he had allowed events to control him with disastrous results. "Guess it kind of backfired," he added. He couldn't shake the feeling that he had been kicked in the stomach. The sense of dislocation and injury had stayed with him, a waking constant ever since the sentence was passed. He pushed his hair back with one hand.

"Why can't we appeal?" John asked, his rough, deep voice almost a whine.

"You can't appeal a guilty plea, for Chrissakes," Bruno muttered.

DeMicco stretched out a long arm and wrapped it around Michael's head, pulling him off balance. "Take it easy, Mikey," the big thug growled. "No one likes doin' time, but it ain't as bad as you think. Sal. He's right. You just go through it." He shook the boy, his version of an affectionate hug. "Don't be scared, kid."

"Well, I am."

"Course you are," Bruno chuckled. "Who ain't, first time?" He reached out with a huge fist and tapped Michael lightly on the crown of his head. "That's natural." He smiled, his wide face softening uncharacteristically. "No one wants to do time, you better believe it."

"That's the truth, Mikey," Angie laughed without humor. *Dat's da troot.* "It's just something you get through. That's all. Take my word." He shook the young man's body once more and released him. He leered at Sal. "We ought to take Mikey over to Half Day, to the club. Get him laid at least before he goes inside." Bruno rumbled out a laugh.

"Can it," Dom snapped.

"I've got to go," Michael muttered. He looked across the desk and smiled sadly.

"John, give him a lift," Dom said. He walked from behind the desk and opened his arms. "It'll be okay, Mike," he said softly as he embraced the young man. He glanced at the others. They moved away. Dom spoke softly. "Mike. You remember when you and John were ten, when he rode his bike into the back of that car, that Cadillac with the fins?" Dom waited until Michael nodded. "How long did it take you to walk him back here with his broken collar bone?"

"A couple of hours, I guess."

Dom laughed gently. "I don't mean literally. How long did it feel like it took?" When Michael shrugged, Dom pressed lightly on his shoulder. "It felt like forever, didn't it?" Michael nodded, looking into Dom's face. "This'll feel like forever, but it ain't. Just remember who you are, and get it over with." He smiled slightly, trying to be reassuring as he stared into the young man's eyes. "Just remember who you are, Mike."

21

"This is terrible!" Linda said, her voice more awed than anguished.

"Yeah," Michael replied, clenching the telephone receiver. He squeezed his eyes shut, picturing her on the phone. Was she in her family's den or in the kitchen? He loved Linda's home, a big, white Victorian-styled fortress in River Forest. He could clearly see her upscale, tree-lined street. He wanted to be there.

"How long? This just isn't right!"

Michael sighed. "A maximum of ninety days."

"You'd miss the start of school!"

"That's pretty much the least of my worries."

"Oh, Mike!"

He pictured tears starting in her green eyes. "Listen. Can I see you tonight?"

The long pause was devastating. "Oh, Mike," she repeated. "I can't. My folks, they... I couldn't."

Michael raised his head and smiled furiously, staring through the living room window at the trees outside. He tried to picture how Linda's parents had reacted to his arrest, imagining raised voices in their elegant living room. They weren't hateful people, and they liked him, but he assumed his current problem had utterly changed their view of his character. "Forget it," he said softly.

"I'm so sorry," Linda breathed.

"Forget it," he said again, almost whispering.

"I don't know what to say."

He laughed. " 'Good luck' would be nice. 'Goodbye' works too." He dropped the receiver into its cradle and pushed a hand through his hair, still staring out at the street.

22

"Do we have anyone there?" Dom asked. He held his palm steady on the blotter on top of his desk, then straightened and shifted his weight away from his chair.

Bruno shook his head. Dom walked to the French doors, agitated and straining to control his rage. "I'll try to find someone," Sal said. After a pause that was freighted with confusion, he added almost mournfully, "He's gonna have a rough time."

Dom turned away from the panes with quick anger flashing across his face. "The kid's tough where it counts," he snapped.

Sal stared back, shrugging finally. "It's short time," he said. "He'll be okay. The same, I wish we could get him in segregation."

"It ain't that kinda joint," DeMicco said. "There's nothin' we can do. Can't even get a word out."

Dom sat behind his desk and lit a cigarette. "Stupid," he barked with sudden intense vehemence, thinking he should somehow have insisted on using his lawyer, not some incompetent third-rate small-town asshole. He exhaled a cloud of smoke and shook his head.

"Mikey's a stand-up kid," Bruno said. "He'll handle it."

"Yeah," DeMicco echoed. "It's a work farm. He'll be all right."

"God damn it!" Dominick shouted, his face red with fury. "It's fucking time that kid shouldn't be doing! I give a shit how short it is!" He slammed his open palm down on his desk. "Don't 'try,' Sal," he growled, pointing at Bruno with his cigarette. "Fucking do it! *Find* someone! A goddamn guard. I want that kid taken care of like he was my own son, you hear me? Like my own fucking son!"

23

"Just drop me in the parking lot," Michael said, his voice tight with bitterness and fear, "and take off." His mother gasped suddenly, horrified and somehow startled by the long fences of Astoria Adult Correctional Facility, as if the reality of a prison had not before crystallized in her mind. She had been bizarrely confident the whole long ride from Barrington, but the sight of the walls and wire put an end to the upbeat charade. Michael hadn't spoken more than twenty words during the three-and-a-half-hour trip.

His father turned into the drive, his breathing ragged. As he neared the guardhouse, he said brokenly, "This is my fault."

"It doesn't matter now," Michael said venomously. "Stay in the car," he snapped, jumping out of the back seat. His mother rolled her window down, and he leaned inside to briefly hug her. "Don't cry, Ma," he said softly. "It's not a long time." He looked fiercely at his father and added, "Don't come back here. I'll get home all right."

"We'll pick you up," his father began, but Michael cut him off.

"No. I'll get home fine. Don't come back here." He then turned as bravely as he could and walked without a backward glance to the gate, where a guard stood watching with a clipboard in one hand.

24

After his tenth day in Astoria, Michael spent all but the last two days of the thirty-four days he served of his sentence in the small prison infirmary recovering from a concussion, a dislocated jaw, multiple facial fractures and lacerations, several broken bones in his right hand, a fissured rectum and cracked ribs. It was an unfortunate accident of timing, because the assault occurred the day after Salvatore Bruno finally reached a guard who was willing to do business, and the protection Dominick Calabria was attempting to purchase arrived twenty-four hours too late.

It happened in the usual way, following a predictable path that Michael in some part of his mind perceived as it was in process, beginning his first afternoon in the cells. Even as he went through the orientation—an amusing word, he thought at the time, to describe the most disorienting experience of his life—and was assigned a cell, other inmates were howling at him, the cacophony of their voices blending into a constant background noise of smacking lips, epithets, laughter, threats, "Hey, fresh meat!" "Here, chickie, chickie, chickie," and spit flying onto his shirt, his hair, "Come git a piece of my big job, baby!" like the immense disjointed noise of hundreds of crows gathered in early morning oaks. It wasn't like the movies, but it *was* like the movies, he thought as he tried to sleep the first night. Maybe even more so. A year later he would wonder if the growth spurt that began shortly before his twentieth birthday might have made a difference and concluded it would not have.

Unable to even theorize the efficiency of a prison grapevine, it frightened him to realize that before he had been inside twelve hours all the inmates and guards seemed to know he was a college student and despised him for it so thoroughly that he might as well have delivered himself to the prison gates in a Boy Scout uniform. After receiving his clothing, toiletries and instructions and following the towering guard through a milling mass of jeering prisoners to his small cell with two pallets arranged like bunk beds, a toilet and sink with a small steel shelf for toilet articles, on the second tier halfway down one ell of the large, barn-like, modern cellblock, he did not utter a word for four days. Not in the mess hall, not in the common areas, not in the fields, not in the yard. On his fourth day inside, the man who shared his cell was released. They had not spoken to one another. No one replaced the man in the cell.

The taunting continued without pause until the afternoon he was carried to the infirmary, but no real direct contact occurred with anyone. Contrary to the ignorant, lurid, fanciful scripts of his mind, nothing happened to him in the shower, or as he carried his trays of food, or in the work buildings, or the fields, or the common room of his cellblock, yet he was harassed constantly, almost obligatorily. By the evening meal of his third day inside, he became aware that a big blond inmate with sculpted muscles like a committed body-builder was focusing on him, catching his eye and kissing the air, rapid series of two or three loud smooches, then laughing with such omnidirectional violence that the young man began to harbor childish fantasies of effective self-defense. The blond was invariably accompanied by an equally muscular black convict and a smaller but likewise built white man, and by the end of his fifth day inside, all three were giving him an uncomfortable amount of attention, the blond in particular flexing his massive arms and displaying his amateurish jailhouse tattoos. The young man knew what was coming but had no idea of any kind as to what to do about it. And still the screaming of crows battered him wherever he was, whatever he was doing.

Michael had imagined that in prison, even a lower-security installation like Astoria, he would be under constant observation. He was surprised to discover that this wasn't at all the case, that the men had substantial freedom of movement in the cellblocks and common areas. It was typical for inmates coming off their work details to return to their cells to change shirts or retrieve laundry, to gather basically at will in the yard or exercise areas. Nor was their time as regimented as he had anticipated. Softball games weren't uncommon at the diamond in the yard. It was as if the total abnegation of self—once in the hands of the prison system, any concept of 'me' an inmate might cling to was stripped away more quickly and indifferently than someone on the outside might discard junk mail—was sufficient, that within the double rows of tall fences topped with concertina wire, there was no urgent need to restrict the caged animals further, which was how it was possible that in the middle of his tenth afternoon at Astoria he could return to his cell for a clean undershirt to find the hulking blond standing next to his bunk with his two leering henchmen crowded against the walls on either side of the steel door.

"Hello there, honeybunch," the blond minced, smiling with such rapacious delight that the young man was barely aware of anything beyond the sudden burst of adrenaline boiling in his stomach.

He turned swinging his fist to struggle out of his cell, but the big blond threw a hard right cross that seemed to instantly split the skin of his left eyebrow, and he spun with the blow into the black convict's rising forearm, lights flashing too brightly for him to recognize anything else that was happening, surprised that the pain wasn't greater when he was wheeled around from behind and the blond's knee slammed into the bottom of his face, his teeth piercing the skin below his lower lip in a splash of blood as his chin bounced off the floor. He heard a strange clashing sound as a tooth chipped but heard nothing more for a moment as a bright orange pain exploded in the back of his jaw with a grinding noise that seemed to originate within his ear. His teeth were no longer aligned, and his mouth hung open, his jaw no longer under his control. He tried to push off the floor when a second kick cracked the side of his head into the toilet and his awareness became tenuous. One of them grabbed the belt of his pants, lifting his hips off the floor, then the black man picked up his head by his hair, drew back his left arm, and punched him in the right eye. More dazzling bursts of light. At the same moment, a boot blasted his ribs, and he heard the black convict whoop as mucous burst out of his nostrils.

"Lookee there! Ah punched the snot out of 'im!"

"Bullshit!" crowed a voice from above. "I kicked his skinny ass!"

"Ah'll show ya," the black man announced, switching his grip to clasp a handful of hair with his left hand as he carefully cocked his heavily muscled right arm, and Michael stared uncomprehendingly as he saw the brown fist draw away, then come hard into his left eye, the black man grunting with gleeful satisfaction as Michael's cheekbone cracked and blood spurted from his eyebrow. A new blossom of pain flowered from his twisted jaw when his face again bounced onto the floor. He vaguely felt his pants being tugged away.

"Ride that cowboy, Mac!" the kicker's voice hooted again from above.

"Ah'm gonna give this bitch a taste o' mah ole' johnson," he heard the black voice announce as his head was once again lifted by his hair. "You suck, bitch," the man instructed him, but his jaw wouldn't move one way or another, and he passed out momentarily as the pain in his jaw filled his head with a pale rose glow when the black man's bumping and pushing shifted the position of the dislocated mandible. He didn't really feel anything at all outside of the vortex of general pain so consuming that it became a separate reality of its own as his face pushed rhythmically across the floor to bump against the base of the toilet, but for some reason the hooting laughter remained very clear in his mind, along with the big blond's voice announcing, "You Mac's punk now, little pussy!" and lip-smacking mock smooches in the air above him.

He wasn't discovered for another forty-five minutes, when a guard at the station in the center of the cellblock heard him retching in his cell and found him semiconscious on the cement floor, unable to rise to his knees although he pushed weakly at the floor with his hands, lying face-down in a pool of blood and vomit, whimpering softly with his pants around one ankle and a small trickle of blood leaking from his anus.

25

John paused at the entrance of the narrow infirmary ward. The guard pointed along the wall to the fifth bed, where the young man lay. John glanced at another prisoner in the bed closest to the steel door and walked to Michael's side. At first, John couldn't tell if his friend's eyes were open or not, they were so swollen. His purple and yellow jaw was so thick it distorted the shape of his face to such a degree that John would not have recognized him at a glance, even without the bandages surrounding his chin and taped over his stitched left eyebrow. His right hand was wrapped and seemed to be splinted; John couldn't tell. "Jesus, Mikey," John said softly, his face contorted with rage and pity. John had never seen anyone beaten as badly as Michael. He waved his hands in confusion, unsure what he could touch without causing pain. Michael raised his left hand to grasp John's fingers. He forced his eyes open to look up from the pillow, and John could see that his left eye was red with blood. When Michael shifted the position of his head, John glimpsed another cluster of stitches in a swollen, shaved patch of his scalp, above and behind his left ear.

"I got stitches in my asshole," Michael said. Through his wired jaw, his voice lisped, so what came out was, *I got shtitchesh in my ashhole,* and as he clenched fiercely onto John's hand, tears leaked out of his bruised, bulbous eye sockets. John began to cry with impotent fury.

"We'll get the motherfuckers, Mikey," he blubbered. "God damn it!" He pulled a sleeve over his eyes. "Who done this to you?" he finally asked.

"Three guys," Michael answered. "Big blond guy called Mac, big black guy, 'nother guy."

"Christ! They beat the shit outta you!"

"They *fucked* me," Michael said, and John started to cry again, his fists clenched. He choked out inarticulate vows of vengeance, asking who are they, who are they?

"They broke my tooth," the young man said. "The black guy's gotta have a cut up dick from it."

"The jig fucked you in the mouth?" John sobbed brokenly, aghast. Michael grunted assent. John reached out to lift the young man's upper lip with his thumb. "It's just a little chip outta a front tooth, Mikey," he said, as if it mattered. Michael grunted again, confused. To his tongue it felt like half the tooth was missing, leaving a jagged serration. John glanced over his shoulder at the guard in the doorway, then leaned forward. "Those guys are dead, man," he promised. "You hear me, Mikey?" The young man closed his eyes.

"They fucked me," he repeated softly. "Two of 'em, anyway."

"They're dead, man," John repeated. He stared at his friend's battered face. The color of the bruises repulsed him. "You hurting?" he finally asked.

Michael rolled his head slightly on the pillow. The motion made him queasy. "Little buzzed," he muttered dreamily. He opened his eyes and stared at the ceiling through an unfocused red scrim. "Here's what I want," he said at last.

"Anything, man. Tell me."

"I want this Mac fucker to fall off a roof with a broomstick up his ass. And I want the black guy to strangle on his own prick." He felt incongruously calm and mildly addled by painkillers. He let his eyes fall shut again.

"You got it, Mikey," John said hoarsely. "The day the fuckers get outta here, I swear," holding the young man's left hand tightly between his palms.

"Don't know who they are." A fog was descending.

"We'll find 'em, Mikey. Don't worry." John's jaw clenched; the skin around his eyes felt tight. "We'll have a blowtorch party with the third cocksucker."

"No," the young man said quickly, his eyes open and almost alert. "No. I want him to think about it."

That night, when John recounted the details of his visit in his father's office, Salvatore Bruno and Angelo DeMicco grinned at one another.

"Kid don't fuck around," Bruno chuckled.

"Always said he was a smart kid," DeMicco added.

Dominick Calabria lifted a cigarette from the gold box on the edge of his desk and tapped the filter on the blotter. He fingered the cigarette without lighting it and stared sadly at the night through the mullioned panes of the French doors.

Lights were on in the barn. "None of this should've happened," he said finally, the anger in his face like a mean dog straining against a leash.

"Hey, whaddaya want?" Sal protested, raising his hands. "It took a while to reach one of them hick guards."

Dominick glanced from the windows without turning. "You were too late, Sal. Too fuckin' late." He swung around in his chair, staring at Bruno. He finally lit his cigarette, still glaring through the wreath of smoke as he regained control over his voice. "You find out who these three..." he paused with his teeth grinding, no word in his vocabulary seeming adequate to express his rage, "...pieces of shit are. I want to know when they're getting out of that shithole. If it's ahead of Mike, I want to know where they go. Nothin' else until Mike's out of there and I get a chance to talk to him." He looked from face to face, finally staring at his son. "Nothin' else. Understand?"

"They beat the shit outta him, Dad," John almost sobbed. "They fucked him up bad."

"It ain't permanent," Dom answered, spinning in his chair to turn his back on the room. He sent a spire of smoke toward the ceiling. "Nothin' else, God damn it."

26

"I told you not to come back here," Michael said through his immobile teeth. He felt an overwhelming desire to snatch his unbandaged left hand from his mother's grasping fingers, wanted her to stop worrying over him and get the hell out. His father stared at his eyes, his thin lips trembling, unable to read any expression on his son's misshapen face. Michael's head was hammering with pain, the sunlight through the barred, west-facing infirmary windows dripping through his eyes like hot wax. His brother paced back and forth behind his father's head, his jumpy discomfort giving the young patient a repulsive feeling of vertigo.

"You couldn't expect us to sit home," his father gasped, "when…"

"Oh, honey," his mother groaned. "What have they done to you?"

"It was a fight, Ma," Michael said softly. "I got beat up, is all."

"I bet you gave it back," his brother blurted.

Suddenly his older brother seemed like a small child to him. "Not really," he finally said, as his mother continued to gently grip his hand. Later, as they made the long, desolate drive back north, his brother would repeatedly reassure himself that Mike had given as good as he could, that's how he broke his right hand, fighting back, but the young man would have laughed at the idea. He had half-thrown precisely one punch with no effect whatsoever, although he may have cracked a knuckle on the floor when he first fell, but the broken bones occurred beneath a boot, after the attack ended, a playfully vicious parting shot at a point at which his consciousness was so questionable that he had no idea which of the three men had amused himself with one last bit of cruelty. In the end, the broken bones in his right hand would prove to be among the most durable of his physical injuries, because the ring finger would never again completely straighten.

His father lowered his head, biting back tears as his hand rested on the young man's knee. Only through an effort of will did Michael manage to keep his leg still. When his mother reached out, sudden tears glistening on her cheeks, to caress his face, he involuntarily flinched away, the sharp anger in his eyes cracking her courageous façade and releasing a torrent of frightened tears. He softened with regret and lisped, "Sorry, Ma. It's sore."

"This is all my fault," his father moaned with his head down, as if he felt the weight of the enormity of blame he was trying to claim for himself.

"How's it your fault, Pa?" the young man muttered. "I got in the fight," thinking, *Don't try to make this your responsibility, Pa,* I'm *the idiot who followed your advice.*

"You shouldn't even be here!" his brother said in confused anguish.

Michael whispered, "'Should's' got nothing to do with it," but none of them heard him.

27

He recognized his assailants sitting together on the small tier of benches next to the baseball diamond. They smirked in unison as they saw him approaching.

"Well lookee here," said the black convict, flexing his muscular shoulders. "Ah bet this bitch wants another taste of mah sweet thang." He smacked his lips suggestively, grabbed his crotch and cackled.

"Funny you should say that, Sam," Michael said, squinting at the black man. "It's the last thing you're ever going to eat."

The black man raised his eyebrows in mock fear, but a trace of anger crossed his eyes as he glanced past the young man at a huge guard who was moving toward them. The big blond, Mac, sucked air through his teeth and spat at the young man's feet.

"You don't know me, asshole," the young man said to him.

"But you're dead. A corpse. Hear me? A fucking corpse." Mac shook his hands as if he was trembling. Michael smiled, his face distorted by his wired jaw. "You don't know me," he repeated, "but you're going to meet some of my friends. Let me teach you a new word. Defenestration. I'd say you can look it up, but you probably can't. It means you better learn how to fly, you hopeless piece of shit. You're going to take a walk off a building with a stick out your ass." The blond laughed with hard bravado, but the muscles of his jaw worked with rage. Something about the kid's uninflected declaration was making him nervous.

The third convict mimed masturbation and laughed, but the young man felt an inner surge when he recognized something, a small glint of insecurity in the man's dull eyes. The young man kept his voice flat, still delivering guarantees, not threats. "Don't worry, dog shit. I won't forget you," he said directly to his third attacker.

"Where you think you can hide, punk?" the blond snarled.

"I'm leaving, fool," the young man answered. "But that's a better question for me to ask you. And believe me, you'll want to find a hole to hide in." He smiled crookedly, his lips parting slightly as his speech lisped between his closed teeth. "Here's a promise. You won't live a month after you're out of here." He turned away without ever changing his monotone. "Not a month." He walked past the approaching guard, feeling a small ache in his jaw.

28

"Don't look so bad today," John said, gazing at the long double fence extending along planted fields out into the distance. From inside the air-conditioned car, the late-July sun made the seemingly endless rows of corn look fecund beyond imagination.

"Every joint's bad," Salvatore said, shifting his bulk behind the wheel. He stared at the guard station.

"Get out to meet him. Give him these," Dom said, reaching into the backseat to hand John a pair of wraparound sunglasses. He leaned back in his seat and closed his eyes, as if he was about to take a nap. Bruno reached into the inside pocket of his jacket and fished out three photographs. He glanced at the prints, then set them down on the seat. Dom picked up the photos, looked at each in turn, and set them down again. They waited in silence.

After some thirty minutes, the door of the gatehouse opened. John got out of the car into the clanging sunlight and stepped around the trunk to meet his friend. Michael walked to the gates accompanied by two guards, his face set. One said, "Good luck, kid," as he opened the gates.

"Ayyyy, Mikey!" John crowed, opening his arms and holding onto a broad grin, but his eyes narrowed as he studied the swollen scar across Michael's left eyebrow, the pink line beneath his lip and the stubbled patch on the side of his head. They embraced briefly, and he handed the sunglasses to the young man. "You okay?" he asked, squeezing Michael's shoulder. Michael nodded and climbed into the back seat of the Cadillac, adjusting the shades over his eyes and thankful, because he was already tearing up. Salvatore and Dom reached across the seat to shake his hand. Dom held his hand for a moment, pressing softly as he studied the damage to the young man's face. His jaw twitched once.

"Thanks for coming," Michael said, an almost imperceptible tremble in his voice. The men turned forward.

"Let's get the fuck outta here," Sal said, throwing the car into gear.

The two guards stared at the car as it pulled out of the parking lot.

"Who picked him up?" one said.

"Got me," the other replied. "Let's get someone to run the plate." That evening, he invented an opportunity to walk past Mac's cell so he could ask him maliciously, "You know who gave your boyfriend a ride home, asshole?"

"Which boyfriend?" the blond answered belligerently, squinting through cigarette smoke with his lip curled.

"The college boy you and your buddies worked over," the guard said with a nasty grin. "He rode away with Dominick Calabria."

"Who the fuck's that?"

"A mobster, shithead. A big-time mobster in Chicago," the guard answered, stretching out the 'big' and grinning. "You and your pals better find a way to stay here for a long time. Hear me, hardass? A long, lonnnng time."

"Fuck you!" the inmate shouted as the guard strolled away laughing.

The Cadillac rolled east toward the Route 66/Interstate 55 construction project. Michael stared through the window at the passing fields of soybeans and corn. He brushed his fingers beneath the sunglasses. No one said anything until they reached the highway back to Chicago. As Bruno accelerated onto the four-lane interstate, Dom lifted the photos from the seat beside him.

"Sal has some pictures," Dom began, holding the photographs over his shoulder. The young man reached up to take them. As he looked at each in turn, Dom asked, "Those the guys?"

"Yeah," the young man answered through his wired teeth, thinking that the mug shots finally put names to his assailants.

John McVee, Darryl Jackson, Robert Andrews. He handed the sheets back to Dom, who passed them back to Bruno. Sal set the photos on the seat with a grunt.

"When do they get out?" Michael asked.

"Don't worry about it," Dom answered.

"I'll take care of it," Sal said.

"Keep your pants on," Dom said. "I want to talk to Mike when we get home."

"About what?" Michael asked.

"When we get home."

29

Dominick walked into the kitchen and said, "I'd like to speak with Mike alone for a few minutes." He stepped toward the door and turned. "Then John can give him a ride home." Michael placed his soda on the counter and followed Dominick from the room.

Calabria gestured to a chair in front of his desk. He walked to the French doors and glanced across the sweep of his property, lit a cigarette, then returned to sit behind his desk. He gazed appraisingly, fondly, without speaking for a minute. Finally, he said, "Do you still want what you told John?"

"Yes," Michael replied.

"Let me say something. If you wish it, it will be taken care of. It will never be mentioned again by you or me, or Salvatore or Angie." He paused to drag on his cigarette. Smoke trailed from his nostrils and mouth as he spoke again. "No one will ever ask anything of you in return. No favors. No work. Nothing."

"I want to work for you."

"This kind of job, it's by invitation only. Maybe I don't want you to."

Michael had no answer. This possibility had never occurred to him.

"What you said you want, maybe it isn't such a good idea."

The young man shook his head in confusion. "You mean I have to hunt these guys down on my own?" he said finally, his voice sounding high and thin in his own ears.

"Would you do that?"

"Yes." He met Dom's flat gaze. The man's dark eyes were completely without expression. "Or, rather, I'd try."

"How?"

A baffled shrug. "I guess I'd have to know when they got out," he began, but Dom interrupted.

"What would happen if you found them?"

The young man stared, trying to determine if this was a challenge of some kind. "One way or another, I... I'll kill them."

"All three?"

"No. Just the two, like I told John."

Dom nodded slowly, almost sorrowful, but then his face set. "Listen to me, Mike. Before you swim in the dirty end of the pool, I want you to think about it for a week."

"I've thought about it for a month."

"That's an even better idea. A month." He crushed out his cigarette and leaned back in his chair. "You thought about it inside. Now you'll think about it outside. You'll go home and get ready for the next term at school. If you bring it up again before a month is over, it will never happen." He paused for effect. "Do you understand what I'm telling you?" The young man nodded. Dominick smiled, but his eyes were still strangely flat. "You didn't plan for any of this to happen, and it was a bad time. Maybe you shouldn't make it go on."

"What if I don't change my mind?"

"Then we'll talk." He stood and walked around the desk, smiling now with genuine warmth. He reached to embrace the young man.

"Thank you," Michael said, but he couldn't continue.

"We were glad to pick you up," Dominick said. "Go home, spend time with your family, and forget about the last five weeks. Think about school instead. Then finish your probation and put this shit behind you forever."

1994

1

Detective Larry Klinger was bored and already sick of Bobby Andrews' voice as the muscle-bound felon insisted for what seemed like at least the tenth time in five minutes that he never killed anyone, he didn't know the shooter was gonna do it, he just happened to be along, he didn't know nothin' from nothin'. Klinger stared briefly at the manacles attaching Andrews' wrists and ankles to a metal ring in the floor. He held up one hand and said, "Hang on a minute, Bobby. I want to get a cup of coffee. I'll be right back." He stood and indicated the door of the dull-beige interview room with his eyes. The young homicide detective who had asked him to listen to Andrews followed him into the drab hall.

"Tell me again, Tim. Why am I talking with this bustout?" Klinger ran a meaty hand across his patchy, graying brown hair, his wide face suffused with weary impatience. At fifty-one, he couldn't count the number of lowlifes just like Andrews whose whining jive he had endured, and he realized almost every morning that an ever-greater daily effort was needed to motivate himself to deal with the endless litany of stupid, stupid lies, childish evasions and pathetic, ignorant chest-puffing of almost all criminals. "Truth be told," he had said to his girlfriend only the night before, "I'm just sick to the teeth of street rats." Even in Area Six, where some of Chicago's most inventive murders occurred, it almost always came down to the same dumb things—money, sex or some clueless notion of power. His disappointment had been acute, three years earlier, when he transferred to the organized crime division and discovered that even the highest-rolling bigtime mobsters were often pretty much the same as hopelessly uninformed street crooks, at least in terms of their motivation.

"It's like I said," Tim O'Driscoll answered urgently. Klinger liked O'Driscoll and envied his energy; dealing with the tall, young detective made him miss homicide. "Bobby says he can give us Dominick Calabria."

"That I doubt," Klinger answered. "A scumbag like Andrews couldn't get close enough to Dom Calabria to find his spit still wet."

"Absolutely," O'Driscoll agreed. "But I checked out his story, and he ain't lying. At least, he knows something unusual."

"That's gotta be a new experience for the shithead," Klinger muttered. He rubbed his nose. "What's he looking at?"

"He's gone for good this time." O'Driscoll handed a manila folder to Klinger. Klinger glanced through Andrews' jacket, thinking again how tired he was of lifetime felons like Bobby Andrews. "We got three solid witnesses say he came into the bar with the guy who whacked José Perez six hours ago, he stood by when the shooter did Perez, and he left with the shooter. Unbelievable. We picked them up like immediately, brought the assholes in here, and Bobby starts in on Calabria. I'm like, whoa, what have we here?" O'Driscoll continued. "So I let him cool off for a couple of hours while I checked his story. Quick, I mean, just a few high points. He wants outta the life sentence, for sure, but it's not just bullshit. Says he has information on a pair of murders he says Dom Calabria committed twenty, twenty-two years ago. The thing is, the killings weren't run-of-the-mill, and he's got the details right."

"What do you mean?"

"One guy got thrown off a roof, and the other guy got mutilated, specifically, castrated. His own cock was in his throat. Neither case was officially closed."

"That sounds like the Dom Calabria I know and love," Klinger said. "What's this moron got to do with it?"

"He was in Astoria with the two victims back in '72," O'Driscoll answered. Klinger again studied the abbreviated rap sheet.

"Early in his illustrious career," he mused.

"Bobby's your complete asshole, no question," O'Driscoll said. "He's spent fifteen of the last twenty-three years either in the joint or waiting for trial."

"That explains the prison bod," Klinger grunted.

"Yeah, muscles on muscles," O'Driscoll nodded. "Here's the thing. He says the two victims raped a college kid in Astoria who was Dom Calabria's foster son."

"How could that be?" Klinger asked with a start. He'd known of Dominick Calabria for decades and had spent a fair amount of time studying him since he joined organized crime in 1991, and he wasn't aware of any foster son. He tried to reconstruct the Calabria family tree in his mind.

"I don't know. That's what he says. I only checked the murders. He had the names and the details right, like I say. Superficially, anyway."

Klinger stared at him pensively, chewing his lower lip. Finally, he asked, "Who's the state's attorney on it?"

"You mean, on Calabria? Nobody. I called you first."

A broad smile crept over Klinger's thick lips. "You're okay, Timmy boy. I like you micks." He grinned and turned back toward the interview room. "Okay, let's see what the asshole has to say."

"Don't you want your coffee?" O'Driscoll asked.

Klinger looked at the younger detective as if he had just proposed they go to bed together, a deep scowl furrowing his fleshy cheeks. "I don't drink that shit," he snapped. He hiked up his pants beneath his belly and opened the door.

2

Interviewing scumbags has to be the most tedious damn thing in the world, Klinger thought, as Bobby Andrews jumped back and forth over the same explanations, tripping over one lie after another. *They think while they're talking, and then they forget what they said.*

"Listen, Bobby, you're starting to piss me off," he snarled. "You walked into the goddamn bar with Montoya, Montoya clipped Perez in front of fifteen people, you left the bar with Montoya, you were picked up in Montoya's car, and the effing gun was under the effing seat! So drop it!" he shouted. The nasal whine of the man's central-Illinois accent was like sandpaper against Klinger's eardrums. "I can't cut a deal with you, you stupid shit. That's up to the state's attorney. But you aren't gonna *see* one until I get some straight answers outta you. You follow me, Bobby?"

Andrews rolled his muscular shoulders and tugged at the sleeve of his dirty tee shirt, fumbled with a pack of cigarettes and finally nodded sullenly.

"Good," Klinger said. "No more bullshit about Perez and Montoya, okay? I don't want to hear it." Klinger sat across the table from Andrews. "You're looking at a life stretch now, Bobby. What the hell does Dominick Calabria have to do with it? You wouldn't know the man if he walked into this room."

"I'm telling you, man," Andrews insisted, "he kilt two guys I knew in Astoria back in '72! He done it!"

"Tell me again. Who were these two guys?"

"Jack and Mac. That's Darryl Jackson and John McVee, man. They was partners in the joint. Like I tole him," he drawled, pointing at O'Driscoll, "Mac 'n' Jack worked over a little bitch what was Dominick Calabria's foster son. He tole 'em they's gonna be killed when they got out. He tole 'em how they's gonna be kilt, and that's just how it happent."

"What do you mean, they worked him over?"

"You know, man. Beat 'im down and fucked 'im up."

Klinger stared for a moment, thinking. He picked up O'Driscoll's folder and held it in front of him. Tim had made a couple of notes confirming that Andrews had been in Astoria Adult Correctional Facility at the same time as Darryl Thomas Jackson and John Michael McVee, both deceased since 1973 and, Klinger concluded, probably missed by no one, least of all, society at large. But, Klinger thought, there just wasn't any possibility that someone related to Dom Calabria had done short time in that particular medium-security work farm; it made no sense whatsoever. He closed the folder and picked up his pen. He wrote the names on a legal pad to show Andrews he was making progress, and then he asked, "How do you know about it?"

Andrews fumbled briefly with his cigarettes and glanced at O'Driscoll. "You know, man. I heard it. Everybody did."

Klinger drew a small asterisk next to the names to remind himself of a lie to pursue later. "Who was this kid?" he asked.

"I don't know, man," Andrews answered quickly. "Some runty college punk what Mac wanted as a bitch."

"How do you know that?" Klinger asked, writing COLLEGE STUDENT in block letters under the names.

"Ever'body knew when Mac wanted a bitch," Andrews said. Klinger added an asterisk.

"Was the kid Mac's bitch?" Klinger asked.

"Nah," Andrews said. "Him 'n' Jack did 'im once, I guess, and then he was to the infirm'ry the rest of his time." He chuckled.

"What was the kid in for?"

"I don't know, man. I think some drug bust. It's a long time ago."

"How'd you know he was a college kid?"

"Ever'body knew that." Andrews lit a cigarette.

"You aren't giving me much here, Bobby."

"Man, I don't know what the punk's name was. How I'm s'posed to know that? Hardly saw the little fuck. Shit." *Shee-yit.*

Klinger looked at his notes. "What did the kid say to McVee and Jackson?"

"He tole 'em they was gonna die. He tole Mac he was gonna fall off a building with a stick up his ass, and he tole Jack he was gonna eat his own dick," Andrews said quickly, nodding his head. Klinger glanced over his shoulder at O'Driscoll, who did a *told-you* with his eyebrows.

"How do you know that?"

"I overheard 'im," Andrews said. Klinger drew another small asterisk.

"How was that?" he asked.

"Just 'fore the kid got out, he come walking across the yard with his teeth clenched together. Mac 'n' Jack's settin' on this little bleachers next to the ball field. I's there too. The kid walks right up to 'em and says they's gonna get kilt."

"You just happened to be there, huh?" Klinger said with an irritated sneer. "And these two hardasses, McVee and Jackson, don't do a thing when this kid walks up and threatens them?"

"Oh, man, they's guards everywhere around that kid his last two days in the joint," Andrews moaned. "That's how we's sure he's Calabria's son."

"Let me clue you in on something, Bobby. Dom Calabria isn't a good name for someone like you to be dropping, you follow me?" He stared and noted a small flush of fear in Andrews' face. "What makes you sure this college kid was related to Calabria?" His eyes never left Andrews'.

"It's like I tole him," again indicating O'Driscoll. "When the kid got out, Calabria picked him up."

"How do you know that?"

"Ever'body knew it." Another small asterisk. "One of the guards tole Mac." After the asterisk, Klinger drew a slash and added a question mark. He made a note to find out who the guards were at Astoria during the summer of 1972, then gazed at Andrews for a minute without speaking and waited while the prisoner stubbed out his smoke. Then Klinger asked, softly, "Did you do the kid too, Bobby?"

"Hell, no," Andrews said quickly. "Just Mac 'n' Jack did that kid." Klinger set his pen down.

"Okay, Bobby. We'll talk again." Andrews seemed relieved. "Listen up. You're going down to County now. I personally don't much care one way or the other, but I'll give you some free advice: Don't mention Dom Calabria again except to me and a state's attorney named Dan Whittaker." Andrews nodded fearfully. "That's a name that could be very hazardous to your health. You follow me?"

3

"What's got you in such a high mood?" Dora asked as Klinger trailed his fingers across her ass. She shifted her heavy hips to one side, coquettishly tilting a shoulder and cocking an eyelid above her slinky smile in a wrinkled imitation of the movies. Klinger found Dora's vamping irresistably charming. Despite her jeans and cardigan, the image worked.

"Dunno," he answered happily. "Let's go down to Hogen's, have some weiner schnitzel."

Dora's eyebrows rose in pleased surprise. She turned into him, pulling his paunch against her stomach. "No objection here, baby," she crowed, her brown eyes delighted. She grabbed his cheeks and kissed him loudly. It occurred to Klinger that Dora was just about the only bright spot in his life. He wrapped his arms around her ample back and hugged hard. Dora laughed, her pleasure gleaming as her eyes nearly disappeared into half-moons in her round face. Larry was so infrequently in this kind of mood. She kissed him again, then leaned away to stare into his eyes. "What's the good word, sweetheart?"

"Got an interesting case," Klinger announced with satisfaction, disengaging to walk to the refrigerator. "Least, I think it'll be interesting. Gotta get Dan interested too." He scratched his head. "I think he will be." Dora picked up the vegetables she was going to prepare for dinner and waited. Klinger found a beer in the refrigerator and glanced over his shoulder, acting as though he'd said enough.

"My God! You *are* in a good mood!" Dora laughed again, the alluvial fans around her eyes again swallowing her irises. When Klinger persisted in his innocent act, she demanded, "Are you going to tell me, or what?"

Klinger chuckled with pleasure, then briefly recounted the interview with Bobby Andrews.

"Are we talking about *the* Dominick Calabria?" Dora emphasized.

"The same," Klinger boomed. "Mister Number One. Top dog in the Outfit."

"Isn't this a little far-fetched?" Dora asked. She'd spent the last six years with Larry Klinger, and she knew enough about police work to know that a routine arrest didn't often lead to someone like a low-level mobster, much less the head of one of Chicago's organized crime families, whether the old Sicilian connections or more-recent street organizations.

"No doubt," Klinger agreed. "That's what makes it interesting. Once I get Dan's go-ahead, I gotta dig up whatever I can, find out if it's real and worth takin' somewhere. Start by talkin' with this asshole again, see what I can see."

Dora reached out suddenly to touch Klinger's hair. She smiled fondly. She had watched Larry work for three years in homicide and three years in organized crime, always awed by his focus, his intelligent concentration when an investigation captured his imagination. Delighted now that something other than loneliness and fatigue was gripping his mind. "It's amazing what you can do when you're into it," she said softly.

"Dora, you're too much," he answered, staring. *Someday,* he thought, *I'll tell this wonderful fat woman how spectacular she is.* A smile slowly moved across his face. "Think dinner can wait for a little while?" he asked, reaching out to encircle her waist with his beefy arm.

4

"Who you looking for?" a uniformed Cook County Sheriff asked. Dan Whittaker didn't know the man. The tall state's attorney glanced around the huge lunchroom at the Criminal Courts building.

"Larry Klinger," he finally answered.

"Over in the corner," the uniform said, pointing across the crowded room. He stared suspiciously up at Whittaker and glanced several times at the ID clipped to the pocket of his tan coat.

"What's the matter? My tie crooked?" Whittaker asked, glaring down at the officer, but he was distracted by Klinger waving. Whittaker weaved a tortuous path through the chairs and tables, nodding to attorneys, officers and detectives he recognized. Klinger was gnawing on a corned beef sandwich. He sat at a table with three uniformed city cops. Whittaker assumed the officers were giving testimony. They looked up as he approached, classic aggressive give-a-shit cop stares as they studied his expensive suit.

"I know you," one said. "You played for DePaul, right?"
"Wrong," Whittaker snapped.
"Somewheres else?" the officer ventured.
"Why is it," Whittaker interrupted impatiently, "that whenever you idiots see a tall black guy, if he's thin, you assume he plays basketball, and if he's heavy, you assume he plays football?"
Klinger laughed merrily and thrust the remainder of his sandwich into his mouth. "Glad to see you're in a good mood," he said cheerfully.
"For God's sake, swallow before you start talking, will you?" Whittaker scowled with distaste. "You've got sauerkraut on your face."
Klinger laughed again and swiped his fingers across his chin, then wiped his hands with a napkin and stood. "Don't take it so hard, Dan," he said. "They think tall white guys played basketball too." He picked up his tray and moved away from the table. "It's just a general lack of imagination." The three uniforms sneered but said nothing, too disinterested to break balls in return.
"It's not the same," Whittaker replied. "And you know it." Klinger shrugged and nodded. "Besides, I'm about as athletic as that fork," Whittaker said.
"Really?" Klinger dumped the remains of his meal into a trash can and placed the tray on its lid, smiling up at the prosecutor. He shifted a brown accordion file stuffed with manila folders more comfortably under his arm. His outdated, worn sport coat wrinkled up around his shoulders. "You know, Dan, to be honest, I always thought you played basketball, too. This comes as a real disappointment to me."
"Don't start," Whittaker answered, rubbing one hand across his close-cropped hair. "I'm too tired for it."
"Prickly today, are we?"
"Not especially." Whittaker glared.
"You know, Dan, these guys see God's own amount of black attorneys. It's not like you're a novelty to them."

"You trying to develop racial harmony, Larry? Little one-man crusade?"

"Nope," Klinger answered. He understood Whittaker's annoyance as much as he could, but he also understood that he could never truly understand it. He doubted any white person could. The only times he had come close were when, at Dora's insistence, he read *Beloved,* and maybe when he read *Invisible Man* in college. Those were the only moments in his recollection when he had understood in a visceral way, and then, only very briefly. *No surprise if they hate us,* he thought. He had no clue what to do about it.

"Thanks for meeting me," Klinger said, shuffling behind the lanky attorney. "You got the time to talk to Andrews now?"

"I'll listen to him," Whittaker said slowly. "But look, Larry. It's practically impossible to try a twenty-year-old murder. If it wasn't you, I wouldn't even be wasting my time."

"I'll take that as a compliment," Klinger said happily. He walked toward the exit, shifting the waist of his pants under his belly.

"I'm not kidding, Larry."

"I hear you. But I figure, the Calabria connection's gotta be worth a little time, right?" He pulled a folder from the accordion file and handed it to Whittaker. "That's the guy. Bobby Andrews. A complete bustout. He's scramblin' to get outta this Perez murder rap and thinks he can drop a dime on Dom Calabria." Whittaker stopped in the hall and studied the file, frowning and slowly shaking his head. "I agree," Klinger said quickly. "Absolutely. It's unlikely as hell. But I talked to this scumbag a couple times now, the night he got arrested and again two days ago, before I called you. Like I said on the phone, there's something odd here." He waited while Whittaker scanned his notes and the photographs he had inserted into the file. "Plus, Calabria's what? In his seventies now? How many more shots are we gonna get at him?"

"You have any of the reports on these murders? When were they, '72 and '73?" Whittaker had worked with Klinger for eight of the ten years he'd been in the state's attorney's office and considered him one of the three wholly trustworthy cops he knew, so he held his overwhelming skepticism in check.

"They're on the way," Klinger answered. "But the basic details are confirmed." He paused while Whittaker again studied the file. "There's enough here to be worth a second opinion," he added. The attorney frowned thoughtfully and handed the file back to Klinger. They walked toward the elevators.

"What's your gut say on this?" Whittaker asked at last. This was a shared joke; neither man placed much faith in cop intuition.

"It says the corned beef was too greasy," Klinger announced, slapping his protruding stomach for emphasis. "You want the truth, Dan? I got a feeling this could be interesting, you follow?"

"Well, we could all use a little of that, couldn't we?" Whittaker said softly. Klinger had a strong feeling that the younger man was reading his mind. "Let's see what our friend has to say," the prosecutor said, still shaking his head as they made their way through the checkpoints leading to Cook County Jail and Bobby Andrews.

5

Dreading another episode of Andrews' whining, nasal, incompetent prevarication, Klinger groaned inwardly as the prisoner was led, manacled, into the stark interview room. He glanced at Whittaker, who leaned against the wall and studied Andrews. Andrews met his stare, his lip curled with distrust.

Klinger exhaled slowly, feeling a persistent sense of fatigue. "Siddown, Bobby," he said. He paused as Andrews arranged himself and fished a package of cigarettes from the pocket of his county coverall. "This is Dan Whittaker, with the state's attorney's office," Klinger began. "Try to tell the truth for a change, okay?"

"I'll call a spade a spade," Andrews answered with a leering smirk, staring at Whittaker. Whittaker's face remained impassive, but his eyes turned cold. It was almost a visible change, Klinger thought, like a sheet of cheesecloth had been drawn across the bright gleam of Whittaker's dark irises.

"Not a good opener, Bobby," Klinger said with a heavy sigh. "Lemme start over. This is Dan Whittaker. He's the *only* person in this room who can do your sorry ass a bit of good, you follow me?" He leaned forward with one hand on the table and glared down at Andrews. The prisoner stared back belligerently. "You know how many cards you're holding, Bobby?" Klinger held up his right hand to form a zero. "You can cooperate with Mr. Whittaker, or he can send you away forever. It means shit to me, but I'd advise a little respect." Klinger leaned forward suddenly and slapped the unlit cigarette from Andrews' lips. "Am I getting through to you, Bobby?" Andrews' face flashed sullen rage. His eyes darted to Whittaker, who still leaned against the wall with his arms crossed. "Now answer the man's questions," Klinger went on. "Politely," he added with forced patience, "and maybe you won't get yourself a permanent room in Joliet, you follow?"

Andrews nodded, sulking. "Good," Klinger announced. "Much better." He fished the same manila folder from his accordion file and again handed it to Whittaker. The state's attorney sat facing Andrews. He opened the folder and flipped through the computer printouts on Darryl Jackson and John McVee while Andrews lit a fresh cigarette. Whittaker reached inside his coat for a pen and glanced at Klinger, who handed him a legal pad and moved to one end of the narrow interview room, slouching comfortably with his rump pressed against the wall and his arms crossed on his stomach. He gazed indifferently at Andrews.

Whittaker stared briefly at Andrews as if lost in thought, then slid a black-and-white photograph from the folder and turned it on the table so it faced the prisoner. "Do you know this man, Mr. Andrews?" he finally asked.

Andrews shook his head.

"No?" Whittaker said with mock surprise. "You claim to know something about him. That's Dominick Calabria." He paused while Andrews stared at the photograph. Whittaker and Klinger both noted fear creasing the skin around Andrews' lips. "He doesn't have any foster children," Whittaker continued without changing his tone of voice. "No one related to him ever spent any time in Astoria." He paused again as Andrews puffed nervously on his cigarette. "So who was this young man, this college student, you, Jackson and McVee raped there back in 1972?"

"I never raped that kid!" Andrews protested.

"I have a hard time believing that, Mr. Andrews," Whittaker said. "I just can't see how you would know Jackson and McVee raped him if you weren't part of it."

"I never!" Andrews whined, almost pouting, a habitually dishonest child accused when for once he's telling the truth.

"Why don't you tell me what really happened?" Whittaker asked with commiserative patience. "How did you know Jackson and McVee raped this young man, whoever he was?"

"Ever'body knowed it," Andrews said, still sulking.

"Maybe everyone knew they'd sent the boy to the infirmary. Did 'everyone' assume they'd also raped the boy?" He paused as Andrews shook his head in rising confusion. "Was that their reputation?"

"No!" Andrews barked. He crushed out his cigarette.

"So how would you know about it, unless you were in on it?"

"I never done that kid!" Andrews fumbled with his cigarettes and stared at the tabletop. He flicked his eyes away from the photo of Calabria.

"Listen to me, Mr. Andrews," Whittaker said, still with calm forbearance. "If you are hoping for favorable consideration in your trial, I'd suggest you become considerably more forthright with your answers to me. As in right now." He waited long enough for Andrews to begin squirming in his chair. "Let's keep it simple," Whittaker said at last. "How do you know Jackson and McVee raped this young man?"

"I jus' heard it."

"Care to try again?"

"I never fucked that punk!" Andrews shouted.

"So what did you do?"

"I jus' beat 'im up a little."

Klinger allowed himself a tight smile. He was glad Whittaker was pulling the teeth on this one; he didn't think he had the stamina for it anymore. The sound of Andrews' accent drove him to irritated distraction as it was.

Whittaker backed off a little. "How did you know McVee and Jackson?"

"I hung with 'em in Astoria. They's good friends to have, you know?"

"Why was that?"

"No one fucked with Mac, you better believe."

"He was one of the tough guys?"

"Yessir," Andrews answered, nodding rapidly.

"So you hung around with him for protection?"

"No!" Andrews said quickly. "I's no punk. I jus' hung with him 'n' Jack. Gotta have friends in the joint."

"I see," Whittaker said, faking a thoughtful tone and nodding in agreement. He picked up his pen and prepared to make notes. "So what happened with this college student?"

Andrews drew in a deep breath and held it briefly. Finally,

he said, "Mac had 'is eye on 'im from the first day he was to Astoria. Said he wanted to give 'im a wider a-hole." Andrews laughed with his lower lip jutting out over his bottom teeth. "Show 'im somethin' they don't teach in no schoolbooks." Whittaker jotted notes and waited without saying anything while Andrews chuckled over his memories. Andrews lit another cigarette and glanced from Whittaker to Klinger. *Now that you've started,* Klinger thought, *the bitch is going to come all the way out.*

"So, anyways," Andrews continued as if on cue, "after the punk's there a week or so, we's jus' waitin' in his cell one afternoon." *It never fails,* Klinger thought. His theory was that the novelty of telling the truth was a powerful drug for people like Bobby Andrews.

"And what happened?" Whittaker asked.

"Mac 'n' Jack made a san'witch outta the punk," Andrews snickered. "Mac in the back, Jack in the front."

Klinger shook his head with disgust but masked the intensity of his feelings. "No room for you, huh, Bobby?" he threw in.

"Hey, man! That ain't my thing," Andrews said angrily, glaring toward Klinger at the end of the small interview room.

"So what did you do?" Whittaker asked. "Hold the kid down?"

"Hell, no," Andrews chortled. "That weren't necessary. I guess I kicked the punk once or twicet."

"Just a couple a taps with your shoe, right, Bobby?" Klinger said.

"The fuck difference it makes?" Andrews replied defiantly. "I already tole you I beat on 'im some."

"Why were you there?" Whittaker interjected.

"Armed robbery," Andrews said.

Whittaker looked down to fight the smile from his cheeks. "I meant, why were you along when McVee and Jackson assaulted the student?"

"Oh. I tole you, we was partners, me, Mac 'n' Jack."

"That's fine, Mr. Andrews," Whittaker said reassuringly. "We know how it is inside." He flipped sheets in the file folder, scanning Klinger's notes from his earlier interviews with Andrews. "Tell me, what's the connection with this man?" he asked, tapping the photograph on the table.

"This college pussy was his foster son. Leas', that's what we thought."

"Why'd you think that?"

" 'Cause the kid got picked up by Dom Calabria."

"How do you know that?"

"One a the guards tole Mac the day the kid left. He come by his cell and tell 'im the pussy got picked up by a heavy mobster name Dom Calabria."

"Who was the guard?"

"I don't know, man. I never cared about no guards' names."

"What made you believe him? The guard, I mean."

"Like I tole him," Andrews said, nodding at Klinger, "the kid's like on a leash with a guard the las' couple days he's inside. They's always a guard to hand wherever that kid is." Whittaker again waited, adding notes on the legal pad. "We din't think it 'til after he's gone, you see," Andrews explained. "Then the protection made sense."

"I see," said Whittaker. He glanced at the notes. "You told Detective Klinger that this college student threatened McVee and Jackson?"

"Yessir," Andrews answered brightly. "The day he's from infirmary he comes walkin' acrost the ball field, straight up to me, Mac an' Jack. We's settin' on the bleachers, and this kid come right up to us, holdin' his teeth tight together, an' he starts in."

"What did McVee and Jackson do?"

"Jack said he musta wanted to suck 'im off again," Andrews cackled, remembering the *bon mot.*

"What did the kid say?"

"I can tell you zackly what he said. He says, 'Funny you

should say that, nigger. It's the las' thing you's gonna swallow.' "
Andrews laughed again when the skin around Whittaker's eyes tightened. "Hey, I din't say it. *He* did."

Whittaker's face set in a tight frown. He adjusted his glasses and held his expression. "Anything else?"

"The kid tole Mac he's gonna walk off a building with a broomstick stuck up his ass." Andrews leaned back in the chair. "He says, 'Here's a promise. You ain't gonna live a month when you's outta here.' That's what he said."

"What did he say to you?"

"He din't say nothin' to me, an' I din't say nothin' to him." Klinger shook his head at the floor.

"How did McVee and Jackson react?"

"They's nothin' they *could* do," Andrews said simply. "Like I say, they's guards everywhere. Big motherfuckers too." He nodded as if this confirmed something. "Then the kid's gone jus' two days after."

"Would you be able to identify this student?"

"I dunno. I s'pose, less he looks a lot diff'rent." Andrews shrugged, flexing his shoulders. "He's a runty guy with brown hair."

Whittaker jotted a few notes and flipped a page on the legal pad. "Jackson and McVee, they both got out of Astoria before you did, right?"

"Yeah. Couple months."

"When did you learn they had been killed?"

"I knowed Mac got kilt right after it happent, like 'fore Thanksgivin'. After that, me 'n' Jack knowed for sure it's Calabria's son, like I say."

"How did you find out?"

"Jack tole me. He come over in the yard scared pissless and tole me Mac got throwed off a roof in Peoria, stuck up his ass with a broom, zackly how the kid say he would."

"How did Jackson know about it?"

"Got me. I don't know."

"Jackson was frightened?"

"Fuck, yes. Said he was gonna disappear, day he got outta there."

"When did he get out?"

"I ain't sure. Ahead a me. I din't get out 'til February." *Fibwary*. Klinger felt almost physically sick of Bobby Andrews.

"Did you know Jackson had been killed before you were released?"

"Yeah. I did." Andrews' face flashed a hint of fearful recollection.

"How did you find out?"

"A guard tole me."

"Do you remember the guard's name?"

"His firs' name, not his las'. Dick. Dick the Prick. The motherfucker."

"Why'd he tell you?"

"How I'm s'posed to know? He was a mean sumbitch."

"How did this occur?"

"How did what occur?"

"When the guard told you about Jackson."

"Oh." Andrews lit another cigarette. Klinger was starting to gag in the small room. "It was jus' a couple a weeks 'fore I got out, like in January sometime, maybe third week or so. Maybe Fibwary. I dunno. Dick come by my cell jus' 'fore lights out and tells me my friends is droppin' like flies, the motherfucker," Andrews snarled. Whittaker again waited without reacting. Andrews frowned but continued, "So I says, 'What the fuck you talkin' 'bout?' An' he goes, 'Your second buddy's done bit the big one.' He's talkin' 'bout Jack, see. Then he tells me Jack's whacked down to Cairo with his cock in his mouth." Andrews nodded morosely.

"That's all?" Klinger blurted.

Andrews glared at the detective and started to pout again.

Klinger strolled casually away from the wall, around the room to a position behind Andrews. He leaned back with one foot against the wall and rested his meaty chin in one palm. "Hey, man," Andrews whined over his shoulder. "Don't be standin' behin' me like that. I don't like it." *Ah doan like hit.*

"Too bad," Klinger answered. *You wretched piece of absolute shit,* he thought.

Andrews turned to face Whittaker. "Hey, man. Get him the fuck around from behin' me."

Whittaker forced the smile off his face and gestured with his head. "Come on, Larry," he said. "Give Mr. Andrews a break."

Klinger grinned across Andrews' head and moved to the other end of the room, opposite his earlier position. Andrews glared suspiciously at Klinger. The detective returned his stare with a blank look on his face, but trying to give an idea of potential violence, as if some sort of third-degree was about to occur.

Whittaker asked, "Would you be able to identify the guard?"

"Sure could. I ain't forgot that bastard." Andrews hitched up the crotch of his coverall.

"Did the guard, this Dick, say anything else?" Whittaker asked, smiling at Andrews as if they were sharing a joke on the pun.

"Couple things, making fun a me, mainly. He says I better learn to run mighty fast in a couple weeks."

"Did you?"

"Shit, man."

"Did the guard also mention Dominick Calabria?"

"No." Klinger shook his head at the floor again.

Whittaker made a few more notes to give Andrews the impression that they were becoming partners. Now that Andrews was shifting into monosyllables, he decided to quit for the time being. He looked up at Andrews for a few beats and smiled. "Well, thanks, Mr. Andrews." He tore his sheets of notes from the legal pad and folded them. "I think we'll be able to work together."

"You gonna help me out with this Perez bullshit?" Andrews drawled.

"Perhaps. I want to check a few more things, but I'll be in touch."

Klinger stepped to the edge of the table and stared at Andrews until the prisoner started to fidget, then he said, "Remember what I told you about name-dropping, Bobby. Try to stay healthy, you follow?"

6

"So. What do you think?" Klinger asked, increasing his pace to keep up with Whittaker's long strides. They left the jail behind and moved into the long halls of the Criminal Courts building.

"I think trying a twenty-year-old murder with that halfwit at the center of the case is doomed," Whittaker said casually. He didn't slow down or glance at Klinger. "Dead. I wouldn't even propose it."

"That's your call," Klinger said cheerfully. He knew Whittaker well enough to be pleased by the response. He shifted the subject. "You going to give Andrews a break?"

"For this? Not likely. But if he also gives evidence on the Perez murder, I won't push for too much. But we can get to that later."

"So I should keep him thinking this is what will help him?"

Whittaker stopped and thoughtfully rubbed the fingertips of his right hand in the palm of his left. The characteristic gesture gave Klinger even more confidence. He smiled as two paralegals hustled past, thick files in their arms. "Yes," Whittaker finally said. "We'll want him to identify this college student, whoever he may be, and the guard or guards, once you find them." He smiled at Klinger's conspiratorial grin.

"I told you this might be interesting," Klinger beamed.

"I'll tell you, Larry, Andrews isn't the key here. If we're going to get any shot at Calabria out of this, it's going to have to come from this John Doe student."

"Or a guard Calabria did business with," Klinger agreed.

"Yes," Whittaker replied. "Both would be better. But don't get too excited, okay? This one's got long shot written all over it."

Klinger shrugged noncommittally. "I got the time," he said.

"I'm not trying to be discouraging. Just realistic."

"I follow you," Klinger said, still smiling. "But keep in mind the times that sack of shit was lying just now. I mean, Bobby lies mosta the time, so I don't mean in general. Here's a laugh. The other night, when I asked him how old he was, he said forty-one."

"And?"

"The asshole's forty-five." Whittaker laughed and started walking again. His heels clicked on the worn linoleum. "I figure, most times when Bobby tells the truth, it's by accident," Klinger added. "But what I'm getting at is this. Just now, Bobby lied about the guard, right? This guy told him that Calabria was waiting outside, that was the whole point of telling him about Jackson. Probably the same guy told Jackson about McVee. This is the guy I want to find."

"Definitely," Whittaker said. "Here's where twenty-two years can be a problem."

"True enough," Klinger said. "But now we got a name, maybe, so if the guy's alive, I'll get hold of him."

"Let's assume you find him. There still won't be any direct connection between the killings and Calabria, even if Calabria bought him back in 1972. The guard wouldn't know enough for anything."

"Just one step at a time," Klinger said cheerfully. "You know how it is, a connection here, a little link there. I want the guard, but mainly I want this college student. He's the guy I really wanna find."

"Do you have any idea who the student might be?"

"Not really," Klinger answered. "Or I should say, not yet. I been through the Calabria file a few times, and I can't find anyone specific. His youngest son, John, never did any time. He ain't even been arrested for maybe fifteen or twenty years. And there's no cousins the right age." He pursed his lips pensively. "It ain't anyone else's kid, either."

"What do you mean?"

"Bruno or DeMicco or any of the other usual suspects. None a them got children the right age. Besides, none a their kids went to college." He thought for a moment. "And I can't believe anyone in the family woulda ended up in a place like Astoria. That just don't figure. 'Sides, I took a look at the sheets on everyone in Calabria's crews, and no one did any time there, least, as far as our records go."

"You know," Whittaker said, stopping again in the hall leading to the elevators that would carry him up to his office, "Andrews could be making up every word of this. He could have heard about McVee and Jackson and just grabbed a name out of the air to get our attention now."

"Dom Calabria ain't exactly the smartest name to grab, if you want to stay alive," Klinger said.

"Maybe it's the biggest name Andrews knew."

"It would have been safer to use the governor. Or the president." Klinger chuckled. "More to the point, I don't think Bobby's smart enough to make this up on the fly. He's not what I'd call an inventive liar, you follow me? The same, I'm gonna confirm everything he's said so far. That's first. Once I have the details, we can go from there." He nodded, mapping the architecture of the investigation in his mind and rolling speculations against one another like dice in his hand.

"Well, let's go ahead with it," Whittaker said.

"Matter of fact, Dan, I kinda already have."

"Why doesn't that surprise me?" Whittaker laughed, his deep voice bugling in the hall.

"I got faxes of the coroners' reports on McVee and Jackson last night. The case files should be here tomorrow, if they ain't already in my mailbox. Plus," Klinger concluded with a self-effacing smile, "maybe a hundred-fifty college students got busted for drugs in 1972, and I gotta assume one a those names'll show up on the list of guests at Astoria that summer. Here's my guess. Some friend of John Calabria's is the guy we want to find."

Whittaker raised his eyebrows. "Now, that might make sense."

"Yeah," Klinger said enthusiastically. "The age is about right, give or take." He bobbed his head with the intensity of the inspiration. "I think I'll take another look in the Calabria jacket," he said quickly, his voice rising slightly with excitement. "Maybe I been giving too much attention to Dom, when John's the one I should be tracking here." He pinched his lower lip and nodded, concentrating, and stepped into an elevator. "Maybe the Feds got something I can use," he speculated.

"Hey, Larry," Whittaker said from the hall. "Don't have too much fun now." He smiled as Klinger turned in the elevator.

"You sure you didn't play for the Blue Demons?" Klinger asked as the elevator doors closed.

7

Klinger scanned the old autopsy reports on McVee and Jackson, making notes. On November 5, 1972, McVee had been beaten and bound with wire, the coroner theorized from the deep, thin lacerations on his wrists and ankles, and a broom handle had been forced through his rectum and into his intestines, perforating his lower colon. The pain must have been unspeakable, Klinger thought, assuming McVee was conscious when it happened. He had then fallen or been thrown from the roof of an unoccupied six-story industrial building or warehouse in Peoria. The cause of death was massive injuries sustained in the fall, although the coroner had noted that intestinal trauma or potentially peritonitis probably would have killed him anyway. The coroner set the time of death between midnight and 4:00 AM. Klinger wondered why the restraints had been removed, since none were found on the body. Were they taken off first, or down on the ground? Had McVee been forced somehow to walk off the edge of the building? No speculation existed in the short summary of the investigation, such as it was.

Jackson had likewise been beaten, more severely than McVee, on January 14, 1973, in Cairo, Illinois. He had been castrated, and his severed penis was lodged in his throat. The cause of death, according to the autopsy, was asphyxiation. His partially frozen body had been found in a field outside of the small city, his wrists tied behind his back with baling wire. The coroner had concluded that he had been dead two days when he was discovered.

Klinger flipped back through his file for the dates the men had been released from Astoria. McVee had been out less than three weeks—sixteen days, to be precise—but Jackson had been released at the end of November. As Andrews had said, truthfully for a change, he had finished his sentence in February 1973. Klinger constructed a timeline, adding a question mark after Andrews' release date. If Andrews was telling the truth about the connection between the killings, Klinger thought, why had he been spared? If these were vengeance murders, and they definitely felt like it, why hadn't Andrews been killed as well? Klinger was startled to feel a surge of angry revulsion. From the case reports, it seemed that no more than half-hearted efforts had been made to discover the perpetrators of a pair of gruesome murders.

"Why are you surprised?" Whittaker asked when they met later. "These guys weren't even thirty yet, and between them they had what? More than a dozen assault raps, three armed robberies, and one rape—Jackson. They'd each been in and out since they were teenagers. McVee was in Astoria because he'd beaten a fourteen-year-old boy so severely that he crippled the kid. He may have been a sadist. It's hard to figure why they weren't locked away in some max somewhere. Would you have given it a huge effort?"

"I don't know," Klinger answered thoughtfully. "I mean, I mighta thought, good riddance, sure. It's probably true. They were the scum of the earth. If they got shot or stabbed in a bar, I woulda thought, big surprise. But these were pretty ugly killings. Plus, no leads of any kind. No fingerprints, no clues, no nothin'. Basically meaningless physical evidence. So little they practically scream, 'Pros at work,' 'specially considering what was done. I think I woulda pursued it, just to satisfy my own curiosity, you follow?"

"Maybe you're a better cop than those investigators were," Whittaker laughed. "But I don't see any egregious incompetence in it. Back then, maybe there were more important things going on. Why would anyone connect these two murders?"

"At least one of the Astoria guards coulda connected them."

"No doubt. I'd say he did, since he told Andrews about Jackson. But that guy was dirty, right?"

"You'd think other guards there could have made the connection too," Klinger said with grumpy disgust.

"Well," Whittaker shrugged, "they didn't. Or they didn't say so. So why would the investigators in Peoria and Cairo? As you've pointed out, it's not like the world was going to regret the absence of those two. If Andrews had opened his mouth at the time, sure. But otherwise, why would anyone put it together?"

"That's a problem. Why didn't he spill it to someone? He says he knew Jackson and McVee had been killed before he got out of Astoria himself. If this guard, this Dick whoever, told him he better be ready to run—and I believe that part of Bobby's story—he must have been scared shitless when he was released."

"He tried to disappear, remember? His next stretch was in Colorado."

"Yeah," Klinger mused, "that's true. But do you think that would have kept Dom Calabria away from him, if he wanted him dead?"

"Not at all," Whittaker said, shaking his head. "I think the safe assumption is that Calabria, if in fact he killed the other two, had no interest in Andrews. Like you say, that's a problem with this. It wouldn't be in character for Dom Calabria to leave a loose end floating around."

"Hey, these Outfit guys aren't as efficient as everyone thinks," Klinger began, but Whittaker cut him off.

"Don't talk yourself into something, Larry. You just said it yourself. If Calabria had wanted Andrews dead, he'd be dead." Whittaker chewed on his lip for a second or two. "This could be a big hole in Andrews' story. Don't get me wrong," he added quickly as Klinger started to fume, "I'm not questioning the Calabria connection yet. At least, not between you and me. But why *is* Andrews alive? It's a hole in this case, if you think in terms of trial. As long as the possibility exists that Andrews invented the whole story, we're vulnerable." Whittaker paused, thinking. "It could be that the student himself killed Jackson and McVee, without Calabria's involvement at all. We can't ignore the possibility."

"These murders couldn't have been committed by a single guy alone," Klinger protested. "I mean, think of the forensic evidence. Besides, Bobby keeps referring to the student as a small guy."

"It's not out of the realm of possibility," Whittaker replied. "All I'm saying is, we need the student."

"I'm workin' on it," Klinger answered. "None of the names of the college students arrested for drugs in 1972 matches up with the Astoria inmates for that summer, but that don't necessarily mean anything. I mean, these are all old records, and maybe the state computer files I've searched ain't complete, or maybe some got expunged, who knows? I never figured this'd be easy. Plus, none of the student names is anyone with known ties to the Calabrias. At least, none of them jumps out at me."

Klinger opened a folder containing a small stack of six black-and-white photographs. He spread the photos on the table. "These are all old surveillance shots of apparent friends or associates of John Calabria, none of them positively identified."

Whittaker looked over the photographs and lifted a pair that included young men in tuxedoes. "Where are these from?"

"Those are federal 'loans' from John Calabria's wedding in 1976. From what I understand, it was a big affair. The guys you see there, other than Johnny boy, weren't ID'd by the feds. Don't know if they were ushers, groomsmen or what. All I know's they ain't related to his wife, and no one knows who they are." He gathered the photos back into his folder. "Maybe one a them's our guy," he concluded.

"Any luck finding the guard?"

"Not yet. Likewise, my search for the personnel files ain't complete. Bobby says he was an older guy, so he's likely retired. I'm gonna get hard copies of inmates, personnel records and—most important—infirmary records from 1972," Klinger said triumphantly. "I figure, if Bobby's story is true, and I think it is on the big stuff, for the most part, the student's gonna be easy to identify. Then I'll get confirmation from the guard, once I find him, and Bobby."

"Then we go to work," Whittaker said with a hungry smile.

"Then we go to work," Klinger echoed.

8

Whittaker groaned when his beeper interrupted his dinner conversation. Fried calamari had just been delivered to the table at Avanzari, a slick Italian restaurant east of Michigan Avenue near the Hancock Center. He apologized to his date, a handsomely lovely newscaster, and fumbled for the pager, but he smiled inwardly when he saw Klinger's office number. He apologized again, rose from the table and asked a passing waiter where the telephones were. This was for the sake of his companion, whom he wanted to impress—he felt it would be crass to use his bulky cellular phone at the table.

"Duty calls," he said with a self-effacing smile. "I'll be back in just a moment." He moved away with studied nonchalance.

"Michael J. Pollitz!" Klinger bellowed joyfully through the receiver, his jubilance instantly elevating Whittaker's mood.

"Talk to me," the prosecutor said, smiling at the detective's excitement.

"That's our student! I got no doubt about it!" Klinger slapped the surface of his desk.

"Who is he?"

"Beats me," Klinger almost sang. "I'll find out. But this is the guy. He was in Astoria the summer of 1972, short time. He was nineteen. And here's the clincher. He spent all but a couple weeks of his sentence in the prison infirmary!" Klinger laughed, overcome with glee. Whittaker couldn't remember the last time Klinger had been so enthused about an investigation. "And if that ain't enough, this guy Pollitz? His address when he was an inmate was Barrington!"

"You've been busy," Whittaker said. He glanced at his watch.

"That ain't all," Klinger added with pride. "There were just three guards named Richard working that joint in 1972, all still alive."

"Where's all this coming from?"

"I got a guy down there to fax me the rosters outta their morgue, plus the infirmary logs," Klinger said blandly. "Told him I'd buy him dinner tomorrow if he'd dig through the files this afternoon. Then I just did a little cross-checking. I was right about the info I got from the state. It was incomplete. Probably got screwed up when they computerized their records. The thing is, there's no record anywhere of this Pollitz kid being arrested, least, not with the state. So his name never came up before. But this is him."

"Is that your gut talking?" Whittaker chuckled.

"Nope. There's no other candidates." He had received ten pages of infirmary log summaries, and Pollitz was the only inmate who was both the right age and remained in the infirmary for a length of time that was consistent with the sort of beating Andrews had incompletely described.

"What about the guards?"

"Two of the Richards are retired, one's still at the prison. All three still live in the area. Piece a cake."

"You're planning to look them up tomorrow?"

"What tomorrow? I called 'em just now."

"You did?" Whittaker glanced at his watch again and smiled.

"Sure. It ain't *that* late. I can even give you a guess about which one did business with the Calabrias, 'cause the other two didn't mind talking to me. But I'll confirm that tomorrow. I haven't been downstate for a while, anyway. Maybe Astoria's got a photo of this Pollitz."

"You never cease to amaze me, Larry."

"What? This stuff's routine."

"At ten at night?"

"I don't follow," Klinger said, half-listening as he scanned the guards' addresses.

"Never mind," Whittaker laughed. "What's the connection between this Pollitz and the Calabrias?"

"No idea, my man," Klinger replied cheerfully. "Except the Barrington address fits. But—and this time it's my gut talkin'—I bet I find one, once I know more about him."

9

Klinger pulled his car onto the small gravel shoulder of the two-lane highway running past the attended entrance to Astoria Adult Correctional Facility and spent a few minutes studying the fenced prison. In the distance he could see the cellblocks inside a second fence. A couple of smaller buildings were visible as well, outside the enclosed cellblock area. He wondered if it had looked the same in 1972. The small buildings looked new. A double row of tall chainlink fences topped with razor wire marched away into the distance, set in a hundred yards or so from the road.

The drive down had been immensely enjoyable to him, and he wished he had asked Dora to come along. He had left Chicago before dawn to avoid rush-hour traffic and hadn't stopped for breakfast until a sign advertising 'Pig-Hip Sandwiches' led him to a small restaurant in Broadwell, a town whose name he had never before heard. He had laughed at himself when he recognized that he had forgotten that the word 'town' could mean such a small collection of buildings—just a couple of businesses and a big concrete silo next to the train line surrounded by, he thought, no more than thirty houses. It had intrigued him, making him speculate about whether he could adjust to life in such a setting. He had concluded he would love the absence of Chicago street rats, but otherwise he probably wouldn't be able to handle the apparent inactivity.

He climbed out of the car and stretched, ruminations about rural life still powerful in his mind. *On the other hand,* he thought, *it's peaceful.* His stop in Broadwell had occurred because he had daydreamed past the closest exit to Astoria, and he was forced to follow small rural routes northwest to Havana and the Illinois River. The drive had been lovely and so foreign from his usual milieu that he naturally yearned for an urbanite's imagined solace of bucolic ease. Not even the ominous aura of a prison across the road could dilute the fanciful feeling. He told Dora late that night, "It made me think it might be time to retire." She laughed gaily in response, "Well, if you're thinking central Illinois, you're doing it without me, buster."

Klinger assumed the fields on his side of the road were all part of the work farm, and he leaned on the roof of the car and looked around. There was a chill in the air, and the sky had a threatening look, but Klinger was still aware that he was visiting a different climate zone. It felt like the Astoria area, unlike Chicago, might even experience spring. The harrowed earth seemed to go on forever, broken only by distant lines of bare trees, a fence and one new metal building. He stretched again and sniffed deeply. The dirt smelled good.

At the gatehouse he identified himself and announced, "I'm here to see Phil Arbuckle and Richard Shaw. Where do I go?" The wide gates in the double fence stood open. Next to the road was a small, roofed three-sided enclosure with a bench. Klinger concluded a bus ran along the road to Astoria.

The guard checked a clipboard and sent him on to the small visitors' parking lot. No other cars were parked there. The gatehouse guard had said he would call ahead for Arbuckle, and a small man with wire-rimmed glasses was waiting at the station near the gate in the interior fence as Klinger climbed out of his car. Klinger waved.

"You Phil?" he said as he walked across the lot. The man nodded and smiled as Klinger neared. He was slightly built and looked to be in his early thirties, his sandy hair close-cut in a military style. Klinger shifted his accordion file to his left hand and extended his right with a broad smile. "Thanks again for faxing me all that info last night. I really appreciate it."

"Glad to help."

Klinger noticed the man had no accent. "Are you a native?" he asked.

"Actually, I grew up in Rockford," Arbuckle answered, "but my wife's from here." He grinned and led Klinger to the gates. "We went to college together, at Bradley, in Peoria."

"You like it here?"

"Yes," Arbuckle replied with a smile. "It's a real nice place to live."

"Yeah, it seems like it," Klinger said a little wistfully. "I had no idea the Illinois River was so beautiful."

Klinger checked in with the guard at the inner gatehouse, receiving a visitor badge and locking his weapon in a safe.

"Can you tell me what this is about?" Arbuckle asked as they moved onto the grounds.

"Like I said yesterday, we're investigating a man who was here in 1972," Klinger replied conversationally. "Rather, I believe he was here in 1972. I'm hoping to confirm it. He was nineteen at the time. His name was on the infirmary logs you sent me. Evidently, he got raped and beaten, a pretty good beating."

"I'm told the facility was a little looser then," Arbuckle said, "so it doesn't surprise me." He frowned. "Rick Shaw could tell you more about that."

"You mean that couldn't happen now?"

"Oh, it happens. You know, though, it's a lot rarer than people think. There's this common fantasy about what goes on when people are incarcerated. It's not totally inaccurate, but it's overblown."

"Sure." Klinger nodded.

"I'm not as involved with the inmates, so you ought to ask Rick about it. But from what I understand, most of the sex here is consensual."

"Plenty of people would argue that rape has nothing to do with sex."

"I'd probably agree with that," Arbuckle nodded. "In here, you could argue that *sex* has nothing to do with sex. Who was the guy?"

"His name's Michael J. Pollitz," Klinger answered. "Do you keep photographs of the inmates?"

"We do, but I don't know if we have records going back that far." He noted the disappointment in Klinger's face. "I'll try to find one," he added. He looked at his watch. "Rick's on duty for another hour," he said. "He'll meet you in the staff lunchroom during his break, okay?"

"That's perfect," Klinger replied. "I'd like to take a look around, get a feel, if that's no problem."

"Not at all."

Klinger studied the three-story structure. The windows were small and covered with steel grilles. "Can I see the cellblocks too?"

"Sure. But we call it a dormitory," Arbuckle laughed.

"Whatever," Klinger chuckled. "I was told there was a ball field with a little bleachers, back in 1972."

"It's still there, back on the other side of the dorm." Arbuckle led Klinger across the grass. "The bleachers aren't that old, but there's still a small set of benches."

"Does the facility look pretty much the same as in 1972?"

"I've only been here four years," Arbuckle answered. "Rick's an old-timer, though. He ought to be able to tell you what's changed." He gestured toward the dormitory. "But anything that's new, it was done no later than 1985."

"Why's that?"

"That's the last time we had any additional funding." The guard laughed ironically.

"How crowded are you?"

"Too crowded," Arbuckle answered simply. "You'll see, once we're in the dorm."

Klinger paused to look around again. "Man, I hate a prison," he said.

"So do the prisoners."

10

"Thanks for taking the time, Mr. Shaw," Klinger said, sitting across the lunchroom table from Richard Shaw. The heavyset, balding man looked about Klinger's age, maybe a couple of years older, he thought, *in better shape than me.*

Shaw nodded pleasantly, cupping a coffee mug between his thick palms. "Whyn't you call me Rick?" he said with a slight central-Illinois twang. Klinger smiled, thinking he probably sounded like a classic Chicagoan to Shaw.

"Deal, if you'll call me Larry," he replied. He shifted his weight in the seat and pulled a couple of folders from his accordion file. "How long do we have?" he asked, glancing up at a clock on the wall.

"I go back on in forty-five minutes," Shaw answered.

"Should be more than enough. Like I said last night, I'm investigating a man who I believe was here in 1972. That's one of the things I'm trying to establish. You were here then, right?"

"Yessir," Shaw answered. "I started in 1967." He nodded with a smile in his watery green eyes, as if absolutely nothing Klinger might ask would come as a surprise.

"How much has the place changed since then?"

"Phil showed you around, din't he?" When Klinger nodded, Shaw continued, "Well, physically, not a lot of changes. In 1972 the arrangement of the fences was different. There was a double row like we have on the perimeter now, but it started inside the parking lot, like, where we have the interior fence now, if you can picture that." Klinger nodded some more and sipped a soda. "So it was a single pair of fences. The smaller buildings you saw outside the interior fence? They weren't there in 1972. And the dormitory was shaped like an L, not a T. We added the east wing in 1983, the same time the new fences were built."

"Don't sound like big changes," Klinger said.

"Nope," Shaw agreed. "Added about a hundred beds and improved security some, but that's about all. When we added the east wing, we din't even have to move the guard station. Made it a little bigger." He raised his mug. "I'm not sure if I can remember many inmates from 1972, though."

"You may remember this one. The name I'm looking for is Michael J. Pollitz."

Shaw squinted as he concentrated. "Seems like that's a name I know," he began, tentative and trying to remember.

"He spent most of July, 1972, in the infirmary here after a pretty severe beating," Klinger added, opening a file folder. In it he had the six old photographs of young men who seemed to have been friends or at least acquaintances of John Calabria, none of whom had been positively identified by either his department or the FBI.

"Yeah!" Shaw said. "Yeah, I remember that kid!" He frowned. "He was a college student. And you're right, he got beat pretty bad."

Klinger studied Shaw for a few seconds, and then he slid the six 'John Doe' photos from the folder and arranged them on the table. "You see the guy here anywhere?" he asked.

Shaw slurped some coffee and studied the photos. He took his time. "There he is," he said at last, pointing at the photograph taken outside the church at which John Calabria was married. In addition to Calabria, there were two young men in the shot, standing on the church steps and smiling at the groom. Both were wearing tuxedoes.

"Which one?" Klinger asked.

Shaw tapped a slender man with longish brown hair. "This one. That's your guy."

Klinger turned the photo back toward himself and studied the shot with predatory triumph. "You're sure," he said, a perfunctory declaration.

"Absolutely."

"Can you tell me anything about him? I mean, did you know him at all?"

"Everyone knew *of* him, after he was assaulted," Shaw said, "but I didn't know him personally. Never spoke to the kid."

"He got raped, too, right?"

"That was my understanding."

Klinger produced the three mug shots of McVee, Jackson and Andrews. "You recall these guys?"

Shaw's lip curled with disgust. "Yeah, I remember those pricks. Hard cases. McVee in particular. A real bastard. We heard he got murdered right after he was released."

"How'd you hear that?"

"Me? Just through the grapevine."

"They were the guys who worked Pollitz over, am I right?"

"I'm sure of it, but it was never confirmed. The kid wouldn't name his assailants. Said he wasn't conscious enough to identify them."

"Were you aware that Jackson was killed as well?"

"No, I didn't know that. It sure ain't a surprise, though." Shaw shook his head. "Him an' McVee, they shouldn't have been in this facility, if you ask me. They'd been better put away in Menard, Pontiac, somewheres with tighter security. Those boys were bad news. If you'd asked me then, I would've said they's going back to jail within a year."

Klinger nodded. "Yeah, that's the impression I got of them," he said. He put his file folders away. "I'm told the scuttlebutt around here had it that Pollitz left with a mobster, when he was released. Had you heard that?"

Shaw looked confused. He shook his head, his brow wrinkled. "No, I never heard that," he said. He thought for a moment. "When was the kid released?"

"Toward the end of July that year," Klinger answered.

"Well, then, I wouldn't've heard about it. I got married on July 20, 1972, and we took a three-week honeymoon. Rumors about the prisoners don't last all that long among the guards. Especially one that's gone."

"You said you thought McVee and Jackson belonged in a different prison. Was security lax around here in '72?"

"Not in the sense that someone could walk through the gate, if that's what you mean. But we had a real mixed bag at the time. We got a lot of first-time offenders, a lot of them small drug busts, back in the early '70s. In '72 the big push from Springfield was 'cleaning up the campuses,' which according to the governor were overrun with drugs. So I guess a few college kids found themselves in the system. It wasn't that different from the statutory requirements we're seeing these days in some facilities, where guys that aren't your tough criminals get medium-

or even maximum-security-type sentences for drug busts, but 'cause the other choice was really heavy time, some bad customers got sent here instead of where they really should've been. Back then, I mean. Now, of course, most of our inmates actually are medium-security-type offenders. Not the hardened cases you get in Joliet, say, but men with records. Back in '72, guys like your fella were thrown in here with sumbitches like McVee. Those days, the work details and unscheduled time were geared more toward the minimum-security types, guys who were going to be here less than six months or a year. So internal security was a little lower."

"And that has changed."

"Definitely. We're organized different now. I'm not saying what happened to that kid couldn't ever happen now, but it's a little harder for bastards like McVee and Jackson to pull it off." He sucked at his teeth thoughtfully. "Plus, we have a lot fewer first-timers these days."

"That makes a difference?"

"Sure does. A guy who's been inside already knows the score. Fewer cherries around, as the inmates call 'em."

"Phil Arbuckle claims most of the sex here is by consent," Klinger said. "That true?"

Shaw raised his eyebrows. "Yes and no," he answered. "I mean, succumbing to intimidation doesn't imply consent, to me. But if you mean as opposed to violent rape, like what happened with the kid you're asking about, that surely isn't a regular thing. Like I say, this prison has changed over the years. The men are monitored more closely than they were in the 1970s." He sipped coffee. "And very few of the sentences being served here exceed three years, lots less. Most of the men who come here, they tend to be younger, almost always under forty, though. I'd have to look it up, but it would surprise me if less than, say, three-quarters of the inmates aren't out of their twenties. Some violence occurs." Shaw shrugged. "We do what we can to prevent it."

Klinger glanced at the clock. "Well, Richard, I don't want to take up any more of your time. But I really appreciate the insights." He looked at his notepad. "Just a couple more questions, if you don't mind." Shaw smiled and stopped half out of his seat. "I'm going to see two more guards named Richard, same as you, Richard Kranz and Richard Taylor. I gather they're retired now, but they were here in 1972. Did you know them?"

"Oh, sure, I knew 'em. You'll like Rich Taylor. He's a real good guy. He just retired three, four years ago. Lives on a little lake north of here about twelve miles." He nodded and finished his coffee.

"What about Kranz?" *The dirty one,* Klinger thought.

"Him I didn't know very well," Shaw answered, his face guarded. "He was partial to the graveyard shift, so I only worked with him a few times. He retired a long time ago, like in 1983 or so."

Klinger noticed without surprise that Shaw did not make eye contact as he spoke.

11

"Here you go," Arbuckle announced proudly.

"What's this?" Klinger asked, reaching to take the photocopies the guard held.

"It's an induction photo of the guy you're asking about, plus all the records about his stay here that I could dig out of our morgue." The size of his grin suggested that the search hadn't been simple.

Klinger held the copy next to the shot from John Calabria's wedding and smiled slowly. "Yeah, it's the same guy," he announced. He winked at Arbuckle. "You pick the place, Phil, the best around here. Whatever your favorite is. I owe you a good meal. Bring your wife."

"Ahhh, forget it," the guard replied, still beaming with self-satisfaction. "I'm glad to help. Besides, it was fun to do something out of the ordinary."

"Took some time, did it?"

Arbuckle shook his head with a self-deprecating frown. "Just the time you've been with Rick Shaw," he answered. He shifted his position to one side and looked down at the admission photo. "That's kind of an unusual shot," he offered.

"What do you mean?" Klinger studied the photo. The face was young, almost boyish, with the unruly hair of a student.

"I should show you a few admission shots," the guard explained. "Almost always, the inmates look, like, totally zoned out, or they try to look hard. So their faces are either basically completely blank or sneering. This one looks more like a high school yearbook photo."

"You think so?" Klinger asked dubiously. To his eye, it looked like a frontal snapshot of a confused, scared kid; there was nothing benign in the photo's message.

"He's too alert," Arbuckle concluded, chuckling. "When I was digging through the old files, there were a few guys like this. Don't look a thing like what we always get now." He shook his head with a short laugh. "I can't really put my finger on it. I guess he just looks too soft, you know what I mean?"

Klinger couldn't tell if the shot showed softness or fear. "Well, he definitely looks outta place," he snorted. "But it's my guy."

"Check out the infirmary detail."

Klinger nodded slowly as he scanned the record. "Looks like he got worked over pretty good."

"I'll say," Arbuckle agreed. "He must've been beat nearly to death, to stay in the infirmary that long."

Klinger paused as he reread the record. "Seems like a long time," he agreed, thinking out loud. "But the injuries they got listed here ain't exceptional, you follow? Busted jaw, some ribs, nothin' too far outta the ordinary."

"Who knows?" Arbuckle answered with a nonchalant shrug. "It's twenty-odd years ago. Maybe the care was different." He read the sheet over Klinger's shoulder. "Maybe it was the concussion."

"Could be," Klinger muttered. He flipped through the sheets. "There's nothing here about his charges or any of that."

"I couldn't find any of those records. There's nothing in the file."

"That unusual?"

Arbuckle shook his head quickly. "Not for a file this old. I'm pleased I found what I did."

"Hey, don't get me wrong. This is more than I coulda hoped for. You did me a big favor here. Huge." He tapped the sheets on the lunchroom table. "Can I keep these?"

"They're yours." Arbuckle pulled open the door. "Mind giving me some details on what you're doing?"

"Fishing, mainly," Klinger replied. "But I'm happy to give you what I have. Wanna show me to my car?"

"You'll have a tough time getting to it without me," Arbuckle laughed. He gestured down the hall. "Right this way."

"You ever heard the name Dominick Calabria?"

"Sure. That Mafia guy."

"You got it. But in Chicago, it's called 'the Outfit,' not the Mafia."

"Why?"

"You got me," Klinger answered. He followed the small guard toward a security gate. "Anyway, there's some connection between this guy Pollitz," he continued, flapping his file folder, "and Dom Calabria. Don't know what it is yet. And two of the guys who gave this Pollitz the beating when he was here, they ended up dead not too long after he was released from this institution." Klinger breathed deeply, feeling relieved, once they were outside the building. "I don't know how you guys stand it in here," he said. "My hat's off to you."

Arbuckle shrugged. "And you figure the mobster killed those other guys? Or are you investigating Pollitz as the perpetrator?"

"That's what I'm trying to determine," Klinger answered, smiling inwardly as the prison guard sought a collaberative union in law enforcement. "You sure you don't want a nice dinner tonight?"

12

After a brief hunt for the right street on the western side of Astoria, Klinger located Richard Kranz's small home, a standard-issue one-story clapboard structure with a gable roof and covered with wide aluminum siding, a kind of house found in farming communities throughout Illinois, almost as ubiquitous as bungalows in Chicago. He parked on a short gravel apron behind a big, mid-1970s Buick that was in a narrow carport on one side of the house. The trim needed paint, but the house wasn't dilapidated. A railed porch extended across the narrow front facade, four steps up from the lawn, one end shaded by an overgrown lilac. A skinny old man with slicked-back thin gray hair sat in a lawn chair near the lilac. He wore a windbreaker even though the intermittent early-afternoon sunlight reached the porch. He glared as Klinger climbed with a grunt from his car and waved.

"Richard Kranz?" Klinger called, fighting down a smile as the old man nodded angrily, a quick, sullen jerk of his head, his thick-rimmed eyeglasses flashing in the hazy glow. Klinger opened the back door of his car to retrieve the brown accordion file. He grinned happily as he approached the porch. "I'm Larry Klinger," he boomed, "the guy who called last night. Thanks for seeing me." Kranz didn't move. There was only one chair on the porch, so Klinger stopped at the stairs. He smiled up at the old man and nodded, then glanced up and down the street. He made a show of watching some sparrows in a spirea next door. "Nice town," he said. "You lived here long?"

"All my life," the old man answered.

"What, the whole time in this house?"

Kranz nodded. Through the collar of the windbreaker Klinger could see grizzled chest hairs above the scalloped neck of a sleeveless undershirt. An inane thought popped into his head: *I wonder how long it's been since he washed his hair?* "You raise a family here?" he asked.

"Wife died six years ago," Kranz grumbled.

"I'm sorry to hear that," Klinger frowned. He shook his head. "That's too bad," his face still filled with sorrow and concern. He sighed and smiled in a forlorn way. "And you retired from the prison, when? In 1985?"

"In 1984."

"Ah!" Klinger announced, fascinated by the revelation. "So what's a retired guy do, here in Astoria?"

"Whyn't you tell me what you want?"

"You got something planned? Am I interrupting your schedule?" Klinger grinned again. "I can come back in an hour or so," he offered.

Kranz shook his head, his sneer parting his lips slightly to reveal gold-edged teeth.

"Do you go by Richard, Mr. Kranz?" Klinger asked.

"Dick," the old man answered.

Klinger pulled a manila folder from his accordion file and scanned its contents. "I won't take much of your time, Dick," he said, smiling. "Like I said on the phone last night, we're investigating some ancient history, here, and I need a little help with identification."

The old man nodded distrustfully.

"What I'm concerned with," Klinger continued, "is the summer of 1972. I realize that's a long time ago. There was an incident at Astoria involving, I think, this young man." He slid the copy of Pollitz's admission shot out of the folder and stepped onto the stairs to show it to the retired guard. "Do you recognize him?" He watched the skin around Kranz's eyes tighten slightly as his eyes narrowed. When the old man shook his head, Klinger marked a small asterisk next to the word PHOTO on his notepad.

"I don't remember him," Kranz declared.

"You sure? He got worked over bad enough that he spent like four weeks or so in the infirmary. Here's another shot of him." He displayed the surveillance photo from John Calabria's wedding.

"I jes' told you he don't look like no one I know." Kranz hawked and leaned his head over the porch rail to spit.

Klinger removed the old mug shots of McVee, Jackson and Andrews from the folder and showed each to Kranz. "How about these guys? Any of them ring a bell?"

Kranz frowned and shook his head again. He barely glanced at the mug shots.

"You don't know any of them? They were all guests at Astoria when you worked there."

"So were a thousand other guys."

"True, true," Klinger agreed. "But I'm only concerned with these guys. You sure you don't know 'em? Never talked with any of them? Their names are Robert Andrews, John McVee and Darryl Jackson," he added helpfully, flapping each mug shot in turn.

"You allus ask the same questions over 'n' over? You a dummy?"

"Well, it's a long time ago," Klinger said, affably unoffended.

"I'm just trying to jog your memory. This blond guy, McVee, he got killed right after he was released from Astoria." Klinger bobbed his eyebrows at Kranz. "Not too far away from here, just up in Peoria. Kind of an unusual thing. Got tossed off a roof. Somebody had jammed a broomstick up his ass. Not exactly what you'd call run-of-the-mill. You sure this don't bring up anything out of the old memory bank?"

Kranz shook his head, frowning.

"I gather these three guys hung around together in Astoria, way back when there in '72, so I was hoping you'd remember them." He smiled with feigned patience. "They weren't a very lucky bunch, you follow me? Not only did McVee get murdered, like I say, in Peoria right after he left your care, so to speak, but then the black guy, Jackson," Klinger again displayed the photocopy, "he ends up likewise, murdered in Cairo. Castrated, no less. Ended up with his own cock in his throat. The sort of thing someone might notice, you know?" He grinned expectantly.

"I don't know 'em." Kranz again spit over the porch rail.

"Ah, well, that's the way it goes," Klinger sighed. "Lemme show you one more, okay?" He took another folder from the accordion file and removed a fifteen-year-old photo of Salvatore Bruno. "You ever meet this guy?"

Kranz squinted at the print for a moment and said, "Nope."

Klinger nodded. At last, a truthful answer. "His name's Salvatore Bruno," Klinger went on. "That name mean anything to you?"

Kranz sniffed a couple of times and scratched his ear. "Never heard of him."

Klinger nodded, a small smile lifting the corners of his mouth. He didn't need to produce DeMicco's photo. "How about Dominick Calabria? Is that a familiar name?"

"No."

"No?"

"I just said so, din't I?"

Klinger made a show of rearranging the photocopies and

prints, tapping them on the porch deck to align their edges, and replacing them in their folders. He slid the folders back into the accordion file and reached into his shirt pocket for a package of chewing gum. He offered a piece to Kranz, who shook his head and glared suspiciously. Klinger leaned forward, one foot resting on the top step of the porch, with his arms crossed on his thigh. He affected a weary sigh and stared at the old man, chewing the initial burst of flavor out of his gum. "You know what, Dick?" he said at last. "I think you're lying to me. Fact, I *know* you're lying to me."

"Time for you to get your ass gone, mister," Kranz barked, gripping the arms of his chair.

Klinger dropped the easygoing act. "Don't try to threaten me, asshole," he snapped, his eyes unblinking and coldly furious. Kranz flinched, although Klinger hadn't moved.

"Git off my property!" the old man hissed.

"You did business with Dom Calabria, shithead. You know it, and I know it. You knew damn well what happened to McVee. And I'd say you told Andrews and Jackson that Calabria was waiting for them to get out of Astoria. That's another thing we both know. What's odd here is the kid got worked over anyway. Did Calabria stiff you on the payment, or did you do other work for him to compensate, Dick? You musta been a little scared. Maybe you're how they got their hands on McVee so fast. Whaddya say, Dick?" Kranz's breathing was ragged with impotent rage. Spit collected on his lip. Klinger felt a laugh building in his throat. "Here's some free advice, Dick," he concluded. "Unless you're willing to perjure yourself—and trust me, it would take nothing to prove it—all the answers you just gave me better change in a courtroom, you follow?"

13

Klinger felt an uncharacteristic surge of envy as Richard Taylor led him through the trees surrounding the retired guard's tidy lakeside home, and he laughed as he acknowledged the emotion. Taylor turned back and grinned down at Klinger. *This is a genuinely enormous slab of beef,* Klinger thought. *Even seventy and overweight he'd be an imposing guard.*

"Yeah, this is a real nice place," the retired guard agreed. "My son and I built it back in 1985. I say, 'my son and I,' but really, it was my son." He paused, his mottled face filled with pride, and gazed down the lawn to the small, tree-lined lake. "He's a hell of a carpenter, and he's got a great eye. I mean, look at how he set the house!" Taylor beamed.

Klinger studied the property, feeling old and tired. The single-level home was sited beautifully beneath tall old oaks at the end of a long gravel drive, with what looked to Klinger like two acres or more of mowed grass encircling the house and leading down a gentle slope to a small pier that extended only twelve or fourteen feet into the water. The house was sided vertically in stained cedar, with battens covering the joints between the planks and trellises for climbing roses facing the drive. Large windows overlooked the lake. At the edges of the mowed area, Klinger could see rhododendrons and other ornamental plantings, a large vegetable garden and a path leading into the woods along the water. He walked slowly behind Taylor. The big man walked with a slight limp and held a briarwood pipe in his right hand.

"Is maintaining this property a lot of work?" Klinger asked as he glanced around. "I mean, is it a lotta hours every week?"

Taylor smiled and gestured with his pipe toward a small metal shed set half into the underbrush beyond the house. "Couple of hours on a tractor's all." His slow drawl fit the setting, Klinger thought. "My wife takes care of the flowers, and we probably work the vegetables a day's worth each week. Easy like, you know?" He nodded with pleasure and moved toward a small flagstone patio with a stone barbecue pit behind the house.

"You aren't from this area," Klinger said. He shifted the waist of his pants and settled himself into a wood deck chair. He rested his accordion file on his lap.

"Well, I been here near thirty-five years now. But you're right, we moved the family up here when I took the job at Astoria. From Tulsa."

"You were at the prison since 1960?"

Taylor nodded his huge head, chuckling at Klinger's incredulous expression. "It was a good job. Great pension too."

"I don't think I coulda stood the scumbags that long, you follow?"

Taylor spread his large hands and raised his eyebrows. "How long you been a cop, Detective Klinger?"

"Good point. Definitely a good point," Klinger laughed. "You always been a mind reader, or was it something you picked up in Astoria?"

A deep laugh rolled out of Taylor's throat in response. He leaned back in his chair and stared, an amused light in his eyes. He ran a thick hand across his face, and Klinger noted a network of broken capillaries on the fleshy sides of the big man's nose and across his cheekbones.

Klinger looked across the lake with his lips pursed. Crows were clustered high in a distant tree, providing a dual image in the lake's surface. He focused on the view for a few seconds, then wrapped his sport coat around his torso and rubbed his hands together. "Even on a gray day like today, this'd be real easy to get used to," he said. He sniffed and rubbed his nose, unconsciously echoing Taylor's gesture. "Well, I guess I oughta get down to business. Like I said last night, I'm investigating a man who was a guest at Astoria back in 1972." He removed the photocopy of Pollitz's admission shot from the file and handed it to Taylor. "His name's Michael Pollitz. He was assaulted in the summer of the 1972, spent most of his term in the prison infirmary." He watched Taylor's face. "Mainly, I want to confirm his identity, plus maybe a couple other guys."

Taylor's eyes narrowed with sudden anger and a touch of sadness, it seemed to Klinger. "I know this kid," Taylor rumbled softly. "I wouldn't've remembered the name, but for sure the kid." He shook his head.

"How so?" Klinger asked.

"I walked him through orientation, for starters. Saw him in the infirmary too."

"What can you tell me about him?"

"He was a college student. Quiet kid. Scared. Nothing odd about that, I should say." He again shook his head with a sorrowful frown. "It's not like I got to know him, but after what happened, I took an interest."

"Think you might recognize him now?"

"Sure."

"When you say you took an interest, what do you mean?"

Taylor met Klinger's eyes, his expression still slightly pained but washing into fury. "That kid was beaten savagely and raped by one of the worst human beings it was ever my misfortune to meet," the guard declared. "And I met some evil people. I have no idea what the kid did to get sent to Astoria, but whatever it was, it wasn't bad enough to deserve that."

Klinger stopped rummaging through his files. "You know who attacked Pollitz?" he asked with surprise. Taylor nodded once, sharp with rising anger. Klinger continued, "My understanding is the kid couldn't identify his assailants."

"I don't believe 'couldn't'," Taylor answered. "I'd say 'wouldn't' is the operative word."

"Who beat him?"

"An animal named John McVee," Taylor said, his voice tight. "A piece of human garbage, a walking argument for eugenics."

Klinger stared. "I take it he made an impression," he said at last.

"That *incident* made an impression," Taylor replied. "Almost made me take a different job."

"You're kidding."

"Not in the least."

"Why? Doesn't that sort of thing happen?"

"Sure it does."

"What was so unique about this incident?"

Taylor shrugged, squinting slightly, and bit his pipe. "I don't know for sure," he said after a lengthy pause. "Somethin' about the kid, I guess, or about McVee." He thought some more. "For a few years back then, the damn judges were sending a real mixed bag to places like Astoria, made a lot of us pretty mad, to tell the truth. Kids like Pollitz got tossed into open institutions with genuine psychopaths like McVee," he went on, disgustedly flapping the copy of Pollitz's photo, "and then we were supposed to keep evil from occurring. It was just plain wrong, Detective. Just plain wrong." He shook away the anger and calmed himself. "Sorry I'm gettin' so hot about it."

"Don't bother me any," Klinger said. He smiled warmly and fished in his files. "Well, I'm impressed by your memory, Rich," he went on as he removed the three old mug shots. "For the record, is this who you mean? McVee?"

"That's him," Taylor replied. He handed Klinger the photo of Pollitz.

"You recognize these other two guys?"

"Sure. Jackson, the black guy, was McVee's partner in crime. He wasn't real bright. McVee took the lead, but Jackson was more of a crony than the other guy, Andrews."

"What do you mean?"

"Andrews was one of those toady types who attaches himself to a hardass. Jackson was more in the hardass category himself."

"What made you sure these three assaulted Pollitz?"

"It's not always real obvious, but you can see these things developing, if you're paying attention. But more likely, you just recognize the signs, like, after the fact. In hindsight. Once the kid ended up in the infirmary, I realized McVee had been giving him the eye, you know what I mean? Little things add up."

"I follow you," Klinger nodded. He returned the photocopies to his file. "Something else I wanted to ask about," he said, fumbling in his coat pocket. "I just spent a few minutes with Dick Kranz, before I came over here." Klinger offered Taylor a stick of gum. Taylor shook his head with a smile, displaying his pipe. He leaned aside in his chair to pull a packet of tobacco from a back pocket.

"What'd you think of him?" Taylor asked.

Klinger studied the retired guard, but his face was blank. *May as well see where it goes,* Klinger thought. "Well," he began, "no offense if you're friends, but I didn't think much of him." Taylor nodded with a slight frown. "I figure he did business with a gangster named Dominick Calabria, back when Pollitz was in Astoria. He denies it." Klinger shrugged and chewed.

"It would be in keeping."

"Yeah?"

"Sure." Taylor smiled and clenched his teeth around the stem of his pipe. He lit up and released a cloud of aromatic smoke. "Dick was an old-timer, from the head-bustin' school. Angry guy. You're telling me he was on the take, and I say that's no surprise."

"Are those kinds of deals very common?"

"Pretty rare, far as I know, but they happen. You know, some kid from a gang comes in, wants special treatment, whatever. Someone might call a guard." Taylor sucked on his pipe with a slow smile. "How do you know when a cop's getting paid?"

Klinger laughed. "Usually, the tip-off's when he starts showing up in thousand-dollar suits."

Taylor chuckled, shaking his head. "Around here, it's more often a new boat."

"Did you know Kranz was working for Calabria?"

"No." He frowned. "I had no idea. But Dick was the type."

"The name's familiar, though?"

"Oh, sure."

"In what way?"

"In the first place, I know the name same as I know 'Giancana' or 'Gotti.' Mafia in the news, you know?" Taylor gestured with his pipe stem. "But you mean in relation to Pollitz or Kranz, right?" His eyes twinkled with amusement as he waited for Klinger to nod. "I heard Calabria picked the kid up when he left Astoria. That got around fast, hot news for a few days."

"Why was that?"

Taylor laughed. "How many of our guys you think left with some heavyweight Mafioso?" He chuckled and puffed softly on his pipe, releasing a series of small smoke signals. "More likely, it was some trashy girlfriend or some loser buddies, you know. Crying mamas. You'd be surprised how many of their rides showed up drunk. I'd say more'n half of 'em jus' walked out to the bench and waited for a bus."

"How did you hear Pollitz left with Calabria?"

Taylor thought for a moment, tapping his pipe into an ashtray. "You know, I can't remember. It was just one of those rumors that circulated." He fiddled with his cooling pipe. "What happened was, one of the guards who was detailed to Pollitz when he was released ran the plate on the car that picked him up. That's what I heard, anyway."

Klinger studied him for a moment. "Was it Kranz?"

"No idea." Taylor shrugged. "I doubt it. Dick Kranz liked the night shifts."

Klinger rubbed his chin and stared across the lake. He stretched comfortably in the cool air. "Boy, this is a nice place," he repeated himself. "I could get used to this." He smiled at Taylor. "Lemme ask you something else. One a those three assholes, Andrews, he's in custody in Chicago right now. He's the one that started the Calabria connection. Basically started my whole investigation. He claims 'everyone' thought Pollitz was

Calabria's foster son because he was so heavily protected before he was released." He paused to study Taylor's contorted eyebrows. "Did the kid get any special treatment?"

"You mean, like bought protection?" Taylor asked, a disbelieving frown forming. "Like from Kranz or someone? Not that I knew of. You say Kranz was working for this Calabria, but you sure couldn't tell it by me." He shook his head doubtfully. "But the truth of the matter is, the kid got special treatment in the sense that we kep' him in the infirmary longer than ordinary, and I guess most of the guards paid extra attention the couple of days he was back in the general population, 'fore he was released."

"I don't follow."

"It was kind of an informal thing. Usual policy, since the kid wouldn't identify those three pieces of trash, would've been to put him back in the dorm soon as he healed up. In his case, that would've meant maybe five or ten extra days in the block, maybe even a couple of weeks, so one of the records guys just assigned him to the infirmary for some extra time, you see? Then, when he was due to be released, we—the guards, I mean—just kind of agreed to keep an eye on him. You know, informal, like I say." He put his pipe between his teeth again.

"Was this unusual for you guys?"

Taylor shook his head slowly, his lips pulled down around the pipe stem. "Not at all. Especially back then, when a first-timer with a lightweight offence got thrown in with the McVees of the world. Still happens all the time. You get someone who seems vulnerable, or whatever, the guards talk to one another. Remember, Astoria's not a lock-down type of facility."

"Why'd you do it for this Pollitz?" Klinger asked, opening his file folder to again study the admission photo. The more he studied the shot, the more frightened the young man's expression seemed to be.

"Why?" Taylor asked, searching his memory. "Because a lot

of guys felt like me. We felt pretty bad for that kid. We didn't want nothin' else to happen to him. That simple." He shrugged and smiled. "That's what makes your idea about Dick Kranz sort of odd, far as I'm concerned. He was one of those guys who wouldn't have given two hoots for what happened to Pollitz."

Klinger squeezed his lower lip as he thought about it. "Did you know McVee was killed after he got out of Astoria?"

Taylor nodded. "I heard that." He shrugged indifferently. "And I was glad to hear it," he added defiantly. "Personally, I would have been happy to get my hands on him for a few minutes, away from Astoria."

"You serious?"

Taylor leaned back in his seat, his expression unchanged. He cocked one eyebrow.

"Andrews says Pollitz confronted McVee and Jackson, once he was out of the infirmary. Do you know if that's true or not?"

"No."

"Andrews says there were guards around. Any idea who it might have been?"

Taylor shook his head, again reaching for his package of tobacco. "Could have been anyone," he said.

"You hear what happened to McVee?" Klinger asked.

"No." Taylor carefully packed tobacco into the bowl of his pipe.

"He got tossed off a roof in Peoria, impaled on a broom handle. Through his rectum." Klinger's eyes narrowed as Taylor lit the pipe and gazed across the lake. "You never heard those details?"

Taylor shook his head, his face wreathed in smoke.

"Jackson was also killed, early the following year, down in Cairo. Did you hear about it?"

"Nope." Taylor pursed his lips and sent a stream of pipe smoke into the air.

"I woulda thought people at Astoria would connect those deaths, what with the Calabria connection, you follow?" Klinger said, wondering why Taylor had suddenly stopped telling the truth.

Taylor raised an eyebrow and smiled across his pipe. "Well, if you're right about Dick Kranz," he said, "I guess he would've."

"Seems like other guards coulda done the same."

"None of us paid much attention to what became of people like McVee and Jackson, once they were out of our hair," Taylor replied, still smiling. "I mean, 'cept we never wanted to see 'em again."

14

Klinger tapped the file folder against his palm while he waited in the interview room at Cook County Jail. His fervent hope was that this morning's interview would be one of his last lifetime encounters with Bobby Andrews. If at all possible, he wanted to see Andrews' ignorant, leering face only twice more—right now, and when he testified at Dom Calabria's trial.

When the steel door from the holding cell opened, Klinger noticed a change in Andrews, a certain cockiness that led him to give a sauntering air to his manacled shuffle. *He's loving all this attention,* Klinger thought. *What a nasty surprise the idiot's got coming.*

"Don't get too comfortable, Bobby," he said as Andrews sat and lit a cigarette. "This won't take more than a minute."

Andrews exhaled a huge cloud a smoke and sneered. "Seems to me you oughta show a little respect, the help I's givin' you'uns."

What's with the big-shot routine? Klinger wondered, staring suspiciously at Bobby's face. He pinched his lower lip, his eyes narrow. "Who you been shootin' off your mouth to, Bobby?"

he asked slowly. "I hope it wasn't anyone who speaks English."

"Fuck you," Andrews snarled.

"You are one slow-on-the-uptake kinda guy, aren't you, Bobby?" Klinger said with weary irritation. "You think I warned you to keep your ugly trap shut for my benefit?"

"Way I reckon it, you need me's much as I need you," Andrews retorted, clearly pleased with himself.

"That so? The way *I* 'reckon' it, a guy sitting in Cook County jail oughta have enough brains to keep Dom Calabria's name outta conversation."

"Shit," Andrews said, his lip curled. "Fuckin' Mafia's nothin' no more."

"You're even dumber than I thought," Klinger said, shaking his head. He wondered if they ought to get Andrews into isolation somehow. "It's like talking to this chair." Andrews cackled contemptuously and blew smoke across the table. Klinger sighed with disgust. "However you want it, Bobby," he said at last. "This'll only take a second." He slid the Astoria induction photograph of Michael Pollitz from the folder and laid it on the table facing Andrews. He got the confirmation he wanted from the gleam of recognition in Andrews' eyes, but for the record, he asked, "Is this the guy McVee and Jackson worked over back in Astoria?"

"Maybe it is, maybe it ain't," Andrews said with pompous stupidity. "What I wanna know is, what's in it for me?"

Klinger picked up the photograph and closed it inside the file folder without a word. He turned away and rapped on the door with his knuckles.

"Hey!" Andrews barked. "Hey! Where you goin'?"

"Good luck, Bobby," Klinger said, glancing back across his shoulder as he waited for the guard to unlock the door.

"What's that s'posed to mean?" Andrews said loudly as the guard opened the door.

"We're done here," Klinger said to the guard. "Thanks."

"Hey!" Andrews shouted at his back. As Klinger walked down the hall, he again heard Andrews shout, "Hey!"

15

"What d'you think? Time for an initial interview with Pollitz?" Klinger glanced around Whittaker's office at the Criminal Courts building, noting the prosecutor's framed diplomas, citations and other accolades. He admired the wood paneling. Klinger leaned away from Whittaker's cluttered desk and stretched his arms with his knuckles laced in front of him. His knuckles popped and snapped under the pressure, drawing an annoyed glance from the attorney. Whittaker shifted his gaze over the photographs and records spread across the desk surface.

"Where is he?" he asked.

"I don't know for sure," Klinger answered. "Assuming he's still in this area, there's just one Michael J. Pollitz listed in Chicago, and it's gotta be him. It ain't a real common name. There's only one other Pollitz in the Chicago phone book. Astoria listed his address as Barrington back in 1972, and there's two Pollitz listings out there. I'm guessing one's his parents. Could be the other's him." Klinger yawned and stretched again. "I could go through the DMV and match up a license, but why bother? This is the guy." He waited for a reaction from Whittaker, but the attorney didn't look up. "I figure, I want him surprised, so I haven't pursued anyone yet." He looked at his watch. "If the time's right to get things moving, then I'll get a work number, if I can. But I wanna do it the same day."

Whittaker picked up the enlargement from John Calabria's

wedding and studied the young man in the old surveillance photo. He looked like a harmless kid, his dark hair long, stylish for the time, cut in a sort of shag and falling onto the collar of the tuxedo, smiling on the steps of the church and appearing very trim next to John Calabria's overweight bulk. "I wonder what he looks like these days," Whittaker mused. "I wish you had confirmation from Andrews," he added.

"Gimme a break," Klinger said without conviction. "I've had all I can stand of Bobby. He recognized him, whether he said so or not. So did all three guards, even the asshole. You want Bobby to confirm it directly, you can do it yourself. I've had it with that bustout," Klinger snorted.

Whittaker chuckled. "It doesn't really matter. I'll get him to ID the guard, this Kranz, too," he said, lifting the photocopy of the Astoria admission shot from his desk and holding it beside the wedding photograph. "This is the only connection between Pollitz and the Calabrias?"

"As far as I know," Klinger answered. "Hell, until yesterday that wedding photo was a John Doe. But take a look at the old logs from Astoria. Right after Pollitz got worked over, John Calabria visited him at the prison infirmary. I mean, right away. He was there before Pollitz's family. Interesting, no? And according to one of the guards, it was common knowledge around there that Dom Calabria picked him up when he was released."

Whittaker started to rearrange the sheets and photographs, shuffling them into file folders. He glanced briefly at the old mug shots of McVee, Jackson and Andrews. "This is good work, Larry," he said with a congratulatory grin.

"It's pretty routine, so far," Klinger answered modestly, but he returned Whittaker's smile.

Whittaker shook his head. He couldn't think of another detective who could have pulled the file together as quickly as Klinger had. He closed the folders and handed them across the desk. "Yeah, let's go ahead," he said. "Now's as good a time as any to get started. How do you plan to follow this?"

Klinger looked at his watch again. "Guess I'll call the Michael J. Pollitz number first. He's located just a couple a blocks from the Addison station, if the address is correct. If he's employed, he's gotta be gone to work by now," he said, thinking aloud. "I'll try the Barrington numbers and the other Chicago number and see what I can see."

"Why do you want to surprise him?" Whittaker asked without much interest. He could think of several reasons for an ambush in this case but didn't feel any were especially important. "I mean, what if it doesn't work out that way?"

"It don't really matter," Klinger answered. "But I figure, I'd just as soon talk to him before he discusses this with Dom Calabria, if I can. Plus, I'll probably learn more if at least one of our conversations doesn't include one a you damn lawyers, you follow me?" Whittaker laughed. " 'Sides," Klinger continued, "I don't think he's connected with any of Calabria's crews. I mean, if he is, he's totally invisible. Maybe if I can catch him off guard, he'll do a little talking." He stood, grinning. "Is there any empty office around here with a phone?"

16

Michael was sitting in his fifteenth-floor office, staring south at the downtown Chicago skyline and pretending to be thinking about a lineup of rough designs for a Sears point-of-purchase campaign. The advertising agency that employed him was just one of several that Sears used, but the giant retailer was by far his firm's biggest account. The layouts required serious attention, and Michael was trying to force himself to deliver it. *I should get some binoculars in here,* he thought as he scanned the buildings, *or maybe a spotting scope,* when one of the senior account executives walked into his office. Michael found the woman passingly attractive, tall and athletic and always dressed in expensive, flattering clothing, and he sat up as she followed her peremptory knock through the door. She worked in a different division of the company, with a different boss and a separate chain of command, and he wasn't sure precisely where in the mildly Byzantine organization chart each stood in relation to the other. He had a feeling she was a notch or two above him, maybe more. It was sometimes hard to tell, because practically everyone with any seniority, including Michael, carried a vice-president label. He guessed he was ten years older than the woman, not that it mattered.

She glanced at the layouts on easels in front of his desk and said, "I don't like them. The word 'now' should be bigger."

"What possible difference could that make?" Michael asked. His phone rang.

She gazed at him with the uncomprehending self-involvement of micromanagers everywhere and said, "Everything's important." *Oh, brother,* Michael thought as his phone continued to ring. "Go ahead and get that," she said magnanimously. As she turned to leave, she added, "I want to get your input on the Connor direct-mail package, when you get a minute. Could you stop by? I want everyone's buy-in on this." Michael nodded, and she left. He lifted his phone's handset.

"Pollitz," he said, distractedly dreading the tedious 'buy-in' meeting.

"Is this Michael Pollitz?" Klinger asked.

"Yes."

"This is Detective Larry Klinger of the Chicago Police Department, Mr. Pollitz. How're you today?"

"I'm fine."

"That's great, great," Klinger said. Michael could almost hear his smile. "Listen, we're involved in a rather large investigation that I think you could help us with. At least, I hope so." He paused, and when Michael said nothing, went on. "It's a long story, but to keep it short, it involves the Calabrias."

"Which Calabrias?" Michael asked calmly, successfully masking an immediate uneasy feeling and kicking himself for the dumb stall.

"Dominick and John Calabria," Klinger replied. "Do you know them? Is this the right Michael J. Pollitz?"

"Yes, I know them," Michael answered.

"Good, I got the right guy," Klinger said happily. "It's no big deal, but I'd like to ask you a few questions, if you don't mind. It shouldn't take more than a few minutes. Would it be convenient if I stopped by this afternoon?"

"Where are you located, Detective...?"

"Klinger. Larry Klinger. I'm calling you from the station at Addison and Halsted. Why?" Klinger was actually still sitting in an empty cubicle at the Criminal Courts Building at 26th and California, southwest of the Loop. He smiled in the dull government office.

"That's very close to my home," Michael answered. "How about if I stop by instead? It'll give me an excuse to get out of here early."

"That would be great, Mr. Pollitz," Klinger said, his wide face glowing with triumph. "I really appreciate it."

"I can't get there for a couple of hours," Michael said.

"That's no problem at all, Mr. Pollitz. I'll be here all day. Just ask for me at the desk." Klinger was relieved. He could take his time and still get to the station first.

"Can you tell me what this is about?"

"Oh," Klinger said in an offhand, nonchalant voice, "it's nothing spectacular. I'll fill you in when you get here."

Michael hung up the phone in a state of consternation. *This is a first,* he thought. He picked up the handset again and dialed the office number at John Calabria's restaurant in Palatine. A woman answered. Michael didn't recognize her voice. She sounded like one of John's bimbos.

"Is John there?"

"Who's calling?" She pronounced it, *Hooze cawlin?*

"This is Mike Pollitz." He picked up a pencil and tapped it on his knee until John's loud voice boomed through the handset.

"Mikey! What's up?"

"John, I could live to be two hundred, and I'll never understand why you guys want to sound like morons."

"What the fuck you talkin' about?"

"Your girl."

"You wouldn't believe the tits." John laughed. "You just call to bitch about how she talks, or is there somethin' else?"

"I just got a call from a CPD detective who wants to ask me some questions about you and your dad."

John's tone of voice didn't change. "About what?"

"He didn't say."

"Where is he?"

"At the station at Addison and Halsted, near my house. I told him I'd meet him there in a couple of hours."

"Blow him off."

"That won't make him disappear," Michael said patiently.

"What's the fucker want?"

"How should I know? I was hoping you could tell me."

John didn't say anything for a few moments. Michael could picture his old friend's heavy face contorted with thought. "Beats me," John said at last. "We haven't had any shit from those assholes for a while." He paused again. "You say he's Chicago?"

"Yeah."

"Guy's off his yard," John said. "He give you any details?"

"No, he was pretty vague."

"What's the guy's name?"

"Klinger," Michael answered.

After another brief delay, John said, "It don't ring a bell for me. Tell you what, Mikey. Gimme a call after you talk to the asshole. I'll call my dad, maybe he knows this guy. Don't do nothin' I wouldn't," he closed cheerfully.

Michael replaced the handset with a mixed feeling. John's casual attitude was reassuring somehow. Unless Klinger was after something else. He walked down the hall to his inconsequential meeting and was glad to use the excuse of an appointment with a police officer to leave after a pointless hour.

17

The police station was a ramshackle old dump, made of limestone blocks and with a stair facing Halsted Street and a side door on Addison. Inside the double doors facing Halsted was a big common room that echoed with people complaining loudly in every direction—at the desk sergeant, at the cops who ushered them to the desk, at one another. The chaotic noise and movement of people did nothing to reduce the menacing, uncompromising atmosphere of power common to all urban police installations that made even its worn wooden floors intimidating. The desk sergeant indifferently picked up a phone and told him to wait. Michael hadn't yet decided to take a seat when Klinger barreled out of a hall from the back of the station and marched directly across the open room with his hand outstretched.

"Michael Pollitz? I'm Larry Klinger." As they shook hands, Klinger said, "Thanks for coming by. Come on back." He turned and led the way, slowing his pace so Michael walked beside him. Michael eyed Klinger's blue herringbone sport coat and gray slacks. Klinger hitched his thumbs in his belt and hiked his pants up beneath his belly. He glanced at Michael with a smile. "Nice tie," he said. "Where'd you get it?"

"It was a gift," Michael replied.

Klinger led him into an interview room with a filing cabinet, a metal-legged table with a formica top and three wooden chairs. The chairs were chewed up, scratched and gouged. On one wall was a tackboard. Beneath it was a dented gray metal trash can. Klinger looked around with a wry smile and gestured for Michael to take a seat, saying, "Good enough for government work," with rueful humor. Michael smiled. "What do you do, Mr. Pollitz?"

"I'm in advertising."

"That sounds fun."

"Not really," Michael said.

"No?" Klinger asked, feigning interest. "Well, I guess there's good and bad days everywhere. What's it like?"

"Everyone wants to make the movie," Michael said, smiling. "That's the bottom line."

"Yeah? You get to do that?"

"Once in a while." Michael sat and looked questioningly across the table. One of the seats opposite was stacked with brown accordion files stuffed with manila file folders and loose sheets. Michael glanced at his watch. "You said on the phone you'd explain what this is about," he said.

"Yeah," Klinger answered, nodding as he sat and adjusted his pants and jacket around his girth. He rubbed his hands together. "Like I said, we're involved in a large investigation. I won't get into the details, but it centers on Dominick Calabria. I don't suppose that surprises you."

Michael said nothing.

"You do know him?"

"Yes."

"His son John as well?"

Michael nodded.

Klinger waited for a few beats. He leaned back in his seat with his hands behind his head, then went on. "In the course of the investigation, your name came up."

"How?"

"That's another long story." Klinger leaned forward again and smiled. "Don't worry about it. I'm just tryin' to clear some things up, get some background. To be frank, I was surprised by the connection, you follow me? You aren't involved in any of the Calabrias' operations, are you?"

"If you mean their businesses," Michael said, staring across the table, his face a perplexed mask, "no."

"Well, if you don't mind, I'd like to ask you a few questions. Bear with me. Some may seem kind of dumb, but I'm working in the dark here. Okay?"

"Go ahead," Michael said without betraying the nervousness he was feeling.

"None a this is actually on the record, so to speak," Klinger said reassuringly. "But I may take some notes, okay?"

Michael said nothing but nodded calmly. He crossed his legs. Klinger stretched and smiled, then leaned to the side to lift a yellow legal pad from the floor. He fished a ballpoint pen out of the inside pocket of his jacket and clicked it a couple of times. "First," he said, "let me make sure I got your name spelled right." He printed it on the legal pad and showed it to Michael. This was pure theater.

"That's correct," Michael said.

"Would you mind jotting down your addresses and phone numbers?" Klinger asked, proffering the pen. Michael complied.

"Great!" Klinger exclaimed heartily. "Thanks." He adjusted himself in his seat again and leaned on the table. "Ready?"

"Sure," Michael said, again glancing at his watch. They had

already killed a good slice of time without even approaching a point, as far as he could tell.

"Tell me, how do you know the Calabrias?"

"John and I are friends from early grade school," Michael answered.

"How did you meet?"

"We were in class together."

"Do you know him well?"

"He's my oldest friend."

"Were you neighbors?"

"No. Classmates."

"What, all through school?"

"We weren't always in the same classes, but we went to the same schools."

"So you're close?"

"I guess."

"Did you spend time at the Calabrias' home?"

"Sure," Michael answered, raising his eyebrows quizzically.

"Were you there often?"

"Often enough. I slept over from time to time."

"So you know Dominick Calabria fairly well."

"I like the man."

"He's a criminal," Klinger declared flatly, as if this fact could not mesh with a child's friendship.

"I don't know anything about his business," Michael replied.

"How about Salvatore Bruno? Or Angelo DeMicco? Do you know them?"

"Sure. They work for Dominick Calabria."

"They're crew bosses. And they're button men," Klinger snorted.

"I don't know what you mean by that."

"They're killers. Enforcers."

"I don't know anything about that. As far as I'm concerned, Sal and Angie are simply business associates of Dominick Calabria."

Klinger stared for a few beats, his nostrils dilated with impatience. He finally exhaled loudly and shrugged. "You know, Mr. Pollitz, this would take a lot less time if you gave me, how should I put it? Somewhat more complete answers? You keep playing it cool, we could be here for hours, you follow me?" He drummed his fingers softly on the table. "For the sake of argument, let's assume you know the nature of Dom Calabria's sources of income, okay? Let's not worry about that now. I'm just trying to get a little insight into your relationship with the Calabria family, okay? This ain't testimony, you ain't under oath, but you are sitting in a police station, and I can't imagine you want to be here all night, am I right? So gimme a little help here, okay?" He stared, waiting for Michael to nod. "Let me start over. John Calabria is Dom's youngest son. You and John were friends. Am I correct so far?"

"Yes," Michael answered, smiling slightly.

"Would you tell me something about that?"

"Why do you want to know?"

"Aw, for Christ's sake!" Klinger squawked, but a small amusement wrinkled the skin around his eyes. "Gimme a break, will you? I'm a cop. Why do you suppose I'm interested in Dominick Calabria? I'm just tryin' to get some background here, okay?" Klinger lifted one of the fat accordion files from the chair beside him. "As far as I know, just about everyone associated with Dominick Calabria is in one of these jackets. But not you," he lied smoothly. "Don't make it so tough, will you? I don't care if I waste your time, but I hate to waste mine. Between you and me, you're breaking my heart, Mr. Pollitz. Maybe three times a year I get to interview someone like you, who can actually form a sentence when he talks, you follow me? Don't ruin it for me." He suppressed a smile when Michael chuckled.

"Okay," Michael said. "John and I were in the same fourth-grade class. We kind of found each other, because neither of us really fit in."

"Why's that?"

"We grew up in Barrington. Our classmates were pretty well-heeled. But my dad was a Polack plumber, and John's dad was a disreputable guinea. So we became friends, since no one else seemed to like us." Michael shrugged. "I'm not trying to dramatize it, just telling you how we imagined things, you know what I mean? It's not like we were pariahs or anything like that. But that's how we became friends. Better?"

"Yeah," Klinger smiled. "So you remained friends throughout school?"

"We're still friends. We stood up in each other's weddings." Michael smiled wryly. "John's marriage proved a little more durable than mine."

"Well, I know about that," Klinger groaned, shaking his head sadly. "Your ex-wife, is she still in this area?"

"Yes."

"What kind of work does she do?"

"Marketing. What difference does that make?"

Klinger rubbed his thick cheeks in his palms. "None," he said, smiling with a slight shrug. "I was just curious. My ex, she works in retail sales. We're pleasant enough to each other. You have kids?"

"No."

"Me, neither," Klinger said with a sigh. He looked away for a moment, then glanced down at the legal pad. "How often do you see John Calabria?"

Michael waited a moment, trying to sort out what Klinger was after. There was something disconsonant about the digression. "A couple of times a month, I guess, at most. As I'm sure you know, he runs one of the restaurants the family owns. I eat there sometimes. I like his kids."

"Do you know his older brothers?"

Michael shook his head. "Not really. They're several years older. I mean, we're cordial when we see one another, but I rarely see them. In fact, I don't think I've seen either of them more than twice in the last ten years."

"They live out of town, don't they?"

"I guess, but I don't really know. I mean, I don't know where." Michael shrugged. "I hardly know his brothers."

Klinger stared appraisingly, wondering how tuned in Michael might be. Did he know Dom Calabria's older sons were among the Outfit representatives in Las Vegas and Kansas City? Klinger decided to skip it. After a few seconds, he asked, "Is John as hotheaded as everyone says?"

"Who's everyone?"

Klinger shrugged. "Forget it. Do you know the rest of the family?"

"You mean John's sisters and mother? Sure. I don't know Nina or Mary very well, his sisters. Same reason as his brothers. They're a little older. They're good-looking, Nina in particular. But John's the baby of the family, you know? They're all older. John was a 'caboose,' as the saying goes. I think Mary's six years older than John, and she's the next youngest. I'm fond of his mother."

Klinger wondered briefly if Pollitz was lying about Mary's age—she was only four years older. Maybe he simply had it wrong. "How about Dominick? Do you still see him?"

"Occasionally, like at holidays. Some other times. I send them a Christmas card. I send his wife a birthday card."

"So you'd say you're close with them?"

"Close enough. Sure. They're childhood friends." Michael looked up with a trace of impatience at the repetition of questions. "Why are you asking me about the Calabrias? I really don't know anything about their business."

"Please, Mr. Pollitz. I thought we agreed you'd stop playing dumb."

"I'm not playing dumb. I'm serious. Even if I was willing to incriminate people I like, my oldest friends, I couldn't help you.

I don't know anything that would make any difference. I mean, if you're looking for criminal evidence, I don't have any. Offhand I couldn't even tell you how many cars they own."

Klinger gazed across the table for a moment, his face blank. Michael never averted his eyes. Finally, Klinger shook his head. "I can see you're going to be a puzzler," he grunted. He leaned back and rubbed his eyes, yawning broadly at the ceiling. His paunch trembled over his belt. "Tell me, Mr. Pollitz, are you as cool as you seem or just extraordinarily inattentive?"

"I'm neither," Michael laughed. "What? You think Dom and Sal talked about business with John and me? We were kids. I was more interested in the horses and whatever we could catch at the pond."

"Horses?"

Michael paused and stared with his eyebrows raised. "Who's playing dumb now, Detective Klinger?" He pointed at the stack of accordion files. "You going to pretend you don't know the Calabrias raise horses out in Barrington Hills?"

Klinger smiled and shook his head. He fished in the pocket of his coat for a moment and produced a pack of gum. "Care for a piece?"

"Sure."

Klinger chomped noisily for a few seconds. "Forgive me, Mr. Pollitz. I'm not trying to be cute. I guess that was a shorthand way of saying I want to get a picture from your point of view, you follow me? But just between you and me, these files," he tapped the pile on the chair beside him, "contain less personal information than you might think." When Michael's lips puckered skeptically, he added, "Of course I know Dom has horses. Arabians, if I remember correctly. That ain't the point."

"What is the point?"

"Like I say, I'm just tryin' to get a little background here. I wish to hell you'd stop making it so difficult." He pinched his thick lower lip thoughtfully. "Here's the point," he said at length, pulling a folder from the top accordion file. He opened it, removed three photocopies of the old mug shots and slid them across the table. "You recognize these guys?" he asked casually, masking a small thrill when he saw the skin tighten on Michael's face—very briefly and quickly resolved into a frown, but there, definitely there. The unmistakable rush of adrenaline.

"Why do you ask?" Michael looked at each photograph without touching the table. His stomach was boiling.

"They were in Astoria in 1972." Klinger was interested to note genuine anger rising into Michael's eyes.

"I was told those records would be expunged when my probation period ended," Michael said abruptly.

Klinger was caught off guard. He wasn't sure whether Michael was betraying a certain naïveté or buying time. He shrugged, trying to decide how far to push it. "They aren't part of the public record, if that's what you mean."

"What I mean is, some prick in the state's attorney's office told me those records wouldn't prevent me from running for public office."

Naïve, Klinger concluded. "Why? You planning to run for alderman?"

"What the hell does that have to do with it?" Michael snapped, using anger as camouflage. "It pisses me off that records I was told were deleted obviously weren't."

"Hey, don't get worked up, okay? The fact that I could dig up those records doesn't mean they're actually near the surface, you follow?"

"What difference does that make?" Michael fumed. He looked away to be sure of his composure. "I thought that crap was long over with," he said with a touch of sorrow, almost to himself. When Klinger said nothing, he added, "So, you know I did a short sentence in Astoria twenty-two years ago. So what?"

"Why were you there?"

"Isn't it in the record?"

"I meant in your view."

"I showed a couple of IBI agents to a room. Where they bought some drugs. I had a shit lawyer, got stuck with a felony and got sentenced to a couple of months." He shrugged, his anger dissipating in the drab room as he turned his thoughts away from the people in the mug shots.

"You don't feel it was justified?"

"Please," Michael snorted. "Nowadays I might not even be picked up for questioning. Ogilvie was running for re-election, and one of his promises the first time around was to 'clean up' the campuses. I was one of his major victories. On April Fool's Day in 1972, coincidentally Good Friday, all kinds of easy arrests took place on college campuses. Here's the laugh, though. I thought it was political, like using drugs and protesting the war were the same thing. So at the time, I figured that was why I was getting busted. How's that for clueless? Let me ask you, since you've read the case file, do you think I'd be anything more than a witness today?"

Klinger met his stare and decided to come clean. "Actually, I haven't read any 'case file,' as you put it. There is no record of your conviction that I know of. I got your name from Astoria's morgue files, and all I knew until now was that you'd been there in 1972." He glanced down at the folder. "And that you spent most of your time in the prison's infirmary," he opened the folder and consulted a sheet inside, "recovering from a broken jaw and assorted other injuries." He snapped the folder shut and looked across the table. "From an altercation with these three men," he added, nodding down at the photocopies.

"Is that what your file shows?" Michael asked mildly. Klinger said nothing. "I never identified those guys," Michael said.

"So you don't recognize them?"

"I didn't say that." Michael slowly released his breath. "Sure, I recognize those assholes. They raped me. In the process, they beat the hell out of me." He traced a finger across the scar in his left eyebrow. "They left this little reminder. This, too," he said, holding up his right hand to show the small crimp in the ring finger.

"Fought the good fight, huh?" said Klinger, somewhat taken aback by Michael's candor. Later, he would remark to Whittaker, "This guy intrigues me. I looked over my notes, and the fact is, he gave me nothing at all, but he did it without even once telling me anything but the truth, as far as I can tell."

"Not really," Michael answered. "It was all part of the same thing."

"I don't follow you."

"The rape, the beating. It was all of a piece."

"Must have been terrible," Klinger said with a tone of regret. Michael couldn't tell if it was real or fake.

"I wasn't aware of all that much, to tell you the truth."

"I'm sorry I brought it up."

"Spare me," Michael said caustically. "You've got me here specifically *to* bring it up. I just don't understand why. This is ancient history."

"What?" Klinger began, but Michael cut him off with an angry wave.

"Just get to the point, will you? Why are you interested in my puny little prison record from over twenty years ago?"

Klinger chewed his gum thoughtfully. The interview had turned in an unexpected direction. He tapped the copy of Bobby Andrews' old mug shot. "We recently arrested this one. The other two were murdered in 1972 and early 1973."

"Glad to hear it," Michael said. When Klinger raised his eyebrows, Michael asked, "You expect me to be sorry?"

"You aren't surprised?"

"It's news to me. I wish I'd known it years ago. But surprised?" He laughed harshly. "Hell, no. Those guys were born to be murdered."

Klinger stood and stepped to the trash can. He spit out his

gum, then returned to the table and picked up Andrews' photo. He looked down at Michael. He seemed to hesitate, but then he said, "This one says you know something about the murders."

"He's wrong," Michael snapped. "So that's why I'm here? You're investigating me for murder?" He shook his head. "We're done talking without my attorney in the room."

"Did you kill them?"

"No. But we're done talking."

"Did Calabria kill them?"

Michael smiled slowly. "I want to leave or call my attorney now."

18

Michael left the station and crossed the street to a pay phone mounted on the wall outside a convenience store. *Shit!* he thought. He had to control his hands to insert the coins.

"So, how'd it go?" John asked without preamble.

"Why don't I drive out to the restaurant tonight?" Michael answered.

"Good idea, Mikey!" John shouted. "The asshole say what he wants?"

"I guess he's a homicide detective," Michael replied slowly. "He was asking me about those three guys who fucked me up back in Astoria. Says one of them says I killed the other two." *Shit!* he thought again. *What could they know after all these years?*

"Jesus, that's a long time ago. What the fuck?" John exhaled loudly into the receiver. "But this guy, Klinger, he ain't no homicide detective. My dad knows who he is. He useta be in homicide, but now he's in organized crime or whatever the fuck they call the division." Another noisy pause, pregnant with expectation. "My dad says he wantsta talk to you."

"Can he meet me at your restaurant?"

"Sure thing. Why don't you get here around nine-thirty or ten? Hell, you can stay over."

Michael walked the short distance to his apartment, then climbed the stairs to the second floor of the graystone building, his keys rattling nervously in his hand. He removed his tie and took a beer from the refrigerator. He stared into the appliance, feeling weary. The apartment felt as desolate and sparse as the refrigerator. He picked up a container of yogurt and checked its expiration date. He returned it to the wire shelf.

On his answering machine was a pair of messages from the morning, one from Larry Klinger, asking him to call unless they'd already spoken, and a second message from his mother explaining that she'd given his work number to "a Detective Flint." "You'd think she'd get a detective's name right," he muttered, then chuckled to realize he was thinking aloud in an empty room. He looked at his watch and decided to eat dinner in Palatine.

It could be an expensive irritant, he had often said, to keep a car where he lived in the city, but it was a greater inconveniece to use the trains to visit his family or John's family out in Barrington. He rented a garage just up the alley and across the street from his apartment, and his reasonably new Toyota was always available, except when the alley was blocked with snow. On reflection, getting to his car wasn't much different from when he lived in the suburbs. "It's a pain in the ass, no matter how you look at it," he had told John. He walked to the garage to retrieve his car to drive out of the city. He sighed with regret as he got into the car, because even on the best days, it still consumed more than an hour to drive the forty miles to Barrington.

John had been managing the same restaurant for more than

twenty years, a big supper club with extensive grounds on Rand Road in a location that had become steadily less remote with each passing year, as subdivisions moved inexorably toward it across the farmlands and wooded tracts that had been open land when John and Michael were children. The restaurant was situated on a slight glacial rise and approached by a long circle drive from the divided highway at the base of the hill. It had a huge concrete bear ravening inside the circle drive, but the statue was too far back from the highway to be a useful landmark. To hear John tell it, he had no concerns with the restaurant beyond avoiding income and property taxes. "Here's the kicker, Mikey," he had bragged. "The place makes a profit! Nowhere near what we report, but it could stand on its own. Weddings make a ton." His pride wasn't consistent with his claimed indifference to actually running the place.

Despite the real estate developments that were approaching from every direction, the restaurant's immediate environs still had an open, unincorporated feel. But the area around it was clearly becoming residential. Michael didn't know if this was a good or bad thing for the Calabria family. He finally arrived at the restaurant and left the car running for the valet. As he walked inside, the *maitre d'* deferred to a busty, attractive young woman who, once he had identified himself, immediately led him across a large dining area toward a back room. The main room was busy, with perhaps sixty patrons at the tables and red leather banquettes. The décor was garish, but not tastelessly so, a type of overdone-restaurant styling that verged on being fashionable.

John jumped out of a chair, grinning and expansive, the glowingly confident owner of a successful restaurant. "Mikey!" He reached to hug his old friend. "Come in, man! Come in. Siddown. You gotta try the veal parmesan!" He led the way back to the table and poured a glass of red wine. He glanced across the room and gestured to a waiter. "Try it! The gravy's outta this world. Best you ever tasted." He ordered several courses. Years before, Michael had asked why all the Calabrias called pasta sauce 'gravy.' John had stared blankly. "That's what it's called, man," was all he could think of in reply.

Still standing, they toasted one another. Michael nodded at John's gut. "Man, I think you put on five pounds since last month. You're moving into Sal's territory, John." He smiled.

John slapped his stomach and laughed. "Got a ways to go, Mikey." He jiggled. "Still, you got a point. I gotta lose a few." He glanced around again, beaming. The room was small compared with the main dining area, but still it could easily have held forty people. Gilt mirrors were on the walls. "Siddown, man," John repeated. "Pop ain't here yet, but he ought to be in any time. Let's have some wine."

"Do you guys still own that 'gentleman's club' back down Rand Road?"

"You mean the strip joint at Lake-Cook? You passed it on the way here, right? Sure, that's one of ours."

"I'd think you'd be managing that place. Seems more your style." Michael grinned across his wine glass.

John's laugh boomed into the room. "Hey! I like it here. Keeps me outta trouble."

"How about that strip place up in Half Day? The Lioness. That yours too?"

"What, you know every titty bar around here? You're makin' me wonder about you, Mikey. You need to get plugged, man, say the word. We'll take a drive later on. Go back down to Lake-Cook." His laugh exploded again. He cuffed at Michael's head, bouncing a meaty hand off his shoulder. He gulped some more wine. "Yeah, we got a piece of that joint. Marbles runs it. Mostly his place. Angie's. You know."

Michael briefly considered Marbles, thinking, *the less I see of that goon, the better.* He changed the subject, asking about John's wife and children, then about his brothers and sisters. He couldn't keep up with John's litany of nieces and nephews, the relationships of all the cousins to one another. He was relieved when Dom and Salvatore Bruno appeared in the room's doorway.

Michael stood with a smile opening his face. It surprised him sometimes, how glad he was to see Dominick Calabria, as if his favorite uncle had suddenly walked into the room. They embraced, and it seemed to Michael that Dom held him for an atypically long time. He kissed the elderly man's cheek and moved away. Dom held his arms, gripping lightly as he stared into Michael's face.

"You look good," Dom said. "When I told Toni I would be seeing you, she asked to be remembered to you."

"That's nice of her. Give her my love." Michael pictured John's mother, a little heavy and physically generous, but not a thick-ribbed potato like Sal Bruno's wife. There was an air of glamor about Antonia—Toni—Calabria, even in her seventies, that was echoed strongly in her female children. Echoed strongly in the sense that they were very sexy. As a teenager, Michael had often wished he were years older so he could make a play for Nina. He loved her sharp face—her father's face—with her narrow cheekbones and glittering eyes. Her mother had the same beauty, but her face lacked the hard edge. Toni's aura of sophistication was out of sync with her behavior, which was solidly Franklin Park Italian Mama motherly. "Please, greet her for me," Michael repeated. "I'll come by and see her soon." He meant it.

"Good," Dom nodded. "That would make her happy." He finally released Michael's arms and moved to a seat at the table. He smiled and lit a cigarette.

Michael turned with an apprehensive smile toward Sal. Even past seventy, Sal was physically imposing, as if brute force incarnate simply did not age. The massive thug grabbed Michael's shoulders and wrapped his thick arms around his torso, squeezing with a power that Michael was oddly glad to feel, as though time was not diminishing these men as much as he feared. Sal rubbed a thick hand over Michael's head, smiling, but he said nothing.

Michael sat next to Dom. John filled their glasses and sat across the table.

"Where's Angie?" Michael asked.

"He had to stay home tonight. Got an ache, he says." Dom smiled again. Michael assumed this meant DeMicco was with a girlfriend.

"So let's hear it. What does this Klinger want?" Dom set his cigarette on the edge of the ashtray and lifted his glass of wine.

"You remember the three guys who worked me over back in 1972? In Astoria?"

Dom nodded. He set down the wine and retrieved his cigarette.

"Motherfuckers," Sal spat out.

"I gather that one of them was arrested not too long ago. This Klinger said the guy claims I killed the other two. It's now being investigated."

"Did he specifically accuse you of it?" Smoke trailed away from Dom's face.

"Not directly. It's what he seemed to be getting at, though." Michael shrugged. "What do you know about the cop?"

Dom thought for a second or two. "He's been on the force a long time. Worked homicide until a few years ago. He's now in the organized crime division, which makes me interested in what he might have asked about us." Dom moved one hand slightly, as if to incorporate everyone at the table, in the room, throughout his organization.

Michael nodded in turn. "He asked about it, about you or John and the dead guys."

"Give me the details." Dom's face was casual, but he was intent.

Michael recounted the entire interview, from beginning to end.

"Cocksucker's fishing," John muttered.

"Yeah, but for us," Bruno echoed.

"Who the fuck else?" Dom snapped. "You think this guy's gonna waste time on this shit so he can nail Mike?" His lips pursed with annoyance. "The question is, what's he got beyond some history?"

"The guy's name is Andrews," Michael said. "Robert Andrews."

"Where the fuck is this pile of dog shit?" Sal asked.

"In custody, I think," Michael answered. "All the detective said was 'recently arrested.' I don't remember anything else."

"That prolly means County," Bruno speculated.

"Most likely," Dom agreed. He thought for a moment, leaning back in his chair with his elbows propped on its arms. He sat with one hand beneath his narrow chin, smoke drifting slowly from the cigarette between his fingers. "He asked if I killed those assholes," he said at last.

"That was his last question," Michael answered.

"What'd you say then?" Sal was grinning.

"I said we were done talking without my lawyer." Bruno and John glanced at one another and started laughing. "What?" Michael was confused.

"Angie always said you was a smart kid, Mikey," Bruno chuckled. "We's done without my lawyer," he echoed. *Widdout.*

Michael laughed softly, infected by their amusement. "You think he had any idea I don't even have one?" Renewed laughter from Sal and John.

"I'll give you the same guy I woulda given you twenty-two years ago," Dom said. "Jim Allegretti." He glanced at John, who left the table.

"If you'd used him then, you wouldn't be calling him now," Sal inserted with a small flash of peevishness. Michael said nothing. John returned and handed a pen and order pad to his father.

"Ancient history," Dom said, glancing at Bruno. He wrote the number on the pad. "Allegretti's the best," Dom concluded, coughing softly as he tore the sheet free and handed it to Michael.

"Thanks," Michael said. "I really appreciate this."

"Forget it," Dom replied. "I'll give Jim a call to let him know."

"Otherwise, forget about reaching him," Sal laughed. "If he don't already know you, he'd don't wanna know you."

19

Klinger strolled into Whittaker's office at the Criminal Courts building and passed the time examining the prosecutor's artworks and a few photographs with dignitaries of one sort or another. Dan had risen high enough in the division's hierarchy to rate a fairly plush office with a secretary nearby. Klinger thought he was talented enough to weather even a change in administration, his rank notwithstanding. A couple of years earlier, when a small reverse-discrimination flap erupted about allegedly race-motivated promotions in the Chicago Fire Department, a *Chicago Tribune* reporter who worked the police beat had asked Klinger about racial hiring, and Dan Whittaker had come immediately to mind. When the reporter asked if African-Americans and Hispanics were given preferential treatment in hiring decisions, Klinger had replied, "People talk about that, but I've never noticed it." He didn't add that in his opinion, the opposite was still more often the case. The reporter had asked if minorities received special preferences for promotions within the department, and Klinger had answered, "I think they ought to do more of it," thinking again of Dan Whittaker. He hadn't been quoted in the story.

After fifteen minutes, Whittaker loped in, lugging a stuffed briefcase and an armload of case files. He glanced at Klinger as he dumped the pile onto his desk. The detective had placed a fat law book on the floor and was standing on it to look through the window. "Make yourself at home, Larry," Whittaker said. He removed his suit jacket and arranged it on a hanger in his small closet.

"You know, this is a nice office," Klinger announced. "But the view stinks." He stepped off of the book and stooped with a grunt to put it back on the shelf. Whittaker walked to the window and glanced outside, rolling his sleeves. Klinger adjusted his coat more comfortably on his thick torso and smiled jovially. "You look tired," he said.

"You don't know the half of it," Whittaker groaned and dropped heavily into his chair. He watched Klinger wandering around the office with a file and a legal pad clasped in both hands behind his back.

"I'll tell you, Dan, a guy with your brains could make a helluva lotta money on the other side of the courtroom."

"I like what I do," Whittaker answered with a slow grin. This was a common refrain from Klinger; it came up almost every time he was in Whittaker's office. "What's on your chin?"

Klinger ran his fingers self-consciously beneath his lip. "Cut myself shaving," he replied. To Whittaker it looked more like a bite.

"Oh," the attorney said innocently. "I thought maybe this morning's unusually buoyant mood might be related to something else."

"Let's leave Dora outta the conversation," Klinger replied.

Whittaker bit down on his tongue to keep from laughing. Klinger's girlfriend was built very similarly to Klinger, and the notion of their overweight couplings was an amusing image. "So," he said at last, "what was Pollitz like?"

Klinger sat in front of the desk and flipped pages on the legal pad. "He's smart," the detective said, "and he's cool. Like I said on the phone, he didn't try to bullshit me, but he was pretty cagey." Klinger rubbed his chin thoughtfully. "I can't really put my finger on it."

"What do you mean?"

"Well, think about it. The guy's an ad exec, right? Mosta the time, a guy like that, you haul him in a police station and start asking questions, he gets real nervous. A lotta times, you can't get a guy like that to shut up."

"You think he was too composed?"

"I can't say," Klinger answered. "Hell, who knows? Maybe he's like that all the time. Maybe that's his personality."

"Well, something about him's bothering you."

"I don't know if I'm bothered or just intrigued." Klinger paused, lost in thought.

"This is new," Whittaker said with surprise.

"Yeah," Klinger agreed. "It is."

"How did he react when you showed him the mug shots?"

"He got pissed off."

"Did he deny recognizing them?"

"No. He was a little hesitant, but like I say, he was pissed. Fact, he confirmed Bobby's basic story about what happened in Astoria. Like, immediately."

Whittaker raised his eyebrows.

"Yeah," Klinger nodded. "Hardly missed a beat."

"How was he hesitant?"

"I couldn't tell if he was thinking about denying it or if it was just a bad memory. I mean, according to two of the guards, he had a pretty rough go."

"Is that what he was mad about?"

"No. He was pissed because," Klinger consulted his notes, "he was told the record of his time was expunged. Here's the thing. The records *were* expunged. Even with his name I can't produce an arrest or conviction record anywhere, not with the state, the county or the town."

Whittaker shrugged. It wasn't all that unusual. "Nothing else anywhere?"

“He had one traffic ticket three years ago. Otherwise, he squeaks.”

“If he was direct about what happened to him, how was he cagey?”

“It’s hard to say. You’ll see what I mean if you talk to him. Like, he got pretty quiet about the Calabrias, but he did it without lying about anything. At least, not obviously. I shifted him around some, tried a few different angles, but except for getting pissed about Astoria, he stayed cool the whole time.” Klinger shook his head. “The guy’s a puzzler.” He scanned his notes again.

“Did you tell him what this is about?”

“Eventually.”

“How did he react?”

“He cut off the interview. Said it was time to call his lawyer.”

“Was he upset?”

“Nope. Not rattled at all.” Klinger shook his head. “Then he goes straight across the street to a pay phone.”

“Really?” Whittaker was mildly startled. “It’s like he knows the drill.”

“Yeah,” Klinger agreed. “Isn’t that odd? That’s what I mean about how cool he is. Anyone else, is this how they’ll be? Professional guy, no record anywhere? It’s as if I’m dealing with Dom Calabria himself. And I’ll give odds that’s who he called, ’less he knows his lawyer’s number off the top of his head.”

“How much of Andrews’ version did he confirm?

“I didn’t get into everything. Fact, I didn’t actually *ask* about any of it. He volunteered that he was raped and beaten.”

“What’s his connection to Dom Calabria?”

“It’s social, if you can believe that. He’s a childhood friend of John Calabria’s.” He glanced again at his notes. “They’re still pretty close. I mean, that one photo of him is from standing up in John Calabria’s wedding. As far as his time in Astoria goes, we already know John was his first visitor after the incident with

McVee, Jackson and Andrews. And we know Calabria picked him up. I didn't ask him about either of those things, by the way, but I'll bet a week's pay he wouldn't even consider denying it."

Whittaker leaned forward with his arms on his desk. He propped his chin in one hand and idly scraped his teeth with a fingernail, staring into space. "I can't stop thinking these murders have Dom Calabria's signature on them," he said at last.

"Seems that way to me," Klinger replied. "And I'd say what happened to Pollitz gives us a motive."

"But nothing to take to a grand jury," Whittaker said. He returned his gaze to Klinger. "How do we know it was Dom? How do we know it wasn't John Calabria or this Pollitz himself?" he asked rhetorically. "Did he seem like he could have been responsible?"

"You mean, physically? I don't know. He's built solid enough, I guess, but I just can't see one guy committing the murders, you follow? Plus, how would he have found McVee and Jackson?" Klinger shook his head. "Like you say, these things have a signature."

"I meant in terms of his psychology. If he's a lifetime friend of the Calabrias, he may have had his own access to men who could have done it." When Klinger frowned, Whittaker added, "It's a theoretical possibility."

"Yeah," Klinger finally agreed. "I guess so. I couldn't say. I don't have a read on Pollitz yet. Maybe you should get him under oath."

"You mean issue a subpoena? That's problematic. This isn't even a formal investigation yet." Whittaker chewed his lip. "But it's not a bad idea. Maybe he'll agree to a voluntary deposition. It's worth a try, anyway."

20

Michael asked the pleasant female voice to put Jim Allegretti on the line. She asked him to repeat his name, and then said she'd see if Mr. Allegretti was available. Michael tapped a pen on the side of his shoe, feeling envious. He wished he too had a secretary who could function as a guard dog.

"Michael Pollitz?" Allegretti said into the phone, his well-modulated voice warmly cordial. "Dominick Calabria mentioned that you would be calling."

"Did he?" Michael said pleasantly. "That was nice of him." Michael smiled, thinking how nice it can be to be wired once in a while. "He recommends you highly."

"He's too kind," Allegretti answered.

"Did Dom describe my situation?"

"Only in very brief terms."

"Well, I seem to be the focus of a murder investigation. I'd like you to represent me."

"We should talk, then. Let me put my secretary on to schedule an appointment."

"I hope we can do it soon," Michael interrupted. "I just got a call from a state's attorney asking me to appear for a deposition next week."

"A call? Were you served a subpoena?"

"No. He described it as a 'voluntary deposition,' whatever that means."

"It means he wants to depose you without having to take it before a judge," Allegretti chuckled. Michael could hear the attorney clicking his tongue in thought. Finally, Allegretti asked, "Who was the state's attorney?"

"His name's Dan Whittaker."

After a brief pause, Allegretti said, "Okay. I can clear my schedule. Why don't you come down to the office? I'm in the Dirksen Building."

"You mean, right now?" The haste made Michael instantly nervous.

"Sure," Allegretti answered. "If Whittaker wants to see you next week, then we should meet. How soon can you get down here?"

"I can be there in about twenty minutes, I guess."

"Good. In the meantime, I'll call Mr. Whittaker to inform him that I am representing you and that all future contact should come through me."

Michael told the company receptionist that he was leaving for the day, forgetting a scheduled meeting with two Sears representatives. He left the building and walked through a light rain to the subway for the short ride south to the Loop.

21

Michael had never been deposed, and he had no idea what to expect. Allegretti had advised him not to worry about it, to answer all questions as directly and briefly as he could, ideally with a simple 'Yes' or 'No' if at all possible. Allegretti's suggestion was to treat it as a conversation with someone he didn't know, but who was predisposed to dislike him. In other words, keep it cool, and expect revolving questions that kept returning to the same themes, but from different directions.

What Michael had not expected was the instant adversarial tone, and the immediate move into meaty subjects. After simple procedural preambles, establishing the correct spelling of his name, his address, and so on, plus his voluntary involvement with the proceedings, the state's attorney jumped straight to the heart of things.

Whittaker removed the three photocopies of the old mug

shots from a folder and placed them face up on the table. "Can you identify these men?" he asked.

"Sure," Michael answered without rancor. "Those are the guys who beat the shit out of me and raped me in Astoria prison back in 1972."

"All three?"

"No. All three beat on me, but just the black guy and the blond raped me."

Whittaker lifted the shots of McVee and Jackson and said, "You have identified Darryl Jackson and John McVee, correct?"

"Yes."

"The third man, Robert Andrews, did not participate in the rape?"

"I think he just kicked me a few times," Michael answered, "but I'm not sure."

"Can you describe the event?" Whittaker asked.

"I'd rather not. It's not a pleasant memory."

"How is this germane?" Allegretti asked abruptly, imperiously angry. If he also was surprised by Whittaker's direct approach, it didn't show.

Whittaker stared at Allegretti for a few moments but said nothing. He shifted sheets in the folder and studied his notes. Finally, he changed direction, asking, "Did John Calabria visit you in the Astoria infirmary?"

"Yes."

"Did you discuss the assault?"

"Of course. That's why I was there."

"He visited you even before your family did." Whittaker's remark was a statement, not a question.

Michael wondered what difference timing made. "That's true. John was my closest childhood friend. I appreciated his visiting me. He was concerned about me."

"His speedy arrival isn't odd, in your view?"

"Not at all. I would have done the same."

"He visited you the day after you were attacked?"

"Yes."

"How did he know so quickly? Your parents came the next day."

"I assumed my parents or my brother told him, but I really don't know." Michael had never thought about the timing before and had no idea that Dom Calabria knew about the assault, through Sal, even before his lip had been stitched. It had always seemed natural that John arrived first.

"You don't find it unusual that John Calabria came to the prison before your family did?"

"As I said, I appreciated it," Michael replied. "My parents are not wealthy, Mr. Whittaker. My father was a plumber. He couldn't just drop everything and drive down. John was able to come immediately."

"Did you tell him you wanted him to kill your assailants?"

Before Allegretti could erupt, Michael answered, "No." Michael blandly met Whittaker's gaze. "I'm sure I said angry things, but I was pretty beat up, and I was on painkillers."

"Did John Calabria offer to take revenge on your assailants?"

"No."

"Was he aware that you were sexually assaulted?"

"Yes."

"And he took this news calmly, without any vengeful desires," Whittaker said sarcastically.

"Keep it questions," Allegretti said softly, as if he was instructing a student.

Whittaker laughed harshly. "Fine," he said. "How did John Calabria react when he learned of your sexual assault?"

"He was upset about it," Michael answered, smiling slightly. "So was I."

"Did John Calabria kill your assailants?"

"What kind of question is that?" Allegretti barked.

Before Whittaker could react, Michael interrupted. "To my

knowledge, John Calabria has never had anything to do with the death of anyone." Klinger thought about it. Pollitz's statement was undoubtedly true. There hadn't been an Outfit killing in Chicago in years.

Another long pause as Whittaker flipped sheets in the file folder. Michael leaned back in his chair and crossed his legs, his face blank. Whitttaker again changed tack. "How did you get home from the prison?"

"John and his father gave me a ride."

"Just the two of them?"

"No. Salvatore Bruno drove."

"Why did they pick you up instead of your parents?"

"I asked them to," Michael answered, his face wrinkled in a confused smile.

Klinger hid a grin behind a cough. He was beginning to admire Michael's composure. Later, he said to Whittaker, "See? Like I told you before, he gave us *nada* without lying, as far as I can see." Whittaker didn't find it entertaining.

Whittaker leaned forward with his arms on the table. "Did you discuss the assault with them?"

"They asked how I was feeling, if I was okay."

"That's all?"

"Basically, yeah," Michael said with a shrug. "I was pretty shaken, to tell you the truth. I didn't think I should have been in prison in the first place." He shook his head. "It was a lousy experience."

"I'm sure," Whittaker said indifferently. He stared intently across the table. "Did you ask Dominick Calabria to kill your assailants?"

"No. I didn't even know their names."

"Did Dominick Calabria have anything to say about the assault?"

"He didn't mention it. But I can remember exactly what he said after we got home, before John dropped me off at my house.

He said, 'Go home and forget about the last five weeks. Think about school instead. Then finish your probation and put this shit behind you forever.' Until a few of weeks ago, I thought I had," he added with a trace of anger.

"Can you recall where you were on November 5, 1972?"

"You mean specifically, on that date? No. But I couldn't have been anywhere but at school. Under the terms of my sentence, I wasn't allowed to leave the county."

"What do you mean, 'under the terms of your sentence'?" Whittaker adjusted his glasses and studied Michael's face.

"After I was released, I was given probation for the remainder of two years. In this case, it meant about twenty or twenty-two months, but I was actually released from the probation when I graduated from school. During that time, I was still technically a felon and required to stay in the county and report to a probation officer once a month. I had to request permission to leave the county. At the end of the probation, my arrest record and sentence were supposedly going to be expunged." He drew a long breath, and, when Whittaker said nothing, he added, "Obviously, that wasn't true."

Whittaker shifted sheets in the folder, hiding a small sense of amusement. Finally, he asked, "How about January 14, 1973?"

"Same place," Michael said. "I had to get permission to go home for Christmas, and I had to report back to the probation officer when I got back to school."

"Can anyone verify your presence on those two dates?" Whittaker was indifferent to the answer. He was a good interrogator and only wanted to get Michael on the defensive, if he could. He was becoming frustrated with his inability to do so.

Michael snorted derisively. "How should I know? I'm sure there's plenty of people who can establish I was in school on those dates, but offhand, I couldn't begin to tell you what classes I might have been in or anything like that. Why don't you check the probation officer's records? My whereabouts were known, as the saying goes."

"Which saying is that?" Whittaker muttered. He lifted the old mug shots from the table and looked at each in turn, then set them down again. "You know who your assailants were, am I correct?"

"Thanks to Detective Klinger."

"We've already been through this," Allegretti said. Whittaker ignored him.

"You didn't know their identities prior to your interview with Detective Klinger?"

"I might have recognized them on the street. Otherwise, no."

"And you are aware that two of the men, Darryl Jackson and John McVee, were murdered shortly after their own releases from Astoria, in 1972 and 1973?"

"Detective Klinger told me that, yes."

"You did not know they had been killed until Detective Klinger told you?"

"No."

"Are you aware of the manners of their deaths?"

"No."

Whittaker described the autopsy reports and stared expectantly.

"Too bad," Michael answered. "It couldn't have happened to nicer guys."

"You're indifferent to torture and mutilation?"

"I resent your tone," Allegretti barked.

Michael's dark eyes flashed with anger. "You expect me to care?" His face reddened. "A couple of minutes ago, you casually asked me to recount the worst experience of my life. Now you want me to shed tears over those assholes? Forget it. It took me years to get over what those men did to me." He self-consciously rubbed his eyebrow. "I've still got scars. You think I give a shit what happened to them?"

In Michael's fury that seemed to be filling the room with a

heated mist, Klinger thought he sensed something. He wasn't sure and jotted *guilty conscience?* on his note pad, but later Whittaker disagreed about the nature of undertone, although there was no doubt he had touched a nerve. Finally.

"I'd like to take a break now," Allegretti said.

Whittaker looked at his watch and shook his head. "We're almost done," he answered. He waited while Michael poured a glass of water, then he continued, "The third man you identified as one of your assailants, Robert Andrews, says you confronted Jackson and McVee in the yard at Astoria Prison before you were released. Is that true?"

"I spoke to them, if that's what he means." When Whittaker paused to glance through his notes, Michael added, "I saw them sitting on the bleachers next to the baseball diamond and walked over."

"Why did you do that?"

"I don't know. I think I wanted to take a good look at them before I left."

"What did they say to you?"

"Jackson suggested that I wanted another taste of his prick," Michael said coldly.

"Andrews says you told Jackson," Whittaker paused as he read from a sheet, "Quote, 'Funny you should say that, nigger. It's the last thing you're going to swallow,' referring to his penis. Do you recall that conversation?"

"It's funny," Michael answered uncomfortably, "that when push comes to shove, it always comes down to the racist crap."

"I don't find it amusing," Whittaker replied.

Michael looked away. "No, I guess not."

"Did that conversation occur?"

"Who knows what I said? I was a squirt, probably talking tough."

"That's not a yes or a no."

"Yes. Although I called Jackson 'Sam,' not 'nigger'. And I

didn't tell him his prick was the last thing he was going to swallow. I said 'eat,' not 'swallow'."

Klinger's eyes widened with astonishment, but Whittaker seemed unmoved. The prosecutor continued his questioning without missing a beat.

"Andrews also says you told McVee that he would be thrown from a building," he again consulted his notes, "and that something would be jammed through his rectum. Is that true?"

Michael glanced at Allegretti and shrugged. "Yes, I did," Michael answered. "I tried to seem tougher than I am."

Klinger stared. Why didn't he just say he didn't remember?

"And to you," Whittaker said, "it's just an amazing coincidence that the men were murdered in exactly those ways."

"Mr. Pollitz is here voluntarily," Allegretti interjected angrily, his voice almost shaking. "If you're going to persist with an aggressive, adversarial tone, this interview is over."

"This is a deposition, Mr. Allegretti. Mr. Pollitz is under oath."

"I repeat. My client is here voluntarily. If you intend to treat him as if he's on trial, we're leaving." He slid his chair away from the table. "Produce a subpoena, and we'll be back."

"It's no problem," Michael said calmly. "Let's get this over with." He looked at Whittaker and smiled ironically. "I'd say it's a pretty damning coincidence that makes me wish I'd kept my yap shut," he said. When Whittaker's taut face betrayed annoyed disbelief, Michael added, "I have no idea who might have overheard my childish threats. Maybe I gave someone else an idea."

"We're leaving until you produce a subpoena," Allegretti said again. "If this is your treatment of a cooperative witness..." He shook his head. "Produce a subpoena," he repeated. "And call me when you have it." Allegretti stood and gestured to Michael.

Whittaker paused as he studied the file, trying to ignore Allegretti. Before Michael could rise, Whittaker leaned back and briefly stared into his eyes. "I guess that's enough for now," he said. "Thank you for coming in, Mr. Pollitz. If we need additional information from you, I assume you'll be available to meet with us again."

22

"What in the hell is the matter with you?" Allegretti almost shouted in the back seat of the car. Michael noticed that the driver's head didn't move in response to the attorney's furious tone and concluded that the limousine's barrier was soundproof. Allegretti was on the verge of apoplexy. "Why?" He paused to control himself, and then continued, measuring his words. "Why, in the name of God, did you admit to saying those things? I couldn't believe my ears! No reasonable person would expect you to remember a conversation from twenty-two years ago!" He fumed, almost at a loss. "Don't you realize your admission could be enough for them to make a case? Why on earth didn't you just say you couldn't remember?"

"Because I have no idea who else overheard what I said," Michael answered. "There were a lot of people around, including a couple of guards. What if they have other witnesses?"

"Then let them produce them, for Christ's sake!"

Michael shrugged. "It's simpler if I minimize any lies," he said.

"What? You think you'd trip up over saying you can't remember a conversation? Do you want to go to trial over this? If no one other than Andrews can corroborate his claim about what you said, they won't even take it to a grand jury! Now, they don't need anyone else!"

"I didn't kill those guys. If they take it to trial, they'll lose.

They can't possibly prove I killed those assholes. And if they do have other witnesses besides that shithead, and it seems like I'm lying, then everything else is questionable too. In the meantime, if I appear to be consistently forthright, what do they have to go on?"

Allegretti breathed deeply. "Okay," he said at length, "that's a naïve thought. They can move with whatever they want to use. And you're wrong about what might happen in court. You have no idea, if it goes to trial, what a jury might or might not go for."

"Listen, Jim. You know as well as I do they aren't trying to get me for these murders. They're after Dom. I'd rather they concentrated their attention on me."

Allegretti looked through the window at the wrecked industrial neighborhood south of the Criminal Courts building. He said nothing until the driver swung onto the ramp to the in-bound Stevenson Expressway. Finally, he leaned forward to press an intercom button and give the driver Michael's home address. As he settled back into the seat, he sighed heavily and said, "Fine. Have it your way. Just remember, Mike, innocent men go to prison all the time."

"Not innocent white men with good attorneys," Michael laughed.

They rode in silence for a while, then Michael asked, "What's next?"

"I don't know," Allegretti said. "Klinger will probably keep after you. They may try to depose Dom or John. Maybe. It depends on how far Whittaker intends to take this. I can't believe he thinks he has enough to go to a grand jury for an indictment, but who knows?" He clicked his teeth pensively and looked out at Lake Michigan as they drove north on Lake Shore Drive.

After they dropped Michael off at his apartment, Allegretti instructed the driver to follow the familiar route to Barrington Hills.

23

"Thanks for keeping me informed, Jim," Dom said as he rose from his desk. He walked with the attorney to the front door. While he was gone, John, Sal and Angie sat in silence. When Dom came back into the office, John blurted, "Mikey's a stand-up guy, Dad. You know that. There's nothin' to worry about." Bruno and DeMicco exchanged a glance as Dom walked to the French doors and looked out into the night for a second or two, then returned to his desk. "This is Mikey, Sal," John said, almost in a plaintive whine. "You guys gotta remember who we're talkin' about!"

"Hey, I know," Bruno said irritably.

"From what Jim said, it sounds like Mike's trying to turn the heat on himself," Dom said at length. He sat in thought for a moment. "John, give Mike a call, will you? I want to talk to him. Maybe he can come for dinner Sunday." As John left the room, Dom winced and pressed a hand against his side.

"What?" Sal asked.

"Nothin'," Dom snapped. "A little pain. Don't mean shit." He shifted his weight and glared at the two men.

"What about this Andrews piece a shit?" DeMicco asked.

"That's another matter entirely," Dom answered.

24

Shortly before noon three days after the deposition with Whittaker, the receptionist at Michael's advertising agency buzzed his office to announce a visitor. Michael was perplexed at first, but by the time he reached the lobby he remembered who 'Larry' was. He found Klinger rocking on his heels in front of one of the two wall-mounted television screens the company had installed to continuously run its own commercials. The detective gazed appraisingly at a Sears ad, his lips pursed. He looked as though he was studying a work of art that he wasn't sure he understood. He glanced over his shoulder and grinned as Michael approached.

"You do this?" he asked, thrusting a stubby thumb at the screen.

"No," Michael answered.

Klinger extended his hand. "You feel like some lunch?"

Michael shook his hand, staring in mild confusion. "Why not?" He turned to the receptionist to tell her he'd be back in about an hour, then led the way out to the elevators.

"Nice offices," Klinger said.

"Yeah," Michael agreed warily. They boarded an empty elevator.

"You want to know what a nice guy I am?" Klinger asked, smiling. "I didn't identify myself when I asked for you. Just told that little doll I was Larry."

Michael laughed. "Well, I guess I appreciate that," he chuckled, "but they'd probably find it glamorous if they thought I had trouble with the police."

"Ignorance is bliss," Klinger replied. "Where's a good place to eat?"

"I like a Chinese joint around the corner," Michael answered as they left the elevator. "It's quick and good. That okay with you?"

"Oh, sure, sure. I eat anything." As they stepped into the May sunshine, Klinger stretched luxuriantly, his arms wide. "My God, what a fine day!" he announced, breathing deeply. Michael nodded. "We get so few like this in Chicago," Klinger added happily and gestured for Michael to lead the way.

They walked to the restaurant without speaking. It was a

small, noisy, unassuming place. Klinger was pleased. He never felt entirely at ease in upscale restaurants and said so. Michael smiled as they sat in a booth and placed their orders. He sipped water and waited while Klinger looked around and shifted his bulk comfortably into the corner of the padded vinyl bench. The waiter brought the first part of their order.

"Boy, you weren't kidding about the 'quick' part," Klinger beamed.

Michael smiled and nodded.

"You know," Klinger said, "you really surprised me the other day."

"How's that?" Michael asked. He picked up an egg roll and dipped it in sweet sauce, then pushed the plate across the table to Klinger.

"When you confirmed Bobby Andrews' claims about what you said. Anyone else woulda said he couldn't remember."

"I did remember," Michael answered. "Actually, I was more embarrassed than anything else." Klinger sneezed violently into his napkin, his eyes watering. "That mustard's hot, isn't it?" Michael grinned.

"Christ!" Klinger grunted. He dabbed at his eyes with a fresh napkin.

"Clears the sinuses," Michael added. He chewed slowly while Klinger puffed out his cheeks, coughed and gulped water.

"Man, that's strong," Klinger moaned. He wiped sweat from his forehead and inhaled deeply. Finally, he composed himself. "Why do you say you were embarrassed?"

"It was such sophomoric bravado. It reminded me of what a dumb kid I was."

"Hey, I like that phrase," Klinger said. "Sophomoric bravado. I'll have to remember that one. I should write it down." He smiled. "You have a good memory?"

"I'm notorious for it."

"Yeah, me too. 'Course, most detectives have good memories."

"I'd assume it's necessary for the job."

"It helps," Klinger said. He loosened his tie. "But you know, most people get serious amnesia when it comes to, how should I put it? Potentially incriminating conversations? Or events. Your answers were kinda unusual, you follow me?"

Michael could see how Klinger's conversational tics could get on a person's nerves. He wondered if it was intentional. He shrugged. "Why lie?"

"That's just the point," Klinger said joyfully. "There's a lotta good reasons to lie." He grinned. "And when I asked you out just now, I was almost sure you'd say not without your attorney." Michael shrugged again. He had considered it. "You know," Klinger continued, "I'll let you in on something. Just about everyone I interview, and I mean practically *everyone,* tries to lie to me. You wouldn't believe how stupid mosta the lies are. But in this case, it wouldn'ta been a stupid lie. It woulda been a *believable* lie. You had what they called 'plausible deniability' back when I was a kid." He paused, his lips still drawn back in a wide smile, as the waiter placed bowls of soup on the table. "That's why you're such a puzzler to me," he said with immense pleasure.

"I'm glad to be entertaining, Detective Klinger."

"Hey! Call me Larry," Klinger said affably. He slurped some soup. "Boy, that's good," he announced. He slurped some more, then wiped his lips. "See, Mike," he said with confidential familiarity, "most people don't realize that mosta the work cops do is just plain tedious. I mean, ninety percent of the job. You just keep grinding away. It ain't like the TV shows. Lotsa times, you're just packing some moron off to prison. Everything's obvious, and you just make sure you do everything legal so some judge doesn't let the bad guy walk." He finished his soup and smacked his lips with satisfaction. "But when things are more complex, which is hardly ever the case, then you gotta grind away until you get it together. A little piece here, a little piece there, until you get the whole picture, you follow?"

Michael nodded, wondering where Klinger was headed.

"Lemme give you an example," Klinger said. "One a the best cops I ever knew was a guy who worked in accident investigations, of all things. That ain't exactly the glamor division of the department. A few years ago, we had a hit-and-run down on Western Avenue. A couple kids were crossing the street like at nine at night, and a car hit 'em and drove off. They were killed. Now it's a homicide, so I'm there. We had a couple a witnesses, but they didn't know what kinda car it was, what color it was, whether the driver had hit the hooks, which he had, from the skid marks. They didn't even all agree on which direction it was going when it hit the kids, even though we could figure that out from the street. Lemme tell you, juries love eyewitnesses, but a lotta times, they aren't too helpful. They think they saw something, but they really didn't." He paused to dish some Mongolian beef onto his plate. "So this guy from major accidents gets a flashlight and spends I-don't-know-how-long crawling around the street, collecting all these little pieces of glass and plastic. He had the idea that it was a side mirror from the car that hit the kids. So he takes this bag fulla plastic and glass back to the station and sits at a table with a roll of Scotch tape, and for hours he tries to fit all these little, tiny, busted up pieces together again. And you know what? It *was* the side mirror from the car. We were able to ID the make and model, and finally we found the driver and prosecuted him. All because that cop had the patience to put that mirror back together." He lifted a huge forkful of food into his mouth and looked up expectantly.

"Sounds like admirable dedication," Michael offered.

"I guess," Klinger said dismissively. He sounded disappointed. "Hand me the rice, will you?" He shoveled more food onto his plate. "Tell me, way back then, were you a draft dodger?" From his tone, Michael didn't think he was serious with the pejorative.

"You mean during Vietnam? No, I was pretty apolitical,"

Michael replied. "Once I went to Astoria it was a moot point, anyway."

Klinger laughed merrily, his stomach jiggling against the table. "You never know," he said. "By 1972 the Army might've taken anyone who was willing to go."

"How about you?" Michael asked.

"Oh, I served. Back in the '60s. Lotsa cops my age were in the service then. Stationed in Vietnam too."

"Did you see any action?"

"As a matter of fact, I had the dubious privilege of participating in the first open engagement with the NVA."

"You were in Ia Drang?"

Klinger's mouth dropped open. "How in the hell do you know that?" When Michael shrugged, the detective exclaimed with wonder, "My God! No one knows about that fight! How in the world? You couldn'ta been ten!"

"I was thirteen, but that's not how I know about it," Michael answered. "I read a lot."

"Now, I'm impressed," Klinger beamed.

"So you were a Marine," Michael said, smiling and infected by Klinger's enthusiasm. "Were you with the unit that got overrun or the one that held a solid perimeter?"

"My God!" Klinger bellowed again. "You really *do* know about it!" He shook his head, laughing and awestruck. "I was with the disciplined battalion," he answered at length. "Thank God." He shook his head again. "You amaze me, Mike."

"Yeah? Well, like I say, I read a lot. If I recall correctly, Ia Drang is what convinced the North Vietnamese that American air power would make any pitched battles a losing proposition."

"Who knows?" Klinger said happily. "I was just a grunt. I got to come home after that."

"Were you wounded?"

"Yessir!" Klinger boomed. "Shot in the ass!" He laughed loudly, drawing glances from other diners. "Want to see the scar? No? For some reason, nobody ever does." He kept chuckling as they divided the bill and stood to leave. "Jesus," he said, still abashed, "what a memory. You're the first person I ever met who knew the name of that valley."

Michael followed him back out onto the street. "Tell me something, Larry. Do you think about it much? Have nightmares, anything like that?"

"Not really. Never did, to tell the truth. I haven't even dreamed about it for years," Klinger replied. "I rarely think about it now." They walked back toward Michael's building.

"Well, that's sort of how I feel about my little episode in Astoria," Michael said. "I don't even want to think about it."

"Point taken, kiddo," Klinger answered with a smile. "Point taken."

Michael stopped near the building entrance and looked at the detective. "Why are you so concerned about a couple of really rotten guys who got killed more than twenty years ago?"

"Why?" Klinger asked with his forehead wrinkled by his eyebrows. "You may not believe this, Mike, but I don't think anyone should get away with murder, you follow me?" He met Michael's gaze soberly. "Murder's *wrong*," he said.

Michael nodded without breaking eye contact and smiled. He turned to go back to work. As he reached for the door, Klinger called after him, "Hey, Mike!" Michael turned back. "Nice restaurant," Klinger said.

25

As he walked toward his car, Klinger patted his shirt pocket to feel the sheet he had torn from his desk calendar that morning. He decided to blow off an hour and stepped into a florist's shop in the middle of the block.

"What can I do for you?" the clerk chirped as he walked to the counter.

"I need some flowers to put on a grave," Klinger answered. He looked around the shop.

"What would you like?" the clerk asked. "We just got some nice carnations this morning. They last a long time."

"Nah," Klinger replied. "Somethin' seasonal. Maybe some tulips. You got a half-dozen red tulips?" He fished in his pocket for cash.

"Sure."

Klinger carried the flowers to his car and drove north to Rosehill Cemetery without bothering to call in. He turned through the gate on Western Avenue and followed his customary route through the cemetery grounds to a point on the lane that was near the plots he had purchased almost thirty years earlier, right after he joined the police force. They were near Rosehill's northeast corner, within sight of a few of the fancier parts of the cemetery, the best he could afford at the time. Nearby were a few of the dramatic, expensive monuments, but adjacent to the plots the tall concrete cemetery wall was replaced by a wrought-iron fence. The opening to Peterson Avenue noticeably increased the intrusion of traffic noise, but not jarringly. He walked across the well-tended grass in the bright May sunshine, glancing casually at other visitors here and there around the nearest sectors of the cemetery's huge acreage. No interments seemed to be in progress. A train rolled across the bridge over Peterson and past the eastern boundary of the grounds without seriously disturbing the tranquility of the cemetery. He stopped at a small granite marker set nearly flush with the ground and sighed, holding the wrapped tulips in his crossed hands. The marker was inscribed,

MATTHEW ORMOND KLINGER
1966–1972
BELOVED CHILD

Klinger's shoulders sagged. He closed his eyes briefly, and an observer would have assumed from the movement of his silent lips that he was praying, but he was simply mouthing the rhythmic syllables of his son's name. Sometimes, when he visited the site, the constriction in his chest would become too much to bear, and he would return to his car with a guilty sense of embarrassment that some stranger might see him crying. More often, he felt like he did today, heavy with sorrow and years, and he would stand quietly at the grave, enduring for a few minutes the agony of unmet possibilities, and then he would leave his flowers, if he had brought some along, and return to his duties with a small pressure in his throat that soon went away. He lowered himself to one knee and laid the tulips against the stone, remaining in the position for a moment while he said a brief prayer with his closed fist pressed against his forehead. He stood again with another sigh and adjusted his pants. Momentarily lost in thought, he didn't hear his ex-wife walking up behind him.

"Larry?" she asked, sounding surprised. He glanced over his shoulder and nodded.

"Hello, Marie."

"I didn't expect to see you here," she said. She smiled stiffly. They had divorced twenty years before, and their paths had crossed less and less frequently as time passed. In the previous decade, they had met at the gravesite only once, on Christmas Day eight years earlier.

"I always come on his birthday," Klinger said.

"I didn't know that," Marie answered. "I've never seen you. I mean, I've seen flowers once in a while."

"I don't bring 'em every time," he replied. "Guess we just miss each other, like we arrive at different times. I usually come earlier in the day." He looked down at the marker. "Always reminds me of you," he added with a soft smile, nodding at their son's middle name, which they had chosen to honor her parents.

"I come four or five times a year," she said.

"Yeah?"

She nodded. "Whenever the mood takes me, holidays, you know."

"Yeah," Klinger answered. He crossed his hands and tried to suck in his gut. "How've you been?"

"I'm fine," Marie answered. "How about you?"

"Still goin' along," he said with a shrug. "Can't complain. Bob okay?"

"He's fine. His son's working with him now."

"Yeah? That's nice." Klinger nodded. "Any grandkids yet?"

"Yes, two girls, two and four."

"Ah, that's nice," Klinger repeated. He felt asinine. She smiled briefly and looked at the grave. She closed her eyes. Klinger studied her face, feeling a remote, sad fondness. Her pale brown hair was cut short and permed in loose curls. He noticed more gray than the last time he'd seen her, but she was still trim.

She looked at him again, her eyes glistening, and said, "He would have been twenty-eight today." Klinger nodded unhappily, then reached out to hug her. She returned the embrace and trembled slightly. Klinger struggled not to cry. He disengaged awkwardly and patted her shoulder, glancing away to conceal the moisture in his eyes.

"Hey, listen," he said, "I don't wanna intrude."

"You were here first," Marie answered, fumbling in her purse for a tissue.

"No, don't worry. I gotta get going." He patted her shoulder again and cleared his throat. "It's nice to see you, Marie. You look great."

"Thanks," she said, sniffling with the tissue held to her nose.

"Okay," he said. "You take care now."

"You, too, Larry."

"I always do," he said as he turned away. He trudged back to his car while Marie dabbed at her eyes with her tissue.

26

Michael weaved slightly as he left the bar on Clark. He rarely drank enough to feel tipsy, and he didn't think he'd had enough to be drunk now. Yet his pace was unsteady as he walked toward the subway. He began to catalog everything he had eaten that day when three young black men, or perhaps older teenagers, appeared from what seemed to be nowhere a dozen yards ahead.

"Yo!" the tallest of them called. "Hey, man, you OK?"

Michael noticed that the immediate area was unusually dark, but he didn't look around for a malfunctioning street light. He stopped, for some reason feeling an overwhelming urge to grin as the three boys/men moved toward him. They spread out, triangulating him as they neared. He said, "Do you squirts really want to die? Here? Like this?" maintaining unwavering eye contact as he slid a hand behind his back and into the waistband of his pants.

His laughter chased the trio as they sprinted east and away.

27

"You miss her?" Dora asked. She set a plate of flank steak on the table, a new recipe from the newspaper.

"You mean Marie?" Klinger looked up. "No, sweetie." He smiled. "No. I think well of her, but things fell apart for us. You know that."

Dora spooned green beans into a bowl. She shrugged. "I never know exactly what's happening, Larry," she said. "You're kind of quiet." She looked at his face and saw more sorrow than he seemed willing to admit.

He stood from the table and put his hands on her arms. "Doll," he announced, "you know better." He hugged her briefly. "I miss Mattie," he added, "but there ain't a thing I can do about that." He thought about it. "We split up twenty years ago, and all."

"Since when is that a long time?"

"You think it isn't?"

"Snap your fingers, Larry."

He laughed and hugged harder. "You always get straight to it, no doubt about it." He disengaged and squeezed her shoulder lightly.

Dora stared at his face. "Hard day, wasn't it?"

"Nah. Nothin' outta the ordinary." He turned away. *I don't miss Marie,* he thought, *but we were young together. I miss our hopes.*

"How was she?"

"Marie? She looked good. Guess she's got a couple a grandkids now, Bob's boy's kids. Couple a little girls." He moved to the refrigerator. "It was kinda tough, seein' her there, at Mattie's grave." He shrugged and reached for the refrigerator door. "Mattie mighta had some kids by now. Who knows? Coulda been." He ducked behind the open door, reaching inside.

When Klinger remained out of sight for an unusually long time, moving things around in the refrigerator, Dora smiled sadly. "I gotta go to the bathroom," she said as she slipped out of the kitchen. "Be right back." Some pains deserve privacy, she thought.

28

"Pollitz," Michael said, cradling his phone's handset in his shoulder as he flipped through a stack of prices and specifications for a Sears Sunday insert.

"Ayyyy, Mikey!" John Calabria shouted in his usual greeting. Michael smiled and shifted his position to hold the handset. He glanced through his window. Clouds were building above the city and across Lake Michigan. "How's it going?" John bellowed. "Can you get me a deal on a power drill?"

"Funny you should mention that. I'm looking at a promo for a new cordless."

John laughed. "I shoulda known. No thanks, man." Michael could hear a hissing inhalation as John paused and assumed his friend was smoking a joint. He glanced at his watch and waited. Finally, John continued, slowly releasing his words with his captive breath, "Well, I got some news. Angie had a heart attack last night."

Michael straightened in his chair. "Serious?"

"Not too bad," John answered. Michael heard him inhale again. "He's still in intensive care, I guess, but it ain't like he's about to die or nothin'." He chuckled softly and took another drag on his reefer.

Michael asked, "What happened?" anticipating some explanation for John's inappropriate amusement.

"It's kinda funny, in a way," John grunted. "I guess he was

with his girlfriend, over at her apartment. I don't know what was goin' on, but it musta been good, 'cause Angie has a heart attack while it's happenin'. Whatever it was." John started to laugh. Michael grinned slowly, thinking about Nelson Rockefeller. "Here's the funny part," John went on, "Angie don't want his wife to know where he is, see." He laughed harder.

"So what did he do?"

"He gets his pants back on or whatever, puts his dick away, and he drags his ass out to his car and drives to a gas station, like, while he's havin' this heart attack! Then he goes to the jamoke at the station and says, 'Call a fuckin' ambulance,' and passes out right there on the cement!"

"How do you know all this?"

"Angie told Sal this morning." John cackled over the phone. "He's like, 'Don't tell Yvonne, don't tell Yvonne.' Then he asks Sal to get his piece back from the ambulance guys!" John could barely control his voice. "Sal goes, 'Fuck your gun. Who gives a shit about your piece?' But Sal says he means Angie's girlfriend!"

Michael exhaled impatiently through his nostrils. Sal's double entendre wasn't even amusing, much less funny. Michael couldn't imagine that DeMicco's wife was ignorant of the girlfriend, but he understood that the basics of the arrangement dictated that the tough old mobster's infidelities not be thrown in her face. He shook his head to think of DeMicco enduring crushing chest pain as he climbed into his car and drove away. "Where is he?" he finally asked.

"At the Humana Hospital down on Barrington Road, in Schaumburg or Hoffman Estates, whichever the fuck it is."

"I know it. You got an address?" Michael reached for a pad of paper.

"Sure," John stammered, still chortling. "Send him some flowers and a copy of *The Joy of Sex*."

"Maybe I'll drive out and visit him," Michael said. "When's he get out of intensive care?"

"I dunno. He may already be outtta there," John answered. He paused, and Michael could picture him still shaking with humor.

"Hey, that's you in twenty years, pal," Michael laughed.

"Forget about it," John answered, laughing harder. He finally paused for breath. "Hey, Mikey, there's somethin' else. This state's attorney, this Whittaker asshole, he asked me and my dad to come in 'voluntarily' for a deposition. Says he wantsta ask us about you and 1972. How 'bout that?"

"What did you tell him?"

"We told him to eat shit." Michael assumed this was a direct quote. "He can jam 'voluntarily' straight up his ass. We turned him over to Allegretti." John paused, and when he continued, Michael detected a slight undertone of discomfort. "Anyways, my dad wanted me to ask you if they subpoenaed you or anything."

"No," Michael answered. "That detective, Klinger, came by my office the other day, but that's it."

"When?"

"Five days ago."

"What'd he want?"

"Nothing, as far as I could tell. He asked me to come out for lunch, and he said he was surprised by my answers at the deposition, but that's all. He didn't ask any questions about those three assholes or Astoria or anything else." Michael thought about it for a second. "I think it was his way of reminding me that he's around," he added.

"Hey, Mikey. Do me a favor, okay? Whenever this guy or anyone else wantsta see you, or talks to you, or anything, lemme know, okay? My dad'd like to keep informed, you know?"

"You know you'll hear about it whenever something relevant happens, John."

"Ah, sure I do, Mikey," John answered. "Hey! If you go see Angie, stop by, okay? Come have some more veal parm. Did you like it, few weeks ago?"

"Yeah, it was real good."

"Yeah, I think so too. That new chef's doin' a great job." John coughed. "Well, I'll letya get back to work."

Michael hung up the phone and stared south at the Chicago skyline, wondering what pattern of thought might be developing out in Barrington Hills.

29

Klinger was gnawing on a Snickers bar and watching the patchy sunlight gleaming off the wet street while he half-listened to two other detectives and one of the station's civilian employees discussing the NBA playoff schedule. *It's funny how fast I get sick of rain,* he thought, gazing at the sky through the dirty windows. *After only three days, it feels like it's been raining forever.* He was glad to be distracted by another investigator calling his name; the conversation was boring. How could anyone spend a long time debating whether or not Michael Jordan is the greatest basketball player of all time?

"Dan Whittaker's on line three," the man said.

Klinger swallowed the candy bar as he walked to his desk. He knew he was considered an oddball because he had absolutely nothing of a personal nature on top of his desk. Klinger's assigned workspaces had changed often enough over the years that he didn't try to personalize any particular banged-up desk or chair. It was unconscious at first, but in recent years it had become a deliberate decision. He kept a photo of Mattie in a drawer, and he tended to put his revolver in another drawer. After all his years on the force, he had never become accustomed to the weight of a gun on his belt, under his arm, or anywhere else. As he told Dora, "Truth be told, I hate the goddamn thing." He had yet to fire the service revolver anywhere except on the department's firing range, and if he got his preference, it would stay that way until the day he retired. He punched the blinking button on his phone.

"I have bad news, Larry," Whittaker said without any preliminaries. His voice was tight and agitated.

"Tell me," Klinger replied.

"Andrews was killed last night at County," Whittaker said.

Klinger stopped with the wadded-up candy wrapper in his hand, held close to his head as he aimed it at a trash can across the room. He clenched his fist on the paper and ground his teeth. "Shit!" he spat out with intense distress. His first thought was, *I knew that asshole was shooting off his mouth.* "How?"

"There was a mess there last night. I don't know if you heard. A couple of guys tried to escape. There was a melee, and when it was over, Andrews was bleeding to death."

"Who were the attempted escapees?"

"I don't think they were connected. It was a pair of brothers. A couple of northside Croats who were arrested for some burglaries."

"God damn it!" Klinger barked. He dropped the candy wrapper into his wastebasket and sat, rubbing his forehead with his fingertips. "They have anyone?"

"No suspects as of this morning," Whittaker snapped.

"*Son* of a bitch!" Klinger shouted. The basketball conversation stopped as the three men turned toward his raised voice.

"Any doubt in your mind about who's behind this?"

"Of course not," Klinger snarled. "God *damn* that bastard!"

"Which one, Andrews or Calabria?" Whittaker asked rhetorically. "This creates a problem."

Klinger shook his head, muttering furiously. Without an unlikely dose of dumb luck, they couldn't expect to ever find the person or persons who had handled the assassination. "Christ, they got to him quick," he grumbled.

"It's been over two weeks since I deposed Pollitz. That's plenty of time," Whittaker said, his voice measured in fury.

Klinger thought about a possible connection with Michael. "What does this do to us?" he asked.

"Like I said, it creates a problem." He paused, thinking. "It takes away part of the case."

"What are you saying? We're fucked?"

"I'm not that negative. But you need to remember what a long shot this has been from the start."

"Well, Andrews' testimony wasn't worth much."

"No, but it provided leverage," Whittaker replied.

"Doesn't his murder add ammo?"

"No," Whittaker answered, suddenly sounding weary. "Even a lousy litigator would find some way to pin it on Montoya, to keep Andrews from testifying about Perez, and Allegretti's one of the best." Klinger closed his eyes and pinched the bridge of his nose as the prosecutor continued, "What's worse, from my point of view, is this. Without Andrews around, it's going to be a lot harder to put pressure on Pollitz." He paused as Klinger exhaled loudly in frustration. "And Pollitz is all we've got, now."

30

Michael flinched and almost groaned aloud as he approached his apartment on foot, walking from the bus stop at Addison and Halsted. Ahead he could see Klinger's bulk lounging against a parked car, apparently lost in thought. The detective leaned forward with his broad rump on top of a fender, his arms crossed over his gut and with his chin cupped in one hand. He stared at the cracked pavement of the sidewalk until Michael was only fifteen or twenty yards away, then glanced up with a tight-lipped smile.

"Hey, Mike," Klinger said as Michael neared. "You feel like a hot dog or something? I gotta get some food in my stomach."

"What, are you stalking me?"

"Huh?" Klinger started, but then he laughed, a short, barking burst aimed at the sky. "You know, I've often figured it's gotta seem like that to people I have to interview repeatedly," he said. He shook his head and chuckled as he straightened away from the car. "It's like I told you before. Sometimes, I just gotta keep plugging away. I try to keep it as pleasant as possible." He grinned slowly. "Why don't you take a walk with me? There's a hot dog stand up the street on Halsted. I'll buy you a dog. My car's parked up there anyway."

Michael shrugged and turned back in the direction he had just come. "I know the joint," he said. Klinger fell in step beside him.

"Nice day," Klinger said.

"For a change," Michael answered. "This has been a really lousy year, even by Chicago's shit standards."

Klinger grunted in half-hearted assent. They walked to Halsted Street in silence. Finally, Klinger began, "Well, I hate to be a pest..."

"Why do I find that so difficult to believe?" Michael interrupted, his forehead wrinkled in a wry smile. Klinger laughed, more genuinely this time.

"So sue me," he said. "See, I figure the best way to get things straight in my mind is just to keep asking questions, you follow? I mean, maybe it gets annoying, but it's part of the job."

"So I get ambushed, right?"

"What ambush? I was at the station here," Klinger protested, pointing across the intersection of Halsted and Addison, "and I figured I'd wait and see if you had some time. That ain't an ambush." They waited for the stoplight to change. "I mean, you don't have to come for a hot dog or anything else, you know?"

"It's okay," Michael sighed. "It's just been a long day." He rolled his shoulders with fatigue. "What's on your mind?"

Klinger glanced at him and seemed to hesitate. "I'm just tryin' to clarify some stuff," he said. "Like chronology. Back in 1972, you got out of Astoria when? July?"

"July twenty-fourth, to be exact."

"And then McVee got out late in October, and Jackson in November," Klinger said, almost musing. "When did you get sent to Astoria?"

"Come on, Larry. You already know this."

Klinger shook his head and walked to the order window at the little hot dog stand. "Not really," he replied. "I mean, not as much as you seem to think. What'll you have?"

"A hot dog, fries, a small Coke."

"You got it." Klinger turned to the order clerk. "Gimme three dogs, two fries, and two Cokes." He turned back to Michael. "What do you want on your dog?"

"Everything, whatever they have."

"Yeah?" Klinger smiled. "Gimme one dog with everything. Make the other two Chicago dogs." When the clerk stared at him uncomprehendingly, Klinger explained, "Mustard, onion and celery salt. I'm a purist," he said over his shoulder to Michael. "Put the pickle on the side."

"You want peppers on the everything?" the clerk asked.

"I just said 'everything,' didn't I?" Klinger snapped. He passed cash through the small window.

"Ketchup too?"

"For God's sake!" Klinger glared through the opening. "Everything, okay? By everything, sport, I mean everything. Why is that so difficult?" He glanced back at Michael with a look of supreme exasperation. Michael smiled and shook his head.

"Listen, Larry," Michael said after a moment. "I know you

can't let a crime like murder drop, okay? You already told me how you feel about it. But to me, the biggest crime that occurred in 1972, for me personally, was that I was in Astoria at all."

Klinger gazed at him for a moment, then turned with a shrug to collect their food. He handed a cardboard tray to Michael and said noncommittally, "Well, you were convicted of a felony."

"That's not quite true," Michael answered as they moved to a small, midriff-high concrete table. "It was a negotiated plea. And none of my classmates did any time, not even the guys who were actually selling drugs."

"Classmates?" Klinger began, but Michael interrupted again.

"I was arrested along with four other students, plus a few townies. Only the townies and I went to jail. The other students ended up with misdemeanors and short probations." Michael stared across the table and lifted his hot dog. "How come you don't know all this?" He bit into the sausage.

Klinger met Michael's angry stare as he chewed. He swallowed and sipped his soft drink. "I know most of it," he admitted. "I'm not tryin' to trip you up. It's a just a habit I get into. Like I say, mosta the people I interview are tryin' to lie to me, and it just gets habitual to ask questions in a certain way." He shrugged and chewed fries. "Actually, I know more about those other arrests than yours. Their records weren't expunged."

"I would gladly have traded places with them," Michael said.

"You know, I've never talked to a guy in jail who's guilty," Klinger said with a wicked smile, lifting his second hot dog to his lips.

"Don't give me that crap. The only thing I was guilty of was stupidity. I never sold drugs and didn't even use them all that much. I walk a couple of guys to a room where they actually *can* buy drugs, and I'm the one who ends up fucked up the ass in Astoria!" He paused to stifle his anger and threw some fries into his mouth. "That's a crime, to me," Michael muttered. He picked up his Coke.

"Maybe so, maybe so," Klinger mused, but his tone was distracted.

"You can't know how much I wish we weren't even having these conversations," Michael said. "I mean, aside from the fact that I'm part of your investigation, 1972 was really a rotten year for me."

"Yeah, I guess so. Matter of fact, 1972 was about the worst year of my life too," Klinger answered. He looked away, studying the passing traffic.

"Why's that?" Michael asked. "That when you got divorced?"

"No. That's the year my kid died. It was tough."

"God! That's terrible!" Michael wished he'd kept his mouth shut. "Christ! I'm sorry to hear that." He squinted with distress. "I thought you said you don't have kids."

Klinger smiled sadly. "I'll have to keep your memory in mind."

"It's what you said."

"I know. Thing is, I don't anymore."

"What happened?"

"It was an accident. Mattie was riding his bike and got hit by a car." Klinger exhaled slowly. Why was he telling this to Politz? "He was on the sidewalk but crossed the alley."

"Jesus!" Michael exclaimed again. "I'm sorry. Just a kid."

"He would have been twenty-eight, couple weeks ago."

Michael studied the detective's face. "Still hurts, doesn't it?" he said, cautiously stating the obvious.

Klinger met his eyes. "Yeah. Matter of fact, it does. It never stops hurting." He shrugged. "I'm sure you've heard your Outfit buddies use the expression, 'the calendar cures everything,' am I right?" Michael didn't respond, but he knew the saying. "Well, it don't. Not in all cases."

"No, I guess it doesn't," Michael answered, sorrowful and confused by the undertone of anger in Klinger's voice. It seemed to be directed at him. Klinger looked away and finished chewing the remnant of his hot dog.

"It kind of strikes me as odd that you and Dom Calabria have the same attorney," Klinger said suddenly.

"In what way? Given his history, he knows a lot of good attorneys."

"Well, yeah," Klinger nodded. "Dan says Allegretti's pretty good."

"I'm glad to hear it," Michael said. "I found out the hard way what can happen when you've got a bad one."

"I hear you," Klinger nodded. "On the other hand, as a cop, I don't exactly love it when a 'good' lawyer gets a bad guy off."

"So it goes. As a potential defendant, I want a heavy hitter at the table with me." He stared at Klinger.

"Prosecution ain't my part of the program," the detective answered impassively.

"No, you just gather the evidence that makes it possible."

Klinger shrugged. "That's me," he said. His smile had a hard edge. "Anyway, I got some news for you, Mike. You know that guy, Andrews? Your third assailant from way back when? He's no longer among the living. Somebody stuck a knife in him down at County." He didn't hide his anger well. He was unsurprised to note genuine shock on Michael's face. "I don't suppose that matters much to you."

"Hey, come on, Larry. I didn't have anything serious against that guy." He shook his head. "All he did was beat me up a little a long time ago. I certainly didn't want him dead."

"Yeah, well, someone did," Klinger said coldly. "Care to guess who?"

"How should I know?"

"The way I figure it, there's only two people who coulda told Dom Calabria about Bobby Andrews," Klinger said, "you and Allegretti. You follow me?"

"People get killed in jails," Michael answered.

Klinger frowned speculatively. "It happens," he said with a slow nod. "But it ain't as common as you may think, and mosta the time, it's gang-related. See, it's pretty unusual for an unconnected mope like Andrews to get his throat cut." He was unable to keep the rising heat out of his voice.

"You can't think I had something to do with this."

Klinger stared with his lips pursed, then looked away up the street while he fumbled for a pack of gum. He jammed a stick in his mouth and offered the packet to Michael. Michael shook his head. "No," Klinger said at length, chomping on the gum. "I think Dom Calabria had *everything* to do with it." He straightened his coat and gazed at Michael. "And I think someone pointed Dom Calabria in that direction. That's why it don't seem so smart to me that you got the same lawyer he does, you follow?"

"No, I don't 'follow,' God damn it." Michael dumped his half-eaten hot dog into a trash can and wiped his hands with a napkin.

"Which client do you think is Allegretti's top priority?" Klinger asked blandly. He started to walk away. "Guess I'll get going," he said.

"Let me ask you something, Larry," Michael said softly. Klinger turned back and raised his eyebrows. "If everything you think about Dominick Calabria is true, and if I actually have the information you seem to think I have, what do you think'll happen to me if I'm helping you?"

Klinger met Michael's eyes, his face emotionless. "I thought the Calabrias are your oldest friends," he said with savage irony.

"What do you think will happen, Larry?" Michael repeated.

He turned and walked quickly toward his apartment without looking back at Klinger staring after him, his lower lip pinched thoughtfully between his thick thumb and fingers.

31

Carole Meyer was a surprise to Klinger. He didn't know exactly what he had been expecting, but it wasn't a disarmingly beautiful blond. A stylish male receptionist had led him back to her office, which was situated in a corner of the Illinois Center and commanded an outstanding view of the Chicago River, and while she finished a phone conversation, he glanced around feeling an unaccustomed awkwardness. He laughed at himself inwardly when he recognized the feeling—Carole's regal beauty was atypically generating a dopey male response. He was thankful she remained on the phone for a minute or so because it gave him the time to recognize his own foolishness and drag up his cop personna.

She finally finished her conversation and stood, apologetically waving him into the room. "Detective Klinger?" she asked, stepping away from her desk and extending her hand. *She deserves a wolf whistle,* Klinger thought as he crossed the spacious office. To Klinger's uneducated eye, it looked like Carole bought her clothing at one of the hip, sexy Gold Coast boutiques where women paid $500 for a skirt. He smiled and introduced himself, consciously averting his glance from her legs. "I'm rather surprised to see you."

"Why is that?" Klinger asked.

"I haven't seen Mike in years, and it's a long time since we were married. Did he give you my name?"

"No," Klinger replied, smiling. He knew what was coming.

"Then how?" Carole began, but he held up a hand.

"I found a wedding announcement in the newspaper morgue. Not what you'd call sophisticated police work."

She smiled gently as she returned to her chair. Klinger imagined construction workers chewing the heels of their hands.

"How can I help you?" she asked as she sat.

"Like I said on the phone," he answered, "I'm trying to get a little background regarding Mike Pollitz." Her face closed slightly as she glanced at her watch. "This will only take a couple of minutes," he added reassuringly, "and none of it really involves you at all." Carole nodded slowly. "But I'd appreciate any insights you can give me, if you don't mind."

"Not at all," she replied. "But I should warn you, it's a long time ago, and Mike and I have no contact at all. I don't know that I can offer much." She flashed a wistful smile; Klinger decided to concentrate on his notepad or he'd never hear her answers. Already he was thinking how the creases at the ends of her lips reminded him of some movie star whose name didn't immediately come to mind. *A man could get lost,* he thought.

"No?" Klinger said. "I take it your divorce wasn't amicable."

"Oh, the divorce was amicable enough," she answered with a slight shrug. "So was the marriage, as far as that goes. There was just nowhere for it to go."

"Sorry to hear it," Klinger said, shaking his head.

"So," Carole interjected briskly, idly smoothing her skirt. "What can I tell you? Is Mike in some kind of trouble?"

Klinger continued to shake his head and added a slight frown—misleading without lying. "Our investigation is actually directed at Dominick Calabria." A hooded look crossed Carole's face. "Do you know him?"

"I just met him a couple of times, many years ago," she answered. "He came to our wedding, along with a few other gangsters. It was weird."

"Why do you say that?"

"I always wondered what my parents thought when these mobsters handed me envelopes in the receiving line."

"You mean at the church?" Klinger was surprised. Cash gifts were usually given at the reception.

"Yeah, right outside the church," she laughed, "all these envelopes with hundred-dollar bills in them. It was probably the crassest experience of my life." She laughed again. "Totally out of my experience. Mike said it was because we had such a small reception, just family."

"Was that the only time you met Dom Calabria?"

"No, there were some other encounters while Mike and I were married. Like when we went to christenings for a couple of John Calabria's children. I think we attended two or three parties, if you could call them that, out in Barrington Hills, too."

"Did you know Pollitz in college?" Klinger asked.

"No. We met at Leo Burnett," Carole replied. Klinger masked his disappointment. "I was twenty-four. Mike was twenty-five."

"When did you get married?"

"About two years later," she said. "Right after he took a job with the agency where he still is." From her tone, Klinger concluded that she felt his tenure in his current job was a failure of some kind.

"How long were you married?"

"Just over four years." She pushed a strand of hair away from her face.

"What went wrong?" Klinger blurted. "I mean, if you don't mind me asking."

"It's a natural question," she smiled. "We had different ideas about the future, I guess. I thought Mike might even own the agency where he works. He seemed to be on that path. I imagined our marriage would become comfortable, that we would be raising children, all the usual things. That's what I would have wanted. But it wasn't ever going to happen with Mike."

Klinger thought about it. There was something canned about her response. He glanced at a photo of two nicely dressed, smiling children on the credenza behind her desk. Carole followed his eyes and smiled. "Adam is ten, Jessie's seven," she said, letting her gaze linger on the posed shot.

"I guess life went on," he said.

"It's supposed to, isn't it?" she answered. "But that was the problem. Nothing was going to 'go on' with Mike. It wasn't a lack of love or sympathy, really. The stasis was impossible."

Carole stopped and smiled, self-conscious, it seemed to Klinger. After a moment, he asked, "How much do you know about his past?"

"You mean his childhood?" Klinger shrugged. "Or his trouble with the law? Or that short prison sentence?" She raised her eyebrows expectantly.

"Anything," Klinger answered.

"He told me about all of that," she said with an air of resignation. "He cried about it once, when we were dating."

"Did he?" Klinger rubbed his nose. "In what way?"

"What do you mean? Like heartbroken sobs? Or sniffles?"

Klinger had a momentary insight into how withering it might be to endure such intense sarcasm from such a beautiful woman. He wondered why her tone had turned caustic. "No. I'm just trying to get a picture. I meant, how did it come up, how was it that he became upset about it, that sort of thing."

"He became upset because he'd had too much to drink," she answered. "It was the first I'd heard the story. Maybe it upset him to describe it to me."

"What brought it up?"

"I asked about the scar over his eye, in his eyebrow." Carole paused, thinking back. "I think I teased him about it, said he must have been a boxer or something. A little later on, he told me the story, how he'd been in jail back in college and three men raped him. He cried, much later on."

"Did he say who the men were?"

Carole stared blankly. "Not to me," she replied. "Why?"

Klinger shrugged. "Just asking. Did he describe them or add any other details?"

"He said the rapists were two white guys and a black guy and that they'd beaten him first. That's really about all."

"Were you surprised when a guy you were dating admitted to being raped?"

"Oh, you know it. That was part of his appeal, very open honesty."

"But he became upset."

Carole nodded. "Yes. He cried about it."

"I take it that was pretty unusual," Klinger prompted.

"Unusual?" Carole's eyebrows rose. "Mike just didn't get worked up about much. I can't think of anything dramatic during the six years we were together. That one night is the only time I ever saw him that upset about anything. Not even when people died, like his grandpa." She shrugged. "Mike wasn't all that expressive as a general rule. But like I say, he'd had too much to drink." Carole gazed across her desk at Klinger, her face expressionless as she searched her memory. She smiled again. "It's such a long time," she apologized.

"The rape must have been a lousy experience," Klinger said.

"No doubt," she agreed, "and it's one that countless women have endured."

"That's true," he nodded, thinking, *but none of them comes through it unchanged, and some never recover.*

"Men too," she added. "But bad things happen to all of us. The question is what you do afterwards. I suggested he get therapy once, when we were married."

"Did he take your advice?" Klinger asked.

"Not that I know of."

"Did he talk about the incident often?"

"No, not really," she answered. "It came up once in a while, I guess. I mean, if you're asking, was he tormented by it, I'd say no. At least, not as I recall things." It never failed to impress Klinger, how invariably forthcoming educated people were when he interviewed them, and how often they tried to second-guess the information he was seeking, all of their assumptions based on TV cop shows and movies. He could have told Carole Meyer that her ex-husband's demons or lack thereof meant nothing to him. But he acted as though he was fascinated by her insights.

"How did it come up?"

She thought about it for a moment, her forehead creased.

"I couldn't say," she answered at last. "To be truthful, I think I brought it up more than he did. In fact, I don't think he ever initiated a conversation about it, after the first time. I was curious, you know. In a strange way, I think I might have found it intriguing or romantic, something like that, a man with a past and shady friends, that sort of thing." She chuckled at herself. "I definitely had that wrong."

"How so?"

"The romantic part. That isn't Mike Pollitz. You want to know something else? He has very little interest in sex." Klinger didn't react. "And I don't think it was me or 'us,' or anything else like that," she went on. "It was him."

Klinger asked, "Are you saying you think this was related to what happened to him?"

"I have no idea," Carole dismissed the subject. "Mike and I didn't connect the way we needed to, so I really can't offer much about him. To me, it's an empty space. If the problem was what happened in jail, so be it. There was nothing I could do about it."

Klinger considered the pronouncement. Carole's imitation of soap-opera dialogue notwithstanding, he was beginning to view Michael as one of the most complicated people he had ever met.

"Whatever might have been there once upon a time, if it ever was there, it was gone. But of course I didn't know that at first. I didn't see the reality for a while," Carole added. "The poor guy has no relationship with his family. On the rare occasions we went out there, it was unbelievably uncomfortable. He makes no friends. There's just nothing there," she said.

"I thought he and John Calabria are friends."

"They're friends because they've *always* been friends."

"What do you mean, he has no relationship with his family?" Klinger was confused. Weeks earlier, when he had obtained Pollitz's work number from his mother, her references to her son had been warm. *Normal,* was Klinger's thought about it.

"You've talked to him, haven't you?" Carole asked.

"Sure," Klinger nodded.

"Then you know how remote he is," she declared. "Well, when he gets with his parents and brother, 'remote' isn't the word. He disappears. He says practically nothing. I can't remember him ever directly saying anything to his father. If he discusses the weather with his brother, it's big news."

"What's his family like?"

"His father is kind of a classic, confused son of an immigrant," Carole answered slowly, clearly recalling ancient encounters with her ex-husband's family. "When I knew them, he was still working. I don't know if he's retired now or what. Had a small plumbing business that Mike's brother went into. Out in Barrington, they're probably doing pretty well. Rehabs and new construction, if they're getting the jobs. That's the main thing Mike's father and brother talked about. Work. Jobs they were doing. His mother is deferential to a fault, but she's a warm person. Even with her, Mike had barely two words." She frowned. "It was like he was stuck in one place without any ideas about moving along."

To keep her talking, Klinger protested, "He's successful in his work, though."

"That depends on how you define 'success.' Mike's very intelligent, and he's willing to work like a mule." She paused and leaned back in her chair. "Do you know much about advertising and marketing, Detective Klinger?" When he shook his head, she continued, "Well, it's a cutthroat world for ambitious people, lives down to the usual stereotype. But plenty of smart, creative people can cruise along, advancing slowly, for years."

"You mean that's the case for Pollitz?"

"Basically," she said, nodding. "With his brains, he could be doing a lot more than he is."

Klinger thought about it, and when she added nothing more, he changed subjects. "What did you think of John Calabria?"

"He's warm enough," she answered. "He and Mike acted

like 'pals,' if you know what I mean. In a word, I'd call John a 'follower,' someone who needs to follow another person's lead. That's the way he was with Mike."

"How do you mean?" Klinger asked, suddenly very tuned in, wondering about Michael's role in the Calabria family. "How was Pollitz taking the lead with John Calabria?"

"I mean in the way that groups of friends sometimes have a leader, and sometimes other guys in the group are followers," Carole answered, missing Klinger's line of thought. "It wasn't anything significant."

"Was it something Pollitz needed?"

"No, it was just the basic nature of their relationship. Mike took the lead."

"That don't sound much like John Calabria to me," Klinger said.

"No? Well, I scarcely knew him," Carole replied. "John was loud. 'Boisterous' would be an accurate word. He got on my nerves, to be honest."

"It's a different sort of background," Klinger began, guessing accurately that John Calabria had probably been too unrefined for his old friend's wife.

"I didn't say 'uneducated'or 'ignorant,' even though both apply," she interjected, "and as far as different backgrounds go, mine wasn't that far away from Mike's. My dad was an electrician. He wasn't a first-generation tradesman, but he wasn't a college dean, either. I shouldn't have said John got on my nerves. It wasn't a personal thing. It was that whole milieu. The whole scene made me nervous. Some of those guys are scary. No joke. Their eyes have that matte finish of brutal stupidity." Carole shuddered dramatically.

"Hey, I like that expression. 'Matte finish of brutal stupidity.' I'll have to remember that one. That's good." He shifted his shoulders with pleasure. "Describes ninety percent of the guys I arrest."

Carole smiled and shrugged slightly. "Glad you like it, but I can't claim credit. That was one of Mike's phrases. It's a good line."

"Something he said a lot?"

"Never inaccurately."

Klinger thought about it. The phrase could never be used to describe her eyes. "I thought you didn't see much of the Calabrias."

"I saw more of them than I ever wanted to, you can be sure," she laughed. "Mike saw them more than I did. But it didn't take a lot of contact to know what those people are like, if you know what I mean."

"How about Dominick Calabria? Did you have enough contact with him to get an impression?"

"Not really. Chain smoker, or he was when I saw him. I was there only, say, three times, but one really clear memory is the stink of cigarettes on my clothes." Carole paused in thought. "He's a handsome man. He behaved in a courtly way." She shook her head. "I really couldn't say. I mean, I don't have an impression of him. In a way, I was intrigued by him. I mean, I'd never known any mobsters, so I found him interesting, you know? A different world. Kind of frightening. Intriguing at first, but that wears off pretty quickly." Klinger nodded encouragingly. Carole gave it some more thought. "Well, one impression stayed with me. He had a pretty strong air of authority."

"What do you mean by that?"

"Well, the men that were sometimes around, and John, they basically jumped whenever he snapped his fingers. I don't mean that literally," she chuckled. "But you know what I mean."

"How did Pollitz act around him?"

"Very respectfully, but pretty much the same as he is with everyone. Actually, he was more open with the Calabrias than with his own parents, in my opinion. At least he would converse."

"Lemme ask what might be a dumb question," Klinger interrupted. "In your opinion, could Michael Pollitz have murdered the men who attacked him?"

"*I* could have," she replied with a brittle laugh. "But I have a hard time imagining Mike ever getting motivated enough." She thought about it for a moment and softened visibly. "Listen. I didn't know him then, so I couldn't answer that question. But unless he was very different, completely unlike the man I knew, I don't see him responding directly." Carole shook her head. "I'm not expressing myself very clearly," she added with another self-conscious shrug. "Maybe 'unmanned' is the right word for the way Mike is. I just can't see him killing anyone."

Klinger surprised himself with a strong reaction to the sexist phrasing. He had dealt with enough assault victims in his career to know that what happened was dehumanization, a loss of self that had nothing to do with sexual identity. "Is it 'manly' to kill someone?" he blurted, immediately regretting the sharpness creeping into his voice.

"Oh, no. That's not what I meant. Sorry. Not at all. I was referring to the way he is." Carole shook her head and smiled briefly. "Actually, I don't think Michael would hurt a fly." She laughed. "I mean that literally. He used to catch moths in our apartment and let them go outside."

Klinger snorted with amusement. "What's so odd about that?"

"Don't tell me you do it too."

"No, I'm not that kindhearted," Klinger chuckled. "My ex-wife used to do the same. She didn't like to set mousetraps."

"Same with Mike. We even fought about it."

"What? He didn't object to mice in the house?"

"He said mice have a right to live too," Carole laughed. She shivered with amused disgust.

"Sure, but not underfoot," Klinger said, shaking his head.

"That's how I felt about it."

Klinger sat in thought for a moment. Carole glanced again at her watch. Finally, Klinger mused, "A lotta times, a person can be gentle with animals but have a different attitude about people, you follow?"

Carole nodded in agreement, but then shook her head with a small frown. "In Mike's case, I'd say it applied either way." She smiled softly, the rueful cast of her face breathtakingly lovely to Klinger. "Our marriage didn't work," she said, "but I would never say Mike wasn't gentle or kind. He is both those things."

Klinger doodled on his note pad, pretending to make notes. "How about the Calabrias? Could Pollitz have asked them to kill his assailants?"

"Why? Did they kill them?"

"I don't know."

"I didn't know Mike then, so I have no idea if he asked them to or not. But from what I saw of the Calabrias," she declared, "they are capable of anything."

32

"You gotta hear this," Klinger announced, breathless from chasing Whittaker down the long hallway leading to the elevators in the Criminal Courts building. The tall attorney looked alarmed at the sheen of sweat on Klinger's face.

"What's so urgent?" Whittaker asked.

"I got a copy of some Feeb surveillance on Marbles Soto."

"Yeah?" Whittaker said slowly, finally stopping to face Klinger.

"Yeah, Angie DeMicco's right hand got into it with Pollitz and John Calabria. Least, that's what it sounds like to me. But you gotta lissen."

"All right," Whittaker answered. "Let's go to my office."

As they walked, Klinger fumbled with a small tape player.

"I don't want to give the wrong impression, Dan. There's nothing huge or incriminating on this."

"Then why does it matter?"

"How would you put it? It provides insight, my man. Insight."

"How'd you get it?"

"I asked my guy over there for anything they might have recently regarding Dom or John Calabria. He said they had an incident involving John and Soto that didn't seem to be much, but I could have it if I wanted it. So here we are."

Klinger followed Whittaker into the office and sat in front of the desk, setting the tape player on Whittaker's blotter while the prosecutor hung his coat in the closet. "You know," Klinger observed, "that's why pants on a suit wear out way the hell ahead of the coat, 'cause you hang up the coat but keep wearing the pants."

"The pants never wear out while the suit's still in style," Whittaker answered.

"It's why I wear sports coats," Klinger continued. "I can replace the pants and still look sharp."

Whittaker stared in disbelief, but Klinger busied himself with the tape player. "When was this tape made?" Whittaker asked, dropping the fashion discussion.

"Just a couple a weeks ago."

"Why are the Feebs surveilling Sam Soto?"

"Why would they ever *stop* surveilling Marbles?" Klinger answered. "I don't know the specifics here. Does it matter?"

When Whittaker shook his head, Klinger punched the 'play' button. Club noises rattled across the desk, a cacophony of background voices, glasses and blasting music. Then they heard a growling male voice, "Give it a fuckin' rest, will you?" The voice was indistinct against the mass of sound in the background, but it was clear.

"That's John Calabria," Klinger said.

"Where is this taking place?" Whittaker asked, rolling the

sleeves of his shirt as Klinger stopped the player.

"This is at that strip club Marbles runs up in Half Day. John Calabria took Pollitz there for some reason, probably to get him laid, and Pollitz and Calabria got into it with Marbles. Angie DeMicco's there too. Those Feds have incredible equipment—you can hear just about everything. Amazing. Lissen up." He hit the 'play' button again and leaned back in his chair.

"Fuck you 'a rest'," a voice snarled back.

"That's Soto," Klinger said, and Whittaker nodded.

"Fuck the both of you," Marbles emphasized, *fuck da boat' a youse.* "This prick's hanging out with a gang crimes motherfucker now? And I'm s'posed to give it a rest?"

"Hey!" Klinger crowed, mimicking Bozo, "that's me!"

On the tape, another voice said, "Eat shit, Marbles," distorted and almost unintelligible, but unmistakable on a careful listening.

"That's Pollitz!" Klinger announced, punching the 'stop' button.

"Wait a minute," Whittaker said with a start. "Pollitz is picking a fight with Soto?"

"You got it!" Klinger beamed.

"Jesus!"

"Yeah! Kinda casts him in a different light, don't it?" Klinger hit the 'play' button again, and the office filled with raging profanity from Marbles.

"What the fuck! Who the fuck... 'eat shit?' I'll cut out your motherfuckin' tongue, you fucking loudmouth smartass piece a shit!" Crashing sounds came from the tape, John Calabria's voice bellowing inarticulately, then Marbles again, "Who the fuck you think you're talkin' to, huh? Who the fuck? You don't tell me to eat shit, asshole. I tell *you* to eat shit!" More crashing sounds erupted, as if Marbles was shoving a table out of the way and plates or glasses were falling.

"Articulate guys," Klinger observed, chuckling.

"I'll say whatever the hell I want," Michael's voice carried through the background noise.

"You ain't touching nobody," John Calabria shouted.

A deep, gravelly voice suddenly interrupted, "What the fuck?"

Whittaker asked, "Is that DeMicco?"

"Yeah," Klinger answered. The noise on the tape lessened, although shouting voices that sounded like Calabria and Soto continued.

"Get outta here," DeMicco said calmly, and more clattering was followed by Soto shouting.

"You better split, you piece a shit!" he screamed. Similar threats continued, sounding particularly childish from the tinny speaker on the handheld tape player. It went on for a minute or more, interspersed with DeMicco telling the younger thug to relax, take it easy, don't get so worked up. Finally, the tone calmed a little.

"Here's an interesting bit," Klinger announced.

"I'll cut that loudmouth smartass a new asshole!" Soto crowed. "Little fuck thinks he's a hardass now?"

"Take it easy," DeMicco repeated. "And don't get into it. Mike's a shitload tougher than you think."

"Bullshit."

"A shitload tougher than you think. I know. Just forget about it."

"He don't come in here and tell me to eat shit!"

"He was out of line, and I'll talk to him." *I'll tawk to 'im.* The tape went on in that vein, and Whittaker waved a hand.

"Interesting, no?" Klinger asked as he rewound the tape.

Whittaker nodded. "What do you think DeMicco's alluding to?"

"I'd love to know. Maybe just a general thing."

"It sounds kind of specific," Whittaker mused, holding the tips of his fingers together and staring at the ceiling. "This tape makes things a little muddy," he added.

"Maybe yes, maybe no. Who can say?"

"That's true," Whittaker said abruptly, as if things were final. "There was probably booze involved. It's probably nothing. But maybe we have another angle here."

"Yeah," Klinger answered, but his voice trailed off dubiously.

"Well, why'd you share this tape?"

"I think it shows us something about Pollitz that we didn't know."

"You mean you think he might have done the killings himself? Or played a part in them? You think that's what DeMicco's referring to?"

Klinger raised his round shoulders and answered, "Only if Pollitz is the best liar I've ever met. But I've said that before."

33

Michael stepped through the revolving door of his office building and sniffed gladly in the early June warmth. He had spent the afternoon watching the light change on the buildings of the Loop, and he yawned in the shadows of the street. He glanced around and was surprised to see Klinger's rotund form charging through the crowds on the sidewalk. The detective beamed and waved.

"Lemme buy you a beer," he said as he neared.

"I don't drink," Michael said. He smiled when the detective did a doubletake.

"You know," Klinger said after a long pause, "that's the first time you've clearly lied to me."

Michael laughed and almost placed his hand on Klinger's

shoulder. He shifted smoothly into an expansive gesture northward along the street. "Let's go. There's a nice bar on the next corner."

They walked up Clark Street in the early-evening sun. "Days like today," Michael said, "it's real easy to love this city. Just beautiful today."

"Yeah," Klinger agreed. "Except for when I was in the Marines, I've never lived anywhere else." He smiled and scanned the street. "Why would I want to?" He didn't mention that their views of the city were undoubtedly different—what Klinger saw, even in a benign block like the one they were walking, was a collection of past crime scenes.

Michael inhaled deeply through his nose and grinned. "I guess a lot of it rings different bells for a police officer, though," he said. "Especially a detective."

"What, are you a clairvoyant?" Klinger asked. Michael's face closed in bafflement. "I was just thinking exactly that," Klinger explained as they turned into the bar. The tavern occupied a corner. It had wide windows facing the street and a wood bar extending most of the long, narrow room's length. Klinger looked around with a satisfied smile. "You got good taste," he said.

"What do you mean?"

"This place, that restaurant we went to, they're nice. Unpretentious."

"You mean, no ferns?"

"Yeah!" Klinger was happy. "But it ain't a shot-and-a-beer alky joint, either." He sniffed. "At least, it don't smell like it." He nodded with his thick lower lip pushed over his upper lip, an approving frown. "This is nice," he announced. "Lemme order a couple. What kinda beer do you like?"

"Cold," Michael answered. Klinger grinned as the younger man moved to a pair of stools at the counter against the windows. Michael was watching an attractive young woman walk by, and Klinger grunted his appreciation as he placed a pint of beer on the counter. Michael nodded his thanks and raised the glass. Both men drank, then Michael asked, "To what do I owe the pleasure, Larry?" He eyed the detective guardedly.

Klinger smacked his lips. "Well, I kinda wanted to apologize for hard-timing you the other day."

"No umbrage taken."

"No what taken?"

"Don't play dumb."

Klinger chuckled and hoisted his glass. "I also figured I should tell you I talked to your ex this afternoon, in case she calls you."

"Oh, wonderful," Michael groaned. "That's just splendid."

Klinger pretended to concentrate on his beer.

Michael wiped his lips and shook his head slowly. "Great. Let me guess," he said sarcastically. "She gave me a glowing character reference."

Klinger shrugged. "She's a beautiful woman," he said for lack of anything better. In his experience, few divorced couples spoke of one another in friendly terms.

"That she is," Michael agreed. "I haven't seen her in a couple of years, but the last time I did, she was even prettier than when we were married." He sipped some beer and looked away, then he asked, "How pissed off was she about me? Was she harsh?"

Kliner said, "Not at all. She was pretty thoughtful."

"Carole's actually okay," Michael said, sounding relieved. When Klinger said nothing, Michael gave in to an odd urge to explain. "She's sometimes disappointed about me because our life didn't turn out the way she wanted it to. She's really a pretty likable person." He stretched and rubbed the back of his neck. "And she went on to have what she wanted."

"Who filed for divorce?" Klinger asked, already sure of the answer.

"She did," Michael replied. "Isn't that obvious?" He laughed at Klinger's smile. "I probably would have just gone on," he added.

"She says you have no friends," Klinger interrupted.

Michael laughed again. "That's putting it kind of strong," he said, "but I guess it's not entirely inaccurate."

"Really? You seem like you get along with people."

"Sure." Michael sipped beer.

"No drinking buddies or college pals, huh?"

Michael frowned and shook his head slightly, unperturbed. "No, not really," he said. "I mean, I go out with people, but there isn't any regular circle. Why? What difference does it make?"

"None," Klinger answered, his pint at his lips. "I was just curious. Me, I don't hang around with anyone, either. See, everyone thinks there's this close-knit fraternity of cops, which is true a lotta times. Mosta the time. But it ain't the case for me. Maybe I'm just getting old." He rubbed his nose thoughtfully and chewed on his lower lip. He drank a little more. "Your ex, she also says John Calabria got on her nerves."

Michael gagged and coughed on beer when he started laughing. Klinger smiled. "Is that all she said?" Michael sputtered. "She was holding back."

"Actually, I expected something a lot worse."

Michael boomed out a full laugh, the first genuine expression of mirth Klinger had seen on his face.

"I take it she didn't care for your old pals," Klinger said.

"You should have seen her face after our wedding," Michael said, almost choking. "Angie DeMicco comes swaggering over, that big scar on his face, and wants to plant one on her cheek. I thought her mother was going to faint!" He decided not to mention DeMicco's recent heart attack, even though he guessed Klinger would find the story amusing.

Klinger chuckled as he imagined the scene. In his mind, Angelo DeMicco was every bit as brutal as he looked. "Wasn't Dom offended when he wasn't invited to the reception?"

"How do you know about that?"

"Your ex told me." Klinger raised his eyebrows.

"Maybe he was, a little," Michael answered. "He probably

felt vindicated when my marriage broke up."

"I thought you said John Calabria stood up for you."

"He did," Michael answered, but he shook his head. "Come on, Larry. Let's not talk about the Calabrias."

Klinger shrugged. "Okay by me," he answered, lifting his empty glass from the counter. "I'm gonna get some pretzels. You want anything?" Michael shook his head and watched passers-by through the window while Klinger stepped away, waving at the bartender. He returned to his stool, crunching pleasurably, and set down two new beers. He offered the bag. Michael held up his hand to decline.

"So," Klinger said at last. "You never see your ex-wife?"

Michael shook his head with a frown. "Not often. Our paths never cross."

"But you're in the same line of work."

"I don't go to any organized things," Michael said simply. "Do you see your ex?"

"Occasionally," Klinger replied. "Fact, I just saw her last month. We happened to visit Mattie's grave at the same time, on his birthday."

"That's such a shame," Michael muttered. He took another drink.

"Yeah," Klinger agreed. "But shit happens. That's life."

Michael couldn't tell if the remark was macho coptalk or sincere. "So what ruined your marriage?" he asked. "The job?"

"I don't think the job had much to do with it," Klinger answered. "Maybe it played a part, I dunno. After the accident, we had trouble bein' together for some reason. We split up about two years after." He gulped from his beer and finished the pretzels, crushing the cellophane in his hand. "Marie remarried, like in 1980 or so. Nice guy. Now, she tells me they got two grandkids, couple a little girls," he added almost wistfully. "Guess '72 was a pretty bad year for her, too." He shrugged and gazed through the window. Michael sipped some more beer without responding.

"Tell me," Klinger said with a thoughtful pause. "Those guys, McVee, Jackson and Andrews. Do you think they deserved to die for what they did to you? I mean, granted, it was a terrible thing to do. But did they deserve to die for it?"

"I don't know," Michael said slowly. He stared through the window for a moment. "Does anybody 'deserve' to be killed for anything? I don't know. It certainly doesn't bother me that they're dead. At the time, I would've wanted them killed, yeah." He glanced at Klinger. "That's kind of a crazy question, Larry, since you think I had something to do with it."

"Forget the investigation for a minute."

"That's not really possible." Michael took another drink.

"I hear you. But I mean the question as a philosophical hypothetical, you follow?" He drained his glass.

"Hypothetically?" Michael said. "Let me give you a hypothetical in return, then. You get along with your ex-wife, don't you? I mean, it sounds like it."

"Sure. She's a good soul," Klinger answered.

"You have any sisters?"

"As a matter of fact, I have two."

"Okay," Michael said. "Then let me ask you, hypothetically, if three men beat your ex-wife or one of your sisters like I got beat up, and then they raped her, would you want to kill those men?" He stared at Klinger's face. "You carry a gun, Larry. Would you have wanted to use it on them? Or, as a police officer, would you want to uphold the law?" Klinger said nothing. "Which would it be, hypothetically? Would you want to kill them yourself?"

"I dunno," Klinger answered at last.

"Ignore the personal part of it, then," Michael said, "and keep it strictly hypothetical. The men that did something like that to your ex or your sister, or your girlfriend, if you have one, would they 'deserve' to die, in your mind?"

"You know why that ain't a death-penalty crime?" Klinger replied. "Because the victim's still alive. The victim can recover."

"Have you ever handled rape cases?"

"I spent some time in violent crimes," Klinger answered, knowing the point Michael intended to make.

"How many of the victims 'recovered,' in the sense that you'd recover from a broken wrist or an appendix operation?"

"I really never did any of the followup interviews with the victims."

Michael stared, annoyed. "Well, let me guess. I'd give long odds that the percentage is too low to show up. In my business, we'd call it statistically insignificant."

"Could be," Klinger nodded. "But they have the opportunity. They can work on it." He sipped beer.

"Let me rephrase this," Michael said with rising anger. "Three guys really work over your ex. I mean, they really work her over. They break her jaw. But one of the guys jams his cock in her mouth anyway. I mean, if he's trying for a blowjob, it's hopeless. Her jaw won't work. But he's getting off on the cruelty of it, and he does it anyway, even though he finally has to beat off onto her, because her mouth's useless. Meanwhile, another guy's raping her from behind and pounding on her kidneys too. These three pieces of shit are laughing it up. It's a blast for them. They leave her unconscious. I'd say they leave her for dead, but they'd be very unhappy if she died. They want her to have to live with what they've done to her." Michael realized he was ranting and paused to regain control. He inhaled deeply. "If those guys turned up dead, would you be sorry? Or would you think justice was done?"

Klinger flashed across too many encounters with victims, almost unconsciously reliving a sympathetic understanding of the rapid-fire sequence the attacked person lived through, not unlike the savage intensity of combat—the burst of resistance, the descent into a despairing fear that made a person willing to do anything, anything at all, to survive a single moment in the hope of seeing the next moment, and finally, when the pain and outrage reached a certain level, a numb shock that desired nothing more than that the pain and outrage would end, even if dying was the only way for it to stop—his mind faintly echoing the voices of battle comrades crying for their mothers in Ia Drang. "This reminds me of a thought that came to me while I was talking with your ex," he muttered.

"Fabulous. Like I always say, the absurd non sequitur is never out of place."

"Ahh, don't be a prick," Klinger grumbled. "I was just thinking out loud. Calm down, for Pete's sake. Here's what I say. I say, there's a big difference between vengeance and justice."

"You're avoiding the question."

"Am I?"

"I think so." Michael finished his beer and stood. "Let me get this round." He stepped away to the bar and ordered two more pints. When he returned, he said, "So, Larry, you never answered my question. Three men rape and beat your ex so badly she ends up in the hospital for a month. Hypothetically, would you want the men dead?"

"It sounds to me like you think the death penalty should be expanded."

"Really? I don't. I don't believe in the death penalty."

"Huh?" Klinger sputtered. "You sure sound like it. I mean, if the guys who attacked you deserved to die..."

Michael interrupted. "I didn't say I thought they deserved to die, only that I would have wanted them dead."

"Oh, don't play semantic games about whether or not people should be killed," Klinger said. He slurped some beer.

"Why not?" Michael laughed. "You won't answer my question."

"I have answered your question. Murder's murder, is my opinion. And rape isn't punishable by death. Maybe you oughta campaign to get the law changed."

"To what? I already told you I'm against the death penalty." Klinger shook his head. "I don't think the state should have power over life and death," Michael explained.

"But you think it's okay for people to be killed? Individuals should decide who lives and who dies?"

"No, that's not what I'm saying. I think some victims of some crimes may want to kill the perpetrators."

"What happens if they do?"

"Then they accept the consequences of having committed a crime themselves." Michael shrugged.

"Assuming they get caught," Klinger said quickly. "Otherwise, they aren't accepting any consequences."

"Sure they are."

"Like what?" Klinger snorted.

"Guilt. A different sense of themselves. I don't think there are all that many people who can kill someone and just never think about it again."

"Oh, I've met my share," Klinger replied. "You're playing a philosophical game in your head," he argued. "There's plenty a scumbags out there who can kill a human being as easily as you'd slap a mosquito, believe me. You know a few of them." When Michael started to protest, Klinger raised one hand. "Don't pretend you're completely naïve about what kinda guys work for Dom Calabria, okay?"

Anger flashed across Michael's face. "I don't have any illusions about that," he snapped.

"So what's with this cockamamie business about individuals deciding when someone oughta be killed?" Klinger said, diverting the line of speculation. Michael shrugged, still stuck on the Outfit. "I mean," Klinger went on, apparently oblivious, "some guys think keying their Jaguar should be punishable by death." He sucked down a little more beer. "You know that old eye-for-an-eye stuff? A lotta people think that was setting the penalties for crimes, but it wasn't. That was an attempt to *limit* vengeance, so no *more* than an eye for an eye, a tooth for a tooth, or a life for a life would be taken. You follow? What you're talking about is pure anarchy. Blood feuds. That's the kind of shit that happens with the gangbangers. That's why we got laws and police officers."

"I had no idea you were such a philosopher, Larry."

Klinger raised his glass. "I'm not. I'm practical. You wanna know something else that'll probably surprise you? I'm no big supporter of the death penalty either."

"You're an unusual cop."

"It ain't 'cause I care about killing some a these shitheads, so don't get the wrong idea. I don't have any problem with capital punishment in the way you do."

"No? Then what's your reason?" Michael peered across the rim of his glass.

"Simple. Two reasons. First, if we're wrong once, that's too many times. Second, and even simpler. It ain't working." When Michael raised an eyebrow, Klinger added, "The chuckleheads are still killing each other, the death penalty notwithstanding."

"I understand there's a pragmatic argument," Michael replied, "that it costs more to execute someone than lock them away forever and all that, but I think it evades the question. Should the state have the power to kill someone? I don't think so. And a guy who thinks vandalizing his car should get the death penalty, would he actually pull the trigger on someone over it? Not a chance."

"You don't know the same guys I do," Klinger laughed. "You want another one?"

"No, thanks. I've got to drive out to the suburbs tonight." Michael stood, and Klinger joined him. They walked slowly to the door.

"You on your way to your parents'?" Klinger asked, smiling to himself. This was another small test, conducted mainly for his own amusement; he knew about DeMicco's heart attack and wondered how Michael would answer.

"I may stop over," Michael said, "but I've got to drop by a hospital first." Michael spread his arms in the June evening. "Angie DeMicco had a heart attack." He shifted from his yawning stretch into a mildly embarrassed shrug. "He's no particular friend, but I've known him since I was a kid," he explained. "Well, it's been a pleasure, Larry."

"Lemme give you a lift home," Klinger said with a pleased smile, gesturing south on Clark Street toward his car. He glanced around and noticed a new Lincoln Town Car with smoked windows across the street, about eighty yards away in a no-parking zone. The rounded bulk of a large man was dimly silhouetted behind the wheel. Klinger's eyes narrowed slightly.

"That isn't necessary," Michael replied. "Why don't you walk down to the subway with me?"

"You know, I really don't get you," Klinger blurted as he fell in step with the younger man.

"What do you mean?"

"You're going to visit DeMicco? It surprises me. I mean, here you are, you seem like a good guy, but you got me shoving in, curious, yet you're hanging around with the bad guys." He paused and stared at Michael for a moment. "I mean, as far as what you were saying about the death penalty is concerned, a guy like DeMicco, he doesn't feel any regrets, believe me. Like, the year in question for you, 1972, right? There was a guy named Epstein that they had a beef with. You know what happened to this guy? Someone put a chain around his chin and attached it to a car. They pulled his head off. That's what your old pals do! And when they decide someone oughta die, it's for what? Just some money, usually."

"Oh, I'd say their egos are probably in it too," Michael said softly, looking away at the slanting glow of late sunlight on the tops of buildings. He turned to face Klinger. "Look, Larry, I know what kind of men they are. But you need to understand. I've known these guys since I was in fourth grade. They've all—Dom, Sal, Angie, almost all of the others—all of them were always extremely kind to me. They're rough men, but they always treated me with warmth." He moved his hands in the air, for some reason unable to articulate the familiar comfort of his fond childhood memories. "It's like they're family, like uncles. You know what I mean?" He started walking again and didn't notice Klinger's nod. "Dom wanted to lend me the money for my college tuition," Michael went on, "and I don't think he meant it as a loan that needed to be repaid."

"Why was that?"

Michael stopped again. "You want the truth? I think he was proud of me." Michael laughed softly, self-conscious.

"Why didn't he help you out, back in 1972?"

"He wanted to. He even offered to pay for the lawyer."

"Why didn't you take him up on it?"

"My father wouldn't hear of it." Michael shook his head. "And I decided not to humiliate him by ignoring his opinion." Michael shrugged again, his lips pursed in a wry, unhappy smile.

"I take it you think that was a mistake."

"Absolutely."

"Why? You were what? Nineteen? What was wrong with being respectful to your father?"

"It changed everything. Nothing was the same again after Astoria. I made a mistake that changed everything."

"Which mistake? Listening to your father or helping some agents buy drugs?"

Michael made a clucking noise with his tongue and stared. "Take your pick," he answered at last. "The result's the same, either way." He extended his hand. "I've got to go," he said briskly. "Thanks for the beers. Let's do it again sometime when I'm not under investigation, okay?" He turned and jogged down the stairs to the subway platform.

Klinger waited until Michael had descended into the station, then fumbled his notebook from his jacket pocket to jot down the Lincoln's license number.

34

"I ain't talked with Dom about this yet," DeMicco said, "but I'm gonna retire. It's time for me to take it easy. I'm thinking of moving to Florida, once I get this bullshit over with." He paused to catch his breath. "Yvonne likes Fort Myers. Maybe we'll get a nice place where the kids can come and visit."

"Sounds good to me," Michael answered. He'd been in the hospital room for only fifteen minutes, but the smell was bothering him. The tubes and wires attached to the old man made him look smaller and weaker, completely unlike himself. The scar on his wrinkled cheek seemed more vivid against the pale yellowish tint everyone seems to acquire in a hospital. Michael didn't have enough experience of illness to know if Angie's pallor was from the heart attack or something else.

"I gotta tell you something too. You gotta 'pologize to Marbles. You insulted him in his own place, and that ain't right."

"Apologize?"

"Yeah. Drive over there sometime soon. No use getting bad blood there, 'specially now."

"You mean now that you're retiring?" Michael watched DeMicco's eyes lose focus.

"Yeah, I think that's what I'm gonna do." DeMicco closed his eyes. "Thanks for stopping by," he added.

Michael took the hint. He stood and leaned across the bed

to kiss the old man's forehead. He patted DeMicco's arm.

"Mikey," DeMicco rasped, wrapping his large old hand around Michael's wrist. "Don't never do nothin' against Dom. You hear me?"

Michael put his hand over DeMicco's and stared down into his eyes. "I would never do anything to harm any of you, Angie," he said softly. "Never."

DeMicco's chest heaved as he drew oxygen through the nasal tube. He tightened his grip on Michael's wrist, but the intensity in his eyes softened. "That's good, Mikey," he whispered. "You make sure Dom and Sal know that too."

Michael felt alarm rising in his throat but masked his nervousness. "I'm sure they know, Angie," he said. "But I'm going to John's restaurant now." He smiled. "You think I should tell them?"

"Just don't ever go against him, Mikey," DeMicco whispered again, his eyes fluttering closed. "It would break his heart."

"I won't, Angie. I couldn't. That's a promise."

"I know it, Mikey," DeMicco murmured without opening his eyes. "You always been a good kid. Smart. We was always so high on how smart you was."

"Thanks, Angie." Michael leaned forward to kiss DeMicco's forehead again, then squeezed his hand softly before he left to drive north to John's restaurant.

As he walked into the restaurant, Michael saw Sal standing at the bar with three or four thugs. He recognized one of the men. He grinned and waved. Bruno gestured and called out, "Mikey! C'mere!" His smile seemed too wide, and his eyes were flat as Michael crossed the room. Michael embraced him, as always impressed that a man Sal's age had such power in his arms. Bruno shook him from side to side and cuffed his head.

"Christ, Sal!"

"Good to see you. You're lookin' good, kid," he rasped. He studied Michael's face, then glanced over his shoulder. "You know these guys," he extended an arm. "Duke, Jimmy, you ever meet these douche bags?" *Dese doosh begs.* Michael shook hands with the men, nodding to those he had met before. They were all near his age. None smiled. "You doin' OK? You look good," Sal repeated. "How's the job?"

"Dumb, as always," Mchael laughed.

"Still doin' OK?"

"I'm fine," Michael answered. "I'd be better if I didn't have this bullshit with the cops, but otherwise, just fine."

"Ahh, it's just bullshit. Forget about it."

"How've you been keeping yourself, Sal?"

"You know me, kid, same old shit."

"I just saw Angie."

"Yeah? I was there this afternoon. Looks OK, huh?"

"For a guy in the hospital."

"Hey! Angie's doin' fine. Gonna be OK," Bruno grumbled, frowning.

"You watch yourself, Sal. Get yourself too far over three hundred pounds, you might be there with him," Michael smiled.

"Hey! When I want your health advice, I'll ast ya for it, OK, Mikey?" He slapped with a paw. Michael ducked away, smiling. "Hey, Mikey, Dom's in the back room with John. Go on, go on."

In the smaller room, Dom sat with John at one of the corner banquettes. Dom smiled and watched him cross the room. John jumped up to hug him. Michael leaned across the table to take Dom's hand and kiss his cheek.

"I just came from Angie," Michael said.

"I'm sure he was glad of the visit," Dom replied. "How was he?"

"Tired, a little worn down. But he seemed pretty good."

"Yvonne wasn't there?"

"No. I guess she was getting some dinner or something."

Dom nodded, seeming a little distracted. He coughed softly and reached for a cigarette. "Looks like he'll pull through," he said after his cigarette was lit. He chuckled.

"Let me get some food," John said. "Whaddya want, Mikey?"

"Anything that's good tonight."

"You got it. Lemme get some calamari to start. You want some, Dad?"

Dom shook his head slightly. He sipped some water, then picked up a glass of wine. He tipped his head toward Michael. The younger man poured a glass. "To Angie," Michael said. Dom nodded. Michael set down his glass and asked, "How's the family?"

"Everyone's good. John's brothers are planning to visit at Christmas. Nina's girls, they're getting straight A's in school." He smiled. "You should see her second. What a beauty."

"Like her mother."

"Like her *grand*mother."

Michael grinned. "I hope to see everyone sometime soon."

"That would please Toni."

"Give her my love, would you?"

"She asked me to remember her to you tonight."

"Tell her I think about her all the time."

"I'll do that."

A platter of fried squid arrived. John shoveled a mound onto his plate and squeezed lemon over it. "Have some, man," he said, gesturing toward the plate. "It's really good." He jammed a mass of tentacles into his mouth. "The *osso bucco* I got comin'," he slopped out around the food, "it'll blow your mind."

Michael took a few pieces of calamari and slid the platter toward Dom. The older man shook his head. "This Klinger, he's staying after me," Michael said.

Dom raised an eyebrow. "I didn't think he was going to evaporate." He ground out his cigarette and winced as he shifted position.

"What's wrong?"

"Got a pain," Dom said, rubbing his fingertips along his ribs on the right side of his torso. John looked up, worry furrowing his fleshy face. Dom shifted his shoulders and lifted his glass of wine. "Forget it. What's Klinger want?"

"You," Michael said.

Dom grinned, genuinely for the first time, his dark eyes glittering as he stared across the table. "Anybody who doesn't appreciate you, Mike," he said, his smile getting wider, "isn't paying attention."

Michael laughed.

"Anything specific?" Dom asked, reaching for another cigarette.

"Just those three guys, twenty years ago," Michael answered.

Dom stared across the table, his face blank except for the intense concentration of his eyes, almost black in the uncertain light of the restaurant. Without any way of knowing that Dom was simultaneously seeing an eight-year-old, a nineteen-year-old and an adult, Michael began to feel uncomfortable. Smoke drifted from Dom's nostrils. Finally, Michael said, "John said this state's attorney, Whittaker, tried to call you in."

Dom nodded slowly. "Can't imagine what the asshole was thinking," he said. Michael shrugged. "It's OK that you went and talked to him," Dom added.

"But you wouldn't," Michael said. He was feeling nervous and saying things he would never otherwise say.

"Of course not." Dom set his cigarette down for a moment as the main course was delivered. "Are you going to eat your salad?" he asked. When Michael shook his head, Dom picked up the plate. He lifted a fork and stared across the table. "Mike, we all know what we are. You. You don't like what you do. You think it's pointless, and you might be right. You do it to pay the bills. I am what I am. We all do what we need to. If this asshole Whittaker produces a subpoena, then he and I will talk. Otherwise, he can go back to promoting his career on someone else's back." He waited. Michael nodded. Both glanced toward the door when Sal Bruno's voice suddenly boomed out in laughter. Sal and a couple of the men from the bar stood in the back room's entrance, glasses in their hands. Sal glanced in and tipped his glass toward the table. Bruno seemed to focus his gaze on Michael. Dom stubbed out the smoldering cigarette. "So tell me, as much as you can remember, what these guys are trying for."

Michael spent a few minutes recounting, as exactly as he could, every conversation, but skipping the interlude in the bar. Dom said nothing as he ate, but he never removed his eyes from Michael's face. Finally he said again, "We all do what we have to." Then he coughed and grimaced, again reaching for his right side.

"Tell me what's wrong, Dom," Michael said, studying the older man's face.

Dom told him. Michael chewed his lip for a moment. "What was on the x-rays?" he asked at last. Dom repeated himself.

"Doctor's don't know everything," Dom said. Michael said nothing. "They think it might be pneumonia."

"Then you ought to be in bed."

Dom shrugged and tapped a fresh cigarette on the table.

John drummed his fingers and laughed softly. "Ain't it wild? Pneumonia's good news." He glanced at his father.

"Is that what's got Sal in a bad mood?" Michael asked.

"Is Sal in a bad mood?" Dom said, still staring levelly with his eyes expressionless.

"Seems like it," Michael muttered, looking through the entrance of the back room at Bruno. He smiled at Dom. "Well, I better get going."

"Why don't you just stay at the house?" John asked.

"Can't. I got an early day tomorrow," Michael answered. He stood and leaned around the table to hug Dom briefly. "You take care of that pneumonia, okay?"

"Sure."

Michael leaned in closer to clasp Dom's head. "Take care of yourself," he said, wanting to say, "I love you," but somehow unable to do so.

"I will, Mike." Dom answered.

Michael embraced John and again complimented the food. He waved to Sal as the large man lumbered toward their table. "Lose some weight, Sal," he said, grinning at the old bear. Sal shook his hand in the air, waving the comment away.

As he walked through the restaurant, Michael glanced into one of the mirrors on the walls of the back room and saw Dom and Sal studying him as he left. Outside, he tipped the valet and got into his Camry. He drove calmly out of the lot and south to Dundee Road, where he headed east to the expressways. As he swung south onto the Route 53 link to the Northwest Tollway and home, only ten minutes away from the restaurant, he suddenly banged the heel of his right hand on the steering wheel so violently that it vibrated softly in his left hand.

"Shit!" he spat out. "Shit!" He reached to turn on the radio and expelled air in a loud burst when he became aware that he was holding his breath.

35

What the hell? Klinger thought as he studied the pink message slip on his desk. What could Rich Taylor want? *He must have a bitch that's got to come out,* he decided. He picked up his phone and punched the retired guard's number.

"How's summer on the Illinois River?" Klinger asked after he identified himself.

"Beautiful," Taylor replied, but there was a weakness in his voice Klinger hadn't noticed before. "How is it in Chicago?"

"Same as usual," Klinger boomed. He pictured Taylor's tidy

home on the small lake. It was easy to imagine himself sitting in the evening heat on the patio where they'd met before. "Why'd you call, Rich?"

"Somethin's been gnawing at me ever since you were here, askin' your questions, couple months ago," the guard said slowly.

"What's that?"

"Well, I don't like to admit it, but I lied to you, back when you visited."

"Yeah? About what?" Klinger said, all innocence despite knowing exactly where Taylor was headed. *God bless an honest man,* he thought.

"About whether or not I knew about Jackson bein' killed, and whether or not I made the connection between that kid and Calabria and those bastards gettin' killed." He paused. Klinger waited patiently. "I made the connection as soon as I heard about McVee, so I paid attention to what became of Jackson and Andrews after they left Astoria. I'm sorry I denied it, Larry."

"Why're you telling me now?"

"I got my reasons," Taylor drawled. Klinger again waited him out. "Listen, there's a couple of things we didn't discuss," Taylor said at last. "First, I've got a serious liver problem right now. But that's not why I'm calling. Not tryin' to clear my conscience because I'm sick." He paused again. "I'm a recovering drunk, Larry. I was half in the bag for twenty years, didn't get clean until 1987." He stopped again.

"That's no business of mine," Klinger said.

"No, but that's not the point. I'm not trying to explain anything. What troubles me is, when I lied about 1972, I wasn't living like a good AA," Taylor said, a layer of relief entering his apologetic tone. "One of our principles is to be honest in all our affairs, and my dishonesty has been bothering me."

God bless you, Klinger thought again. "So what do you want to tell me?" he asked.

"Just that the truth is different from what I said. It's important to me that you know that."

"Why'd you hide it before?" Klinger asked.

"You mean, from you? The same reason I never told anybody I figured out the connection between McVee and Jackson's murders, back in 1973," he answered.

"You're saying you felt McVee and Jackson got what they deserved."

"Yes." Taylor's voice was flat.

"I have a hard time justifying murder under any circumstances," Klinger said, almost automatically.

"Back then, when I was a practicing drunk, I thought they earned their killings." Taylor paused to collect his thoughts. "I didn't know that kid at all, but I could see he was just a scared kid caught in something. I didn't mention it when you were to my house, but when I took that kid through orientation, I'll tell you, he could've been my son. I'm not joking. He reminded me of my boy, when he reported to the Selective Service office in 1969. Here's this young man, a child, really, scared out of his wits, and he's trying to be brave. What happened to him shouldn't happen to anyone. The cruelty of it. The brutality. And then, after it happens, he decides to tough it out. He won't say who done it to him. I'll tell you the truth, Larry, I wasn't alone in wanting to take care of McVee myself."

"What do you mean?"

"I mean, more than one guard talked about settin' fire to that piece of trash in his cell, you better believe."

"So more men than just you and Kranz could make the Calabria connection," Klinger said. "Did anyone act on it?"

"I'm not too sure anyone else came to the same conclusion as me."

"Why not?"

"I don't think anyone was really aware of Jackson's death, except me and one other guy. Plus Dick Kranz, I guess, but I surely didn't know that in 1973."

"Who was the other guy?"

"Just the guard who ran Calabria's plate, that I know of. He told McVee who picked the kid up that night."

"What was his name?"

"His name was Dennis Morrisey," Taylor answered. "But don't bother to write that down. He died in 1989."

Klinger smiled as he dropped his pen. "What did you think when Pollitz left Astoria?"

"I was as surprised as anyone when a Mafia bigshot picked him up. But I was glad when I heard it."

"Why's that?"

"Because it made me think there might be a payback for what happened to him."

Klinger thought for a moment. Finally, he said, "I take it you feel keeping quiet about your suppositions was the right thing to do."

"I thought it was at the time."

"You may be asked to testify. You understand that, don't you?"

"Yes," Taylor sighed. "And I will if I must. You should understand, though, that I didn't call you today because I have a guilty conscience about McVee."

"No?"

"I regret lying to you, because I have adopted a different way of life that has returned me to sanity," Taylor said. "But in my heart I am not sorry about what became of McVee and Jackson." Klinger grunted and shifted the handset to his other ear. He was familiar with the phrasing of AA and appreciated what Taylor was going through. "There's one other thing," Taylor continued. "You asked if I knew Pollitz had confronted McVee and Jackson, and I said no. It wasn't true. I was on the yard that day."

"Did you overhear their conversation?"

Klinger heard Taylor draw a long breath and release it with a soft cough. "I wasn't close enough," he answered.

"Was this other guard, Morrisey, also on the yard, like you?"

Klinger asked. "Did he see Pollitz talking to McVee and Jackson?"

After another pause, Taylor said, "Yes."

"And he was the one who learned Calabria had picked up Pollitz?" Taylor grunted in the affirmative. "How did Morrisey feel about McVee and Jackson?"

Taylor coughed again. "If Dennis was alive, I guess he'd be unhappy that I'm tellin' you this." He sighed softly. "But I told so many lies... I'm sorry I did, when you were here," he concluded, his voice weakening. "Dennis felt the same as I did. We felt justice had been done."

36

"Mother of God, I hate a hospital," Sal growled. "People die in these dumps."

Dom grunted. Walking across the parking lot and through the hospital had made him feel short of breath. The pain beneath his ribs was alternately alarming and a cause for fatalism. "Two of Nina's girls were born here," he said at last, smiling as he thought of his little granddaughters, not so little anymore.

"Yeah, I guess it goes both ways," Sal said. He was also short of breath. "Shit, Mikey's right. I gotta lose some weight." He yanked a handkerchief from his side pocket and paused in the hall outside DeMicco's room to wipe a light smear of sweat from his wide forehead. Dom pushed the door open. "Where the hell's Marbles?" Bruno muttered, glancing down the hall toward the nurses' station.

"Right here," came a rough voice from inside the room.

"Who gave you that stupid nickname?" Sal grumbled as he entered, squinting at a bulky man in his forties who stood near the windows.

"Your mother," the man replied. He pulled a comb from his pocket and slicked down his dark hair, then studied the comb's teeth and wiped it with his fingers. A diamond pinky ring glittered. He turned and closed the window shade against the glare of the sun as Dom crossed the room to kiss DeMicco's cheek.

"It's a stupid name," Sal repeated.

"Up yours, Sal," the man answered cheerfully. He leaned against the heater and grinned.

"Shut up, the both of you," Dom snapped. "How you doin', Angie?" He held DeMicco's hand and stared down into his face.

"Not bad," the old mobster answered. "There's a blond nurse, got tits you wouldn't believe. You see her?"

"That's all you need," Sal chuckled. He positioned his mass behind Dom and reached to squeeze DeMicco's knee with one hand.

"Mikey was here last night," DeMicco said.

"Yeah, we saw him," Dom answered. "He came by John's, said he'd been to see you."

"I told him I wanna retire," DeMicco rasped.

"He didn't mention it," Dom said.

DeMicco smiled crookedly. "That's 'cause I said I hadn't told you yet." He laughed and coughed for a few seconds. "Nice to know he didn't blab."

"What, you givin' Mikey tests now?" Sal asked with a smile.

"Why not?" DeMicco answered. "Why the fuck not? I don't wanna hafta worry about him."

"You think I should be worried?" Dom asked.

"Forget about it," DeMicco replied, his eyes at half-mast.

Dom glanced over his shoulder at Sal, then across the room at the younger man.

"I'm serious about retiring, Dom," Angie wheezed. He too

glanced at the younger man. "Like I said before. Think I'll take Yvonne to Fort Myers. If no one minds."

"I don't mind, Angie. But let's talk for a minute." Dom directed his attention away from the bed. "Give us a couple seconds, Marbles."

The younger man stood away from the windows, frowning. "I oughta be in on this," he said.

"You will be," Dom answered. "But I wanna talk to Angie." He stared. Marbles left the room.

"What's the matter, Dom?" Angie asked, once the door was closed. "You got a problem with Marbles?"

"No," Dom answered, sliding a chair next to the bed. "He's no problem." He sat and gestured for Bruno to sit as well. "I wanna talk about Mike."

37

"The thing is, I got a few doubts about this one," Klinger sighed. He set his fork next to his uneaten plate of spaghetti and stared up at the ceiling.

Dora glanced across the table, chewing thoughtfully and wondering how to respond. The antecedent for his remark was at least an hour old. "You often have doubts about an investigation," she said at last.

"Not like this." He flicked his eyes at his girlfriend and ran his thumbnail through the label on his empty beer bottle. He picked up his fork and toyed with his pasta.

"Either eat it or leave it alone, Larry," Dora said. She smiled when he dropped the fork into the plate. He fiddled with his water glass for a moment, frowning down at his food. "You want another beer?" He shook his head without looking up. Dora smiled again at his morose preoccupation. "Well, let's hear it," she said after a few seconds. "What's the problem?"

"It's odd," he began. "I'm not sure about what I'm doing here, with this Pollitz guy, you know?"

"What do you mean? Like you're on the wrong track? Missing something?"

"No, more like I'm not so sure I should be chasing after him at all."

Dora raised her eyebrows and frowned, then wiped her lips and dropped her napkin onto her plate. "You mean you think he's the wrong guy? You were so enthusiastic about this case."

Klinger shifted his weight back in his chair with a mournful shake of his head. He looked up. "No, I mean like maybe I oughta leave Mike alone."

Dora lifted her head with surprise, then crossed her arms across her chest. She tilted her head to one side, resting her chin on her left fist, her forehead wrinkled with puzzlement and concern. It was a characteristic expression of concentration that Klinger absolutely loved, like the way her flat nose flared and her entire body jiggled when she laughed. He smiled and shrugged.

"Are you saying you think he's innocent?" she asked.

"Lord!" He rolled his eyes toward the sink. "There's a tough word." He chewed his lip briefly. "Well, hang on. This one's gonna blow your mind." He drew a long breath. "I don't know if he's guilty or not. Maybe he is, maybe he isn't. If he is, he's the best liar I ever met. That he may be. But here's the thing. I'm starting to think maybe even if he is, he don't need to be punished, you know what I'm saying?"

Dora dropped her hands, punching up a look of shock with her mouth hanging open. "What happened? Did your benevolent twin sneak in for dinner tonight?" She laughed at his awkward smile, faking overblown amazement to cover a genuine astonished feeling. When he said nothing, she leaned on the table, concerned by the troubled look that creased his thick cheeks. "Can you tell me about it?" she asked. "I mean, is it okay for you to discuss it?"

"Huh? Oh, sure. I ain't the jury."

"So. What's the problem?"

Klinger shrugged. "Well, basically, I'm probably putting Mike in danger with all this, and I kinda like the guy. More to the point, I may be causing him a real problem, and this case may not be going anywhere."

When he raised a hand from the table, Dora reached across to stroke his palm. "You were enjoying this one, weren't you?"

"Absolutely," he nodded. "You know how it is. It's never complicated. It was a lot of fun trying to find out who the players were here. Made me feel sharp, chasing it down, like finding that asshole in Astoria."

"So?"

"So the complexity's deeper than just that."

"You're going to have to explain it, sweetheart. I'm not with you."

Klinger yawned suddenly. "I don't really know where to begin," he said.

"Is this all because you had a couple of beers with this guy last night?"

"Yeah, I guess. That and the fact that we were being watched."

"What?" Like most people who are close to police officers, Dora was always aware, on some level, that Klinger's job carried risks.

"One a Calabria's crew bosses was outside when we left," Klinger sighed.

"I don't like to hear that," Dora moaned.

"Huh? Nah, don't worry. I ain't in any danger. It's Mike who might have a problem."

"Mike."

"Yeah, you know, Pollitz."

"Of course I know. I meant, *Mike*."

"What?"
"Since when are you first-names with a suspect?"
"Too familiar?"
"He's the guy you're investigating."
"Sort of. We're really investigating Dominick Calabria. That's who we want to nail, 'specially Dan. I mean, Dan *really* wants Calabria." He shrugged again.
"You're losing me again," Dora said. "What about Dan?" Her feelings about Whittaker were ambivalent; she considered him overly ambitious.
"Well, you know how it is in the state's attorney's office. A lotta what they do is political. Calabria's about as big a fish as you can fry." When Dora's face closed in confusion, Klinger explained. "The deal is, we had a witness who got all this started, said he knew Calabria had killed a couple a guys twenty-odd years ago. Long shot for sure. The connection is Mike. He was a childhood pal of John Calabria. That's Dom's youngest. Mike did a short stretch all those years ago and got roughed up by a couple of guys. Those are the guys Calabria killed, least, according to the witness. Personally, I got no doubt about it, since the witness is also recently deceased."
"Don't worry, I remember the day it happened," Dora said.
"Yeah, I guess it put me in a mood," Klinger chuckled.
"So what's so complex?"
Klinger thought for a second or two. "Mike's complex," he finally answered. "His situation is complex too."
"And he's got information about these old murders?"
"Dan would swear to it."
"How about you, Larry?"
Klinger paused again, thinking. "He may, or he may not. He probably does, one way or another. I mean, there's even an outside chance he committed the murders himself, or was a participant somehow with others. That I doubt, but it's a theoretical possibility, as Dan would say. In a way, it may not matter,

though. If he actually committed the murders, then Calabria is no threat to him, because Calabria would know. But if Calabria knows that, there'd be no need for Bruno to watch Mike have a drink with me." He nodded quickly. "So that settles that. Calabria did it. But proving it's another matter, a whole different kettle of cats."

"Why can't you guys prosceute Calabria for income-tax evasion or something?" Dora asked, trying to lighten the tone.

"No one's done that since Capone," Klinger replied. "The only way you get top-echelon mobsters is if you can flip somebody." He shook his head. "Assuming Mike knows something useful, that's what Dan's hoping Mike will do. I hoped so, too, before I got to know him. He's never going to give up anything, even if he knows it."

"Why not?"

"He just won't. Here's what I think. It would violate his sense of loyalty. And I don't mean loyalty like *omerta* or something along those lines. I mean his sense of loyalty to trusting people when he was a child, before things broke apart for him."

Dora leaned back, surprised. "You mean his time in prison?"

"No, not that. I don't think even the assault screwed him up in a permanent way, kinda freezing things the way he is now, according to his wife, anyways. I think it wasn't what was done to him that changed things but what he decided to do about it."

"So you're saying he committed the murders."

"No. I think he regrets wanting the murders. I think he considers himself guilty of murder, even if he didn't ask Calabria to do it. And now, he's never gonna give Dan anything."

Dora watched Klinger's face, waiting for him to continue. "So what's your worry?" she asked softly. "That the case is going to fall apart, or that you're about to lose a friend, now that you've found one?"

Klinger was startled. "I hadn't thought of it in those terms," he said.

"What are you thinking?"

"I got a call from a prison guard who knows what happened to Mike, what the two dead guys did, all those years ago. He claims he knew about the murders. So why'd he say nothing to anybody? Because justice was served, he says." Klinger gazed across the table, almost plaintive. "Justice was served when a mobster murdered two scumbags."

"Maybe it was."

"You know what Outfit guys do, when it's personal? It gets pretty damn ugly, let me tell you. How can that be justice?" Klinger answered. "How can murder be justice? How come we got laws and courts? How come there's people like me?" He stared at Dora for a couple of beats. "How come I ain't sure I'm doing the right thing?"

38

"So, I had a couple of beers with Pollitz just two nights ago," Klinger announced without preamble.

"What? You mean socially?"

"Yeah." Klinger squeezed the back of his neck and rolled his round head on his neck. "I figure, since I can't seem to get the guy rattled on any level, I'll just try to get inside his head, maybe learn an angle."

Whittaker stared across his desk, raising one long hand to remove his glasses. He pulled a tissue from a drawer and cleaned his lenses. He eyed Klinger carefully, his face composed and watchful.

"And it's having an effect on someone, that's for sure," Klinger added, "'cause Salvatore Bruno was sitting outside when we left the bar."

Whittaker replaced his glasses and ran his hand across the top of his head. He leaned back with his fingers laced on one knee, a grin spreading across his slender face. "We're getting to them."

"How's getting Pollitz killed going to help us put Dom Calabria away?"

"Who said we'll get him killed? Maybe knowing Calabria's watching him will turn him over." When Klinger shrugged noncomittally, Whittaker spelled it out. "Give Pollitz a call, now that you're getting to be drinking buddies. Let him know Bruno's following him around. I guarantee you it'll improve his memory," Whittaker cackled.

"I'll call him, but you're wrong, Dan. Pollitz isn't ever going to give us anything," Klinger said softly.

"What does that mean?"

"I don't think we're ever going to get anything out of Pollitz. Assuming there's even something to get."

"I don't like what I'm hearing, Larry." Whittaker's voice was sharp.

"Sorry." Klinger shrugged, a little uncomfortable. "There's another wrinkle here too. I got a call yesterday from that third guard, Rich Taylor. You know, the one who remembered everything so clearly?" Whittaker nodded, his face distrustful. "Remember how I felt he'd been lying about a few things, and I couldn't figure why? Well, he called to clear his conscience."

"In what way?"

"He owned up to lying about knowing about McVee's and Jackson's deaths."

"Why?"

"You aren't going to believe this one," Klinger grinned. "Taylor's in AA, and lying goes against the program."

"You're kidding."

"No, I am not," Klinger emphasized. "What's more, he knew the guard who learned Calabria's identity when he gave Pollitz a lift home. This other guard died in 1989, so I can't confirm it. But Taylor says he and this other guard paid attention after McVee and Jackson left Astoria. Says justice was served when they got killed."

"Go on," Whittaker said suspiciously when Klinger paused.

"Yeah, there's more. Taylor and this other guard were present when Pollitz threatened McVee and Jackson."

"What are you saying?"

"They may have overheard the threats."

"You mean you think they could have murdered McVee and Jackson?"

"I guess not, but it's a theoretical possibility, Dan. Like Pollitz said, maybe he gave someone else an idea, when he threatened McVee and Jackson. This Taylor, he's a giant. At least six-five. Twenty years ago he would have been capable, 'specially if another guard or two were in on it. And he said he and other guards woulda been happy to take care of McVee themselves."

"Impossible!" Whittaker exploded.

Klinger shrugged with discomfort. "I ain't so sure..." When Whittaker began to sputter with inarticulate disbelief, Klinger changed direction. "I'm just saying, maybe you should talk to him. Taylor, I mean."

"I can't believe my ears! You're suggesting that I introduce a witness that Allegretti would immediately turn into a suspect. You played a tape for me that suggests Pollitz might have been up to committing the murders. So, you've given me three possible subjects, when there is no question in my mind that Calabria committed those murders! And Pollitz knows it!"

"Maybe so," Klinger said. "But maybe not."

Whittaker stared in astonished anger.

"All I'm saying's Pollitz has more than one layer to him," Klinger said.

"What in the hell is that supposed to mean?"

"Just that I think I'm starting to understand him," Klinger answered.

Whittaker slowed his voice. "How is that relevant?" he asked, dripping with sarcasm.

Klinger shrugged and let the barb slide. "It makes a difference to me," he said. "Here's the way I see it. In 1972, Pollitz and I both had the worst year of our lives. Bad things happened. Sometimes, when you get whacked by something traumatic, it breaks things apart. In my case, it killed my marriage. For Pollitz, I don't know what happened. How you recover from bad shit is a matter of chance—for one guy, it passes away, for another guy, it don't. It never goes all the way away for anybody, but if you ain't lucky, it can stay inside forever. Sometimes," Klinger said, "the damage is permanent."

"I never realized you were an amateur psychologist," Whittaker snapped.

"I'm just a cop," Klinger replied.

"I think you're getting too close to Pollitz."

"Yeah?"

"Yes."

"Guess it's a possibility, Dan," Klinger mused. "Truth is, I like the guy."

"Oh?" Whittaker asked archly. "And why is that?"

"He's smart, subtle. Interesting. Got a dry sense of humor. And he's cool. Plus, he's basically a nice guy." Klinger shrugged. "I don't think he even realizes how isolated and unhappy he is."

"What the hell is this? You getting some Messiah complex? You want to reach this lost soul?"

"That ain't it," Klinger snapped. "You oughta know better." He shifted his weight in the seat.

Whittaker stared in disbelief. "If he's so haunted, then get him to unburden his heart."

"About what?" Klinger asked mildly. He briefly considered

whether 'haunted' was the right word. *Could be,* he thought.

"I don't like what I'm hearing, Larry," Whittaker said again. "We're investigating murders that Dom Calabria ordered, I have no doubt about it, and you liking our only piece of leverage is not a good thing."

"Hey, you said yourself that trying a twenty-year-old crime is practically impossible." Klinger rose to leave. "Anyway, Dan, that's the call I got."

"I can't believe this."

Klinger raised his hands at his sides. "I'm just gathering the evidence, Dan. What you decide to do with it is your call."

39

Michael was sitting at his desk, unable to concentrate on his work, when the phone rang. He let it chime a couple of times, debating whether to let the voice-mail system take the call, then finally picked up the handset. When Michael heard Klinger's voice, his nervous feeling climbed a few notes on the scale.

"I really think you should get on our side here, Mike," Klinger announced.

"What makes you think I'm fighting you?" Michael answered.

"Ahhh, come on," Klinger groaned. "You know what I mean."

"I told you before, even if I was willing to, I couldn't help you. I just don't have any incriminating evidence."

"You think Dom Calabria shares your confidence about that?"

Michael paused, wondering how Klinger could have known so precisely what was on his mind. "You know, Larry, if I didn't know better, I'd swear you were trying to get me killed."

"Quite the contrary. Your health is very important to me, you follow?"

"Is it? Nothing against you personally, Larry, but it seems to me I wouldn't have to worry about it if you weren't in the pitcure."

"Hey, we can protect you," Klinger said.

"All the people in this room who believe that just raised their hands," Michael replied. "Forget it."

"You're backing the wrong team," Klinger said with a grunt.

"I'm not backing anyone," Michael snapped.

"So, how'd the visit go?" Klinger asked, abruptly shifting gears.

Michael was taken aback and didn't answer immediately. He again felt as though Klinger was inside his head. "It was okay," he said at last. "Angie's doing well. I gather he needs bypass surgery. Here's something you'll find out, I guess, one way or another, but let me be the first to tell you. Angie says he's going to retire."

"Yeah?" Klinger was unsurprised.

"Here's how ignorant I am, Larry. I didn't think those guys *could* retire."

"Oh, sure they can. Happens all the time. An old guy backs out, someone else takes over, whether it's a crew or the whole show. Fact, that's basically the story with Dom, as far as I understand what happened when he moved up."

"Not that I've given it a lot of thought, but I had no idea there were orderly transitions," Michael said.

"That's why we keep organization charts," Klinger replied with a soft, unhappy laugh. "But thanks for the news. We probably wouldn't've found out for a year or so. On the other hand, I'll bet I could make a better guess than you about who's going to replace DeMicco. Unless he told you?"

"You've got to be kidding."

"Not to beat the horse, but I gotta tell you, I'm mystified by your relationship with these guys."

"We've been through this a couple of times, Larry."

"I know," Klinger sighed. Michael was confused; there was something odd about his hesitancy. "Here's my problem," he said at length. "You're clearly a straight guy, and you aren't stupid. I just can't understand this blind spot you have about your old pals. It ain't that I'm insensitive to how you feel, being a kid and all, but some a these guys, they're *evil.* They shouldn't be runnin' around loose."

"I don't have any blind spot," Michael protested after a long pause, his voice low. "How many times do I have to say it?" He ran his hand through his hair and exhaled slowly. "You like to use anecdotes to illustrate your points, so let me give you one. Do you know a guy named Sam Soto? He goes by 'Marbles,' don't ask me why."

"I know who he is," Klinger answered, thinking, *speaking of evil.* He wondered what Michael might want to say about the utterly amoral enforcer. A possible sadist. Klinger could have added that Soto was probably in line for DeMicco's job. And Michael clearly disliked the man, although Klinger automatically knew to be cautious about revealing his own information.

"A year or two ago, maybe three, John and Marbles were driving through Wilmette or Winnetka, one of the ritzy North Shore suburbs. They were on a residential street. Some kid, evidently a teenager, was in the street on rollerblades. You know how that is. The kid was in the way, and he wouldn't move. That's fairly obnoxious, right? So John lays on the horn. But the kid yells, 'Fuck you!' and gives them the finger. I figure the kid assumed it was some North Shore soccer mom behind him in the car. Unfortunately for him, that wasn't the case. Marbles laughs and tells John to pull up beside the kid. When they're alongside this teenager, whoever he is, Marbles opens the car door into him. Knocks him down in the street. Then Marbles jumps out and kneels on the kid's back."

"How do you know all this?" Klinger interrupted. "Were you there?"

"Me? No. I heard about it from them, and I know these guys well enough to picture what went on."

"So what happened?"

"Marbles asks the kid if he can back up his big mouth. Then he pulls a knife and cuts off the kid's earlobe."

Klinger said nothing.

"Bad luck for the kid, right?" Michael continued. "He was being a smartass, irritating as hell, no doubt about it, maybe a little worse than lots of teenagers might be. But not a *lot* worse. Let's assume, given where this happened, that this rollerblader was a child of privilege. He lips off at the car behind him because he just automatically assumes he can get away with it. He's never met a genuinely hard man, you know, in the way people like Marbles are hard. So in a way, what happened to this kid could be seen as a little instant justice."

"You're joking."

"Not serious, but not kidding, either. Don't get me wrong. There's no way I think being a foul-mouthed, annoying teenager is punishable by mutilation, okay? But that's the way Marbles saw it. At least, he had it in his power to decide the punishment was appropriate, and he had no hesitancy about acting on it. He thought it was funny, like they had given a quick instruction in reality to a rich kid. He bragged about it. Marbles said he was going to keep the earring he cut off as a souvenir. As far as I know, he did exactly that. He may even wear it, for all I know."

To Klinger, it sounded like a vastly scaled-down version of what had happened to Pollitz in Astoria. He wondered if Michael intended to draw the parallel. Michael seemed to feel the story was complete. Finally, Klinger broke the silence. "I guess I'm missing the point, Mike."

"The point is, I have no doubts about how dangerous some of these guys really are. How indifferently they'll do things. I mean, in a way, the kid was lucky. If Marbles had been having a lousy afternoon, who knows what he might have done?"

"What are you saying? You think Soto's going to come after you?"

"I'm hoping *no* one *ever* comes after me. I'm hoping no one ever thinks anyone needs to."

"In other words, you doubt their loyalty?" Klinger chuckled.

"You aren't understanding me."

"How so?" Klinger asked, no longer baiting.

"What I mean, Larry, is if they think it's necessary, I'm in real trouble."

"Like I say, we can protect you," Klinger said, but his tone was half-hearted.

"I doubt it," Michael snapped. "And even if you could, it would mean the end of my life as I know it. Christ!" he moaned. "Not that my life is anything so great, but this isn't the way I want it to change, Larry. All I want is to be left alone." He drew air and sighed loudly into the receiver. "The truth is, Larry, I don't have any evidence that would help you put Dom in prison. That isn't bullshit. But it won't matter if someone thinks I'm helping you. You said it yourself. As casual as slapping a mosquito. Maybe not for Dom or Sal, certainly not for John, but..." He stopped. He was losing control of his voice and he wanted to somehow remove the tone of panic that was creeping in.

There was a long pause. Finally, Klinger broke the silence. "Well, listen, Mike. I called to tell you something." Michael said nothing, so Klinger continued, his voice soft. "I had a nice time the other night. It was pleasant having a couple a beers. I'd like to do it again. Here's the catch. Sal Bruno was sitting outside when we left."

Michael swallowed. This explained a lot. "How do you know?"

"I ran the plate on a Lincoln that was on the street when we came out." Michael again said nothing, and Klinger could imagine that even for someone as composed as Pollitz always seemed to be, this news was causing serious anxiety. "I thought you'd want to know," he added.

"So you figure this will turn me, Larry?" Michael asked, his voice tight. "Make me give you something so you can arrest Dom?" He clenched the receiver, struggling to keep his voice stable. "That why you're offering to protect me?"

"No," Klinger said wearily. "You got it wrong. I mean, yeah, the idea was to flip you. That's what Dan hopes will happen. But I know it won't. I'm telling you this because…" he paused in sorrow before he stepped off the moral ledge, "I thought you might want to tell them about our chat before they asked you about it. You follow?"

Michael was stunned, momentarily speechless. He stared out at the buildings to the south without really seeing them, his mouth working. At last, he stammered, "Thanks, Larry." He shook his head in awestruck gratitude. "Thank you."

Michael walked down the hall to the bathroom, where he washed his hands and splashed a little water on his cheeks. He was surprised to discover his hands trembling. He carefully wiped his hands and face, staring at himself in the mirror. He stood motionless for a few seconds, wondering if what he was feeling was nausea. He drank some cold water from his cupped hands and toweled off again. Then he walked back to his phone.

40

"Hey, Mike," John said. He sounded distracted. "What's up?"

"Nothing much," Michael answered, brisk and nonchalant. "I just wanted to keep you up to date. That detective, Klinger, asked me out for a couple of beers two nights ago."

"Yeah?" John perked up. "What'd he want?"

"Not much. I think he's trying to work me, see if I'll trip over something. He doesn't come at it directly. Like, he wanted to know if I thought those assholes from Astoria deserved to die." Michael recounted as much of their conversation as he could remember, indifferently, easily, without betraying any nervousness. "It was more like a conversation over cocktails than what you usually get from a cop," he concluded.

"He wasn't working you about us?"

"Just those few questions I told you about, outside. I assume it's in the back of his mind, in any case. This seems to be his approach."

John snorted out a laugh.

"No big deal," Michael said. "Actually, this Klinger's a pretty nice guy."

"Fuck 'im," John boomed out merrily. He laughed again. "Why didn't you mention this at the restaurant, Mikey?"

"Huh?" Michael responded, his voice suggesting it was a matter of such little consequence that he couldn't imagine how it made a difference. "It didn't seem like big news," he said. "And the timing sucked, what with Angie in the hospital and your dad feeling sick."

"Ayyyy," John crowed. "Timing don't matter. Like I said, we wanna keep informed."

"Well, that's why I'm calling."

"Yeah! Thanks. I'll give my dad a rundown."

"You want me to call him?"

"Nahhh," John said. "It's no big thing. I'm going over in a couple minutes. If he wantsta talk to you, I'll give you a call."

"Fine," Michael answered, still as light as air. He paused for a few beats, then added, "John, you know I wouldn't ever do anything to hurt you or your family."

"Ayyyyy, Mikey! I know that!" John shouted. "We know that, man! Forget about it." *Fahgedaboudit,* this the expansively dismissive intonation of the catchall, a New Jersey Mob affectation John had adopted years earlier, most likely picked up from the movies, Michael had always thought. Michael hung up the phone with a tentative, wary feeling of relief.

41

"This is a change!" Klinger shouted into his phone. "You're asking me out to dinner? Definitely a first!"

"Really?" Michael asked. "I would assume most guys you investigate want to share a pizza with you."

"Naturally," Klinger laughed. "And let me tell you, pizza's the smart plan. A lotta the guys I investigate don't know how to use a fork." He chuckled merrily, thinking Pollitz couldn't have any idea just how accurate his joke could be. "Where and when?"

Michael named a pizza place on LaSalle, just north of the river. Klinger looked at his watch. "Sounds great. How about I leave right now? I'll be there in a half-hour."

"Just look for me inside," Michael replied. "I'll get a table."

"Outta curiosity, Mike, what's the occasion?"

"Thanks, is all."

Dan would have my nuts for this, Klinger thought as he walked into the restaurant and sniffed deeply with immense pleasure. He loved the odors of garlic and pizza spices. He grinned when he saw Michael at a small table against one wall, casually watching the entrance. Michael waved.

"Another great choice!" Klinger bellowed as he took a chair across the table and gazed around the narrow restaurant.

"You've never been here?" Michael asked with surprise.

Klinger shook his head, a smile still broadening his wide face. "The court building's just down the street."

"That's the traffic court, kiddo," Klinger said. "I been in the department a long time, but that ain't one of my regular stops." He shifted his bulk in his chair and looked around again, beaming at the brick walls and simple lamps hanging from the ceiling. "So!" he almost shouted as he grabbed a menu from the table. "What's good?"

"The pizza," Michael answered.

"How did I know you were gonna say that?" Klinger erupted with mirth. "Let's get a pitcher a beer."

"It's already on its way," Michael said.

Klinger nodded and grinned. "Tell me," he began in a rush of expelled air, "How was work? What's the advertising world like?"

"You really want to know?"

"Absolutely!" the detective crowed. "I'm curious about everything."

"It's insipid," Michael answered simply.

"Yeah? What do you mean?" Klinger leaned forward on his elbows, genuinely intrigued. In his mind, no line of work that included people who looked like Carole Meyer could be all bad. "I mean, just about everyone complains about their work."

"I'm not complaining. That was just a statement of fact. 'Insipid' is the most descriptive word I could think of."

"I would think it'd be interesting," Klinger shrugged.

"I didn't say it isn't interesting. Although it's fairly dull a lot of the time. Especially on the account side. Too many tedious meetings." A waitress arrived with the beer and two glasses. Klinger poured while Michael placed their order. "Here's the problem, Larry. I mean with marketing in general. It's ultimately dumb. But a lot of smart people work in the field, and they're paid well. So they convince themselves that it isn't dumb. They all agree on that particular fiction without ever articulating it, so everyone can pretend that what they're doing isn't as insipid as it is."

Klinger laughed gleefully, happily dubious. "Ain't even entertaining, writing those commercials?"

"I don't write the copy anymore. I haven't done that for years. I'm on the account side now. That part's creative."

"What's the dif?" Klinger swallowed some beer.

Michael laughed. "The account people make the money, the creative people, well, they make money, too, but not as much, so they tell themselves and one another they're, well, *creative*." He shook his head, chuckling at Klinger's grin. "As if designing the word 'sale' in two-foot letters takes genius. They even call themselves 'the creative community.' How's that for clueless self-importance?" He laughed again. "One of our favorite words is 'commitment,' like, 'I doubt your commitment, here, Larry.' It's one of those idiot marketing catchalls we use all the time. What amazes me is the endless stream of people who'll buy into that bullshit. There's no shortage of people who are so dumb they don't know 'commitment' is a euphemism for 'unpaid overtime.' Either they don't know, or they just agree to pretend it means something else."

"Ain't it a way to get ahead?"

"That's what everyone tells themselves."

"You don't go for it?"

"I'm only in it to pay the bills, Larry."

"Ahhh," Klinger groaned with amusement, "everyone bitches about their job."

"You seem to like yours."

"You kidding?" Klinger raised his eyebrows. "Lately I'm feelin' kinda burnt out, you follow?"

Michael grabbed the opening to change subjects. "Where'd you come from? I mean, what location?"

"My office," Klinger said with a sly smile, "at the Belmont station."

"Where Riverview used to be?"

"You got it."

"Tell me the truth, Larry. Were you ever stationed at Halsted and Addison?"

Klinger made a *clocking* sound with his tongue and formed a pistol with his right hand, pointing across the table. "You're a sharp guy, Mike."

Michael laughed. "Not really. You had me fooled the first time." He chuckled. "At least, until I thought about it." He refilled their glasses.

"You ever go to Riverview?" Klinger asked.

"Sure," Michael answered. "My pa took us there a few times. It was a fun outing, because we'd take the train in and ride a bus over. How about you?"

"Oh, when I was a kid I practically lived there in the summer. I loved it. A great park. Our place was just north of there, off of Western Avenue."

"It was kind of run down, when I went there."

"Yeah, it got sorta seedy, there toward the end. 'Course, most amusement parks are pretty gross, if you ask me. For me and my friends, in the '50s, it was a ball."

"You went there alone?"

"Sure, all the time. It wasn't a long ride down Western."

"Where'd you grow up exactly?"

"In the Lincoln and Lawrence area, you know where I mean? Useta be lots of Germans around there. A lotta Greeks too. Both ethnic groups have basically moved away, especially the Greeks. My pop was a sausage maker for a meat company that supplied some of the shops. I still live near there, few blocks east of where I grew up."

"You know Bismarck's line about laws and sausages?" Michael asked with a smile.

"Yeah, and it's appropriate, considering I'm a cop. But I still eat sausages," Klinger replied, "even though I've seen 'em made."

"You know," Michael said, "I don't think my ma ever would

have let my brother or me go to Riverview alone."

"She woulda been right not to, by the time you could've gone on your own," Klinger chuckled, remembering his last visit to the amusement park, when he was in the Marines. "Last time I was there, it was on a date with my ex-wife, before we were married. Almost made us break up," he laughed. "Marie—that's my ex—saw a rubber floating in the tunnel of love and said she wanted to puke." He stretched in his chair and gulped from his glass. "Speakin' of families," he announced, "one thing your ex said has me a little confused." Michael released a melodramatic moan. "She claimed you have no relationship with your family. Says it makes the news if you talk to your father." He sipped beer with a sidelong glance. "Yet it didn't sound that way when I talked to your mother."

Michael was startled. "When did you talk with my ma?"

"Hey, don't sweat it. I mean months ago, when I first got your work number," Klinger smiled. "She sounded, like, normal, you know what I mean?" He scraped his chair backward as their pizza arrived. The waitress slid a thick slice onto each of their plates and covered the remainder with another plate. Klinger dug into the viscous cheese with gusto.

"A 'dull normal' would be an unkind way to put it," Michael laughed harshly. "I like her. She's a kind person. Takes too much crap from my father, but they're pretty solid with one another. What's with the personal questions?" He stuffed a bite of pizza into his mouth.

Klinger raised a hand as he chewed and swallowed. "My God! That is great pizza! Next time I take Dora out, I'm calling you for a recommendation," he declared. He carved another bite from his slice and raised it to his mouth. "Anyway. My question has nothing to do with the Calabrias. Honest. I'm just curious, that's all. Your ex's statement didn't jibe, you follow? But I ain't trying to pry or anything. No offense, okay? Sometimes I ask the wrong stuff."

"Forget about it, Larry. I'm not offended. It's a complicated thing." He leaned back, thinking. "I didn't have much of a relationship with my family when Carole and I were married, and that's what she's talking about. How would she know any different?" He shrugged minutely. "Nowadays it's better than it was." He reached to refill their glasses from the pitcher of beer.

"What do you mean, your mother takes too much crap from your father?"

Michael laughed lightly. "Nothing serious. He gets crabby, childish about things, that's all. It's within the normal bandwidth."

Klinger grunted as he chewed, pure pleasure suffusing his meaty cheeks. He swallowed and smacked his lips with satisfaction. "Delicious!" he announced with happy finality. "My folks were the same way," Klinger grinned. "My pop used to tap the edge of his coffee cup, like with his finger," he said, demonstrating on the rim of his glass. "Then Mom would hop up to get him a refill. Marie, she couldn't stand it. Drove her nuts."

"There's nothing that dramatic with my ma and pa, but it's that kind of thing." Michael smiled and raised his eyebrows indifferently. "They get along fine. My ma, she's crazy about my brother's kid. So's my pa, actually." He thought while he swallowed a bite. "I don't have much in common with him or my brother, but I get along with my pa okay."

"You hold what happened in Astoria against him, don't you?"

"No, not really," Michael said, frowning slightly and shaking his head. "*He* didn't attack me. Those three assholes did. I had some bad feelings about it at the time, but that wasn't the problem. I mean, when I think about it now, I like to believe I would have handled things differently, if I was in his shoes. I was nineteen, still just a kid. I think I had a right to expect more help from my pa than I got. I don't think I would force a child of mine to face all of that alone. But I understand what happened. Between his ignorance and inexperience, and his anger at me, he pushed me into a mistake. But that's just the thing. *I* made the mistake. The problem that I had with him was more what that whole period revealed to me about him, what kind of a person he is. It was my first glimpse of his poverty of spirit. His parsimoniousness. I got a true view of him as a human being."

"You're bein' kind of hard on him."

"I don't think so. Here's the kind of guy my pa is. Say there's some leftover potato salad in the refrigerator. If you eat the last of it, it pisses him off. So you don't eat it. But neither does he. It spoils."

"So?"

"So he'd rather it rotted than someone else take it." Michael laughed. "That's just the kind of guy he is."

"That seems like kind of a small thing," Klinger said.

"Absolutely. That's just a little example. A telling one, from my point of view, though. It has a corollary in how he responded to my problems, back in '72. For one thing, he couldn't get around what he saw as my lack of shame about the whole mess. He wanted me to feel guilty. I couldn't see any reason to. We had what you could call an emotional impasse. Or maybe a philosophical impasse. And I thought he should have been less angry and a little more supportive, maybe tried to see my point of view instead of assuming the fact that I was indicted for something meant I deserved whatever the hell came of it." Michael leaned back in his chair and raised his glass.

"Maybe, bein' a plumber and all, he thought you getting in trouble was like throwing away the advantages of college."

"Gosh, do you think?" Michael mocked.

"It still sounds to me like you blame him for Astoria," Klinger echoed himself.

Michael pursed his lips and glanced away. "It's more complicated than that," he said, reluctant to delve any deeper into the insidious sense of betrayal and abandonment he felt.

"It always is," Klinger muttered.

"No, it isn't always complicated. And you've got it wrong. Sure, I blame him for Astoria, at least, a little more than I blame myself. But doing that short bit, even what happened there, it's over. Past. My pa can't comprehend it one way or another. It's the rest of it that's the problem for me."

"What do you mean, 'the rest of it'?" Klinger pounced, but gently, trying to avoid revealing the sudden predatory surge he felt, the confirmation of what he already suspected.

Michael's eyes turned cold as he glanced up. He shrugged. "Our decisions change us," he muttered, "and I used to fantasize that a family could heal some of that." He smiled, and his expression softened. "Let me ask you something, Larry," Michael said, a little tentatively. "When your son's accident happened, didn't you wish…"

"You can say, 'when Mattie died'," Klinger interrupted. His expression hadn't changed, but the skin around his lips tightened, Michael thought. It was Klinger's turn to close up.

"I'm not trying to draw a comparison, Larry. Don't get me wrong. There's no false equivalency here. I can't imagine a worse thing than losing a child."

"There is no worse thing," Klinger said flatly, his face still expressionless.

Michael winced sadly but pushed ahead. "I'm not trying to pick at a scab, okay?" He sipped a little beer and shifted the line of thought. He set down his glass. "I assume your dad was around, back in 1972." When Klinger nodded, Michael continued. "When your son died, how did he react? Your dad?"

"It hit Pop pretty hard. Mattie was just his second grandkid, at the time."

"How was he with you?"

Klinger smiled, his face creased with sorrow and fondness. "He was good," he said. "Pop was more worried about me and Marie than about himself, and he was hurting too." He looked away, but without discomfort, following a private recollection.

"How old were you then?"

"I was twenty-nine."

"Well, that's not that old. But you were an adult, taking care of business, with a life, started a family and all. Even so, didn't you feel..." Michael went on, moving his hands awkwardly in the air, "Didn't you just want someone to take care of you? I don't mean it literally. Just, like, emotionally? Make it so you weren't trying to handle it all on your own? I mean, even though you were nearly thirty, didn't you want your dad just to step up to the plate and take over the responsibility for you?" He shook his head. "I'm not phrasing it very well." Klinger chewed expectantly. "Well, it's going to sound a little foolish," Michael concluded, "but during that terrible time for you and your wife, didn't part of you just want your dad to tuck you in, so to speak, hold your hand and make it better somehow? Didn't some part of you hope your dad could be your protector again?"

Klinger gazed across the table, thinking he'd never wished for it because it was basically exactly what his father had tried to do; it was nothing you would want unless you couldn't have it. He shrugged the memories away. "I never really thought about it that way," he said at last. "I mean, I'd been on my own for a while, you know? But, yeah, I see your point." It occurred to him that what he'd said to Whittaker wasn't entirely correct. "It's not just a matter of chance," he said thoughtfully. "It's where you are and the people you've got around you too." He realized that this line of speculation applied more often than not and in more situations than he cared to acknowledge.

"I'm not with you," Michael said.

"Huh? Oh, I was just thinking aloud." Klinger shook his head with a smile. "Anyways, I gotcha," he concluded. "Like you say, it's complicated. Give me another slice of that pizza, will you?" He grinned and extended his plate across the table.

42

John stood staring dumbly through the French doors, squinting slightly against the July sunlight baking the patio and pool. He barely noticed two of his children splashing in the water. The muscles of his thick shoulders and neck bunched and shifted beneath his knit shirt as he pressed his hands together, struggling to control his fury. For some reason, today the odor of cigarettes was making him gag.

Dom sat behind his desk and studied his son's back. He glanced across the desk at Sal Bruno and Sam Soto, who sat in the old leather armchairs, then returned his attention to the doors. He watched John's back heave with his breathing. Finally, he said, "Marbles has a point. It's nothing we can ignore."

John turned from the doors, his eye red-rimmed, almost like an enraged bull's. He glared at Soto and stared outside again. "Mikey'd turn on you about as soon as I would," he growled, his voice taut. "You know that, Dad."

"Angie agrees with you," Dom answered. "You're acting like a decision's been made here. Nothin's done. We just need to talk about it." He paused to catch his breath. "We can't pretend there's nothing."

"Who's pretending?" John exploded, wheeling away from the doors and gesticulating furiously. "There ain't no problem! There ain't gonna be no problem!"

"If there is, I'll take care of it, is all I'm saying," Soto said, nodding at Dom.

"Fuck yourself, Marbles!" John screamed. "You guinea piece a shit! It's you who's got this bullshit going!"

Soto's face reddened, but Dom intervened. "Knock it off!" His eyes glittered as he stared at John. "What did I just say? What did I just tell you?" He stopped again to draw air. "This ain't Marbles' fault, for Chrissakes. Since when can't he ask a question?"

"He don't know the history!" John shouted.

"All I'm saying's, he's hangin' around with this cop, and I don't like it," Soto said.

"Like I give a fuck what you like," John snarled, moving away from the doors.

Soto started to react when Dom leaped out of his chair, anger radiating from him like heat from an open oven door. "Marbles is the boss of Angie's crew! He can say anything he wants!"

John refused to wilt under the weight of his father's authority. "What does he know about it? He don't know how far back this goes!" John shook his head heavily, trying to sort out his thoughts. "How come Angie's opinion don't mean shit now?"

"Who said I don't care what Angie thinks?" Dom answered.

"Angie's just outta the hospital, for Chrissakes," Soto grumbled.

"What the hell's that supposed to mean?" John raged. "He's soft in the head?"

Soto curled his lip slightly and stared back at John, his dark eyes as flat as a shark's, then turned his gaze to Dom, who was coughing behind his desk. John was distracted by his father's coughing fit.

Sal shifted heavily in the chair. "Take it easy, John," he rumbled hoarsely. "Marbles ain't off base there. Lotsa guys think different after a heart attack."

John was stunned. "You telling me you agree with Marbles on this?"

"What's to agree or disagree with?" Sal asked. "All Marbles said's he wants to discuss it. Ain't nothin' wrong with that."

"I can't believe this!" John almost wailed. "If Mikey's got a problem, why the hell'd he call the other day? Huh? Why'd he tell me about that cop asshole askin' him more questions?" He turned plaintively toward his father. "We already went through this the other night, didn't we?"

"Yeah," Dom nodded, "and we filled Marbles in, and he wanted to talk about it. Where's the problem with that?" He sank back into his chair, his face drawn and weary.

Bruno thought aloud. "You could ask why Mikey didn't mention it at the restaurant, when he saw us."

"What the fuck I been sayin'?" John almost shrieked. "I did ask him. He didn't bring it up 'cause a Angie bein' sick, and..." he slowed and glanced at his father again.

"I don't like no loose ends," Soto announced.

"Mikey ain't no 'loose end,' you goddamn, motherfuckin' asshole!"

"Maybe yes, maybe no," Soto sneered.

"I'll break your motherfuckin' skull, Marbles! I swear to God!"

"Calm down!" Dom barked. He wheezed with the effort of his anger. "Sit down and shut up, the both of you!"

"Listen," Soto said. "That piece a shit in County, whatever the fuck his name was, that was a loose end. This whole fuckin' mess was 'cause of him. Him and your buddy Pollitz. That's what I mean by a loose end. They bite ya in the ass!"

"Stick to the goddamn point!" Dom coughed. He held a hand in the air as he controlled his breathing. "Mike's not a loose end. Get that clear." He stared at Soto until the younger man dropped his eyes. "That asshole in County, you got a case, you wanna talk unfinished business. But that's way before your time, Marbles. Forget about it. It was taken care of." He looked at each of the men in turn and waited for the tension in the room to drop a notch. John finally sat on the couch. "Now," Dom continued at length, "let's talk. Calmly. Like adults." He looked from his son to Soto and back. "This is business, and Marbles has a right to raise a question. Is that understood?" John nodded morosely. "Good," Dom wheezed. He winced and shook his head. "I also want it understood that I don't feel we have a problem here." He shifted his gaze to Soto. "And even if we do, nothing will be done about it until I get out of the hospital." He continued to stare until Soto shrugged and nodded.

"I wasn't sayin' anything oughta be done," Marbles said, raising his hands slightly and shaking his head. "All I said was, I want to talk."

"That's good," Dom nodded. "Good."

"What do you mean, 'even if we do?' There ain't no problem," John insisted.

"What did I just say? We are going to discuss this to everyone's satisfaction. Marbles deserves a discussion. He don't know Mike. He raised a question about Mike's involvement with this cop, this Klinger asshole. The fact is, Sal saw them having drinks. Now Jimmy saw them eating pizza together."

"So what?"

"I don't like it," Soto repeated. "Why don't it bother no one else?"

"Why are we keepin' an eye on Mikey, anyway?" John whined.

The others ignored the question. Dom glanced at Sal, then turned again to Soto. "Lemme fill in the history here, Marbles," he began.

43

"Ayyy, Mikey," John sang into the phone, booming as always.

"How's your dad?" Michael replied, cutting off any small talk.

"That's why I called, Mikey. He's gotta have surgery. Like, tomorrow."

"Why so fast?"

"The news ain't so hot, Mikey."

"Where is he?"

"Lutheran General."

"I'm on my way," Michael said.

"Why don't you stay at our place tonight? Everyone else's gonna be at the farm."

"Sure, if you want."

"I'd like it, Mikey," John replied. "I'll get Deb to make up the guest room. You know where the hospital is?"

"I'll find it."

"I gotta go to the airport, get my brothers."

"I'll meet you at the hospital," Michael answered. He hung up without saying anything more, gathered his wallet from his desk and left without a word to anyone. It would occur to him later, as he sat with Toni, John, and John's brothers and sisters in the family waiting area at the hospital while a team of surgeons removed one of Dom's lungs, that he could be jeopardizing his job. His companion thought was that he didn't care.

44

"You've been a good friend to John. A good friend to me. More than a friend. Like a son."

Michael was startled. "I love all of you," he stammered. He glanced at John and rubbed his free hand across his cheek while he gently increased the pressure on Dom's weak fingers.

Dom smiled dreamily. "Always knew it," he said slowly. "Never had a doubt." He gripped Michael's hand. He looked at John and raised the hand that held John's fingers. "Lemme talk to Mike alone for a second. Okay, kid?" He smiled at his son. "Go down and find Ma and your brothers."

John stood, haggard but smiling. He seemed relieved to get

away from the tubes and monitors, the odor of the hospital room.

"This thing of ours, it's over," Dom said softly once John was gone, looking away through the windows. His face had the pallid sheen of post-surgery patients.

"What do you mean?" Michael asked. In a hospital wrap, Dom looked very old, almost frail.

"This thing. My life. It's ending. Or I oughta say, it looks like it's ending."

"I'm not with you." Michael reached out to touch the older man's leg.

"Talkin' about business here," Dom explained. "They're still chasing us, but we aren't where the action is anymore."

"There isn't anything I can do about that."

"I know, but John doesn't understand it," Dom slurred. "Maybe you can help him see." He struggled to breathe. "You read the papers, we're still a big deal. But they talk about the 'five families' in New York—I ain't sure you could still count three. There's still Jersey, still stuff in Vegas, plenty of other places, still us. But really, maybe just us, here in Chicago." Michael said nothing, but he wondered why Dom was telling him this. "You ever take economics?" Dom asked.

"Just one course, back in college."

"This is strictly economics," Dom said, drugged and musing. "Hungrier competition."

"What do you mean?"

"I mean alla the older shit, there's hungrier guys out there, chasing it. Jamaicans. Russians. Gangbangers. Latins. Whatever. They want the street shit more than we do."

Michael smiled. "Well, your thing is still glamorous in books and movies."

Dom's eyes suddenly took on a familiar glint. He grinned. "Mike, did I ever tell you how much I love your no-bullshit point of view?" He continued to smile for a few beats, then faded back down into a quasi-drugged state. "But you know better, don't you?" he whispered. Michael shrugged. Dom chuckled softly. "I mean Sal, Angie, Marbles. Them." He lifted a few fingers as Michael began to protest. "I know you love Sal and Angie," moving his hand. "But you know better." He smiled and closed his eyes. "And John. They don't get it. But you do."

"Yes," Michael answered.

Dom smiled again. "Still a lotta dough in it, you better believe," Dom coughed. "If you wanna fight for it."

"This really isn't my concern," Michael protested.

Dom chuckled some more, loose with the painkillers. "Here's the laugh, Mike. Who needs the old shit? You know what John's restaurant alone cleared last year? Fuck the books and everything else. You know what it cleared?"

"Why are you telling me this, Dom?"

Dom chuckled again, almost giddy. "John's place netted six hundred large." He laughed some more. "Granted, it's one of our better places. But six hundred large! That's legit dough, no bullshit. So we report twice that to the IRS. Who gives a fuck? Don't need nothin' more. Shit, meat delivery clears three or four million!" He paused, sucking air through the nasal tubes. Michael was thinking that without an enforced monopoly, the net from the meat trucks would probably be a lot smaller. "Fuck the streets," Dom concluded.

"Try to recover, Dom," Michael said.

Suddenly the old mobster's eyes were back. His grip tightened on Michael's hand. "Won't happen," he said. "Not a chance."

"People live with one lung," Michael protested.

"Not when it's fulla cancer," Dom answered. "Not when the liver and pancreas got it too." He paused, almost dreamy. "I ain't a child, for Christ's sake." There was an uncharacteristic note in his voice. Michael squeezed his hand. His eyes felt swollen to the point of leaking. "What's this?" Dom snapped.

"I'll miss you," Michael answered.

Dom smiled warmly, as if at a small child. "That's my Michael," he said softly, "always honest. How I knew I could always trust you." Michael nodded, but his eyes were confused. "Gotta say, Michael, trying to take a murder rap ain't the smartest way to show your loyalty. Appreciate it, but it ain't too bright."

Drugs are amazing, Michael thought. "I don't think they have much of a case."

"Who the fuck knows? They may not get blood, but they can sure fuck up the turnip."

"I doubt they'll stay with it without you in the bull's eye," Michael answered.

Dom coughed out a genuine laugh. "God, I love you, Michael. You're as straight as Sal." Michael shrugged. Dom wheezed. "Yeah," he rasped at length, "with me dead, what's the point?" Michael felt the pressure on his fingers increase. "Sometime, down the road, tell Toni how much I have always loved her."

"She won't need to be reminded."

"I know it," the dying man answered. "But it will make her feel good, hearing it from you."

"I'll tell her," Michael said, composed. He saved his tears for the car.

45

"Dom Calabria's got lung cancer," Klinger said. "They took out one a his lungs yesterday."

Whittaker looked up from his desk, his eyes narrow. He adjusted his glasses and asked, "How do you know that? Please tell me it's from surveillance."

Klinger pursed his lips. "No," he said, after a few beats, "Pollitz told me."

Whittaker nodded deliberately, one finger at his lips. "When?"

"He called me at home last night."

"He called you at home." A flat declaration, still nodding slowly.

"Yeah." Klinger raised his chin.

"That's great," Whittaker said, nodding again. "Splendid. He called you at home. Charming."

"What difference does it make?" Klinger replied. Whittaker stared at the wall, trailing his gaze across his bookcases. "What do you care how I found out?" Whittaker continued to ignore him. Klinger shifted his weight, stifling his discomfort, and decided to wait out the attorney. He glanced at the sky through the office windows. It occurred to him that he hated the Criminal Courts building. It always seemed dirty, even the air around it. And it smelled bad. The aroma of desperation seeped even into Dan's comfortable office.

Whittaker shook his head again and glanced across his desk. He sighed theatrically, removed his glasses and cleaned them meticulously with a tissue. He put his glasses back on with studied care. Finally, he clasped his hands on the desktop and said, "I assume you think this bit of information affects our case."

"What's the line about 'assume'?" Klinger chuckled, trying to find some easy ground. Whittaker moved only his mouth, pursing his full lips as if he was about to kiss the air. Klinger shrugged and dropped the smile. "What I think, Dan, is we got precious little time."

"Your pal gave you the prognosis, did he?"

Klinger bristled. "No, my 'pal' did not give me a prognosis. Who knows? Maybe Dom Calabria's as tough as John Wayne, can lose a lung and keep kicking for four, five years. I kinda doubt it. Maybe you got more confidence. Me, I think Dom ain't all that long for the world, you follow?"

Whittaker inhaled slowly, clearly controlling himself. "You can be an irritating son of a bitch, you know that?"

"Sorry to be annoying."

"Some day, to someone else, you're going to mean that."

Klinger shrugged. They stared at one another in silence, each second exhaling a mist of tension as it passed. Neither man shifted his gaze.

Whittaker blinked first, finally asking, "I reiterate. You feel this has an impact on the case."

Klinger shrugged with his face. "Pollitz wasn't ever going to give us anything, anyway, but this ices it."

"How so?"

"He loves the man like a father. He's practically in tears tellin' me about Dom's operation. He's a dry hole."

"Thanks for the pointless metaphor."

"Fuck yourself."

Whittaker stared again, this time in a rage. He had to work to avoid escalating the argument. At length, he softened his voice and said, "Let's cool down a little," shifting gears, measuring his words slowly, trying to divert the growing anger between them into a more clinical assessment of the problem. "Calabria's sick, probably terminal. Neither of us knows what the time frame may be, but I agree with you. It's probably short. Why does that lead to Pollitz having nothing to offer us?"

Klinger appreciatively grabbed the olive branch. "Frankly, I don't think Pollitz knows much of anything. I've said this before. I just don't think he could be that good a liar. No one—and Dan, I got thirty years a this shit under my belt—*no one* is that good a liar."

Whittaker leaned forward and raised his hands slightly in question.

"Here's the point," Klinger said. "In my opinion, we weren't going to get anything before, but now, he feels protective. He's gonna clam up totally."

"Maybe Pollitz is the one I should be after!"

Klinger laughed. "All I can say is, good luck." He stretched out the 'good luck' into a student's satiric tone. "You wanna try to peel that onion with nothin' but circumstantial, be my guest."

"Look, Larry, I understand how lonely you feel ninety percent of the time, and how tired you are of the job, okay? But getting to be pals with a suspect in a murder investigation doesn't seem like the right solution to me."

Klinger's anger rose at the sarcasm. "You think I'm dumping on this?"

"Yes, I do," Whittaker snapped. "Like you said once before, back when I thought I could count on you, how many more chances are we going to get to indict Calabria?"

"Well, maybe this wasn't the chance. Maybe we never got a chance. Maybe we were grasping at straws. You ever think a that?"

"God damn it, Larry! The idea was, you were going to flip Pollitz! It wasn't supposed to be the other way around!"

"Don't give me any shit about lack of commitment, Dan," Klinger answered, a cold fury building in his mind. "Who started this goddamn investigation? Who moved it forward? Who hadda talk who into pursuing it?"

"What? You think because you got the game going, you get to decide when to call it off?" Whittaker leaned forward with his arms on his desk. "Listen, Larry. You're the last cop I ever would have expected *this* from."

"That so?" Klinger restrained himself with an effort. "And what might that be?"

"Getting close enough to a suspect to sabotage an investigation! If someone had told me you'd ever be dealing with Internal Affairs, I would have said they're crazy!"

Klinger was so astonished he could barely speak. He had never before been apoplectic. "Are you threatening me, Dan?" he finally sputtered. "You got such a hard-on for Calabria that you'd…" He clenched his hands on the chair's rails. "Hey, I realize nailing Calabria makes your career, man, but we aren't even close to it."

"I'll pretend I didn't hear that," Whittaker said slowly. "You should know me better than that."

"Yeah? You oughta know me better than what you're saying, you follow?"

"I thought I did!" Whittaker almost rose from his chair. "*You* follow?"

Klinger stood, too angry to stay in the room. "Take it to Professional Conduct if you want to, Dan. I give a shit. But when I say you're getting nowhere on this, it ain't 'cause I'm soft on Pollitz. It's because there's nothin' there!" He stomped to the door. "Do whatever the hell you want, buddyboy!"

Whittaker leaped upright, nearly trembling with anger, and shouted, "If I have to get another investigator on this, Klinger, you damn well better be cooperative!"

Klinger stopped with his hand on the doorknob, breathing deeply as he stared back at Whittaker. "I'll pretend *I* didn't hear *that*," he spat back. "But if it's me that's screwing this up, how come you never took the investigation any higher? Where's the fucking grand jury, Mr. Prosecutor? Where're the subpoenas, if you're so sure there's a case here? Answer me that!" He yanked open the door and slammed it behind him as he stalked out.

46

Michael had never seen so many flower arrangements in one place, not even at John's wedding. The funeral home was overflowing with floral displays in the parlors, the hallways, the entrances to all of the rooms, the foyer of the building, the head of the huge room in which Dom's service was to be held. His casket was barely visible in a shoal of arrangements. A florist could have told Michael that in excess of one hundred thousand dollars in flowers filled the building, not that Michael would have cared beyond another brief mental cataloguing of stereotypes behaving stereotypically.

He felt pressure against his arm and glanced aside to find Nina leaning against him, still breathtakingly beautiful to his mind despite her streaked mascara and swollen eyes. He reached to put his arm around her. Nina had always seemed big to him, her voluptuous sexiness some kind of unattainable but intensely desired ideal. He was startled to realize that, even wearing high heels, the top of her hair just reached the bridge of his nose, and he would later smile to realize that this woman, now well past fifty, could still seem so immeasurably desirable. Nina Calabria was an erotic talisman for Michael, a first true object of desire.

"Oh, Daddy," Nina moaned, staring at the figure in the casket. She clenched tightly on the shoulder of Michael's suit and said, staring intently up at him, "I hope you know how much he loved you, Michael."

"I knew it," Michael answered.

There were tears now. He wished he had a handkerchief to hand her in some gallant way. Nina fumbled with tissues.

"You were like a fourth son to him."

Michael nodded. "And he knew how much I loved him," Michael coughed, holding Nina tighter and thinking about the scent of her hair.

Unnoticed, Antonia Calabria had moved nearer to them, and she reached out a hand. "Yes. He knew," Toni said, "and it made him glad."

Michael turned, tears nearby, to hold Toni Calabria. She cried softly as they clutched one another, and in their embrace Micheal could feel an almost physical shift, as she laid down the burden of her generation onto him, as a representative of his generation. It seemed late in coming, to him, another sign of the tremendous power Dom had wielded over even ordinary transitions in his life. But then a line of mourners resumed its insistency, and Toni turned away.

Nina remained close, however, and Mary moved up beside them. Michael had greeted Mary earlier, but now he turned to hold her tightly and express his sorrow in a personal way. Her face was as streaked as Nina's. He wrapped his arms around both women and said, "I want to tell you something. I'll tell your mother later on." They both leaned away to stare. "One of the last things your father said to me, the last thing he asked me to do, when I saw him in the hospital, was to tell your mother how much he loved her. How good their life had been." Floodgates opened. Michael marveled at himself, that he could be so overcome with urgency in the presence of these two women, both enough older than him that in a child's view of the world they were almost of another generation, yet he clung to their tears as if he could somehow hold onto childhood and the notion of protection somewhere, a safety net that would never be absent from the void beneath his feet.

As he disengaged from the sisters and left them to the job of accepting condolences from an endless stream of well-wishers, Michael noticed Sal Bruno sitting like a mountain on one of the armchairs, leaning forward across his immense paunch and shaking every now and again as he stabbed at his face with a handkerchief. Michael had never seen Sal overcome by any emotion other than rage. Even laughing madly a lethal control seemed to persist. But now the old thug sagged on the seat, his bulk deflated somehow, as if Dom's death had removed some psychic whalebone from Sal's mass and revealed him as nothing more than an old, fat man. When Angie DeMicco waddled over to hug his old partner, the same sense of a disconcerting paradigm shift invaded Michael's mind. The vague miasma of deflation enveloped John and his brothers too. Gradually, the sense became profoundly disturbing, even threatening. It was like a warning bell clanging in his consciousness, as if Dom was still trying to get a message across from his hospital bed. But Michael understood his own powerlessness, his utter inability to change the trajectory of events he could suddenly see unfolding with a dismal clarity. He was relieved when the receiving line finally thinned and everyone could leave.

The drive from the funeral parlor to the restaurant took him past a street that led directly to his parents' house. The trees were turning. Michael noted it in passing as he thought about the reception to come and the mass and interment that would be held in the morning. He dreaded the food, the talk. He hated the meal that followed so many funerals, and this one, following the visitation and so preceding the mass and the funeral, would be exponentially worse. He detested the circular conversations. In this case, he didn't want to be anywhere near the public version of the positioning wars that were certainly underway. Angie was up from Florida, and Sal lumbered from place to place throughout the restaurant all evening. Between them, the brutality masquerading as politicking was held down, and Michael was thankful. And no one seemed to grasp that something more than a change in leadership was under way.

As much as he wanted to escape, he stayed, reluctant to leave Toni, Nina, Mary and John. Something was gone now, and he preferred not to articulate what it might portend. The meal would go on, perhaps all night, but the empty place was going to remain, and he could feel it. He also felt a visceral sense of risk. Marbles was walking in a different way, at the funeral home and the restaurant, a subtle change to his characteristic swagger that led him to greet even Michael as though they were old friends, as if the apology Michael had delivered erased the distrust that had underpinned their encounters, bizarrely taking on a donnish role, probably as he fancied such a figure would behave, styling himself as his personal imagined version of Don Corleone. Michael couldn't tell if he was being recast by Marbles in the role of a civilian supplicant or as a potentially turnable member of John's crew, as if John had a crew to kick earnings upward in Marbles' direction. But he did know that Marbles was feeling him out, and that made him anxious to the point of fear.

Michael left as quickly as decency allowed, without eating or drinking anything. He would come back for the mass and funeral in the morning, and he would force himself through another meal, and then he would wait a few days. Then he would call Toni.

He sat quietly in his car outside the restaurant. His habit, when someone he was fond of died, was to scour his mind for as many good memories as he could, forcing himself to repeatedly relive the pain of loss. It was an intriguing exercise that he had tried without success to explain to his ex-wife, years earlier. When his grandpa had died, and he spent many private hours reviewing his happy recollections of the old man, sometimes in a state of despondency, Carole had concluded he was torturing himself because he was unable to reach out to the man when he was alive. But she had it wrong, he thought, even though she was partially right. "It's not a guilty process," he had said. "And I don't do it because, as you've told me so many times, I compartmentalize my emotions. It's just a way of honoring the person's memory." He didn't add that the real reason was to prove to himself that he could endure the pain he was feeling, that the trial could only be completed by increasing the anguish as much as possible.

Of Dominick Calabria, Michael found himself concentrating his thoughts on the first time they met, late in the spring of his fourth-grade year, more than thirty years earlier. To Michael, John's home, with its pond, swimming pool, horse paddocks, stables and woods, had seemed like paradise. He had been sitting on the lawn between the house and main barn, studying a leopard frog he and John had caught and placed inside a shoebox. Dom must have seen him from the office and walked outside to find out what was going on. Michael remembered looking up when the man's shadow fell across the box. He recalled the slim man looming above him, his hands in the pockets of his slacks, his dark hair smoothed back and his face almost expressionless. The man had radiated confidence and competence.

"What you got there?" Dom asked.

"A frog," Michael answered. "We caught him at the pond."

"What, you wade in after him?" A small smile touched the edges of the man's lips.

Michael glanced down at his pants, wet to the thighs, and nodded, squinting up against the bright sky.

"What're you going to do with it?"

"John wants to play baseball with him," Michael replied.

"Yeah?" Dom's eyebrows moved, but his expression registered little change. "John go to get a bat?"

"Yes."

"Don't do it where John's mother can see you," Dom said, his voice strangely uninflected.

"We aren't going to use the frog as a baseball," Michael had answered.

"No?"

Michael shook his head. "We'll let him go again."

Another trace of a smile crossed Dom's lips. "How're you going to convince John?"

Michael had looked down into the box and shrugged. "Just will," he answered simply. He squinted upward again and saw something new in the man's face. Dom believed him.

"Stand up so I can get a look at you," Dom said. Michael placed the lid on the box and held it as he rose to his feet. "What's your name, kid?"

"Michael Pollitz."

"You in John's class?"

"Yes."

"I'm John's father," the man said. He extended his hand. Michael had never before shaken a man's hand. "My name is Dominick. People call me Dom. Do you go by Mike?"

"Sometimes," Michael answered. He met Dom's appraising gaze. Standing, he had a clearer view of the man's sharp eyes.

"Lemme tell you something, Mike," Dom said. "We got two new foals out in the barn. Just born this spring. Would you like to see them?"

"Yes," Michael answered quickly, smiling shyly.

"Okay. I'll get one of the men to take you in. But I want you to promise me something," he added, placing a hand on Michael's slender shoulder. "You and John are never to go into the barn without a grownup. Can you keep that promise?"

Michael again met Dom's piercing stare and nodded gravely. "Yes."

"Good. I believe you," Dom said, the smile spreading. Small even teeth showed. He glanced toward the barn, then back at the house. "Why don't you just let the frog go now, before John finds a baseball bat?"

"We can let him go together," Michael replied, still studying Dom's face. The man's expression changed into something new, even as his smile grew warmer. He nodded slowly.

"However you want it," Dom said at last, still smiling down at the boy. He squeezed his shoulder. "I'm glad to've met you, Mike. I hope I see a lotta you." Then Dom turned and walked back to the office doors.

What I saw in his face was something I'd never seen in an adult's eyes before, Michael thought as he reached for the car's ignition. *It was respect,* he realized, and before he could start his car, he had to stop and wipe his eyes.

47

Klinger fumed outside Whittaker's office. He had been waiting for twenty minutes and would wait for twenty more, but, as he told Dora over cheeseburgers that evening, "I got the message after about five minutes, you follow?"

He spent some time reviewing the material in his files—a new organization chart for what remained of the Outfit, a few guesses about who would assume what role in the diminished criminal conspiracy, and a final report on the now-closed investigation. The final report was the only inclusion that was even vaguely necessary. Whittaker had no need for any updates about any crime organizations in the Chicago area absent any potential prosecutions. The folder of information had been Klinger's eccentric attempt at mending fences. As he waited, the effort became ever more obviously a waste of energy.

Finally, he stood and asked Whittaker's secretary for a manila envelope. With a sympathetic smile she handed over a large inter-office memo envelope. "Long time since I seen one a these," Klinger grumbled, but he grinned at the middle-aged woman. "That's a nice brooch," he said, nodding at her left shoulder. She glanced at the jewelry and smiled back, but she said nothing while he crammed his files into the envelope and made a show of twisting the string around the seals.

On the cover, where names had been listed and crossed out, Klinger wrote in large block letters, RECOMMENDATION: DISINTER D.C. FOR ONE LAST SHOT AT AN INDICTMENT.

He hitched up his pants and gazed around the office as if admiring its accoutrements for old times' sake, and then he winked at the secretary. "I gotta go, but give your boss my best regards," he said. "Tell him, better luck next time."

48

"This is good news," Michael said, smiling with greater satisfaction than his voice betrayed after Klinger announced an end to the investigation.

"Take it as a Chistmas present, kiddo."

"Well, Larry, I'd say I'm sorry it didn't work out how you wanted, but I'd be lying." Michael shouldered the phone and grinned as he scribbled his initials onto a layout for a credit-card mailer.

Klinger chuckled softly. "Don't make a difference now," he said, "and to be truthful, I didn't think we were getting anywhere anyway, you follow?"

"It didn't feel like that on my end," Michael replied. He leaned against his desk and stared through the window. *Chicago can be just beautiful,* he thought as he gazed south into the gray December light. He was almost startled by the rush of relief he was feeling. It seemed like years, not months, since Klinger had first called. "How'd you like to join me for a beer today, Larry?"

"Sounds okay to me," Klinger answered. "Let's go to that place on Clark Street. You mind if I bring Dora along?"

"Fine with me. Let's get some dinner then."

"Hey! Great idea. You pick the place, okay?"

49

"All I'm saying, he's gotta know what's what."

"For Chrissakes, Marbles!" Sal exploded. "Quit sayin' that over and over. It's making me nuts!"

He glared across the table, then glanced at the two men from Soto's crew who sat on either side of their boss. In the throb of drums and bass that filled the building, the men seemed hazy in Sal's eyes. Whenever the padded door leading into the back room opened, the blaring sound of horns and synthesizers was overpowering.

Soto shrugged and crossed his arms. "Just so you know how I feel," he muttered.

"I know what you're saying, for Chrissake. I told you a hunerd times, I'm retired. Dom's dead, may he rest in peace. I worked wit' Dom. I been out of it for months. My crew's with you now." Bruno stared flatly at the younger man. A topless woman walked past the table. "You do what you gotta do."

Soto nodded with finality. "So we're straight about this?" He leaned back in his leather armchair and smiled, as if he was holding a meeting in some sedate office instead of the back room of a strip club.

"We're straight. You want my advice, you keep things as quiet as you can. You make more money that way. But if you don't want my advice, I give a shit. I'm outta it. I don't wanna hear nothin' more about it." Sal again looked from face to face and rose from his chair, sliding his hand across the expanse of knit fabric covering his stomach to tuck in the golf shirt. Losing Dom had had an odd effect on Sal, instantly aging the big man. He had decided to retire immediately after the funeral. He dropped his napkin onto his plate and lifted his wine glass. "Okay?" He tilted the wine toward Soto. "It's none of my business no more." He sipped from the glass and wiped his lips with a speckled paw. "Good luck to you, Marbles," he growled without smiling. "You and me, we got no problems. We're never gonna have no problems. I'm out."

Soto nodded dismissively. "Give my best to Angie when you get to Fort Myers," he replied, standing to lead Sal to the door. "My regards to Yvonne as well."

Sal nodded in turn, amused by Soto's attempt to imitate Dom's mannerisms. The effect in the blasting strip club was ludicrous. "I'll do that," he rasped as he turned away from the table.

From the office doorway Soto watched as the overweight old man trudged past the dancers and the bar and out of the club, then turned to his thugs. "See what I just done? I walked Sal to the door. That's the kinda respect the loudmouthed asshole don't have for no one." The men nodded. One lifted a handgun from inside his coat, looked at the safety, and replaced the weapon. "Joey bring the car?" Soto asked.

One of the men laughed. "Yeah, but I hadda send him out again. Fuckin' idiot didn't get it ready. I told him, 'Put some fuckin' plastic in the fuckin' trunk.' He'll be back in a while." He laughed again, a cruel, mirthless bark.

Soto looked at his Rolex. "Don't matter. It ain't even midnight yet. We got a couple hours."

"Where we takin' him?"

"South," Soto answered.

"You want anyone else?"

"Nah. We're plenty."

"Fuckin' big mouth prick," the second man announced.

"Smartass asshole," the first thug agreed.

"Where's that fuckin' broad?" Soto snarled. "I want some cannoli and espresso." He looked around, frowning, and pulled his comb from his back pocket. He smoothed his hair, then studied the comb. He wiped it with a napkin and returned it to his pocket. "Go get the fuckin' broad," he instructed one of the men. "And cover that fuckin' piece," he added, glaring inside the man's jacket. "How can you stand to wear a tee shirt under a coat, anyway?"

"What? This?" The man plucked stupidly at the lapel of his suit jacket. "Hey, it's hot out."

"So don't wear a fuckin' coat," Soto snapped, raising a hand to prevent the obvious explanation, that something was needed to conceal the weapon. "Go find some fuckin' cannoli."

2003

1

"He won't ever ask, but I can tell you one thing Larry would like better than anything else would be to know what really happened," Dora said, leaning close in the banquette while Klinger was in the restroom.

Michael glanced at the empty bottle of wine surrounded by used dishes on the table and smiled. The only way such a question could come out of Dora was if she'd had too much to drink, and he was sure he could count the times he'd seen her lit since 1994—the total number of occasions was probably fewer than ten. "I assume you're talking about me and Dom Calabria, thirty years ago?"

"I think he'd like to know the truth."

"God! There's a big word," Michael answered, laughing as Klinger trundled back to the table.

"What?" he asked.

"Dora says you'd like to know the truth."

"Whoa! Heavy word."

Dora shrieked with laughter. "You guys said almost the exact same thing!"

Michael decided to ignore the line of conversation. Instead he said, "This isn't what I expected."

"What do you mean?" Klinger asked. "Dora grilling you? About something other than your romantic life, I mean."

"No, this. The restaurant. Just the three of us. I thought a cop's retirement party would be a little bigger."

"I'm not your typical copper."

"Don't I know it." Michael laughed again.

"What am I supposed to be seeking the truth about?"

"The meaning of life," Michael answered.

"I'm too old to care," Klinger said, sipping from a glass of wine.

"Oh, please," Dora moaned. "Now he's acting like sixty is old age. Poor old geezer."

"Retirement age in the CPD," Klinger clarified to no one in particular, adding, "and I shoulda said, like any other mope who spent his life on the force, the meaning of life is at the very bottom of my list of concerns."

"I think we need another bottle," Dora said.

"Fine with me," Michael answered. He had scarcely touched his first glass. "I'm driving."

"Good thing too," Klinger nodded.

Michael waved to the waiter and held up the empty wine bottle. He picked at the remains of a Sacher-torte slice on his plate before the fresh bottle arrived, wondering if Klinger would pick up on Dora's lead. "So," he announced to pre-empt the possibility. "Think you're going to miss it?"

"The job?" Klinger looked up from his dessert and shrugged. "Prolly not," he said, stifling a belch. "I mean," he added, gesturing expansively at the nearly empty restaurant, "it will be tough not seeing all my pals on the force." He grinned. "But I suppose I'll get used to it."

Dora fumed. "This place would be filled to the walls if you'd allowed a regular retirement party like a normal person."

Klinger merrily waved a hand in the air. "I thought we'd established long ago that I'm not a normal person."

"Certainly not a normal police officer," Michael said.

"Still curious, though," Klinger replied, eyeing Michael with a familiar air of expectation.

"Some other time," Michael answered as he refilled their wine glasses.

2

"You have to understand what's in Mike's head about this," Klinger tried to explain, still feeling drunk as he lay on his back in the bed and Dora walked in and out of the bedroom, removing jewelry and clothing.

"Do you?" Dora replied.

"I'd say yes. And I'm not playing amateur psychologist."

"Who said you are?"

"Oh, back when Mike was actually under investigation, Dan accused me of it." When Dora frowned, Klinger added, "Dan wasn't the asshole you think he was. Sure, we had a falling out over that investigation, but it wasn't because Dan's an asshole."

Dora shrugged noncommittally. "What about Mike?"

Klinger yawned. "Mike doesn't consider himself an innocent man," he announced. "Like I said all those years ago. He always evades these questions, which is one way I know."

"I thought you'd want the truth."

"I figure I already know the truth," Klinger answered. "All Mike could add would be details. And the reality is, he's *never* gonna give it up." He paused to think about it. "As far as me," he continued, "Mike might sort out a thing or two, but I doubt it. Unless I've got some of the basics wrong. Then again, maybe Mike and I could trade a few truths some day, just for the fun of it."

"What are you talking about?" Dora asked from the bathroom.

"He'd probably like some kind of confirmation about his pal John Calabria's killing, for starters." He exhaled slowly, allowing it some thought, releasing the air in a soft whistle.

Dora called from the bathroom, "What could you tell him?"

"Good point," Klinger laughed. "After all, without a body, no murder occurred." He heard Dora rattling around in the bathroom and glanced toward the door. She walked across the room and dropped an empty pill bottle into a wastebasket. She then returned to the bathroom. Klinger stared at the ceiling for a moment. "Of course, the same question about a body applies to Marbles Soto. No one ever found either of 'em." He pursed his lips in thought. "Kinda makes a person wonder."

"What's that?"

"Nothin'," Klinger replied.

Dora finished changing her clothes and climbed into the bed. She lay on her side with her head propped on one hand. She waited for a few seconds. "So?" she asked at last.

"So, what?" Klinger answered.

"Don't you want to know the truth about it?"

"What for?" He heaved himself onto his side and faced Dora. "More to the point, what more do I need to know? Like Mike said, once, you don't have to jump in the water to get wet. That pretty much sums it up. If we wanna speculate some more, there's even a remote ultra-long-shot chance one a the guards overheard Mike's threat and decided to do precisely what Mike said. I remember a couple of 'em wanted to take those guys out themselves, but I don't think they did." He clamped a hand over his mouth to cover another yawn. "Contrary to the movies," he intoned, "most people ain't killers."

"So you've said."

"Yeah, a time or two, I guess." Klinger laughed and reached out to pinch Dora's cheek. She squirmed away with a laugh. "I'll show you sixty," Klinger smiled.

"I thought you were retired," Dora answered. She smiled in return, doing her coquette look and drawing a laugh from Klinger. He yawned and stretched, waiting for Dora's body language to express impatience. When she shifted her weight, he followed her across the mattress, reaching across the mound of her back to turn off the light.

My sincerest thanks to Jay Amberg, friend, neighbor, encouraging reader who made this possible; Mark Larson for editorial insights and outstanding suggestions; and Sarah Koz for unfailingly excellent taste.

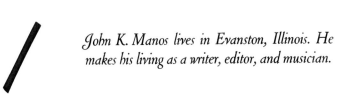

John K. Manos lives in Evanston, Illinois. He makes his living as a writer, editor, and musician.

CPSIA information can be obtained at www.ICGtesting.com
Printed in the USA
LVOW12s1530111113

360874LV00015B/634/P

9 781937 484132